THE SPIRIT WITHIN
TALE OF A FEARLESS HEART
A STORY OF A TEEN'S LOVE AND COMPASSION

BY

ED KIGHTLINGER

Other Works by Ed Kightlinger Writing under his Pen Name Eva Roblins

Eva Roblins and the Enchanted Gate, Book One - Return of the Princess

Eva Roblins and the Enchanted Gate, Book Two - Conquest of the Hidden Valley

Freddy Meets Carmen the Talking Mouse

Gloves for José - A Brief Tale of Love and Compassion

Diana's Incredible Journey, Book One - Fall of Mendacium

DEDICATION

With Love and Respect to my Dear Friend
Stephanie Anne Esmonde

"May your Fearless Spirit and
Unswerving Love and Compassion
Live on Forever in your Heart"

(for they are your raison d'être)

~ ~ ~

"All of our Dreams can come true
if we have the courage to pursue them."
- Walt Disney

PREFACE

I wrote this book for two reasons. The primary reason was to capture the essence of an amazing person through the imaginary makings of written words. To display the intelligence, talents, athleticism, and kindness of that person in an entirely fictional manner.

The secondary reason was to portray the person's passionate métier - *her raison d'être* as it relates to the way she endeavors to treats others in a kind-hearted way. To replicate her fearless spirit through the actions, words, thoughts, and emotions of the book's leading character, Stephanie JoAnne Galanos as she opposed architects of wickedness, be they bigots, bullies, or bull-headed buffoons. All the while bringing to light her sincere love and kind compassion for others - in spite of their failings.

I did all of this by use of fictional scenes in four primary settings - World War II in the Jew-hating Nazi Germany; on a Southern American plantation during the vile slavery era; in an urban town setting before the Americans with Disabilities Act of 1990 became law; and within the violently abusive, bullying walls of an imaginary orphanage.

While many of the fictional scenes in this book depict humanity's shortcomings, they also portray humanity's virtues. Tolerance versus narrow-mindedness. Freedom and self-determination versus prejudice and chauvinism. Strength versus weakness. Love versus hate. Always with an underlying theme.

Believe you can and you're halfway there for *there's a bit of magic in everything, and some loss to even things out.*

Sincerely,

Edward H. Kightlinger, Sr.
Lieutenant Commander, United States Navy (Ret.)
Pseudonym author of Eva Roblins Works

THE DREAMS

Steph supposes she began to experience the frightening dreams about six weeks ago. The heart-wrenching images and sounds she perceived in her dreams were sometimes a bit different, but the location where the dreams occurred never changed. What was even worse, the frightening dreams were the only dreams she dreamt. Continuously.

She thinks that at first, she did not experience the dreams every night. Then again, she believes she dreamt them often enough, perhaps two or three times a week.

That was at the beginning.

The dreams started to appear with regularity about a week or so before she began her journey.

Every. Single. Night. Without fail.

Then the dreams began to repeat themselves throughout the night. As often as four or five times a night. Causing her to think she was on her way to the looney bin.

Unavoidable. Predictable as clockwork.

Dreams of haunting imaginings and disturbing echoing's looping over and over in her mind like a nonstop, low-budget horror movie. So she thought at the time.

Dreams without commercials tailored-made for an unsleeping, late-night television audience.

Zombies. Nightcrawlers or anyone too zonked out to care.

In her semi-conscious, lethargic state of mind, she thought the disturbing visions would never end. And they didn't. Until the morning when sunlight happily streamed into her bedroom window to chase the dreams away. So she believed.

When they returned the following night. Haunting. Upsetting. Frightful.

Scaring the bejesus out of her soul!

CHAPTER ONE

THE CALLING

"It is your Purpose. Your Spirit Within. Your Raison d'être."
- Steph's Fearless Heart, the present

Part I: Nightmarish Scenes and Screams

The recurring, grief-stricken dreams Steph experiences are of an unfamiliar, seemingly foreboding place in a distant, unloved, forgotten land of neglect. Of an imposing, unattractive, seven-story, weathered turn of the century limestone building. A run-down, neglected structure desperately crying out for repair or, perhaps, mercifully, complete demolition.

The scene reminds Steph of a Halloween horror house nightmare gone bad.

With prison-like corroded bars covering grimy, opaque windows on the three upper floors. The four bottom floor windows cloaked with decades-old grime. Unwashed with drawn-out, grayish streaks of too many rains and inattentive, heartless neglect of humanity.

The outside surroundings of the building no better than the building itself.

The decaying building's unkempt entranceway courtyard bursting with soaring weeds and thorn-infested creeping vines. The formerly proud sign welcoming visitors nothing more than peeling paint on rotting wood.

Its once hospitable words faded beyond recognition. No longer welcoming and inviting.

The once paved, handsome sidewalk nothing more than crushed rubble enveloped with thorn-covered weeds, discarded pebbles, and natural decay.

The facility's entire disarray enclosed by a ten-foot-high forbidding fence topped with curved, steel barbs. The corroded, razor-sharp barbs facing inward.

Steph cannot help but wonder.

Is the menacing fence topped with inward-facing barbs purposely made that way? To prevent escape by the unfortunates who suffer within the building? Reminding the unfortunates. "You will never escape! Not ever!"

Bits of wind-swept, threadbare cloth indecently hanging hither and yon from the deadly barbs.

Only the Lord can tell the story about the poor souls that wore the clothing.

Were the souls trying to escape? Did they succeed? Or are the weathered bits of cloth all that remain of those imprisoned, long-lost souls? Their bodies cast to the wind like so many decomposed curses. And who exactly were those souls? Were they, like the decrepit building, neglected rejects of history's past - shameful and forgotten?

Perhaps nothing more than a figment of my nightmarish imagination? Of my haunting dreams?

The dismal scene is an unnatural, human-made blemish of mortality's contempt. Even so, and surprisingly, the fenced-in nightmare sits within the middle of a yawning, as far as the eye can see verdant pasture. The pasture dotted here and there with tiny purple blossoms seeking the sun's golden warmth.

A lush pasture where a solitary handsome horse lazily grazes unmolested. The horse's natural spirit ignoring the ugliness of the imposing building and its fenced-in courtyard.

To the casual onlooker, the decaying building itself looks abandoned. Nevertheless, abandoned it is not. Life teems inside. Barely.

Allow those words to sink in. Life teems inside.

Barely.

Despite the odds of the building's foreboding, shadowy neglect.

The interior of the building is as equally gloomy as its exterior. Dark, dank, somewhat creepy - well, truthfully, plenty of bone-chilling creepy. Like death warmed over.

Capacious, unbelievably depressing corridors meandering at random throughout the entire structure. Most coming to an ending in shadowy dead ends - at the weathered solid oak doors of whatever manages to breathe behind them.

Barely alive.

The ghostly, cobweb-infested pasty white walls of the corridors hideously scarred. Flaking paint sprinkled with lethal mildew and yawning spots of deadly black mold crying out for attentiveness.

The only breaks in the miserable scenery rickety wooden staircases that lead up and down at random from the corridors.

Filthy incandescent bulbs dangling from the scaly ceiling by threadbare wires every twenty feet. Most of the opaque, blackened bulbs burned out long ago. Their former joyful brilliance no more.

Total gloom prevailing over the nightmarish scene. Its foreboding expressing cruelty. Physical and verbal abuse. Untold violence. Outright scorn.

And uncountable broken hearts of forgotten, youthful innocence. Children.

Nevertheless somehow it lives. And breathes.

Barely.

In Steph's coldhearted dreams she can perceive countless unseen tiny footfalls hurriedly echoing through the corridors and staircases like frightened raindrops on a decaying roof in the heart of a ferocious, fatal storm. Begging to be unnoticed, left alone, yet embraced and loved.

Pitter-patter. Pat. Pitter-patter. Pat. Pitter-patter. Pat.

Again and again. Nonstop. Day and night.

Pitter-patter. Pat. Pitter-patter. Pat. Pitter-patter. Pat.

Steph's unconscious sleeping mind wonders time and time again.

Are the footfalls happily dancing steps accompanying the sounds of make-believe music? Or are they running footfalls fleeing in fear, trying to escape an inescapable, horrifyingly tormenting nightmare?

If so, from whom do the owners of the footfalls cower? More importantly, to whom do the footfalls belong?

When out of nowhere the tormenting shouts begin. Shattering the unnerving stillness. Like a thunderclap in the dead of night.

Then the crescendo screams. Echoing. Over and over. Again and again.

Screams followed by barely audible weeping and sobbing. Grief-stricken cries for help.

Please no! Somebody help me! God, help me. Please!

Pitiful cries of broken hearts and shattered dreams.

Of so many orphaned children abandoned. Institutionalized. Neglected and abused.

Society's scorn for those who cannot speak for themselves amongst the throngs of uninterested, uncaring, unsympathetic grownups.

It is when her senses suffer the many tormented screams in the dreams that Steph sits up wide-awake in her bed. Shivering. Her eyes welling up with sorrowful tears. Covers pulled to her neck. Uncontrollable hurting overwhelming her heart.

She stares into the blackness of the night's torment. Her heart nearly racing out of control. Her lips dry. Her throat crying out for hydration. As she waits with breathless, uneasy anticipation. For the tiniest, whispered voice of a young teenager to call out once more in the night like she has many times in the past. Her words very plain.

As though she is standing mere inches away at the side of Steph's bed. Just seven haunting words. Night after night. Tormenting. Pitiful.

Seven simple words pleading silently.

"We need - I need - you! Please, Steph."

If these wrenching sounds and scenes are not enough to scare a person, one night the unthinkable happened. It was as vivid as if Steph were watching a movie. It was the incident that compelled her to decide she was prepared to journey on the adventure of a lifetime.

To hasten to Jordyn and the other - still unknown - children's defense. To lend a hand to the neglected, endangered, less-fortunate, bullied, and abused. For her fearless heart insists.

It is your Purpose.

Your Fearless Spirit Within.

Your Love and Compassion.

Your Raison d'être.

*****

Part II: Roger Clyde

Slap!
Slap!
Slapity-slapity-slap!

Jordyn's head violently snaps to the left and then to the right and then to the left, right, left. Like it is parading to a marching beat. Except for the hearing-impaired Jordyn, the beat is painful silence.

The violent, painful drumming the result of the five rapid, terrorizing blows exploding like bursting bully bullets on the back of her head.

She is already on her hands and knees as she scrubs the grimy wooden floorboards with a bristle brush. Otherwise, she would have collapsed onto her face with the force of the powerful slaps.

Despite being on her hands and knees, she is dreadfully wobbly from the blows. Her fragile, malnourished body totters back and forth. She is in a daze. Feeling as if she is going to pass out. Luckily, she does not. Otherwise, Roger Clyde would strike out at her a half-dozen times. Probably more. Maybe even kick her brutally.

She shakes her head vigorously to clear her vision of the dazzling white lights. They are bursting in her eyes like countless 4th of July sparklers on a starless night.

Tears of extreme anger mixed with intense shame begin to stream down her cheeks.

She can handle the terrible sting from the bullying slaps. Even on the back of her head, which she hates more than anything. Receiving a bullying slap or even a well-placed kick to her bottom or on her legs, or even a violent punch on the arm happens to her all the time. Therefore, as sad as it is for her to confess, she is used to the physical abuse. And mostly immune to the pain.

But not this time. This time Roger Clyde had straddled the sides of her bare waist with his fat legs a split-second before he slapped her. Just the disgusting thought of his grotesque, hairy legs touching the sides of her bare waist nauseates her.

As she looks up at Roger Clyde, she shivers. Just the sight of him standing next to her gives her the creeps. Her eyes are squinting. Washed with tears.

She fully expects him to slap her again. He usually does. For some reason, this time he does not.

Roger Clyde Brewster is the senior boy of the Saint Mary's Home, Doolittle, Ohio.

He is huge in girth and tall in height. He is only a year or two older than Jordyn, but he weighs at least fifty pounds more. He has bulging biceps and strong, fat (and grotesquely hairy) legs. He can out-run, out-eat, out-punch, out-kick, out-talk, out-lie, out-think, and out-curse every other kid in the orphanage. That includes the seventeen-year-olds. He limps badly and does weird things with his head. But that does not stop him from being the meanest dog in the fenced-in orphanage.

Roger Clyde is the leader of the top three orphanage bullies. The three bullies proudly refer to themselves as the "Trio." The orphanage is full of bullies, but the Trio bullies are truly despised and feared the most. The Trio roams the corridors all hours of the day and night as the Saint Mary's predatory Trinity.

The two other boys in the Trio are complete cowards when compared to Roger Clyde. They never walk alone. Always in twos or threes. Only Roger Clyde roams the orphanage alone seeking hapless girls and boys who are by themselves. He is the supreme bully, meaner than the day is long. And tougher than an enraged cat slung over a clothesline.

Roger Clyde gets off sneaking up on kids and smacking them on their rumps with his open hand. He relishes slapping kids on the side of their heads. Sometimes even kicking them. When you make him mad enough, he will pummel you with his closed fists until he nearly knocks you unconscious. Or cry, *Uncle.*

Luckily, Roger Clyde has never punched Jordyn. She reckons it is a good thing. His slaps hurt just fine for her disliking.

And there is the one thing Roger Clyde is an expert at doing when he is on his *bully versus victim patrol.* Making sure there are no witnesses when he terrorizes you.

"Don't you do that anymore," Jordyn cries. She wipes her dirty, tear-streaked face with her torn shirtsleeve. "It huwts, it huwts really bad."

Her sad, now dreadfully frightened greenish-grey eyes are spewing tears that are cascading down her ruddy face like an unchecked, bursting dam. Her eyes usually sparkle like moonbeams. They are that unique, so very beautiful.

But right now her alluring, beautiful eyes are not sparkling. No surprise considering what just happened. She is hurting too much, both physically and mentally, for her eyes to shine. In fact, her eyes are awash with reddish streaks. A mixture of anger, shame, and pain.

"You do that one more time I am gonna tell. 'Specially if you straddle me with your gross hairy legs like some disgustin' naughty dog."

She reads Roger Clyde's lips as he replies.

"How dare you's compare me to a dog you wench! Besides, who you's gonna tell, stupid?" He sneers the nastiest grin imaginable. "No one is gonna believe you's. Not only are you's deaf. You's are dumb. Who is gonna take the word of a fourteen-year-old little snot? No one I dare say. No one."

He bends down and cruelly slams Jordyn's left cheek with his open palm.

Her head snaps to the right as if a brick slammed it. She cannot help but cry out with excruciating pain.

Her open palms splay on the soapy water causing her head to nosedive. Luckily, she can keep her face from smashing onto the floor. She immediately rights herself and stares. Her eyes are misting with fresh tears. She reads Roger Clyde's lips.

"That is for you's calling me a dog, stupid! Serves you's right you dummy. Hah!"

Jordyn continues to grimace at the horrific pain from Roger Clyde's powerful slap to her face. She believes this latest slap is worse than the five slaps that landed on the back of her head.

Because it is especially insulting for someone to slap your face. Everyone knows that, right?

"Ain't dumb," she manages to stammer in between heartbreaking sobs. Her eyes are now gushing tears. They are dropping like little raindrops into the soapy bucket in front of her.

"Deaf and dumb t'gether mean you can't hear or talk. I can talk. Not too good, but I talk just the same. Ain't my fault I talk funny sometimes. It is normal for deaf people." She grins a nasty smirk as she points her finger at him threateningly.

"But I tell you this, Roger Clyde. My thoughts are clear, crystal clear. Nobody can question my thoughts. And right now you do not want to know what I am thinking!"

Roger Clyde clenches his fists. He bends over until his face is mere inches from hers. Jordyn grimaces.

He is going to punch me in the face with his fist. I just know that he is!
But he doesn't. Thankfully.

When at last he speaks, spittle splish-splashes onto Jordyn's face. It is almost as if Jordyn can taste the hate spluttering from his lips. Like vicious thrusts of a murderous knife.

"When I said dumb I meant that you's are stupid. A moron. A stooge. An idiotic, brain-dead nobody. Whatever you's wanna call it. You's are dim-witted. You's are dumb! Since you's be so dumb, ain't no one gonna b'lieve someone like you's if you tattletale."

He glares at the galvanized, dented pail of hot soapy water. It sits on the floor in front of Jordyn. His smirk turns into an evil-looking smile. He suddenly gives the pail a firm kick. Chocolate-colored foamy water splashes onto Jordyn's face. The remaining contents of the overturned pail race across the wooden floor. Jordyn blinks back tears yet again.

The acidic, dirty, soapy water is stinging her eyes worse than the blow Roger Clyde had delivered to her face. All the same, she refuses to give him the satisfaction of knowing the water is stinging her eyes.

She keeps the palms of her hands firmly planted on the floor. As she glares up at Roger Clyde, she blinks rapidly. Her beautiful, tearful eyes speak of disgust. And irrefutable contempt.

Roger notices the hateful look in her eyes. He is a bit scared, so he moves back a few steps. Then he kicks the pail once more. It flies against the wall. Then it ricochets off the wall and bangs noisily down the staircase. Sixteen stair treads in all.

Jordyn's deaf ears could care less. She doesn't even bother to watch as the empty pail noisily bounces on the stair treads then lands with a loud crash at the bottom of the staircase.

All she does is glare at Roger Clyde.

If only he knew what I am thinking. If only he knew what I could do to him simply with my thoughts. How I could call out in the night and end this horrible nightmare! End his bullying life!

"Now clean up that mess, dummy," Roger Clyde's lips say.

"And don't you's dare tell no one or next time I will hurt you's real bad. No slaps on the face for you's next time, stupid. Unh-unh. Nope. Gonna hurt you's with a baseball bat."

With a sickening sneer, he adds, "And I am's gonna hit you's so hard, you's won't want to sit for the rest of you's stupid life! Maybe even kill you's. Sure 'nuff that I am standing here."

Steph awakens with a start. She almost is certain that the side of her face was stinging like someone poured hot water onto it! It is as if she too suffered the brutal blow Roger Clyde had landed on Jordyn's face!

She gingerly touches the side of her face with her fingertips. There is no intense throbbing pain, no hotness that usually accompanies such a blow.

Weird.

All the same in her heart she knows. She had felt the blow. Just the same as if Roger Clyde had struck her.

She has felt similar blows to the side of her face two times before. One such blow was a super-fast tennis ball she had failed to return during a hotly-contested tennis match. The speeding ball smacked her straight on the side of her face. She saw stars. She saw *lots* of stars.

It amazed her that a cloth-covered rubber ball could hurt so darned much.

The other time was when she smacked her face with her tennis racquet. It was during a doubles match. She had dived to return one of the opposing team's high-speed serves. She had missed the ball by inches and lost her balance. Her tennis racquet smacked the ground.

Then it ricocheted and smacked her hard on the side of her face. She thought she was going to pass out with the intense pain.

It was humiliating to be struck by her tennis racquet in the middle of a playoff game. Some of the nastier students in the stands had laughed at her misfortune. Nonetheless, she hung in there. She and her teammate easily whipped their opponents three sets to zero. The bluish-black bruise and soreness lasted for a week.

But to feel the pain of a blow administered by another human being. Goodness no!

Her parents never hit her. Not even her sister smacked her even though they quarreled from time to time. Sure, her parents punished her every once in a while. When she truly deserved a good lesson. Rightly so. By grounding her and taking away some privileges.

But they are truly easy-going, fair, and loving parents. They usually give in before the punishment period is up. All it takes is Steph to roll her big brown eyes and to pout innocently. And often. And admittedly, doing extra chores without being told helps as well.

Steph gets out of bed to look at her reflection in the mirror.

Nothing.

But the effects of the slap and its sting strangely remain in her psyche even so. She can only imagine how Jordyn must have felt since she is the one who was struck by Roger Clyde brutally.

Six times.

She recalls something similar happened to Jordyn once before. It was a few weeks ago.

Steph dreamed that Jordyn had received a kick from behind. She never sensed who did it, and Jordyn's thoughts entering her mind never enlightened her as to who the culprit was. But it was horrifying to bear witness to what had happened!

Jordyn was scrubbing the baseboards near the stairwell landing. After being kicked in the rump - she could not hear the culprit approaching - she had tumbled down the staircase head-over-heels. Sixteen stair treads in all not counting the landings!

A split-second before she hit the lower landing, she had stretched her hands out before her to lessen the impact of the fall. Despite her frantic efforts, her head smacked painfully hard on the wooden landing.

She passed out immediately. That is when all thoughts from Jordyn ceased. Steph was certain she was dead.

To Steph's relief, her thoughts resumed the following night. As usual, she was in a fitful sleep. Her unconsciousness was anticipating the nightly dream.

She envisioned Jordyn was lying in the orphanage infirmary. Three fingers on her left hand were taped together with brown masking tape. No splints, no cast, no nothing. Just masking tape. And nothing to ease her throbbing pain. She had hideous-looking lacerations on her face and knees. She also had a nasty-looking black eye. Worse, she had broken her nose.

She was very lucky she did not break her neck during her tumble down the stairs!

The nurse had scolded her for being clumsy. She had repeated the nurse's words, so Steph would know what the nurse had said. But her repeating the nurse's words was not necessary. Steph somehow sensed the nurse's reproaching reprimand as if the heartless, uncaring woman was standing next to her bed.

"You are one super clumsy idiot, Jordyn. How could you be so reckless? Sliding down the stairs on a cardboard box! Just for fun. When you were supposed to be working! You are fortunate Roger Clyde found you. Lord knows how long you would have bled from your broken nose! Stop being a showoff and fooling around when you are supposed to be working. Do I make myself clear young lady?"

It was right then, just after the nurse had scolded Jordyn, that Steph had awakened from her restless sleep. Her nose was hurting like someone had punched her in the face. And the three smallest fingers on her left hand felt as if they were on fire. She could barely move them no less bend them at the joints. It was as if she also had experienced three broken fingers!

Naturally, her fingers were just fine. All the same, while the pain of her nose lessened within the hour, her fingers ached for nearly a week. Thank goodness she is right-handed. Otherwise, she would not have been able to compete in the school tennis championships!

*****

Part III: Steph Makes Up Her Mind

"Honey, you get that notion out of your head right now. There is no way your dreams are real."

Steph's mother is stirring the family favorite. Homemade chicken noodle soup. Deliciously aromatic steam rushes from the simmering pot. She slowly turns to Steph. The look on her face is troubled.

"Besides, if what you are dreaming is real, and I seriously doubt that it is, there is no way I would ever consent for you to go on an adventure to places unknown."

She shakes her head back and forth disapprovingly. She dips the ladle deep into the pot. When she withdraws the ladle from the pot colorful, delightful-looking morsels come into view. The truly appetizing morsels consist of wide egg noodles sprinkled with cubes of chicken and potato along with thin slices of tomato, sweet peppers, and celery. After blowing on the ladle for a few moments, she places it to her lips. Her nose wrinkles.

Her mother's reaction causes Steph to laugh. Her mother is never entirely satisfied with her chicken noodle soup until it is deliciously beyond perfect. By the look on her face, she will undoubtedly say that the soup needs a bit of *doctoring.*

"Here Steph, try some. I think I need to add more sage. What do you think? Maybe more garlic. Yup." She smacks her lips, and then she frowns.

"It needs a tad bit of doctoring."

Steph laughs again. She downs the ladle's contents. She smacks her lips. As she expected, the broth is perfect. And delicious.

"C'mon Mom. Stop fretting so much. It tastes delicious, just right. Your homemade chicken noodle soup is the best on the planet. You know that! This batch cannot get any more perfect. I do not think it needs a tad bit of doctoring at all." She laughs for the third time.

Steph's mother laughs as well - just as she reaches into the cabinet for the plastic bottles of sage and garlic.

"Nope. You are wrong young lady." She vigorously shakes spices into the soup. "Needs more of this and a pinch of that. Needs serious doctoring." She laughs again.

She suddenly turns to look at Steph. The expression on her face is dead serious.

"Steph, there are too many unknowns out there in the real world. And some of those unknowns are outright dangerous. The wide world is no place these days for an adventurous teenager. Especially a girl." She turns away from Steph to stir the pot.

Steph's mother is a beautiful woman. She has shoulder-length, jet-black hair that reminds Steph of the most delicate woven silk imaginable. Steph loves to comb her mother's hair at night when her mother relaxes in her favorite living room chair. That is whenever Steph does not have homework! Which seems to be every school night these days! Gobs of it too!

To Steph, Mom, as she likes to call her, is the best mother a daughter could have. Her mother is understanding, compassionate, talented, firm when she has to be firm, yet flexible when there is cause for compromise. Her mother never raises her voice at Steph or Steph's sister. Her mother's stern look is all it takes for one to know one is in serious trouble.

On the other hand, Daddy is easy-going and the king of the world, at least in Steph's eyes. Daddy is her hero. So is her Grandpa. Her ninety-two-year-old navy veteran grandpa is her World War Two fighting hero. Her Daddy and Grandpa are the most wonderful men in her life.

Steph has many of her mother's striking features. Same beautiful brown eyes and an infectious smile. A smile that effortlessly compels others to smile in return. Unlike her mother's dark hair color, Steph's hair is a golden brown. It falls in long curls to the small of her back. She also sports a beautiful dimple in the middle of her right cheek. She is a bit shorter than her mother by two or three inches. That is understandable since Steph is sixteen-years-old. She will turn seventeen on Valentine's Day, February the 14th.

She is very active athletically. She is a proven tennis champion and is a member of the school rugby team. She also is an articulate roller skater. She is super-smart, talented, respectful, and very pretty. Steph is a charming teenager.

Her mother frowns as she sets the ladle on the stovetop. She turns toward Steph and opens her arms out wide, gesturing for her daughter to move closer for a loving hug. As she hugs Steph lovingly, she whispers into her ear.

"Goodness, child. I would be horror-stricken if you were to venture out anywhere on your own. For sure, the world is a wonderfully exciting place. It is full of lovely scenes and beautiful people. But it is also a very dangerous place especially, like I said, for a female teenager. I love you very much. You know that. It would wound me terribly if something were to happen to you. And goodness, Steph - your Father! He would be devastated if something were to happen to you. You know how much he adores you and your sister."

She gently pushes away from Steph to look into her eyes. She places her hands on her shoulders and gently squeezes them.

"You know I worry very much about you. I get fretful whenever you are late for supper even though I know you are at a rugby match. Goodness, Honey, I even worry about you when you are at school!" She abruptly turns toward the stove and picks up her ladle once more.

"Please forget those notions of yours and try to ignore those weird dreams you are having. You are not going anywhere, and I mean it. I do not care what you say about a fellow teenager and others that are in distress. I do not care if this girl Jordyn is real or a figment of your imagination. Nor do I care if she is just a person in your dreams. It makes no difference to me. All I care about is you. Please set the table for dinner if you please."

Steph reaches near her mother's head to retrieve the dinner plates from the cupboard. She cannot help but notice that her mother's eyes are welling up with tears. It is as if she is going to cry. As she begins to set the kitchen table, Steph's mind races a mile a minute.

Is she crying? Because she truly is worried about me? Or is she crying because she somehow knows I have made up my mind? That I must leave in the morning? Oh, I am sorry Mom. I truly am! But I have to leave. Jordyn and the other children need me.

I have no clue who Jordyn is, where she lives, or why she needs me. All the same, I feel compelled to do something. Someone is bullying her horribly, and she lives in a nasty-looking place. And I have faith that she will somehow guide me along the way as I journey.

I have to go, Mom! You would do the same if you were me. I know you would! After all, I have this uncanny feeling deep in my heart. That despite everything I must go. It is my purpose.

My raison d'être.

Steph clears her thoughts and momentarily stops setting the table. She reaches from behind her mother to hug her around the waist. She whispers into her mother's ear.

"Mom, I love you. Please do not cry, okay? And please do not worry about me, all right? I am a big girl, and you and Daddy have done a great job teaching me right from wrong. No matter what happens, no matter come what may, I will always be your little girl. And I will always love you just as I know you love me."

Her mother does not reply.

*****

Part IV: Saying Goodbye

Dear Mom and Daddy,

By the time you read this, you will know the truth. I have departed on my journey to visit Jordyn and to help others in need. I know it is difficult for you to understand why I am doing this. I do not intend to upset you. God knows I would never intentionally do anything to hurt you.

Nevertheless, I somehow know in my heart that I will cause you great pain. I also know in my heart that both of you understand that I have to leave. Jordyn calls for me. As I have mentioned before, she is a sweet, adorable girl who appears to be in so much pain. Others constantly bully her, and she lives in deplorable conditions. She is deaf, and when she talks her words sound a bit unusual to those with whom she lives. In my mind, however, her words are as clear as the morning sunshine! I find that to be amazing!

How Jordyn can transmit her thoughts into my mind at night and how I can comprehend them are, well, to be honest with you, beyond my comprehension. However, you have known for a long time that I have a unique ability to foresee things, things that even I cannot explain. As you know, I am also able to read - to a limited degree - thoughts of others, especially those who are hurting. At least I think that I can.

Mom, remember that time you lost your wedding ring? If you will recall, I was at school. You were frantically looking for your ring all morning. Suddenly you called out, "Oh God, where is my ring? I will do anything to find it!" I could sense your grief-stricken words, so I called you from school during my recess.

I pretty much can recall my exact words when I spoke to you over the phone. I had said, "Mom, your wedding ring fell between the bathroom sink and that tiny little crack in the wall. You accidentally knocked your ring off the counter with your hand when you were shampooing your hair. So please do not cry, okay?"

I had asked you not to hang up so I could find out if what I envisioned in my mind was correct. A few moments later you were back on your phone. You were flabbergasted as you tearfully whispered, "Steph, Honey, how did you know? I had the ring on my finger after you left for school! How did you know, Steph? It is impossible!"

I had replied, "I do not know, Mom. But for some reason, I felt your pain and how distraught you were, and then I saw in my mind what had happened to your ring. I hope you are not sore at me for calling you during recess. I just felt as though I had to." You had replied, "Sore? How could I be sore? You have just kept me from having a broken heart. Thank you, thank you, thank you!" As a reward, you served my favorite dessert that night - German chocolate cake. It was delicious as always!

Mom, many other bizarre things like that have happened before and after. You know of some of them, but there are plenty others that I do not have time to go into here.

Jordyn told me to be out of the house and outside on the porch with my packed belongings no later than one o'clock. She also said that you are not to worry. She told me to tell you that she promises that I will be unharmed. She said that yes, some danger would challenge me along the way, but that she would keep me safe. Plus, you know me,

Mom, I am pretty darned smart, too. And tough. Jordyn also said do not bother looking for me because you will be unable to find me - whatever in the world that means. So, away I go. I love you, Mom and Daddy. Bunches. Forever and forever. Please give all my love to Sis and tell her she is the best sister in the whole wide world! Thank you. Love always, Steph.

*****

Part V: Preparing to Leave

It is twelve-thirty in the morning. On a Saturday. Everyone in the house except Steph is sound asleep. The temperature outside is still a bit chilly. No surprise since it is spring, the middle of May. The moonlight is shining brightly through the kitchen window silhouetting Steph in its soft whitish glow. As she quietly moves about the room, she is desperately trying to follow Jordyn's instructions from memory as accurately as possible. And as quickly as possible.

Okay, what was it that she had said? For me to pack a small paper bag with all of my edible goodies. No plastic bags! She had stressed the importance of that. I should be sure to use waxed paper instead of plastic baggies for my sandwiches. Peanut butter and jelly sandwiches work best. Jordyn said they would not spoil. The bread may get stale and harden after a few days. But the sandwiches will be okay to eat and still taste as yummy as if I just made them. She said pack six sandwiches. I should cut them in half, so I am not tempted to eat an entire sandwich at one sitting. She said I would want my sandwiches to last a few days.

Also, I should bring along some Twinkies and other sugary snacks. I am to be sure to remove the cellophane wrappers and wrap the snacks in waxed paper. I should pack a handful or two of hard candies. Stick them in my pockets. She said I would need the extra energy. It is okay if the candies are still in their wrappers as long as the wrappers do not have any lettering on them. I must not forget to pack that plain white mug that I use for cocoa. Jordyn says it is important that it not have any lettering on the bottom. I looked. It does not.

I must not forget to pack my light jacket and extra undies and things like that. Stuff them in the checkered kitchen tablecloth that is in the linen closet. I am to take along at least three T-shirts. Any T-shirt is okay as long as it does not have any lettering on it. I must not pack denim jeans. Only long pants made of cotton. I must not forget to rip off the collar tags from the T-shirts and laundry tags from the pants. I am not to bring anything to drink. Jordyn says I should have plenty of water to drink on the journey. She also said she would tell me what streams and ponds and other sources of water from which it is safe to drink. I certainly do not want to contract giardia during our journey!

Okay, I am all packed. I have written a note to Mom and Daddy. Wait! Oh, my goodness! I almost forgot to pack a long-sleeve shirt and a light sweater. I must not forget to remove the tags.

She tiptoes up the stairs into her bedroom and quietly removes the shirt and sweater from her chest of drawers. After she leaves her bedroom, she peeks into her parents' room. They are sound asleep. She blows them a kiss from the doorway. She opens the door to her sister's room. She quietly tiptoes to her sister's bed. She gently kisses her sister on the forehead. She whispers, "I love you." Her sister briefly stirs, and then she turns over on her side.

There, I have finished packing everything. Now it is time that I get to the porch as Jordyn had asked. Gosh, I am excited and anxious and scared all at once! Am I going crazy? Am I doing the right thing? And Jordyn, are you real? And will you help me along the way as you promised you would?

A voice in her head replies, "Steph, you are not going crazy and yes. Deep in your heart, you know you are doing the right thing. You listen to me. And trust me. If you do everything that I ask all will be okay. I promise."

Steph flings her makeshift knapsack over her shoulder. She heads out the front door to the porch making certain she quietly closes the door behind her. She listens as one of the two door locks clicks into place. She jiggles the doorknob to make certain the door is locked. Jordyn's thoughts are in her mind once more.

"It is almost time for your purpose, your *raison d'être* as you like to say. It will not be long now. And I thank you for your willingness to embark on this journey. Your spirit and fearlessness are admirable as are your love and compassion. I love you."

Steph replies, "I love you, too. And I look forward to seeing you soon."

She glances at her watch. The time is 12:51 am.

Yay, only nine minutes to go before it's one o'clock!

She walks to the left-hand corner of the porch. She sets her knapsack on the floor and sits down beside it. She leans her head against the porch wall, and then she closes her eyes. She is confident she will not fall asleep. She is too keyed up to do anything but anxiously wait for her journey to begin!

CHAPTER TWO

DREAMS CAN COME TRUE

"What dreams invaded the tranquility of my imagination?"
- Steph, the present

Isn't it amazing when you think of something and whatever you were thinking comes true? Say, for instance, you think - perhaps wish is a better word - you wish for a week of gorgeous sunshine during your summer vacation, and lo and behold, it is the perfect sunshine-filled week. Better yet. You are at school or work and crave for something gooey, yummily delicious when you get home. Maybe your favorite meal or dessert? Only to have it waiting for you as you step across the threshold! Maybe it is your all-time favorite snack. Yummy German chocolate cake!

Or perhaps, whenever you are bored out of your mind and want someone to call or text you, to invite you to a fun party, a thrilling blockbuster movie, or to go for a walk? And presto! Your phone rings or the text miraculously appears! Out with the boredom and in with the fun!

A dream can be like that, too. You fall asleep, and then a cool dream appears. Perhaps you are saving someone. Better yet - falling romantically in love. And then there are the dreams where you are flying. Many of us have had that sort of dream, yes?

Maybe you are flying in a horizontal position with arms stretched before you, sort of like superman or superwoman or some other superhero. Then again, maybe you are the type of person who is flying upright in a vertical position in your dreams. Either way, you are flying, or floating, looking at the ground far below, perhaps engaged in something wonderfully adventurous and exciting. Maybe even saving someone's life as you battle evil.

Well, it was sort of like that for Steph as it relates to a horse she calls Spirit.

Steph had a dream one night she was flying high above the ground. No, not in an airplane. No, not like a superwoman. She was flying while mounted on a courageous horse named Spirit!

Spirit was a flying horse with beautiful, elegant, white wings - a Pordonas! Pordonas are members of the Troop, a fighting legion of flying horses and elf archers in a fantasy world of elves and bizarre creatures called Spardom. Steph, also an elf, commanded the Troop as its leader.

Far below on the ground, as far as the eye could see, a vicious battle was ongoing.

In Steph's dream, there were humanmade flying machines spewing fire! And, somehow, someway, Steph - who was referred to by others in her dream as Lady Enna - was chasing a humanmade instrument of war while mounted on Spirit.

A deadly drone!

Then she had saved the day by maneuvering Spirit, so he could down the drone causing it to crash in the desert. She was declared a heroine in the strange land along with her prized, flying horse Pordonas, Spirit!

Steph dreamed such a dream a few nights in a row. Naturally, over time she forgot about the general idea of the dream. Until eight weeks ago, just before she began to dream about Jordyn and the orphanage.

She was Googling the Internet and came across a novel entitled, *The Enchanted Gate, Conquest of the Hidden Valley*. For some strange reason, she felt compelled to read the book. She bought the book and downloaded it in ebook format to her iPhone. And wouldn't you know it? There, toward the end of the story, a few pages told of a courageous Lady Enna (the "Anne" portion of Steph's middle name JoAnne spelled backward!) saving the day as she rode a flying horse - a Pordonas named Spirit! Talk about supernaturally cool!

But the coolest thing is this. Lady Enna in the novel was able to read the thoughts of her flying horse, Spirit! Just like our Steph in this story can read her horse's thoughts as you will soon see for yourself. Even more amazing is Spirit's ability. In the novel, he was able to understand Lady Enna via telepathy. Just like Steph's earthly horse Spirit will understand her! They will enjoy telepathic conversations.

Steph enters the barn. She is pleased to see that Spirit is fully awake. As she places the saddle on his back, she says, "Well, it looks like we are about to embark on one more adventure."

She reads Spirits' thoughts as he replies, "So, you have decided to undertake the journey to visit with Jordyn and the other children? To strange places unknown and perhaps many in between? From what you have told me, Jordyn sounds like a charming teenager. But, desperately lonely and in need of someone to take care of her. That place where she lives seems to be horrible."

"Yes, it certainly is horrible. And oh! That nasty boy Roger Clyde Brewster has it out for her. Remember me telling you that he kicked her down the stairs? At least I presume he was the one that did it since he was on the spot immediately. He probably did not intend to kick her so hard, to cause her to tumble down the stairs.

"However, since she is deaf, she probably was in her own little world of absolute silence. As a result, she could not react properly to the kick like us hearing folk. So, rather than fall flat on her face or try to catch her fall, she must have panicked. Sixteen stair treads darn him! Even if Roger Clyde was not the one who kicked her, he is still one mean character. I am going to have a heart-to-heart talk with him when we arrive at wherever we are going."

Spirit's thoughts convey, "Hmm, which brings me to ask a crucial question. Just where *are* we going? Do you have an idea?"

"Well, to be honest with you, I have no clue where we are going. I am just hopeful that Jordyn will give us some instructions as we journey."

"I see," Spirit replies in his mind. "Well, do you have a clue as to which direction we should proceed? North, south, east, or west? Or do we stay here and wait for something to happen?"

Steph shakes her head and hunches her shoulders.

"I dunno. As I said, I have no clue. You are a horse. Therefore, you are supposed to have the natural instinctive ability to find your way.

Maybe you will be able to get us started in the right direction and also keep us safe as we journey."

"Me?" Spirit replies doubtfully. "Remember, Steph. Horses are renowned for their fight-or-flight instinct. We evolved from small mammals that would rather run than fight. Hence our first instinct, when confronted with danger, is to run away. That is why we have powerful legs and can gallop faster than most beasts. So, as far as keeping us safe, well, we will have to wait and see.

"As it pertains to finding our way, I have to agree. We horses are renown for finding our way. Home, Steph. The emphasis is definitely on the word home. As far as finding our way to Jordyn's domicile and anyplace else to where we will journey, I must say this. Unless she lives in your house, we are out of luck."

Steph laughs quietly.

"I see. Well, I hope you will resort to biting, kicking, rearing, or striking with your deadly hooves anyone or anything that intends to harm us."

"For you, I will do all of that. But remember, we horses consider humans to be predators. So, do not blame me if my fight-or-flight instinct takes over, in reverse order of course."

Steph knows that Spirit is toying with her. He loves to joke around, especially when he knows it will relieve the tension. In spite of this, she is too anxious and nervous right now to play his mind games.

She says curtly, "I am no hunter. And you *will* defend us. After all, you are the biggest. And you can forget about the flight part of a horse's fight-or-flight instinct. You will *fight* unless I tell you there is a need for *flight*. And when it is time for flight, if it comes to pass, you will ensure you have me mounted safely on your back. So there you have it. I implore you to get over your fight-or-flight conflict. That is if you please." She smiles.

Spirit replies in his mind, "Okay. You win. This round." As Steph leads him out of the barn into the morning's chill, he adds jokingly, "Okay, now tell me, miss meanie horse slayer predator who likes to bully poor little me. Which way do we go?"

"Well, for starters we will walk down the path toward the woods behind the house," Steph replies. "We will play it by ear from there."

She looks at her wristwatch. It is exactly 1:00 am.

Then she stares dumbfounded as her wristwatch gradually begins to disappear! After it has vanished completely, she warily touches her wrist.

Yep! The watch is no longer there!

At that moment she senses something else is dreadfully wrong, chillingly wrong.

She cautiously lifts her head as if she expects something frightful to appear before her eyes. She slowly moves her head to the left and then to the right. Then she does a complete three-hundred-sixty-degree turn in place.

"What in the world?"

She stares wide-eyed in disbelieving wonder at the surrounding incredibly unfamiliar scene. Gone is her two-story brick house. The school crossing street sign. The blinking school zone warning light. Her mailbox. The cars in her driveway. The street and sidewalk in front of her house!

Even the elementary school and its expansive parking lot across the street have disappeared!

Everything familiar that she has known all her life and loved with all her heart has vanished!

Her heart begins to race, the muscle's loud pounding in her chest echoing deafeningly in the pre-dawn stillness. She feels nauseous and is dreadfully frightened, a sensation she has never experienced before now. She begins to tremble uncontrollably. Clutching Spirit's reins more tightly, as she lovingly strokes his mane to pacify her rapidly growing fear, tears begin to fall freely from her eyes.

There is nothing but absolute devastation as far as the eye can see!

CHAPTER THREE

KÖHN (COLOGNE), GERMANY, WORLD WAR II

"Nazism is a human parasite. Altruism will eradicate it soon enough."
- Adalard, July 31, 1942

Part I: A World Turned Upside Down

The Royal Air Force (RAF) bombers of the first 1000-bomber raid of *Operation Millennium* had flown over Cologne two months earlier on May 30, 1942. They soared over Germany's third largest city at a calculated rate of one bomber every six seconds. The horror lasted nearly 90 minutes. The raid had two goals - to severely lower German morale and for use as a propaganda tool for the Allies.

Some estimates put the number of incendiary bombs unleashed that night at a hundred thousand. Smoldering fires of the nearly 5,000 ignited by the bombers told of indescribable devastation. Ninety percent of the central city was flattened. Six hundred acres of developed areas were destroyed, resulting in 59,000 homeless men, women and children. Even though most of the city's population hunkered down in underground shelters, nearly 500 civilians had perished. Thousands were wounded. Before World War II would end, Cologne would see its population reduced by 95 percent.

Despite the city's nearly total devastation, the Cologne Cathedral stood proudly, its twin spires a pillar of dignity in a city ruined by war. Allied airmen had used the cathedral as a reference point during their raids. The cathedral would receive fourteen direct aerial hits during the war. Even so, the majestic Cologne Cathedral withstood the horrific, terrorizing destruction of war. It remains standing to this present, modern day. The proud structure is the prime Gothic church in Northern Europe.

The preceding scene of destruction is confronting Steph and Spirit. Complete devastation looms, except for the two tall spires of the Cologne Cathedral off in the distance. Suddenly, familiar thoughts are in Steph's mind. The thoughts belong to Jordyn.

"In the church, Steph. A young boy. His name is Adalard. In the German language his name means *brave*. He lives. Barely. He is very emaciated. Notwithstanding his condition, his heart is bold. You must save him, Steph. Please!"

"How in the world does she expect you to do that?" Spirit's thoughts suddenly inquire. "I mean, take a good look around us. This place is in ruins. The few people who are walking look as though they are in a trance. No surprise considering the horrifying carnage and destruction that surrounds us.

"What is worse, there are German soldiers everywhere! I can sense their presence." His thoughts cease momentarily. "And I bet all of them would love to feast on some fresh horsemeat right about now! We need to get out of here. And fast!"

Steph is in no frame of mind to respond to Spirit's question. His last comment concerning horsemeat has twisted her stomach into knots. It implied death.

Ours!

She wants more than anything to flee with Spirit, to hasten away from this awful scene.

How long has it been? Less than five minutes since we left the safety of our neighborhood? I am already homesick, homesick for normality! Not to mention I am scared out of my wits! Thank God Spirit is with me. Otherwise, I would wish I was an earthworm and bury myself in the dirt to hide!

Despite her fear and longing to be back at home, she knows it is important that she answers Spirit's thoughts. After all, he is the only friend she has right now. Her mind goes off on a tangent as it races a mile a minute yet again.

But hold on a second here! How in the world did Spirit know what Jordyn just said in my mind? Is Jordyn somehow able to send thoughts to him telepathically? If so, that is remarkable! Goodness, the teenage deaf orphan girl is more mysterious and magical than I ever imagined!

"Well, okay, Spirit," she says aloud. "We are here, and something tells me there is no turning back. Even with the horrible misfortune before us, we must courageously face whatever comes our way. But I must tell you this. I am frightened like never before in my life. Before we come up with a plan, let me ask you a question. Did Jordyn's thoughts enter your mind? Did they? If they did, this is the first time. Am I correct?"

"Yes, they did," Spirit's thoughts reply. "And let me tell you something. I certainly do not like…"

Before he can continue relaying his thoughts, a rapid and ear-piercing staccato of gunfire repeats over and over in the morning's quietness. Steph instinctively ducks her head in response.

Rat-a-tat-tat!

Rat-a-tat-tat!

Rat-a-tat-tat! Rat-a-tat-tat! Rat-a-tat-tat!

It is the sound of an unseen machine gun frantically firing in Spirit and Steph's direction. Bullets ricochet everywhere on the shell-pocked wall just above Steph's head causing jagged pieces of weathered concrete to fly in all directions. One piece of the concrete grazes Steph's right cheek. She shouts out in agony.

"Ouch! That hurts!"

She gingerly touches her finger to her face. The tip of her finger is blood-stained. Blood begins to drip from the gash onto the dirt.

"Dismount!" Spirit's thoughts seem to scream.

"Get down and get low. Now!"

He drops to his front knees allowing Steph to dismount easily. She kneels behind the concrete wall beside him. The machine gun ceases firing now that the concealed shooter can no longer see them.

Steph presses the palms of her hands to either side of her temples. She can sense thoughts entering her mind. She knows that Jordyn is trying to communicate with her, but it is difficult to read her thoughts.

The gash on her cheek is throbbing, and her heart is loudly beating like it wants to burst out of her chest. Nevertheless, she knows that she must try to concentrate despite the danger and her fear.

After all, Spirit and I are here in this godforsaken place for a reason, *my raison d'être*. Besides, Jordyn had promised to keep us safe. I can only hope and pray she is true to her word.

Jordyn's thoughts seem to scream in her mind.

"Steph, you must enter the cathedral. Now! Soldiers are on their way to the cathedral. Adalard is in imminent, mortal danger. They want to kill him. Because of his religion. You must recall from your history lessons what happens during the Second World War in Europe. The Nazi's and their partisans murder millions of innocent men, women, and children like Adalard. Because of their religion! Because they are Jews!

"The cold-hearted, bigoted Nazi's will do anything to hunt down those they do not like. Even a small, innocent child like Adalard. And they will ask no questions. They will shoot on sight. Hurry now, Steph, before it is too late. Please!"

Steph scrambles to her feet. She crouches as low as possible. Her voice is shaky as she whispers.

"Spirit I want you to remain here. I do not want anything to happen to you. You are a larger target than I am. If you were wounded, there is no way I am leaving you behind." Tears well up in her eyes. "Besides, I would die if anything happened to you. I would rather give up my life than see you hurt."

She strokes his mane affectionately.

"And promise me this. If you feel like you are in danger, gallop from this godforsaken place as quickly as you can. Save yourself and do not worry about me. I will be okay. Do you understand?"

Before Spirit can reply, Steph takes off running. As she runs the bullets seem to follow her as they strike the other side of the wall.

Rat-a-tat-tat!

Rat-a-tat-tat!

Rat-a-tat-tat! Rat-a-tat-tat! Rat-a-tat-tat!

She abruptly stops running. She is breathing hard, panting. Now she is even more frightened. She is shaking from head to toe.

How is it the shooter can follow my movements? Yes, I know I am in a twilight zone of sorts in spite all that has happened recently. Jordyn talking to me in my mind. Jordyn somehow sending thoughts telepathically to Spirit.

Given the Köhn sign that I saw earlier, I know we are in Cologne, Germany. Given the destruction that surrounds, I know we are here during World War Two. All of what is happening is strange enough. But the unthinkable, the impossible may also be happening.

Is it possible that the unseen shooter can see through concrete walls? If so, I am a goner for sure!

She stares at the heavily pockmarked wall. It slowly dawns on her how the shooter seems to know her location as she runs. She correctly supposes that the shooter is following her movements through the many gaping shrapnel and bullet holes in the wall. To mask her movements, she considers running in a *stop and then go* kind of way.

Maybe that will keep the shooter from knowing my exact location! It is worth a try.

She crouches even lower until she is nearly on all fours. It is at this point she ponders her athleticism.

She is thankful for playing rough games of tennis and rugby. If she were like many of her peers, playing video games all day and not working out, she would be in a world of hurt. Although the bullets still might follow her, she feels relatively safe. Jordyn had said that she would protect her. Nevertheless, despite trying to put a positive spin on her current, deadly situation, serious doubts enter her mind yet again.

But how? How can Jordyn protect me from a blasting machine gun? Heck, I do not even know if Jordyn is real! Then again, perhaps this nightmare is nothing more than that - a terrifying, crazy dream, something abnormal going on in my head! That what I think I am sensing in my mind is nothing more than me talking to myself! Am I going crazy?

If so, I can only hope and pray that I awaken soon, contentedly tucked in my comfy bed with all of my joyful things and a loving family surrounding me.

But enough of this wishy-washy, wishful thinking. I am here. Spirit is here. And I have a job to do for Jordyn, whatever it may be.

Jordyn's words say, "Yes, Steph. I am glad you are working out your purpose in your mind. It is good therapy. After all, it is your *raison d'être* as you like to say."

Her thoughts pause briefly.

"Okay, you have caught your breath. Now you need to run, fast! I will be there alongside you. I will tell you what to do each step of the way. I will protect you, too. I promise. Run as quickly as you can, Steph. Please!"

Steph resumes running, this time more cautiously than before. She maintains a consistent pace until she comes to the next hole in the wall. Then she drops on all fours to crawl past it. She is relieved that the shooter does not detect her movements.

Most of the gaps in the wall are waist high. Now and then Steph comes to a hole that is a foot or more from the bottom. She cannot crawl beneath these holes. She is forced to hop over them. Her hopping over the holes occasionally prompts more gunfire from the other side of the wall. Finally, after more than a minute of running, she arrives at the far end of the wall.

She groans.

The cathedral doorway is more than twenty feet from where she is crouching behind the wall. And, amazingly, she somehow knows the gunner does not want her to enter the cathedral. After all, Jordyn had said people were on their way to harm Adalard.

Do they know I am on my way? To try and save the Jewish boy from almost certain death?

All of a sudden she hears voices. Lots of voices. Men. Lots of men shouting in German. The voices are coming from the opposite side of the wall where she had first cowered with Spirit.

Jordyn's thoughts enter her mind. Her words seem desperate.

"Steph, you do not have much time! The soldiers know you are at the end of the wall. And they know you do not have a weapon and that you are a female teenager! You are now in danger like Adalard if not more so! I promise I will be beside you all the way as you run. Now, Steph - now! You must run to the cathedral! Please!"

Steph does not hesitate to ponder her next move. She fully appreciates her state of affairs. The loud, gruff, commanding voices she hears off in the distance are those of soldiers. There is no doubt in her mind. And the voices are getting closer by the second. She knows the soldiers will not be very agreeable if they capture her.

She sprints toward the cathedral's main entrance as speedily as her powerful legs can move.

The machine gun fire resumes, but this time the gunner shoots bursts of bullets in front of her intended path. It is as if the gunner wants her to turn around and to run in the other direction - back behind the wall! But no matter what happens, Steph is determined to enter the cathedral. She zigzags her way around the bullets that are hammering the ground in front of her. She is scared out of her mind as she sprints in a crazy, crisscross pattern across the rubble-strewn grass.

I hope and pray to God the shooter does not mess up and take one of my zigs for a zag and accidentally shoots me!

If being shot at by an unseen machine gunner is not bad enough, even though the gunner is purposely trying to avoid hitting her on purpose, a male's commanding voice pervades the chaotic scene.

"Halt! Du bist verhaftet! Halt!"

Steph is tempted to stop. But she keeps on running.

She recognizes the word "halt," but she has no idea what the other words that the soldier shouted intend. But she is certain of one thing. She does not intend to halt for anyone. She is going to keep running - as fast as she can!

She sprints the final ten yards to the cathedral's opening.

The cathedral is dark and gloomy inside. Thick coats of concrete dust cover the overturned, cratered pews. Jagged bits of concrete litter the entire wooden floor. Shards of glass are everywhere, consequences of the many shattered windows destroyed by the bombs shockwaves.

Despite the depressing scene, the inside of the cathedral seems largely undamaged, the holy sight purposely spared by the Allied bombing.

To Steph, the cathedral is a consecrated, saintly sanctuary in the midst of an unbelievably devilish nightmare. She curtsies slightly, and then she makes the sign of the cross. She wants to say a brief prayer. However, she knows time is of the essence. She calls out to Jordyn for guidance.

"Jordyn, help me out here. Please tell me what am I supposed to do. Where is Adalard hiding? Please talk to me, Jordyn! I beg of you!"

She notices something in front of the altar. Its slight movement has sparked her attention. Her heart sinks. What she sees is not Adalard.

She is looking at an old-fashioned, handmade, wooden rocking horse. It is by itself to the left of the altar. To her bewilderment, the horse begins to rock from front to back vigorously on its own as if propelled by some magical force. She guardedly walks toward it. After taking a few steps, she abruptly stops in her tracks.

Ice-cold shivers scream up and down her spine. Then they speed across her shoulder blades causing her to shiver. Then thousands of tingling goosebumps cover her arms. The hairs on the nape of her neck come to attention. She begins to tremble wildly.

She is incredibly scared. Too paralyzed to move. Oddly, she feels like bawling; however, she knows that she cannot cry. The tears will not come. She knows that. Besides, she is too scared to do anything but stare at the rocking horse as it crazily rocks back and forth.

That is because her worst fears have come at last.

The soldiers have entered the cathedral!

She winces as a commanding voice shouts at the top of its lungs. "Dreh dick um!"

*****

Part II: Audacity of a Fearless Heart

"You will not turn around!" Jordyn's thoughts shout in her mind. "I repeat. Do not turn around. That is what the soldier is telling you to do. Stay put and do not move until I tell you. There are three soldiers. Do not look at them. Say to them this.

"'I am an American. I do not speak German. I only speak English.' One of the soldiers is a Hauptmann Rittmeister, a German Army Captain. He speaks some English. He will understand you, and he will talk to you in English as well. I do not want you to say anything else. Just repeat my words. Nothing else. Trust me.'"

Steph is now so terribly frightened her knees are shaking. She feels as if she is going to vomit. Or, even worse, she will faint. Then she will be helpless - completely at the mercy of the soldier's kindness or, horrifyingly, their notorious cruelty.

At that very moment her amazing, courageous inner-strength gradually regains control of her senses. She takes a deep breath to regain her composure. As Jordyn had commanded, she does not turn around. She takes another deep breath. Then she softly whispers, her voice firm.

"I am an American. I do not speak German. I only speak English." Then, ignoring Jordyn's direction not to say anything else, she yells.

"And I will not turn around as you have ordered!"

Silence. Deafening silence. What seems like forever. Nevertheless, the silence actually lasts but a few seconds.

Finally, one of the soldiers says in scratchy English, "You? An American?" He laughs. "I seriously distrust your words. Perhaps a very pretty Deutsche school girl educated in English, ja?" He laughs again as he looks at his fellow soldiers, and then he says in a disgustingly mocking tone, "Du bist seher hübsch."

Jordyn immediately translates his German words into English.

"The officer said, 'You are very pretty.' Now, Steph, please do not allow his chauvinistic words to upset you. I know that they will. Try to remain calm. There are three of them and only one of you. You are in more danger than you realize. I will try to figure out how you can get out of this frightening dilemma. Just remain calm. Please!'"

The soldiers jeeringly laugh as they exchange unrecognizable words in German. Steph winces at the sound of the soldiers' hideous-sounding guffaws. She is certain they intend to harm her. She tries to take Jordyn's advice - to remain calm.

Jordyn is right. I am very angry with the rude words from the man saying I am pretty. The officer's insulting, chauvinistic comment and the soldiers' rude laughter feel like sexist daggers piercing my heart! But remain calm? How in the world does Jordyn expect me to remain calm? Three men are standing behind me! And they have guns, while I have nothing but Jordyn's advice. And she's not even here!

The officer who spoke to her a few moments ago addresses her once more. From the tone of his voice, Steph knows that he is annoyed and very angry.

"I said turn around! But, of course, you already know what I said since you said in Deutsche that you would not turn around. So, an American you are not my pretty girl. If you do not obey my command, I will order my subordinates to shoot you. Now, my pretty English-trained Deutsche girl, turn around. At once! Or I will shoot you myself!"

Steph's present state of affairs horrifies her, but she refuses to allow this man to bully her, to mock her. She intends to cut the officer down with her words. When she finally replies her voice is stern and forceful.

"I was schooled in America, ja? I was born in America, ja? And I will not turn around, ja!" She unexpectedly recalls a word that a friend at school had said in German. The German word means *no* in English. She yells at the top of her lungs.

"Nein - nein - nein!"

After a brief moment of agonizing silence, the officer whispers in German to his comrades, "Dummes Mädchen!" Then he yells at Steph in English.

"Stupid girl! Stupid, stupid girl!"

Jordyn's thoughts quickly enter Steph's mind.

"You made the officer very angry. They are going to ambush you. I want you to walk slowly to the rocking horse. Make no sudden, panicky moves."

Once again, terrorizing paralysis is overwhelming Steph's senses. She is afraid that her legs will not move. Miraculously, by some means, she starts to walk slowly, almost nonchalantly, toward the rocking horse. The horse is approximately twenty feet away. As she slowly draws closer, it steadily slows its rocking. Then, with a mixture of both surprise and dread, Steph watches as the rocking horse turns on its runners ever so slowly. It does not stop turning until it is facing her straight on!

The soldier's voice booms in both German and English.

"Halt! Hor auf zu laufen! Stop walking! Dreh dich um! Turn around! Jetzt! Now!"

Steph suddenly winces at the sound of an extremely loud gunshot. Her eardrums immediately begin to scream. She recoils with outright dread as a bullet smashes into the floor just inches from her left foot. Wood splinters fly in all directions. A few of the splinters pierce the calf of her left leg drawing blood. The splinters immediately produce a fierce stinging pain. They feel like someone has stabbed her calf with needles.

Despite the throbbing pain that is slowly radiating up her leg, she does not flinch. She is unable to move. It is as if she is fossilized. Surprisingly, she sniffs the air. She grins as the distinctive odor of gunpowder enters her nostrils.

The smell reminds me of the aromatic odors of exploding fireworks on the 4th of July. Those smells, sprinkled with grayish clouds of smoke, I truly like. They are some of the most enjoyable aspects of holiday outings with my family back home.

Abruptly, her grin vanishes as tears well up in her eyes.

But the smell of this gunpowder is strangely different. Unpleasant. Deadly. Horribly deadly! I truthfully want to escape this invasive smell, escape this nightmare!

At that precise moment, to her complete amazement, the rocking horse raises on its runners and neighs loudly. Steph thinks she could be mistaken, but she believes she hears Spirit's faraway neigh answering in return.

What happens next is absolute chaos.

Two soldiers, undoubtedly the English-speaking German officer's underlings, suddenly charge at Steph from behind.

One of the soldiers roughly seizes her around the waist. The other soldier grasps her right arm firmly. By twisting and turning forcefully, she manages to break free of the soldier that had grasped her arm. She kicks at his shin. He shouts expletives in German as he stumbles to the ground.

Steph immediately kicks sideward to the knee of the soldier that had seized her around the waist. The crushing kick of her leg's well-developed, rugby-honed, powerful muscles impacts his kneecap brutally. He goes down on all fours moaning loudly, his kneecap agonizingly dislocated.

Despite the soldier's suffering as he lies on the floor, he somehow manages to unholster his sidearm. He glares up at Steph. She can see hatred in his eyes. Although his hand is shaking cruelly, he attempts to take careful aim at her head.

She kicks with all her strength at his hand that is holding the weapon. At the same time, she ducks waist-high to her right. The weapon discharges a split-second later. The bullet passes two or three inches above her head and sails through the hand of the other soldier that has clamored to his feet. Finally, the discharged bullet lodges harmlessly in the altar. Splinters of wood fly in all directions.

Steph watches out of the corner of her eye as the soldier's gun continues to soar through the air. It ultimately smashes to the floor twenty or more feet away with a metallic-sounding *twang!* Then it bangs across the wooden, debris-burdened floor with several threatening *thump, thump, thumps!* As one would expect, the gun discharges yet again. Luckily, the discharged bullet does not hit anybody.

The soldier that received the gunshot to his hand is shrieking. He is shaking his wounded hand up and down vigorously as if that will somehow lessen the unbearable pain he must be experiencing. Droplets of blood splash everywhere. Amazingly, despite his shrieking, and the intense pain he must be feeling, he continues to try to seize Steph. He grabs her around the shoulders from behind just as she turns to flee.

He will not give up until he subdues me! He is trained to ignore the most intense, physical pain - even an awful gunshot wound to his hand. Like all soldiers, he is trained to kill! What must I do to stop him?

The soldier with the dislocated kneecap attempts to get to his feet. Despite his efforts, he is unable to stand upright. He is in a stooped position. Steph immediately sees an opportunity to take him out - permanently. She kicks him hard in the face, smashing his nose with a loud *Crack!*

Tottering on one severely injured, useless leg, and now suffering the excruciating pain of a broken nose, the soldier staggers backward helplessly. He falls hard onto his back and smacks his head violently on a piece of concrete debris. He immediately starts to flail on the floor, visibly, witlessly confused.

Despite his bemused condition, he somehow manages to locate his nose with his right hand. He pinches his nostrils with his fingers. It is a futile attempt. Blood gushes from his hopelessly shattered nose and through his fingers like spouting water from a leaky bucket full of holes. Next, he manages to find his kneecap with his other unsteady, shaking hand. He cuddles his dislocated kneecap tenderly. If the agony he is experiencing is not enough for him to endure, he is shaking his head back and forth forcefully as if trying to clear his vision.

Steph is certain, in addition to a dislocated knee and a broken nose, he has a concussion.

As she fleetingly glimpses at the injured man, she experiences a sinking feeling in her gut. She is not a violent person. In fact, she abhors violence. She feels sorry for brutally injuring the young soldier.

Despite her momentary guilt trip, a wide grin appears on her face.

Be that as it may, I have beaten him. Besides, he started it, not me. One down two to go.

She does not have a chance to reflect at length about the soldier flailing helplessly on the floor. The second soldier, the one with the gunshot wound, is still trying to subdue her. He cannot get a firm grip on her arm with his one good hand. This is due to Steph's incessant turning here and there, and as expected, because of the palpable pain rendering his wounded hand virtually useless.

Steph grabs the soldier's wounded hand. She bites severely hard on his fingers instantly drawing more blood. He screams with renewed pain. He begins to cry out, presumably to the officer who, surprisingly, has not yet entered the fray.

"Ich bin verletzt! Hilf mir, Mein Herr! Bitt hilf mir, Mein Herr!"

He manages to get his good hand on Steph's throat. Before he can squeeze her windpipe, she delivers a mighty uppercut blow to his groin with her knee. He immediately recoils from the force of the blow and collapses to his knees. His hands instinctively move to the source of the agonizing pain.

Steph grabs him by his shoulders firmly. Before he can react, she delivers a second uppercut kick with the same knee. The powerful kick connects squarely with his jaw. The knockout blow renders him unconscious. He falls in a heap; his eyelids closed tightly. Steph grins once more as she stares wide-eyed at the two soldiers laying on the floor.

All of this happens within a few minutes timeframe. But to Steph, it seems like hours.

She suddenly notices that the rocking horse has disappeared. In its place stands a frail-looking, emaciated, young boy in ragged, ill-fitting, soiled clothes. Notwithstanding the ongoing confusion and her anxiety, she has enough sense to reckon the little boy most likely is Adalard.

She notices a faded yellow star on the left side of the boy's vest. The star is the telltale mark of a Jew. The Nazi's require Jews to wear the star, to distinguish the Jewish people from those of the so-called pureblood German race. Steph reasons the child must be older than six years. Only Jewish children older than six years have to wear the star on their garments. But she has precious time to contemplate what she is seeing. That is because she is under attack for the third time.

The third soldier, presumably the officer, because he is yelling filthy obscenities in English, rushes her from behind. He attempts to seize her in a headlock. As he struggles with her, he unholsters his sidearm. He tries to point his sidearm at Adalard. Due to Steph's twisting and turning, he is unable to aim his sidearm properly.

Steph screams, "No, no, no! You will not hurt Adalard!" She lunges for the firearm. But she is too slow.

The officer releases his grip on her as he steps back. To Steph's horror, he points his firearm less than an inch from her forehead. She stands motionless, her arms by her side. Her eyes begin to cross as she stares down the deadly darkness of the firearm's sinister muzzle. Her panicky heart begins to swell with a sea of tears as it echoes loudly in her trembling chest. She is afraid she will pass out in sheer terror. She locks her knees and sways ever so slightly on the balls of her feet. Words of a familiar, hopeful prayer lovingly caress her trembling lips. They seem to comfort her as she readies herself for whatever comes next.

The officer whispers, "Gib dich jetzt hin." He smiles an evil-looking smirk. "In English, pretty little girl, what I said in my beloved

Deutsche is, 'surrender now.'" Continuing to point his firearm at Steph's forehead, he glances down at his comrades. He shakes his head slowly. What he says next is in a nearly inaudible whisper. His tone is somber.

"Oder, ich werde dich töten müssen."

He looks up from the floor and stares at Steph squarely in her crossed eyes. She has no clue what he said. She instinctively hunches her shoulders in reply.

"Okay, pretty little girl, let me translate into English what I just said in my beloved Deutsche. What I said is, 'Oder, ich werde dich töten müssen.' That means, 'Or I will have to kill you.' Do you understand what I am saying, pretty English-speaking girl?'"

Steph does not respond. All of a sudden, Jordyn's words are in her mind. What she says provides Steph with a glimmer of hope, a small ray perhaps, but hope even so. She smiles a sheepish grin, and then she crosses the fingers on both of her hands. She slowly tilts her head to the right.

"I understand what you are saying. Please allow me to reply. May I?"

The officer slowly nods his head. His dark eyes remain riveted on her face. "Go ahead, pretty girl. Speak."

Steph's knees are shaking violently, and her lips and mouth are extremely dry. She licks her lips, and then she sticks out her tongue. What follows are insulting words in a spitting scream.

"Du kannst zur Hölle fahren!"

The officer is visibly upset. His face immediately flushes, and the veins in his neck begin to bulge. The hand holding his gun is moving from side to side ever so slightly. Steph knows he is insulted and very angry with her because she told him *where he could go* in his beloved Deutsche.

He gradually regains his composure. Then, as he sneers a disgusting grin, he casually shifts his firearm from his right hand to his left. Steph correctly assumes that his right hand is his dominant hand. And something tells her what he intends to do with his dominant hand is not going to be very pleasant.

"Nur für den Fall hübsches kleines Mädchen."

"Do you want me to say in English what I just said in my beloved German?"

Steph does not reply. Not only does she not care what he has said, but she is also too frightened to open her mouth to speak.

"'I said, 'Just a precaution pretty little girl.'" He glances at his soldiers sprawled on the floor. "Just a precaution considering you were able to do that to my men with your powerful legs. And they are two of my best men!" He leers the evilest grin imaginable. Then he says in a nauseating tone of voice, "Pretty little girl."

If he calls me pretty little girl one more time, I am going to spit in his face!

Despite Steph's anger with the officer's repeated sexist words, she instinctively knows what he is thinking. He intends to crush her face with a knockout punch. That is why he relocated his firearm from his favored hand to the other hand. Then she will be completely at his mercy. So will Adalard.

As if he has read her mind, the officer looks at Adalard. The boy is standing behind Steph to her left.

With clear loathing in his voice as he glares, the officer spits out between clenched teeth, "Du bist der nächste Jude!" He looks at Steph. "Do you want to know what I said to your friend?"

Steph slowly shakes her head no.

"Too bad, pretty little girl. I will tell you anyway. I said to your friend, that disgusting Jew over there, 'You are next Jew!'" He smirks a hideous look. "Besides, pretty little girl, it is his destiny. And then it will be yours." He pauses briefly. "But know this. When I kill the disgusting Jew, I will force you to watch."

Steph cringes in horror as the officer begins to flex his dominant hand in front of her face. Then he clenches a tight fist. Next, he purposely, sinisterly, ever so slowly, rears back with his clenched fist. Steph closes her eyes.

When suddenly! A nanosecond before he can punch Steph in the face, he hurriedly spins on his heels.

Rapidly galloping hooves resonate deafeningly throughout the cathedral. They are comparable to furiously pounding thunderclaps of an oncoming storm.

Steph screams, "Spirit!" Then she pushes away from the officer with all of her strength. He stumbles forward.

Spirit is alongside them in no time. He raises up high on his hind legs. Steph falls to the ground to escape his hooves that are thrashing dangerously in the air. The officer hurriedly turns to escape. He drops his weapon. Just as he bends over to retrieve it, Spirit pummels him in the back of his head with his hammering hooves knocking him out cold.

As she stares at the three men lying on the floor next to her, Steph wants to smile. However, she does not. She feels hopelessly sad. She shouts, "Three down, a whole world war of evil to go!"

She gets to her feet and rushes to Spirit. She hugs his mane.

"Thank you, Spirit. You saved my life!"

She suddenly feels uncomfortably chilly. Sweat caused by the intense physical exertion of fighting three men has drenched her clothes. She also is exhausted. What is more, she is frightened of what may happen next. Not only to her but Adalard as well. She also has to think about Spirit's welfare.

In spite of her exhaustion, her anxious fear of what the future may hold, and her unbelievably sore body, she is determined to carry on. She is unwavering in her commitment to accomplish whatever it is that Jordyn will ask her to do.

After all, it is my purpose.

My raison d'être.

She unexpectedly collapses to her knees. She begins to crawl on all fours to Adalard. Her eyes are streaked with tears.

But I will not cry. I must remain strong for Adalard. He is trying to survive in a world of unbelievable hatred. Because he is here - in the wrong place at the wrong time. Because he has suffered more agony and seen more horrible things, than I would care to imagine.

Because he is a Jew.

Adalard rushes over to Steph. He helps her to her feet with his good hand. The two embrace.

Suddenly, Jordyn's voice cries out in her mind.

"Steph! There is no time to relax. One of the soldiers is waking. The one you kicked in the jaw!"

Steph spins around. The soldier is on his hands and knees. He appears groggy, but Steph knows it will not be long before he is back to his same soldierly self - ready to pounce! Or worse!

Jordyn's thoughts are in Steph's mind yet again.

"Heavily armed soldiers a short distance away heard the gunshots! The gunshots echoed like loud thunderclaps from inside the cathedral. The soldiers are hastening to the cathedral. There are at least ten of them. You do not have much time!

"Now, Steph, listen to me carefully. Gently place Adalard on Spirit. He has a broken arm as you know, so do not worsen it. I will speak to Adalard in his mind, in his language, to calm him. After you place him on Spirit, I want you to mount up as well. Spirit will know what to do when the two of you are safely mounted. Now move! Please!"

*****

Part III: Run Like the Wind!

With Steph and Adalard mounted on his back, Spirit gallops through the cathedral toward the entranceway. Just as he is about to exit, Jordyn's thoughts enter his and Steph's minds.

"Whoa, Spirit! Steph, do not allow Spirit to exit the cathedral. Not just yet. Remove that detestable star from Adalard's vest. Hurry!"

Adalard is sitting in front of Steph. She reaches from behind and rips the cloth star from his vest. She tosses it to the floor.

Good riddance to detestable bigotry!

"What now, Jordyn?" Steph's thoughts say. "Please tell me what we should do next."

Jordyn does not reply.

She attempts to contact Jordyn again, this time in a whisper. "Jordyn! Tell me what we should do! Please talk to me!"

Adalard shakes his head forcefully. He repeatedly taps his temple with the forefinger of his good hand. Steph immediately understands what he is implying with this non-verbal gesture. Jordyn is telling him what to do. She frowns.

Oh, my goodness. Now we have to rely on a child to get us out of this mess. A child who is taking directions from a person who I have never seen!

Jordyn's thoughts are in Steph's mind once more as she addresses Spirit.

"Okay, Spirit. Exit the cathedral. Ensure your gait, your walk, is slow and purposeful. And Steph, please do not worry. Adalard knows what to do once you are outside. No matter what happens do not panic. They will shoot the three of you without any hesitation if you panic!"

Now Steph is even more terror-stricken.

Not only must I trust the wisdom of a child to keep us from harm, but now I must trust the wisdom of a horse? What is worse, Jordyn is purposely leaving me out of the loop! Why is she doing this to me?

Jordyn's straightforward response in her mind consists of seven words.

"Trust me. Trust them. And be quiet."

Spirit slowly exits the cathedral.

Before Steph's eyes can adjust to the bright sunlight, her heart sinks. Standing before them, just outside the cathedral's entranceway, is a squad of worried-looking German soldiers. The hardened expressions on their faces are ones of no-nonsense - *ask few questions, take no prisoners, shoot on sight if necessary.* Their rifles are cocked, loaded, and leveled at Steph, Adalard, and Spirit.

An officer moves to the front of the soldiers.

"Halt! Du machst?"

Steph is about to say something when Adalard elbows her in the ribs. He replies to the officer in German. He anxiously glances over his shoulder.

"Sir, please help us! Allied soldiers are in the cathedral. They have shot one of your Sergeant's! We were lucky to escape with our lives. Now they are hiding from you amongst the pews. A few are hiding behind the altar. Some have escaped from the back of the cathedral."

The officer, an Overleutnant, a senior lieutenant of the German Army, frowns. He unholsters his sidearm, a German Luger. He presses the muzzle of the pistol against Adalard's chest. His words are doubtful, scornful.

He scolds in German, "That is preposterous! There are no Allied troops in all of Germany." He cocks his Luger pistol. "You are lying. Tell me the truth or I will shoot you."

"Overleutnant," Adalard cries, "they do not wear uniforms. I fear they might be rebellious Jews disguised as German soldiers. You must assist the Sergeant. He is bleeding but still alive." He gestures at the cathedral with his thumb.

"Surely you heard the gunshots, Herr Overleutnant?"

The Sergeant that is standing next to the Overleutnant says politely, "Es ist möglich, Overleutnant?"

The Overleutnant replies, his look doubtful.

"I hardly think it is possible. Although I have heard of some Jews possessing weapons, I seriously doubt this boy is telling the truth." Turning his attention back to Adalard he motions with his Luger at Steph.

"And who is this girl? Your sister?"

He holsters his Luger as he approaches Steph. Adalard smiles inwardly. The officer holstering his sidearm is an unconscious sign of respect for the opposite sex. Adalard appreciates that this officer is kindhearted even though he knows the officer still mistrusts them.

The Overleutnant smacks Steph's left thigh hard with his swagger stick. She flinches at the sudden razor-sharp pain. She slowly turns her head to look at the officer. The expression on her face is one of repugnance. She abhors being struck by anyone, no less by a stranger in a foreign land! Who can blame her?

"What is your name?" the Overleutnant commands in German.

Steph does not reply. The expression on her face is one of absolute disgust. She turns her head and looks away.

The Overleutnant removes his Luger from its holster. He places it against Steph's forearm. He begins to tap her stomach with his swagger stick.

He says in German, "I asked you your name!"

Steph slowly turns her head to look at the officer. Once again, she does not reply. That is because she has no clue what he has said.

Besides, Jordyn told her to keep quiet. She narrows her eyes and stares blankly at the officer. She looks down at the swagger stick. The officer's constant tapping of the swagger stick on her stomach is making her angrier by the second.

She turns her nose up at the swagger stick, and then she brusquely rips it from the officer's grasp. She nods at the officer one time with an accompanying straight-faced expression. Then she places the swagger stick into his open hand. She glares at him spitefully before looking away yet again.

If he smacks me one more time with that stick of his, I am going to punch him in the nose! Goodness me, these soldiers are arrogant!

Adalard turns his head to address the Overleutnant.

"She is deaf and dumb, sir. She was born that way. She does not know what you are saying." He makes a few small circles with his forefinger near his temple. "Also, she is not all there if you know what I am saying. So, please do not bother her, sir. She has been through much pain." With a sheepish grin, he adds in a sad tone, "I hope you understand, Herr Overleutnant. She does not know what you are saying. And that is the truth."

Suddenly, without warning, sporadic gunfire erupts from inside the cathedral.

Pop! Pop! Pop - Pop - Pop!

The Overleutnant shouts to his men, "Get in there now! Be careful." He points to the Sergeant.

"Take four of your men and enter the cathedral from the rear. I will remain here with these three. I want to ensure they are safe. Now move!"

Steph assumes that Jordyn is somehow causing panic inside the cathedral - that she is forcing the three German soldiers to exchange friendly fire.

But wait! Are all of the soldiers conscious? I seriously doubt it. But if they are conscious, at what are they shooting? Themselves? Then again, is Jordyn shooting at the soldiers? If she is not, is it possible that she is causing the weapons to fire by themselves? If so, how?

The Overleutnant reholsters his sidearm. He gently pats Steph's thigh with his hand. He steps forward a few feet to address Adalard in German.

"Please tell the girl that I am sorry for hitting her. I can appreciate how she must feel. My youngest daughter is deaf from a serious infection." He strokes Spirit's mane.

"Now tell me, son. How is it you came to have this horse? He is a beauty."

"It is not my horse, sir," Adalard replies. He gestures with his thumb at Steph. "My sister stole it from a Jew when he wasn't looking." He laughs adding, "Being deaf has its advantages I dare say. She is very stealthy when she walks. The Jew did not know she was there."

Surprisingly, the Overleutnant laughs in response to what Adalard has said.

"Yes, being deaf has its advantages despite its cruelty." He smiles as he looks longingly at the dark gray sky. A storm is approaching from the north.

"My deaf daughter sneaks up on me from behind, and I never even hear her coming." Tears are welling up in his eyes. "But that seems very long ago, in a faraway place." He looks at Steph. She continues to avoid his gaze.

"Such a shame to be both deaf and mute." He imitates Adalard's gesture by making a few small circles with his forefinger beside his head.

"And being a little verrückt as well. My daughter is about her age. But, unlike your sister, she does not have intellectual problems. She lives with my wife and three boys on the outskirts of Berlin. Have you ever been to Berlin, son?"

"Nein," is all that Adalard can manage to say in reply.

Even though Jordyn is telling him what to say, Adalard is becoming very nervous. In the beginning, he interpreted the officer's show of kindness as genuine concern for their welfare. But now he is worried. If the situation does not change soon, the Overleutnant will take them back to his Hauptquartier, his headquarters. Then the three of them will be subject to scrutiny, interrogation, or worse!

Gunfire erupts from inside the cathedral for a second time. The sound of this latest gunfire is more intense than that of a minute ago.

Pop! Pop! Rat-a-tat-tat! Pop! Pop! Rat-a-tat-tat!

The Overleutnant looks Adalard squarely in the eye. He taps his holstered Lugar menacingly with the palm of his hand.

"I want the three of you to remain here, son. Do not move from this location. If you leave, I will find you. Since there is gunfire inside the cathedral, I know you were telling me the truth. Nevertheless, I still have more questions to ask you. I want to know why you and this girl were in the cathedral, why you have this handsome horse, what your names are, things like that. Do you understand what I am telling you, son?"

"Jawohl, Overleutnant," Adalard replies smartly. He lifts his broken arm in a feeble but respectful attempt to salute the officer.

The Overleutnant laughs in response to Adalard's comical saluting gesture. Then, unholstering his Luger, he dashes toward the cathedral.

Jordyn's thoughts seem to scream in Steph and Spirit's minds.

"Run like the wind, Spirit. Run like the wind!"

*****

Part IV: Nazism is a Human Parasite

An hour later Steph and Adalard are resting beneath the leafy canopy of a tall elm tree. Spirit is grazing nearby in the meadow of tall grasses. Rays of sunshine seemingly play a lofty game of hide and peep amongst the dark gray storm clouds.

Steph is lying on her side supporting her head in the palm of her hand. She is facing Adalard as he talks. Without thinking, she is snapping off the tips of blades of grass with her fingers and tossing them into the soft breeze. She watches amused as they momentarily sail in the breeze then cartwheel lazily to the lush, green grass.

Now and then she tilts her head to look at the sky. She is uneasy. It looks as if it is going to rain in a little while. Neither she nor Adalard has rain gear. If it starts to rain the two of them will get soaked. Fortunately, so she reckons, she has a light jacket and a sweater in her makeshift knapsack. The outer coverings are not waterproof, but they will help ward off the cold for the two of them if the rain continues into the night. The day is warm enough, so she does not think they will have to worry about hypothermia. That could change when darkness falls or if the temperature drops significantly.

Steph has no clue what month it is nor the day of the month. She snaps another tip from a blade of grass and examines it. Based on its luxuriance she guesses the month is mid to late July. The meadow of tall grass on which Spirit is grazing is a healthy green like one would expect to see in the springtime. Dandelions dot the landscape with their bright yellow flowers. The trees have nearly full foliage. The brisk breeze is warm to the skin.

We should be okay in case of rain. Spirit will continue to graze happily whether it rains or shines, so there is no need to worry about him.

Adalard is sitting cross-legged as he eats a piece of hard candy. He is a handsome boy with sandy blond hair speckled with chocolate-colored streaks. He has deep blue eyes. Steph guesses he is nine, maybe ten-years-old. He is very thin probably due to the lack of nourishing meals and not eating often enough.

His mismatched clothes are in tatters. His soiled trousers are ill-fitting, at least four or five sizes too large for his slight frame. The trouser cuffs are rolled up just below his knees. His long-sleeve, ragged gray shirt hangs loosely from his bent shoulders. Steph reckons it is a man's shirt.

Most strikingly, Adalard's ragged leather shoes do not match. The shoe on his left foot is brown. The shoe on his right foot is black. It is missing its toe tip. It is also a left foot shoe. Adalard explains that he could care less if his shoes do not match or if both shoes are intended for the left foot. Being fortunate enough to have shoes on one's feet during the dead of winter can spell the difference between life and death. He also says that the black shoe is two sizes smaller than his foot, so he had to cut off the toe tip.

He did not have any cutting tools, so he used the jagged edge of a rock. He said it took forever to cut off the toe tip. All the while he was looking out for danger. He goes on to say that he removed the black shoe from the rotting corpse of a teenager. The teenager was a Jew, his body left to rot in the snow. Someone shot the teenager in the forehead execution style.

Adalard goes on to say he found the brown shoe beneath a pile of rubble of a Jewish house. Unknown persons had torched the house. "Nevertheless," he had added with a solemn tone, "undoubtedly those that torched the house were members of the dreaded Geheime Staatspolizei, the Gestapo."

Steph places a clean bandage on Adalard's broken arm. As she tends to his arm, she is relieved to see that the break in the bone did not pierce the skin. If it had broken the skin, he would soon have a raging infection, an infection that would undoubtedly cause high fever or even kill him.

After bandaging his arm, Steph strips large pieces of cloth from one of her T-shirts. She makes a sling. As she ties a knot in the sling on the back of Adalard's neck, he whispers, "Danke, Fraäulein. Du bist sehr nett." He blushes noticeably with an accompanying cute grin. He hunches his shoulders just as he says another phrase in German.

"Und sehr hübsch."

Steph is not certain what Adalard said in his native tongue, but she knows some of what he said was a thank you. While she waits for Jordyn to interpret Adalard's words in her mind, she nods her head and smiles.

Jordyn's thoughts say, "Adalard said, 'Thank you, miss.'"

Steph pats Adalard on his knee a couple of times. In reply for his thanking her in German, she says, "Bitte schön."

She figures the two of them should try to learn a bit about each other's language by repeating words and phrases in their native tongue. She repeats the words in German, and then she says them in English.

"Bitte schön. You are welcome."

Jordyn's thoughts are in her mind once more.

"You may have noticed that Adalard said two additional German phrases. The first one was 'du bist sehr nett.' It means 'you are very kind.' The second phrase was 'und sehr hübsch.' That means 'and very pretty.'"

Much to Steph's surprise, Adalard seems to comprehend what Jordyn has said. He giggles just as his face turns bright red. He quickly looks away from her to stare at the darkening sky. Steph reasons, correctly, that Jordyn had conveyed her thoughts to Adalard at the same time she was conveying them to her. She replies cheerfully with a loud laugh.

"Danke, Adalard."

In the back of her mind, she is thinking, Jordyn is amazing, truly amazing! It seems she can telepathically send her thoughts to two people at the same time - in two different languages!

Adalard has just finished nibbling on a half sandwich of peanut butter and jelly. It is the first thing he has had to eat in four days.

Steph recalls reading somewhere that it is not prudent to feed substantial amounts of food to someone who has not eaten in a while. Otherwise, their stomach will revolt, and they will throw up, or in extreme cases, they could even die. Consequently, Steph tells Adalard, naturally via Jordyn's telepathic exchange, to eat the sandwich slowly. She is happy to see that he is following her instructions.

Adalard had access to ample supplies of clean rainwater while he was hiding from the Nazis. If he had not had water to drink, his suffering probably would have ended by now. He keeps a tiny vial of iodine in his pants pocket to treat water when fresh rainwater is not available.

Now he is sucking on a piece of hard candy and happily smiling as he licks his lips. Later, Steph will surprise him with one-half of a tasty Twinkie. But first, she will wait to see how his stomach reacts after eating a half sandwich.

Adalard begins to describe the widespread misery and suffering of Cologne's inhabitants, particularly the Jews. His account is profoundly upsetting and very moving.

*****

Part V: War Against the Jews

Life in Cologne before the Allied bombing was relatively good. Except, of course, for the Jews. There was an ongoing war of bigoted cruelty long before the Allied bombers began to unleash their death from the sky.

The war, as Adalard's parents liked to call it, was the *German War against the Jews*. It focused on the complete discrimination and total alienation of Jews in Germany. No Jewish person, the German citizen Jew or the immigrant Jew was immune to its narrow-minded hatred. In the eyes of the German Aryan society, all Jews were *verboten*. Translated into English, the German word verboten means forbidden.

Adalard wasn't even born when Aryanization began in Cologne and elsewhere in Nazi Germany. Aryanization was the steady expulsion of Jews and other peoples, referred to as non-Aryans, from the business way of German life. The goal of Aryanization was to eliminate all Jewish influence on the German economy. There were two primary parts of the Aryanization process.

The first part was *voluntary* on behalf of Jewish business owners. It focused on the voluntary exchange of property between a Jew and a non-Jewish German partner. Within this first part, there was a second segment, a *Chapter Two*, as Adalard's parents liked to refer to it at the time.

The second segment, the Chapter Two, of the ongoing persecution of Jews occurred during the Nazi boycott of Jewish businesses. It began in the Spring of 1933 shortly after Hitler was granted plenary or unlimited powers by the March 1933 *Enabling Act*.

Women of the National Socialist organization, abbreviated *NS*, would stand in front of Jewish shops to prevent customers from entering. To avoid confrontations with the NS-organizations, citizens of Cologne, even those sympathetic to Jews, gradually stopped shopping in Jewish-owned places of business. Naturally, Jews steadily lost their means of survival.

The second phase of Aryanization began sometime after 1938. Adalard explains the procedure was quite simple. Exchange of property between a Jew and a non-Jewish German partner was no longer voluntary. State laws were enacted to *force* Jews to sell their businesses. To add insult to injury, Jews had to sell their businesses at prices far below market value.

With tears misting his eyes, Adalard explains how his parents interpreted the Nazi and the Cologne citizenry's attack on their business. It was a business that was in their family for three generations.

"My family's business was our livelihood." As Steph nods her head, Adalard looks at his mismatched, worst for wear shoes. He suddenly bursts into tears. His subsequent words touch Steph's heart as Jordyn repeats them to her.

"I used to help my father, sweeping the floor, fixing things, oiling the machinery, stuff like that. Ironically, our family business was a shoe repair business!"

He buries his face in his hands and sobs.

Now Steph's eyes are welling up with tears. Once again, she tries with all her strength not to cry. She understands that she must remain strong for Adalard and for whatever Jordyn will ask her to do next.

Jordyn has ceased transmitting Adalard's thoughts to Steph momentarily. During this painful, silent period of contemplation, Steph reflects on a curious wonder.

When Jordyn translates Adalard's German sentences into English, she sometimes corrects herself. Her thoughts in my mind will convey things like, *sorry, Steph, that is the wrong word for,* or, *what I should have said was the word so and so.* Of course, that is it! Just as Adalard shakes or nods his head, Jordyn immediately corrects a word or two in her telepathic conveyance to me. Because of these subtle corrections, I must assume that Jordyn is repeating words to Adalard in German just as she conveys them to me in English and vice versa.

Simultaneously! In two different languages!

It is like Jordyn is two distinct people sitting beside us. One listening and talking in German to Adalard. The other listening and talking in English to me. Then, somehow, miraculously, the two of them instantaneously linking the two transferences without a pause or delay!

Telepathically!

But that is not all. How can Jordyn envision what is happening to us, generations in the past and across the vast Atlantic Ocean? Assuming she is somewhere in the United States! And how did she know where the soldiers were, their numbers, the insignias on their uniforms, and other pertinent facts? And was it Jordyn that caused the chaos inside the cathedral when we were outside? There is no doubt in my mind it was her!

Telepathy is one thing. Incredible! Telepathically causing guns to fire. Unbelievable!

At last, Adalard has composed himself. He dabs at the corners of his eyes with the cuff of his tattered shirt.

"To my parents, the slow squeezing of their way of life was like trying to survive as ravaged characters in a nightmarish story in a non-fiction book of horrors. It was a story that, amazingly, contained all the important, required parts that one sees in a book of human history. Please allow me to explain.

"First came the *Characters* of the book, the major players in the story. The Antagonists - Hitler and the Nazi movement along with its dreaded Gestapo, the Schutzstaffel (*SS*) and, for young people like me, its hated Hitler Youth, the Hitlerjugend. And the Protagonists - the Jews.

"Next, there was the story's *Setting* of the book. Spreading hateful propaganda that Jews were a threat to the German way of life. The Nazi's vicious propaganda resulted in insults by ordinary citizens on the street, singing of hateful songs in small gatherings, and scrawling of discriminatory slogans denouncing Jews on street signs and shop windows. Next came the enactment of laws to make life miserable for the Jewish population.

"The third part of the story consisted of the *Plot* of the book. The plot turned our Jewish community upside-down. The verbal hate on the streets, in the newspapers, and in the schools turned a dangerous corner. The hate had intensified to beatings and even random killings of Jews. Lawyers and school teachers, even judges, were rounded up and paraded in the streets. Many had to wear signs mocking Jews. Jewish government workers were loaded into garbage trucks and driven through the streets to be mocked and stoned.

"Yes, Steph, hatred of the Jew was everywhere. And the German government had realized its devious *Plot* as if a dream had come true. The Plot was carved in stone as the Aryan race began to remove all things Jewish from German society.

For the Jews were verboten."

He shakes his head sorrowfully.

"While the entire world watched and did nothing!"

He wipes the tears from his eyes once more.

"Then the unthinkable part of the story began - the *Conflict* of the book. It was the successful alienation of Jews from the business and social life of Cologne and the rest of Germany. Yes, Steph, the centuries-old history of the persecution of Jews had repeated itself. It had revealed its ugly, bigoted head yet again.

"Indeed, the outright quest to battle against the Jew's very existence had begun in earnest. As I mentioned earlier, it was during the second phase of Aryanization, during the Conflict portion of my hypothetical book, that my parents were forced to sell their shoe repair business at one-third of its worth.

"During the Conflict, Jews over a certain age were required to wear the yellow star. Like the star you ripped off of my vest. Jews could not use public telephones. Jews had to walk for hours to get food from public distribution centers because they were not allowed to ride on public transportation. Jews could not buy books in the bookstore. How lame is that?

"What is even more cold-hearted, Jews were forbidden to own pets! Can you imagine? How do you explain to a Jewish child that he could not own a pet? Who does that? Evil does that. I had to give my dog to a non-Jewish friend. Can you believe that?"

Adalard reaches to tie the tattered lace of his black shoe.

"But there are five important parts of any storybook worth telling." Tears are now streaming down his face.

"The last part of a story is its *Resolution*. Regrettably, my parents could not tell me about the final part of the Jewish people's nightmarish story, the Resolution. I had to learn it firsthand. The hardest way imaginable. By myself.

"My parents, along with many others, were moved to a so-called Jewish House. I have not seen them since." Despite his shaky voice, Adalard manages a meek smile.

"I learned about the final, most important part of the Resolution in my make-believe book, from my father's best friend. Please allow me to refer to the Resolution of my hypothetical book by another name. *The Final Solution*.

"The Final Solution - in the German language it is known as the *Endlösung der Judenfrage* - according to Herr Erich Kilbansky, is the Nazi plan for the extermination of all Jews during this ongoing war, this so-called World War II. Herr Kilbansky is, or I should say, was the Schulleiter, the Headmaster of Jawne. Jawne is also known as the Jewish Gymnasium of Rhineland in my city, Cologne.

"According to Herr Kilbansky, this Nazi policy, stemming from the top of the Nazi hierarchy, from Hitler himself, is the official code name for the murder of all Jews within reach of the Third Reich. Herr Kilbansky said he had proof that the policy of the Endlösung der Judenfrage was devised by the Nazi's during a January 1942 conference in Berlin.

"I was at school when I learned that my parents and my baby sister were taken away, relocated to the Jewish House. Herr Kilbansky said that being relocated to a Jewish House is the kiss of death. He believed that Nazi's would transport Jews in the House to concentration camps.

"As soon as I heard about my parents and baby sister's fate, I ran away. Many of my classmates ran away as well. Those of us who ran away were following the suggestions of Herr Kilbansky. He had encouraged us to run away and hide while we had the chance. He told us that we had to survive, to someday tell the story to future generations of Germany's persecution of the Jews. He said, even if it meant that if we were to abandon our family, friends, and neighbors, we must survive.

"Unfortunately, Herr Kilbansky did not heed his own advice. The Gestapo deported him and his whole family a few days ago. Rumor has it that they were all shot in a wooded area during their transport to Minsk and their bodies dumped into a prepared pit. I assume my parents and baby sister may someday share the same fate as Herr Kilbansky if they haven't already."

Adalard shrugs his shoulders.

"I have been running ever since the day they took my family away, over four months now. Sadly, my classmates, those that ran away with me, are all gone. All of them perished during the horrible Allied bombing of my city two months ago."

Adalard looks at Steph, his face expressionless.

"And do you know why all my classmates perished in the Allied bombing?"

Steph slowly shakes her head.

"As Jews, they were forbidden to go into the underground shelters while bombs rained down on the city! I too had to remain outside of the shelters. Nevertheless, I am one of the lucky ones. As fate would have it, I survived."

He buries his face in the palms of his hands once more.

Steph whispers, "That you survived the bombings proves that nothing can scathe your impenetrable will to survive. You are a brave boy, Adalard. Amazingly brave."

She reaches into her makeshift knapsack. She pulls out a Twinkie and breaks it in two. She hands one-half of the pastry to Adalard. His eyes brighten as he takes it. He even manages a timid smile. As he slowly munches on a small portion of the delicious, cream-filled pastry, he mouths, "Danke, Steph."

Steph gobbles her half of the Twinkie in one bite. With a forced smile, she replies, "Bitte schön."

As he eats, Adalard's sad expression slowly turns to one of resolve. Steph is amazed at this transformation. As soon as he begins speaking, Jordyn translates his words and conveys them to her.

"Nazism is a human parasite. Altruism will eradicate it soon enough."

He reaches into his pocket. He withdraws a small, rounded object. He has a huge grin on his face as he drops the object into Steph's open hand. It is a tarnished, weather-beaten coin.

Steph studies the coin for a few seconds. The number "1" is on the obverse side of the coin along with a wheat sheaf. It is like an American one-cent piece except the words are in German. Jordyn interprets Adalard's thoughts as he tells Steph what the coin represents.

"It is called a Reichspfennig. It is the lowest denomination of the coins of the Reichspfennig series. There are also 2, 5, 10, and 50 pieces. The two highest pieces are silver. But the coin you are holding in your hand is made of bronze. It became official coinage in 1924."

Jordyn's thoughts pause for a moment.

"It belonged to Adalard's father, Steph. He wants you to have it."

Steph stares into Adalard's eyes. Like his, her eyes are also welling up with tears. She shakes her head as she says, "Please tell him that I cannot accept this. While I sincerely appreciate his gift, and I thank him from the bottom of my heart, it belonged to his father. He must keep it as a memento, a reminder of his beloved father and his past."

Adalard immediately begins to shake his head back and forth before Steph finishes her little spiel.

In response to his shaking his head, Steph ponders Jordyn's magical telepathy ability once more.

Just more proof that she can interpret and send thoughts to two people in two different languages simultaneously and via telepathy. She is amazing. I cannot wait to meet her!

Adalard looks Steph straight in the eye. His spoken words match the look of certainty that appears on his face. Steph immediately knows her spiel has not had an effect on him.

"Nein. Es ist deins. Du hast mich gerettet. Papa würde wollen, dass du es hast." With a sincere smile on his war-weary, young face, he places his hands over his heart.

"Ich auch. Danke, Steph. Ich liebe dich."

As Jordyn translates Adalard's words, Steph begins to tremble, not so much because of what Adalard said. She is trembling because she prays to God that the poor, innocent child sitting before her does not have to suffer anymore. He has seen enough death and destruction to last a lifetime of a thousand souls.

Adalard's words in German, translated into English by Jordyn, slowly enter Steph's mind.

"Adalard said, 'No. It is yours. You saved me. Papa would want you to have it. So do I. Thank you, Steph. Ich liebe dich.'"

Steph stretches her arms out wide to embrace Adalard.

"Bitte schön, Adalard. Bitte schön."

Jordyn purposely did not translate Adalard's last three words for Steph. For she knows that Steph will understand their meaning.

Steph gazes into Adalard's eyes. When she finally overcomes her emotions, her tone of voice is soft, tender, compassionate, full of feeling and love.

"Ich liebe dich auch.
"I love you too."
Ich werde dick niemals vergessen.
(I will never forget you.)

CHAPTER FOUR

SIN BY ANOTHER NAME

"Freedom without health is infinitely sweeter than health without freedom."
- *New York Daily Tribune*, March 9, 1859

Part I: We are not in Kansas Anymore, Toto

Steph awakens with a start, her mind shrouded by a blanket of heavy fog. She shakes her head vigorously to clear her sluggishness. She is lying beneath a tree, but as she looks up, it doesn't look anything like the tree she and Adalard were sitting under a few moments ago.

Goodness gracious, no! Where in the world are we now?

She struggles to get to her feet. She is sore all over from fighting the three soldiers, and her calf aches where the wood splinter sliced into her. She frantically looks around for some sign of recognition. Not seeing any, her thoughts immediately turn to Adalard. She calls out in a whisper.

"Adalard, wo bist du? Where are you? Adalard! Please answer me!"

Her heart is racing and thumping loudly with apprehension. It feels as if it will burst out of her chest like a cannonball from a big gun. She suddenly feels anxious, her uneasiness cascading from her mind to the pit of her stomach.

Adalard is gone. So are we. At least from Germany.

"Spirit? Where are you?"

She turns around and catches sight of Spirit grazing far off in the distance. She exhales with relief. Her heartbeat gradually begins to return to its steady, normal cadence.

She is uncertain of the time of day. But it feels like it is morning. The temperature is chilly, and there are tiny drops of dew on the blades of grass. Chills race across her shoulders causing her to shiver. She reaches into her makeshift knapsack and grabs her sweater. She drapes it over her shoulders and ties the sleeves into a loose knot around her neck.

As she looks up absentmindedly at the wispy clouds floating in the blue sky, she rolls her eyes. Then she shakes her head back and forth.

I cannot believe this. Where in tarnation are we now?

Spirits thoughts enter her mind.

"Good morning, sleepy head. Have a good rest? I thought you were going to sleep the day away. Early bird gets the worm as they say. It appears like you are going hungry today. Sorry about that, unless of course, you enjoy eating grass like me."

Steph yells, "Spirit, stop joking around!" Her annoyed shout is loud enough to be heard for miles.

"Can't you ever be serious? We are in someplace altogether new. And Adalard is missing. Do you know where he has gone? You are a horse. As a horse, you are supposed to know things that humans do not. Tell me if you know where we are, where Adalard is. Do you know?"

"I do not have a clue, Steph. But there is one thing I know for certain. We are not in Kansas anymore, Toto. That is for sure!"

His loud whinny booms from across the meadow.

"Spirit, I warn you! Stop fooling around. Where is Adalard? What do we do now?"

"Beats me. But as the saying goes, 'when nothing seems right, go left.'" He neighs yet again.

"Darn you, Spirit! I love you, but sometimes I want to smack you!"

She softly whispers, "Jordyn? Are you there? Jordyn, please answer me. I need you now more than ever. Where are we? And where is Adalard? He is gone. Hello?"

Jordyn does not reply.

"Hey, you know what, Steph?" Spirit's mind conveys.

"What now?" Steph replies. She is irritated because he is interrupting her calls to Jordyn.

"I think we are, in fact, uh-huh."

Steph stammers, this time out loud, "In fact what? Tell me. And hurry up if you please! I am trying to contact Jordyn."

"Hold your horses, Steph. I am looking around here. I need to move to a better spot for a better lock." After a minute's delay, while Steph continues to try to contact Jordyn, his thoughts say, "Yes, we may, in fact, be in Kansas or someplace like Kansas. Either way, we are undoubtedly in America yet again."

"Really?" Steph questions excitedly via her thoughts. "Why do you think that? What do you see?"

She raises on her tippy toes to where Spirit was the last time she saw him. Then she jumps up and down in place to get a better look. But there is no sign of him. He has moved beyond her line of sight.

"I see an old wooden barn. And way off in the distance I see a man walking behind a horse. And what is that? Oh yeah. It is a plow, an old-fashioned plow. The man is plowing a small plot of land next to the barn. And will you look at that! There are a couple of outbuildings also made of wood. One of the outbuildings has a porch with a couple of rocking chairs on it. It is much larger than the other buildings. I assume it is somebody's home."

"Oh, yes!" Steph yells gleefully. "We are home. Home at last! Nevertheless, I am worried about Adalard. He is nowhere in sight. I hope he didn't wander off. He doesn't know a lick of English, so he will not be able to ask directions or even ask for help."

She slowly spins in place as she softly calls Adalard's name once more.

"Adalard? Adalard, where are you? Wo bist du? We are safe, Adalard. We are in my country."

"Ah, Steph?"

"Yes? Do you see Adalard?"

"No, I do not see Adalard. You are not going to like me saying this, but I seriously doubt we are anywhere near home or even in the Twenty-first Century for that matter."

Steph's initial excitement knowing they are back home slowly begins to fade. Something is telling her that they are in a fix - a serious fix that is going to get much worse.

"What makes you say that?" She asks skeptically.

"As I said, the barn looks old-fashioned. And the outbuildings are old-fashioned as well." He pauses for a few seconds as he contemplates what he sees. "And now that I can see a house, it also looks old-fashioned like something you would expect to see in the 1800s or maybe earlier than that. I remember you showing me pictures from back then in your history book."

Steph refutes Spirit's thoughts.

"The Amish have old-fashioned stuff. Maybe it is an Amish farm. Did you ever think of that?"

"No, it is not an Amish farm. And it definitely is not an Amish farm from our era either."

"And why would it not be from our era?" Steph asks annoyingly.

"Not too many modern folks plow a plot of land using a horse and an old-fashioned plow. Of this, I know. The Amish use old-fashioned tools. Amish do not even have electricity. I have to disagree with you. I think we are somewhere in modern America. Maybe we are in Pennsylvania or our home state. There are loads of Amish families in both locations."

"Steph, the house isn't right. It is a mansion, almost like one would see centuries ago on a plantation. You remember when we visited the Rippavilla Plantation outside Columbia, Tennessee? It was a few years ago during a Mule Day Festival. Naturally, I was not allowed inside the mansion, but I had a clear view of the mansion as well as the slave quarters.

"What I see looks something like that. Except the mansion is not made of brick. It is made of wood and painted white. It is super huge. Two stories tall with a lovely veranda, four chimneys, and a well-manicured garden with lots of blossoming flowers. A brightly painted white picket fence surrounds it. There's a gate, too. It is open. A little African American boy is playing in the dirt outside of it."

"Oh," is all that Steph can reply. Her heart is now sinking even further with despair as she begins to absorb the scene Spirit has described to her.

Do you want to know what I think?"

Steph replies, "Not really. But go ahead. What are you thinking?"

"I think Jordyn has taken us back in time yet again. I hate to tell you this, but I think she has sent us to the slavery era." He pauses, and then he conveys, "And I thought being in a war and us getting shot at was bad. Being here is worse. Far worse."

"Oh, my goodness, no!" Steph whispers to herself. Then she conveys to Spirit, "This is terrible, and I hope you are wrong. But tell me. Why do you think that?"

"Because a large group, perhaps a few hundred men, women, and children, are laboring in the fields beyond the mansion. They are black men, women and children, African Americans. They are wearing ragged clothes, and all of them are barefooted. I can see a tall white man with a wide-brimmed straw hat as well. He is on a beautiful horse.

"The man has a rifle in the saddle's scabbard. My heavens, Steph! Now the man has a whip in his hand! He is waving it threateningly at a little African American girl that is cowering at his side! She is covering her face with her hands! He is going to whip her, Steph!"

Steph turns to dash to where she last saw Spirit. She suddenly stops in her tracks. She wants nothing to do with the scene unfolding before Spirit's eyes. There is nothing she can do to change the situation.

She muses. What in the world am I supposed to do to stop a man with a rifle from whipping a child? Then again, Jordyn sent us here for a purpose.

My raison d'être.

There must be something I can do to help. Otherwise, what in the world are we doing here? All I have to do is figure out what it is I am supposed to do.

She cries out in her mind, "No, Spirit, no! You must try to stop him from whipping the child. No matter what the child may have done, she does not deserve physical punishment. Especially a sadistic whipping!"

"I cannot stop him, Steph," Spirit's thoughts say. "What is a horse that suddenly appears out of nowhere on the overseer's land supposed to do? He will shoot me if I attack him. Or worse, he will try to capture me. Either way, you will be on your own. I cannot allow that! We need to come up with a plan. Hold a second, Steph." His thoughts cease for a few moments.

"Thank goodness. The man is not whipping the little girl. He only appears to be threatening her. That is good. But what a horrible way to treat a child! A woman, maybe the girl's mother, is scooping her up into her arms. She is hurrying the girl away from the man. But wait! Something is diverting the man's attention.

"Oh, now I see what is taking place. It looks as if two men on the far end of the field are fighting. They are rolling on the ground exchanging blows. I am not certain, but I would guess the men are pretending to fight, to distract the white man's attention. I feel for the two men. Once the white man breaks up the fight, he undoubtedly will punish the two men severely. The white man still has not noticed me although some of the slaves have. I am not going to press my luck. I am returning to you now. You are not safe here. We must figure out a plan."

As Spirit returns to her in a gallop, Steph is pondering this latest predicament that confronts them.

Being in Cologne during World War Two was bad, really bad. And it was frightening. Being shot at was not much fun either. Neither was fighting three grown men. Or, for that matter, being smacked in the thigh by the officer's swagger stick.

She rubs her thigh with her hand. She imagines that it is black and blue from where the officer smacked her.

Then she smiles.

But it was exciting! After all, I beat up three soldiers and Adalard outsmarted the officer. To say nothing of how Jordyn made all of it happen in the first place. More importantly, Spirit and I were able to save Adalard from certain death - from the Jew-hating Nazi soldiers. In retrospect, I know what we had to go through was dangerous. But in the end, it was well worth it.

Thinking about Adalard causes her to worry about his fate once more. She calls out to Jordyn in a whisper.

"Jordyn, can you hear me. Can you read my thoughts? I hope you are okay, that nothing bad has happened to you. Please, Jordyn, answer me. I am worried about Adalard. Besides, I am really in the dark here as to what Spirit and I are supposed to do. It seems we are back further in time to the immoral and wicked evil times of America's sinful, brutal past. Talk to me in my mind, Jordyn, please!"

She gets on her knees and places her hands together in prayer.

"Please give me the strength to confront whatever challenges that Spirit and I must face. I have no idea how to act in this inexcusable, cruel world of intolerance. I have no idea how to confront this appalling injustice of African Americans. And I am worried about Jordyn. She does not answer my calls. Hopefully, she is okay and silent for a good reason.

"I am also worried about Adalard. He is missing. I pray that he is not alone beneath the tree where I last saw him, afraid and despondent yet again. He does not deserve any more heartbreak. He has been through so much. Too much in fact. I ask for your guidance and blessing. Please keep Spirit and me safe. Adalard, too. Thank you."

Steph does not know where they are. But one thing she knows for certain. Jordyn, who uncharacteristically will remain silent, has sent them back in time to the appalling era of slavery in America.

Steph is on the property of the Gray Plantation, Georgetown County, South Carolina. The Gray Plantation is a sprawling, 1500-acre plot of land on Pawleys Island approximately 80 miles northeast of Charleston. The plantation owner, known as the "Monarch of the Southern Rice Planters," enslaves over eleven hundred African Americans. The owner also has the dubious reputation of being the cruelest of all slave owners in the South.

The date is April 12, 1860, exactly one year to the day before the commencement of the American Civil War.

*****

Part II: Realization Sets In

Steph gets to her feet. As she does, she steps on something half buried in the grass. She bends over to get it, but she cannot pry it loose. She kicks at it with the toe tip of her shoe. Once it is free, she picks it up. It appears to be made of iron and is unusually heavy for such a small device. She estimates that it weighs a quarter pound maybe a bit more. Rust has discolored its surface.

She begins to shiver as the realization of what she is holding in her hands gradually dawns on her. She is holding a small set of metal handcuffs. The restraint device has machine stamped words on both keyways below the rotating arms. She moistens the hem of her shirt with saliva. Then she carefully wipes the dirt from one of the keyways. When she reads the words, she barely can contain a scream from escaping her lips. The words on the handcuffs graphically summarize in simple terms the heartless times in which she and Spirit now find themselves.

Property of Georgetown County Plantation Police

She wipes the other keyway. Its stamped words send harsh shivers of agony to run up and down her spine. She chokes back tears as her heart sinks with inconceivable disbelief and an unimaginable sadness. The stamped words only consist of five horrible words. Nevertheless, those five words will forever remain etched in her mind.

Negro woman or child only

Steph has discovered a set of handcuffs that was accidentally misplaced by a member of the Georgetown County Slave Patrol. Slave patrols began in South Carolina in the early 1700s and quickly spread to the other thirteen colonies. Slave patrols were formed to recapture slaves who ran away from their plantations. Slaves that did not have passes in their possession were returned to their owners by the slave patrol. Once returned, runaway slaves were subject to whippings and beatings. Despite the cruelty of the white man's retribution, the slaves feared something even more than physical punishment. The auction block. Being placed on the auction block would mean being separated from family and friends.

The white man who misplaced the handcuffs found by Steph is a member of the Georgetown County Slave Patrol. He is actively involved in what is known as the Reverse Underground Railroad. As the name implies, it is the opposite of the Underground Railroad, the informal system whereby kind citizens would spirit away slaves to freedom in the North.

The Reverse Underground Railroad involves the practice of kidnapping free blacks and fugitive slaves from U.S. free states and transporting them back to slave states for sale as slaves. The Reverse Underground Railroad ended with the Union victory over the south at the end of the Civil War and the passing of the Thirteenth Amendment to the United States Constitution which abolished slavery in the United States.

White's fear of African Americans increased after the Confederate Army lost the Civil War. Former patrol methods resurfaced during the post-Civil War Reconstruction period of 1865-1877. The Southern police officers and the Ku Klux Klan began to prescribe procedures to intimidate African Americans. The slave auction was an integral part of the intimidation procedure.

An enormous slave auction took place in early February 1859, approximately fourteen months before Steph and Spirit arrived at the Gray Plantation. The auction was held at a location about sixty miles south of Charleston. Six hundred forty-nine slaves were put up for auction. The auction block consisted of African American men and women and children of all ages including infants. The auction was very popular, so much so, the Editor of the *New York Daily Tribune* sent a reporter to cover the event.

When the Gray Plantation owner arrived at the auction he, like the other white buyers, was excited. Word had it that the former owner of the slaves was selling his *human goods* at a discount. Just like the other slave owners, the owner of the Gray Plantation was anxious to get a good deal for his money. He prodded the slaves' limbs to ensure they were not lame, poked their muscles to see how strong they were, and he even pried open their mouths to look at their teeth. He made them walk up and down stairs, stoop over, pick up heavy rocks, and he even subjected them to the ultimate humility - ordering them to undress so he could see if they were worth his time and money.

During the auction, some of the more resourceful slaves pretended to be lame. If a slave could prove that he or she was lame (less valuable) - with a bad limp, a dislocated bone, a disfigured hand or foot - then he or she would be auctioned off at a lesser price. Conceivably, a less valuable slave could hope to accumulate enough money to buy his or her freedom.

The 1859 Slave Auction was a grand event. At least in the eyes of the white slave owners. All of the hotels in the nearby town were sold out. The bars were full of patrons, and the mood was upbeat, jovial in fact. Except for the slaves. They felt more like cattle than human beings. They were herded this way and that, day and night, without regard to their privacy. For more than six days. Prospective buyers even roused children and infants from their sleep for one last look at the *merchandise*.

The Gray Plantation owner bought nineteen slaves for $13,205, approximately $290,700 in today's currency. Five women, two girls, three boys, and nine men. The first words out of the owner's mouth when he returned to his plantation were, "A steal at twice the price!"

*****

Part III: Josephine

"Josephine! There you are. You have finally arrived! We were expecting you three or four days ago. Welcome to the Gray Plantation!"

Steph flinches. The last thing she wants right now is company, especially unknown company that has a male's tenor voice. She slowly turns around.

Standing less than three feet from her is a handsome looking boy. He appears to be around eighteen years of age. He is slightly taller than Steph, muscular, and sunburned. He looks a bit silly standing in his brown smock topped with a wide-brimmed straw hat. His attire confirms Steph's suspicions. She and Spirit have arrived back in time once again.

She whispers in a cautious tone, "What? Are you talking to me? Who are you? Who is Josephine?"

The boy laughs as he jokingly declares, "Quit fooling around, Josephine. Your mother corresponded with us that you can be the funniest jokester in the world, but please do not pretend you are not Josephine. Who else could you be? I know every pretty young lady by their first name from up and down the island and from here to the Atlantic Ocean." He glances up at the sun.

"Are you hungry? I expect it is a few hours until dinnertime, but we could give you some leftover breakfast biscuits. They are especially good with Janette's strawberry jam. Janette is my step-mother's slave. Been in the family since last year when Papa bought her at the auction. She is an excellent cook and very obedient."

The boy suddenly looks from Steph to Spirit. Spirit has just returned from spying on the whip-carrying white overseer and watching the hundreds of African Americans hard at work in the fields.

"Goodness, Josephine, is this your horse, Abraham, the one of which you wrote us? He is very handsome. You never told us he was accompanying you to America. How was it he was able to manage such a long trip across the ocean?" He reaches out to stroke Spirit on his mane. Then he slowly walks a large circle around Spirit as he lovingly touches the horse here and there.

"He is gorgeous, Josephine, absolutely gorgeous. As I said, you never told us he would accompany you. That you brought him with you is very surprising. I have heard of horses that seem to fare very well on ships that cross the Atlantic Ocean. To be perfectly honest with you, however, I never did believe the stories. I guess your horse being here proves me wrong."

Steph stares across the meadow for the longest time as the teenager continues to ogle over Spirit.

Okay, for whatever reason, this boy thinks I am someone named Josephine. He said I just arrived from across the Atlantic Ocean! Well, that part is true, I guess, but Spirit and I did not travel on a ship. That is for certain. If only he knew from where we came and the manner in which we crossed the Atlantic. Boy! Would he be surprised! Also, if all that he said is not weird enough, he is calling me a jokester and offering me leftover breakfast biscuits. It is like I am part of the family or something. Weird.

Her stomach suddenly begins to growl noisily.

Oh! How I would love freshly baked biscuits! And who in the heck is Abraham? Goodness, this is weird, totally weird.

She calls out for Jordyn in her mind.

"Jordyn, please help me! I have no idea who this boy is and what I am supposed to do. Jordyn! Answer me!"

Jordyn does not reply. But Spirit does.

"Okay, Steph, I mean Josephine. Play along with the boy. His name is William. He is your step-cousin. His step-mother and Josephine's mother are sisters. Josephine's mother is the oldest of the two. Today is the first time William has met you, so he does not know how you look. You have come all the way from Greenwich, England. Since you, or rather Josephine, was born in America, and she lived a part of her life in our country, you do not have much of a British accent." He pauses, and then he whinnies.

"Now, that would be some good trick, Steph. I would love to listen as you try to mimic a British accent. And oh, by the way, I am Abraham." He pauses once more. Then he whinnies a second time.

"So, my dear Josephine, call me Abraham if you please. I sort of like the name. Makes me sound important, almost holy. Like I am royalty or something. How about you? Do you like my new name? How about your name? Do you like it? Goodness, it is like we are going incognito. Sort of enigmatic. Like a mystery or something."

Steph wants to scold Spirit for fooling around. However, she does not. The boy is tugging at the sleeves of her sweater tied around her neck. He is trying to get her attention. She looks at him with an expression of utter misery.

"Josephine!" William lightheartedly scolds. "What in the world is going on in that pretty head of yours? You look like you have lost your mind as you stare inattentively across the meadow like that! And goodness. A thought just occurred to me." He playfully smacks the side of his head with his open hand.

"How in the world did you get from the Port of Charleston to here? It is a least a full day's ride maybe two. And how were you able to find your way to the plantation without an escort? Goodness, cousin, you truly are an amazing girl."

Then he begins to eye Steph up and down. That he is eyeing her in an entranced way is making her feel very uncomfortable.

"And what is with your clothing, Josephine? Those are men's clothes! Is that what young girls wear in England? If God is my witness, I swear. I have never seen such clothing worn by a young lady. We must have one of our slaves sew you a suitable outfit. Or, perhaps, my step-mother may have some clothing for you that will fit. The way you wear your clothes, you look like one of the farmer's daughters from across the rice fields."

He shakes his head disapprovingly.

"No, we must clothe you in something more suitable. No offense but you look rather funny dressed like a man." He laughs. "Sorry, just saying."

As she fans the side of her face with her hand and rolls her eyes, Steph says in a whisper, "I am sorry, William. As you can imagine, I am a tad bit unsteady from traveling." She extends her hand to shake his.

"Please excuse my uncivil manners. I am very cautious as you can well imagine, and I wanted to make certain you were William." With a wry smile, she adds, "Unescorted ladies must be ever on their guard as you know."

Then, with a serious tone, she says, "And I honestly do take offense with you saying I look funny like I am a man or a farmer's daughter. How do you expect me to appear? After all, I ride Spi..., I mean Abraham, so this attire is very suitable for me. I thank you very much for insulting me. I cannot think of a more hospitable way to welcome a step-cousin to your home."

She places her hands on her hips as she adds with a scolding tone, "And if you do not like the way I appear before you, tough. You do not have to look at me. Especially the way you just did. It is inappropriate to stare at a young lady - to look at her with ogling eyes that say more than his nasty hidden thoughts. So please allow me to be very clear, William. I will wear what I want to wear. And if you look at me like that another time, with your flirtatious, roving eyes, I will knock you senseless."

William removes his hat as he bows deeply. He takes Steph's hand in his. She notices his hands are soft.

Something tells me this boy hasn't done a lick of work in his entire life!

He says in an apologetic tone, "I can only imagine you are a bit unsteady from your long trip. And do not fret anymore about not having an escort." With a sincere smile, he adds, "I am your escort for as long as you visit us."

His face flushes.

"And I apologize for saying you look funny. I beg your pardon. I did not intend my words as an insult. But goodness, Josephine, you certainly are feisty!" He grabs Spirit's rein.

"Let us proceed if you please. My step-mother will be happy to know that you finally have arrived."

As they begin to walk, William asks, "What did you mean when you said, 'I will knock you senseless?'"

Steph laughs.

"It means I will knock you on your behind. Take the wind out of your sales. Kick your butt."

William scratches his head. He replies, "Oh, I see. Well, we cannot have any of that."

As they continue to walk slowly across the meadow, William points out various buildings and other noticeable landmarks.

"That is where the slaves live. As you can see for yourself, their dwellings are quite right and proper. Papa tries to go out of his way to treat the slaves with dignity even if they get rebellious and do not appreciate his benevolent ways."

Steph stares in disbelief at the squalid living conditions, what William referred to as right and proper. Through the open doors, she can see dirt floors and sparse wooden furniture. One bed. A small table. A gas lamp. Mats on the floor for sleeping. Her heart sinks.

She feels no anger toward William. Folks in the South, especially the youngsters, have no concept of how repulsive slavery is and how history will, rightly so, censure slave owners fervently.

Most of the weather-beaten, wooden structures appear to be two-family dwellings with one entrance. They have post-in-the-ground supports. The roofs consist of assorted sizes of wooden boards nailed in place. The dwellings are clustered together in a circle. A large fire pit is in the center of the circle. A circle of assorted sizes of logs surrounds the fire pit. Steph reckons the slaves use the logs as seats when they congregate at night.

Two of the slave quarters are like log cabins. They are a bit removed from the other dwellings, perhaps twenty or thirty feet distant. William explains the log cabin houses are for more important slaves like the one plantation slave overseer. There is also a single-dwelling log cabin for Janette and her family.

Steph knows from her history classes that slaves lived under horrid conditions. They had to toil in the fields for hours on end. They endured horrifying, brutalizing treatment by their white owners. Many slaves were beaten, whipped, or worse. There was always the risk of having husbands lynched for disobedience. Also, slave owners sold wives, husbands, daughters, and sons at auctions on the slave market which resulted in the splitting up of families. And there was nothing the slaves could do about it. To rebel was to suffer even more. To rebel repeatedly was to be sold or worse.

Little did the white owners know, however, that by segregating their slaves from the whites, African Americans focused on and maintained their own culture despite the odds. They pursued their distinct views and goals. By coping with the challenging, nearly overwhelming immoral and dehumanizing conditions, over time, slaves slowly forged a new identity. Eventually, they became the African Americans of today. Like their white counterparts and other minorities, they now are an integral part of the American way of life. They are Americans through and through.

William goes on to say that some of the slaves, particularly the single adult males and females, usually sleep where they work. One slave usually sleeps in the stable even though he is married. His name is Samuel. Others sleep in slave quarters off the kitchen in the Gray House. The Gray House is the plantation owner's mansion.

While slaves live in shanties, twelve people enjoy the most comfortable of conditions in the mansion. Naturally, all of the residents are white. The plantation owner, his wife, William and his brother, two overseers, and six hired hands. There are two spare bedrooms in the mansion for visiting white guests and relatives of the Gray family.

Whenever slaves are loaned out to the cities, they stay in dwellings called shanty towns. The Gray Plantation owner usually loans out his slaves between the planting and harvesting seasons. When the slaves are loaned out, usually to Charleston, South Carolina, they must wear a slave tag.

The slave tag, known as the Slave Registration Tag, is in keeping with a strict law enacted by Charleston in the early 1800s. The registration fee, or tax, brings income to Charleston. The tag is a way of identifying to which plantation owner a slave belongs. The tag also indicates the specialty of the slave. Examples of specialties are servant, seamstress, cook, and furniture maker. The current tax year is also hand-punched on the tag.

According to William, silversmiths and blacksmiths make the tags for a fee. Mister Cleveland M. Grouse makes the current day tags for the Gray Plantation. The tags are made of metal, usually copper. The tags measure approximately one and one-half to two inches square. Slaves wear the tags in a diamond orientation. A slave must wear the tag around his or her neck at all times while on loan from the plantation.

Steph says wordlessly in her mind to Spirit, "Goodness. What William is telling me is nauseating. He seems to be bragging, too. All of it is dreadfully disgusting. I wish Jordyn had not transported us here, to this time and place. I do not know if I can handle it."

Spirit's thoughts say, "You must handle it. Jordyn has a plan, and even if she is not communicating with you right now, her plan is evident. You are destined to help someone in need. And you know you have a purpose here. Therefore, hang in there and try to go with the flow as best as you can."

Yes. My purpose.

My raison d'être.

"Easy for you to say," Steph counters. All you have to do is hang around looking handsome and all. I must interact with these people. What is worse, I have to pretend I am someone I do not even know who I am supposed to be!"

"In the chest of drawers, in the room where you will be staying, you will find all the letters from Josephine's mother. I know you do not want to snoop but read them as soon as you can. They probably will give you some insight as to what Josephine says and does."

"Goodness, Spirit, how do you know these things? It is virtually impossible for you to know about the letters. And how did you know William's name? I am beginning to think Jordyn is communicating with you and not with me! While I am very pleased you know the things that you are telling me, it is disheartening to know Jordyn has abandoned me."

"Not now, Steph. Now is not the time to go into the details of what I know and how I know it. And get in the habit of calling me by my rightful name, Abraham. Or, better yet, try not to mention me at all. I do not want you to slip up. Then everyone will become even more suspicious of you."

Steph is suddenly aware that William is gently tapping her on the shoulder.

"Hey, Josephine, hello. Are you okay? We have been walking all this time, and I have been talking nearly nonstop while you have said almost next to nothing. At least you could say yes, or uh-huh, or even no occasionally. That way I would know you are listening."

"Sorry," Steph replies. "It's just that I have never seen slave quarters before, and I truly dislike what I see. I also dislike knowing about the slave registration system. It is barbaric if you were to ask me. It is very inhumane. How would you like to wear a tag, huh? I dare say you would not like it at all. I know I wouldn't.

"History will someday prove what you are doing here is un-American. History will severely judge everyone who owns slaves. I promise you." She points her finger at William. "Even you, William. Even you."

"Wow," William blurts out, "spoken like a true Limey. I had heard that the British, like the Northerners, dislike our way of life here in the South as it relates to slavery. Give me a break, Josephine. Try to show a little understanding and respect. After all, you are in our country now, so please try to pretend that you respect our culture."

Steph stops walking. She points her finger at William a second time just as she asks Spirit via her thoughts, "What is a Limey? It does not sound very flattering."

Spirit's thoughts say, "A Limey is a derogatory American word for a British person."

Steph says, "William, let us get something straight right here and now. This is the second time you have insulted me.

"You first said that I looked funny in my attire. Well tough. It is what it is, and I will wear what I want to wear. Now you are insulting me by calling me a Limey. It is derogatory, and I do not like it. If you and I are to be more than friends while I am visiting, I implore you to *act* like a friend. Hold your tongue, or you and I will not be on speaking terms. Do you understand me, sir?"

She smiles adding, "I know I am your guest, but please show me a bit of respect as well. I am not one of those, how did you put it? Yes, I can recall your exact words. You said, 'I know every pretty young lady by their first name from up and down the island and from here to the Atlantic Ocean.' While I appreciate the compliment, we are cousins. And cousins respect each other. Pure and simple. Got it?'"

William says in an apologetic tone, "Yes, ma'am, and I am truly sorry. I must correct myself, and I ask for your forgiveness."

Steph smiles. "That is better, and I thank you." She suddenly yells, "What in the world is that?" She points to the stable. "It sounds like someone is screaming from inside the stable!"

"Oh, that is nothing," William replies offhandedly with a wave of his hand. "It is just one of the stable boys getting a well-deserved lashing. That is all. Nothing to worry about. It is probably Joseph. He stole some food from the pantry the other day. Said he needed it for his little sisters. Hah! We give them enough food. Stealing is stealing no matter what the reason. And he deserves punishment. I hope his back is sore for a very long time. If it is Joseph who is being whipped, he will receive thirty lashes if not more."

"What!" Steph cries. "You call the whipping of a stable boy nothing?" She takes off on the run in the direction of the stable.

Spirit cries out in his mind as he gallops beside her.

"No, Steph, no! You are going to make things even more difficult for yourself. Do not, I repeat, do not go into that stable! I warn you. You will not like what you see!"

William races after Steph. Even though he is sprinting, he is no match for her gait. Steph is super-fast when she runs, especially when she is agitated.

William cries out, "Steph, no! White women are not allowed in the stable while there is a whipping!"

When Steph enters the stable, her first reaction is to turn away and race back to the meadow. She wants more than anything to end this terrifying, ugly, slavery nightmare. She wants to return home to normality. Her second reaction is to throw up. Thankfully, her stomach is empty. She has not eaten anything except a Twinkie since yesterday. As she bends over and places her hands on her knees to catch her breath, she grimaces with a mixture of disgust and hatred at the ongoing scene.

A young male slave, perhaps fifteen or sixteen years of age, is hanging by his hands from the rafters. His feet barely touch the ground. His back is bleeding profusely from at least three or four thrashes of a white man's whip. A dozen or so slaves of both sexes and differing ages, including weeping children, are standing a dozen feet to the right side of the young slave. A white man with a rifle is facing them. To Steph, it almost appears as if the white man is daring the slaves to intervene. Then he will have a reason to shoot them or smack them in their heads with the butt of his rifle.

Steph nearly collapses to her knees as the jeering white overseer administers another sickening blow.

He calls out, "This will teach you to steal from a white man's pantry!"

Surprisingly, other than a soft moan that escapes from the boy's foam-covered lips, he does not cry out as the lash cuts into his flesh brutally.

Steph's adrenaline kicks in immediately. Just as the overseer winds up to deliver another blow, she races to stand in between him and the slave. With a defiant look of hatred, she plants her feet wide apart and raises her hand in front of her face. She yells at the top of her voice.

"Stop! Stop, I say! What in the world do you think you are doing? It is disgusting, inhumane, brutal to whip someone! What are you anyway? The devil? How dare you!"

She turns around and reaches up to untie the ropes binding the slave.

The overseer laughs loudly. Then he roughly grabs her around the waist. She spins in place.

"Oh, you must be the British girl. Everyone has been talking about you. Well, what we do here in America is no business of yours, young lady!"

He slaps Steph across the face, and then he crudely tosses her aside. She falls face-first onto the stable floor.

It doesn't take her but a second to recover from the fall. She shakes her head causing bits of straw and dirt to fly everywhere. She looks up at the man and sneers. Her nose is bloody, and she has a small cut on her lower lip. She uses both of her hands to brush straw and dirt from her face. She smells her fingertips.

Now I smell like horse poo. Yuck!

As he stares down at her, the overseer snarls viciously, "Serves you right for interfering where you do not belong." He abruptly turns around and cruelly lashes the slave as he screams, "This one's for the bold British girl!"

Steph scrambles to her feet. She grabs the man by his shoulders. She roughly spins him around to face her. Then she delivers a powerful kick to his kneecap crushing it. The man, still holding the whip in his hand, goes down on all fours moaning loudly. Steph snatches the whip from his hand and hurls it across the stable.

Meanwhile, the other white man points his rifle at her. He says in a whisper, "I wouldn't if I were you."

Steph plants her feet firmly on the ground as she faces him.

"What? Are you going to shoot me? Go ahead. I dare you." She gestures to the slave. "Then you will be the one hanging from these rafters, but not by your hands. You will be hanging by your neck!"

With a sullen look on his face, the man slowly lowers his rifle. Then he turns around and faces the group of slaves.

Steph stares down at the overseer that is moaning on the floor.

"I just whipped a World War Two German soldier using the same devastating kick. Don't you dare slap me or push me to the ground! I am a rugby player, and my kicks are meaner than that of an angry, bucking horse!

"And look at you now! All this time you thought you were a brave, tough guy, huh? Whipping a defenseless boy hanging by his wrists from the rafters. Well, you are not very tough now, are you?"

She turns around and hurriedly unties the binds holding the slave. The boy collapses into her arms. She gently lowers him to the ground. Her eyes well up with tears. She yells at the astonished slaves. They are staring at her with a mixture of tender envy and sheer terror.

"You people there! Get over here and attend to this boy. Now!" She glares at the man holding the rifle.

"Do not worry about him. If he even makes a move to stop you, I will render him unconscious or unable to walk for a long, long time. Now move! This boy needs medical attention!"

William cannot believe what he has witnessed. He was entranced by what Steph said and did. He did not move a muscle the entire time. Finally, having regained his senses, he races over to grab Steph by her shoulders. He steers her toward the opening in the stable.

"Oh boy, now you've done it, Josephine. Let me get you out of here before something else happens!" He looks at the man holding the rifle. "Before he shoots you!"

As Steph and William exit the stable, William's friend Benjamin whispers, "My God William, I saw the whole thing. Who is she?"

"She is my cousin, Josephine. She is from England. She just whipped Boss's backside, crushed his kneecap with one powerful kick. Then she threatened Jess even though he was pointing his rifle at her. The man even lowered his rifle after she threatened him! I would never have believed it if I hadn't seen it with my own eyes. Amazing!

"Then she unhitched Joseph from the rafters. Told the slaves to ignore Jess and help Joseph. She is something else, I dare say. I love her to death as my feisty British cousin. Indeed I do!"

CHAPTER FIVE

MANKIND'S WICKEDNESS

"Slavery's detestable bigotry is like intolerance turned upside-down."
- Steph, April 12, 1860

Part I: Your Kind Ain't Welcome Here

"I do not care who you are!"

The Man is yelling at the top of his lungs. His face is redder than an overripe tomato. If his head were a steam kettle, Steph is certain its top would explode to smithereens. He stares at her with a look of absolute repugnance.

"And I do not care what you think." He points his finger threateningly. "Let me make myself absolutely clear, young lady. You ain't got no business meddling in our affairs. Period. If you continue to meddle, I will confine you to your room during your entire visit." He sneers as he adds in a disgusted-sounding tenor, "I got a business to run. And I got enough problems around here without you interfering. You got that straight, Missy?"

Steph takes another sip of her lemonade. She feels wonderful to be freshened up and sitting at a real table with an elegantly embroidered tablecloth. Especially a tablecloth with carefully sewn, flowery tulips of red, yellow, purple, and green. The embroidered napkin on her lap matches the tablecloth.

She carefully wipes the corners of her mouth with the napkin. Despite how clean and fresh she feels, what she likes the most is devouring warm, homemade, golden brown biscuits smothered with delicious honey. She looks up at the Man with an impassive expression.

"For your information, my name is Josephine. It is not Missy. And, my dear sir, I do not appreciate you pointing your finger at me. I find it extremely rude. As far as confining me to my room, I seriously doubt you will do that. Nevertheless, if you do confine me to my room, I will escape. I have my means." She grins a slight, mischievous smile. "Please allow me to say that once more. I will escape. Let there be no doubt about it."

"I ain't gonna tolerate your rebellious attitude, either!" the Man scolds. "You are a stranger here, a guest. I must ask you this. Will you stop meddling in our affairs? Answer me yes or no!"

Steph takes a huge bite of her biscuit. She chews a bit. When she answers, she purposely replies with food in her mouth. She mumbles a nearly incoherent reply.

"Yes or no."

She runs her tongue across her front teeth. She beams a huge smile fully appreciating that gooey honey and bits of biscuit are sticking to her teeth.

"What in tarnation does that mean?" the Man snaps. He places his hands on his wide hips and glowers.

Steph furrows her brow as she fakes confusion. She tilts her head to the left, and then she says with a grin, "What does *what* mean?"

"Yes or no. What kind of answer is that?" As he angrily waves his hands in the air with frustration, the annoyed Man scolds Steph even louder.

"Answer me either yes or no. One of the two words but not both. And you best make certain it is the right answer." He points his finger at Steph once more. "Or, so help me God."

Steph says in a quiet tone, "You said to me, and I quote, 'Answer me yes or no.' I simply answered you as you had requested, yes or no.'"

She grabs another biscuit from the bowl and begins to smear it with honey. Seeing that the Man is staring at her, she hunches her shoulders and ignores him. She concentrates by carefully layering gobs of honey on the top of the biscuit with her spoon. Then, for good measure, she splits the biscuit in half and covers the bottom part with more honey. She looks up at the Man.

"I honestly have no clue what you would like me to say. Therefore, I have nothing more to say to you." She grins. "At least not until you calm yourself."

She glances across the veranda. Two very pretty African American girls are standing in the far corner facing the table. From their facial features, Steph guesses they are sisters. One appears to be eight or nine-years-old. The other girl looks like she is twelve, maybe thirteen-years-old. Both are wearing drab clothing common to slaves.

Unlike the child slaves who toil alongside the adults in the fields, these young girls are more fortunate, at least as it relates to their attire. Their one-piece cotton dresses that hang below their knees may be dowdy, but at least they are clean. Also, they are not raggedy and worn to shreds like those who work in the fields. Most slaves have only one, or if they are very fortunate, two changes of clothes. So they eat and sleep in the same clothes they wear while sweating beneath the hot sun.

The girls are wearing brightly colored headwraps. Steph correctly assumes the girls are of West African heritage. West African women and girls held in servitude often continue the ancient custom of wearing headwraps. The wraps repeatedly enfold around their heads to cover their hair. Knots and tuckings secure the wraps tightly.

The girls are barefoot which is customary for slaves, particularly children. Unlike the slaves she saw in the stable, their feet are clean.

Steph smiles at them. They grin from ear to ear in return. The oldest girl begins to giggle. She looks at the Man and covers her mouth with her hand to stifle a laugh.

The Man slowly turns his head as he follows Steph's gaze. The girls quickly stop grinning. They immediately avoid the Man's look by staring at the floor.

Steph is relieved they were not caught smiling in response to her silly, rebellious antics. It is bad enough she is giving the arrogant Man a rough time. There is no need to involve the girls. Given the Man's nasty attitude and obvious temper, she would not be surprised if he struck out at them in anger - knowing fully well he cannot strike out at her except using his angry, hateful words.

The Man redirects his attention to Steph. He stares at her, his dark eyes scowling with disgust. His nasty attitude reminds Steph of a rabid dog.

He has his fist clenched at his side. He inhales a few times deeply. His long, drawn-out exhales are accompanied by loud, annoyed hisses. It is quite obvious to Steph that he is frustrated with her antics and desperately trying to control his temper.

She returns his stare as she indifferently takes bite after bite of her gooey biscuit. She pretends to ignore the honey dribbling down her fingers.

After a few moments, the Man breaks their glowering stare. He has closed his eyes and is shaking his head back and forth in disgust. Steph quickly licks the honey from her fingers. When the Man opens his eyes and looks at her once more, the expression on his face is loathing.

"You look like you have not eaten in a week. That is your fourth biscuit."

Steph grabs another biscuit from the bowl. She begins to smear it with honey. She looks up at the Man.

"What of it?" She smiles adding, "Actually, *this one* is my fourth biscuit."

"Okay, Missy. I see we are not going to get along very well. Maybe my wife will have more success talking some sense into that stupid, idiotic youngster head of yours."

Steph throws her biscuit onto the table. She pushes away from the table and jumps from her chair. Her chair teeters on end, and then it falls backward with a loud *thump!*

Because she forcefully jolted the table as she stood up, the half-empty glass pitcher of lemonade falls onto its side. It rolls across the ruined tablecloth and crashes to the wooden floor. It shatters into at least a dozen shards of glass. Sweetened lemonade begins to spread far and wide across the floor. The two slave girls rush to clean up the mess. Their eyes are as wide as saucers, their expressions sheer terror.

Steph waves her hand at them.

"Stop, if you please! Others, especially innocent children, will not clean up my mess. I made it. I clean it. Understood?"

The girls slowly withdraw to the safety of their corner where they had been standing. They nod their heads solemnly. Steph notices they do not know if they should laugh or cry, jump for joy, or turn around and head for the hills. She truly feels sorry for putting them in this awkward predicament.

She addresses them in a soothing tone.

"And now, if you please, I must ask you to leave the veranda."

She glances at the Man. Her tone of voice matches the look on her face. They reflect the disgust she feels in her heart for this hateful Man who keeps children in bondage.

"What I have to say to this gentleman is not proper for your ears. Now vamoose!"

The girls look at the Man expectantly. He does not turn around to acknowledge them. He is staring at Steph with a look on his face that is outright hatred.

Steph commands with a shout, "Go, now! Please do as I ask!"

The girls bow their heads slightly and dash out of the veranda as if someone has just yelled, "Fire!" Once they are out of earshot, Steph addresses the Man.

"How dare you refer to me as a stupid idiot. I have more book-learning and knowledge in my teenager's head than you will ever have in yours. Even if you live to be a hundred-twenty-years!" She breathes in deeply to calm her emotions. Despite her best efforts, her words continue to seethe from between her clenched teeth.

"What you said to me is very insulting! You do not know me very well. Nevertheless, I can assure you of this. I do not take kindly to insults. Nor should I!" With a tone of defiance in her strong voice, she adds, "And let me assure you. I am anything but stupid."

The man cackles a disgusting laugh. He crosses his arms over his chest.

"Well, I'll be. My wife told me you would be a feisty one, but I never expected this. I am glad you are a blood relative of hers and not of mine. If so." He smacks the side of his butt with the palm of his hand. "If you were a blood relative I would smack the devil out of you to teach you a lesson for mouthing off at me."

His expression suddenly turns profane as he growls in a low, menacing voice.

"But let me tell you this, Missy. Your kind ain't welcome here. Let me say that again. Your kind ain't welcome here. We are proud Southerners, and we will do what we want with our slaves. If you do not like what we do around here, I encourage you to get back on your boat and sail back to your prissy English island.

"But if you decide to stay, to enjoy my gracious hospitality at my house, on my plantation, in my country, I must warn you. You best not interfere with a whipping again or else!" He smacks the side of his butt once more with the palm of his hand. Then he turns on his heels to exit the veranda.

Steph whispers, "I wish you would not turn your back on me. I would think it very unwise if I were you, particularly after threatening me with your nasty 'or else' warning. You know what I did to the man who was whipping that young boy. I would hate to do the same to you.'"

Steph knows the Man cannot stand her. She also knows that if she weren't white, he would race across the floor and pummel her with his fists thereby knocking her senseless. Then he probably would put a collar around her neck and link it to her arms and legs with chains.

Earlier, she saw a middle-aged slave who was bound in that exact manner. He was sitting cross-legged beneath the scorching sun. What she saw was horrible, detestable, inhumane. She knew then, as she knows now, that the Man standing before is completely immoral.

She smacks her butt with her open hand as she says, "Nobody threatens to strike me. Period." She adds with a smile, "As far as I am concerned, you are a nobody, a detestable slave owner. Nothing more than a figment of history's scorn. Your threats mean nothing to me."

The Man places his hands on his hips as he scowls spitefully. Steph knows it is evident he is looking for trouble, for some legitimate excuse to smack her. For some strange reason she cannot explain, she is in the mood to oblige him. Even so, she does not want to anger him too much. He looks meaner than a barnyard rat. And as unpredictable as a raging storm.

Besides, if a look of absolute hatred like his could freeze a soul, I already would have a one-way ticket to heaven.

The Man yells, "And what are you going to do about it, Missy? I dare say you shan't do anything. You ain't nothing but a girl, a puny, weak girl."

Steph replies unemotionally, "You do not scare me. No more than an elephant fears a flea. As far as what I am going to do about it, I am going to make you feel pain." She smacks her butt with her open hand yet again. "That is what I am going to do."

The Man threateningly points his finger at her. He says with a hearty, contemptuous laugh, "Oh yeah? You and what army? Eh, Missy? Surely not the British Army, you know, those of your yellow kind, your fellow cowardly countrymen. Our Revolutionaries whipped them up and down the East Coast during the Revolutionary War. It is sad when you think about those gutless British Redcoats and everything. Should have called them yellow coats. Maybe even turncoats.

"They did not even know how to fight proper. Stood in the open when there were trees to hide behind. Ever hear of George Washington, Missy? Well, the founding father of my country is a distant cousin of mine a couple of times removed. Mightily proud he is my ancestor. He was a courageous fella. His blood runs in my veins, and, like him, I ain't afraid of no one. Especially a girl like you. Even if you are my wife's niece."

Steph replies solemnly, "What army you ask? Let me tell you, sir. That army will be me, myself, and I. That is what army. I am a very agreeable person. I am civil. And I loathe violence. Nevertheless, I will defend myself if need be. On the other hand, you, sir, are through and through evilness." She pauses briefly, and then she shakes her finger at him.

"And a conniving, deceitful liar. I know that you told Boss, as you refer to him - Jim is his real name, am I correct? Jim Shane Dewitt if I remember correctly. You told Jim to whip that poor boy because he stole food from the pantry. And all the while you knew the truth. You sent an innocent, young boy to receive lashes and you knew the truth!"

A curious look appears on the Man's face. He says, "What truth? What in the world are you talking about? You cannot know of such lies. You were not here when the theft occurred."

Steph smiles deviously.

"You know that Joseph did not steal from the pantry, don't you? You made up the story. Someone else stole food from the pantry. You blamed Joseph because you needed a scapegoat, someone on whom you could blame the theft. You know I am right, that what I am saying is the truth. I can see it on your face as plain as day."

The Man says in a gruff tone, "I have no idea what you are talking about." He stares at Steph for the longest time, and then he turns to leave the veranda. He mutters something under his breath. Steph cannot discern all of what he said, but she instinctively knows some of it consisted of curse words and something about a female dog.

"Do not call me such horrible names. I am a young lady, and I do not appreciate your evil tongue. As far as what I am talking about, oh, I believe you *do* know. Your oldest son, Henry, from your first marriage, stole the food, didn't he? He intends to share it with his friends."

The man turns around once more. He has an expressionless look on his face. Steph knows she has his attention, so she decides to tell him more of what she knows about the theft.

"You knew your son, Henry had stolen from the pantry, but you did not want to confront him. That is because the two of you seldom speak to each other after you remarried. He is still very upset because you remarried too soon after the passing of your first wife. She passed away less than one year ago if I am correct. Surprisingly, your son William is not upset. That is good."

Steph taps her temple with her forefinger as if she is deep in thought.

"Let me see here. Ah, yes. Your deceased wife's name was Edith. Am I correct?" In a sincere tone of voice, she adds, "And she was very young, too. Thirty-two years old. I believe her birthday was this past Tuesday." Steph's expression suddenly changes, and her tone is sympathetic.

"I am very sorry for you and your sons, Henry and Williams' loss. Losing a loved one, especially a wife and mother to your sons must be very difficult."

The Man does not reply. All he does is stare at Steph with his wide-eyed, coal-black eyes.

"So you made up a believable lie that anyone on this bigoted plantation would accept as true. Didn't you? You said to everyone that Joseph had stolen food from the pantry to give to his sisters. And you recognized from the get-go that everyone would go along with your lie. That is because all of you, except your wife, Mary, believe slaves are no good. All of you believe they are deceitful liars. You hate with all your heart those you enslave.

"In your white workers' racist eyes, as in your eyes as well, slaves are less than human. You hold the firm belief that your slaves steal, lie, cheat, and conspire behind your backs even though they cannot do a thing about the horrible hold you have over their pitiful lives!"

She places her hands on her hips. She is so angry she is shaking.

"If only you knew how loving, understanding, and beautiful their souls are! How amazing their culture is! And all you and other slave owners seek to do is erase their self-dignity and destroy what little remains of their culture and self-esteem. You and everyone who own slaves are despicable."

When the man replies, his tone is skeptical.

"Who told you these made-up lies? Did Henry tell you, simply to impress you? If he did, I am going to thrash that boy behind the woodshed the next time I see him!"

Steph replies, "How could Henry tell me? He and I haven't met. He is away for the weekend with his friends, the very friends for whom he stole the food. They are camping in the hills to the west of here." She slowly shakes her head in disgust.

"William did not tell me either. He did not know what happened until you cooked up your evil lie. Nor do those who you enslave know who stole from the pantry. They were asleep when it happened."

The Man's facial expression suddenly changes. His voice is calm when he speaks.

"How is it you know these things? You have been here less than one-half of the morning, and you have already upset this household like no one else before now. Can you read minds? Are you a witch? Even though I do not believe in such things, a witch around here is treading on dangerous ground. Let me assure you of that fact, Missy."

"I am not a witch. I know things. That is all. I can see things others cannot. Take you for instance. Deep in your heart, you do not enjoy being sinful. You know it is wrong to whip your slaves. You do wicked things so that you can fit in with your neighbors, with your friends. And yes, for profit. You are a religious man. I know that. And it breaks your heart to see African Americans suffer. But, despite your remorseful thoughts and heartbroken pains in your heart, what you do is sinful and contrary to God's will. Just because your father owned African Americans, and his father before him, doesn't mean you have to follow their perversion.

"For your information, that is how I will refer to your slaves this point going forward. As African Americans.

"You can change your ways but only if you want to. And change you should. Before long, a future American President, a man you have not even heard of yet, Abraham Lincoln, will declare in an Emancipation Proclamation that all slaves are free. Also, many fathers, sons, and brothers on both side of the slavery issue will die in a Civil War, a horrible war of the North versus the South. It will be the costliest war regarding the dead in our nation's history.

"And know this. Descendants of the very souls you enslave today will someday in the future refer to themselves as African Americans as I said. While their road to freedom and equality will be long and arduous, they will become legitimate citizens of the United States equal to the just laws of America just like you." Steph smiles as she adds with a somber tone, "So unless you want you and your children's descendants to regard you with disgust for enslaving others, you better get with the program, and soon! Let those who you enslave go free."

The Man looks at Steph for the longest time. His tone of voice is calm and sorrowful when he finally speaks.

"I apologize for calling you an idiot, and although your kind is not welcome here for reasons of your safety, I take back what I said." Then,

ED KIGHTLINGER

with a genuine smile, he says with an affectionate tone, "Josephine. Yes, some of what you say may be true. However, I must tell you this. Be careful what you say around other white men on my plantation. They will not take kindly to your words, your British anti-slavery words."

He suddenly turns around and yells, "Hannah, Patsy. I know you are out there eavesdropping. Get in here!"

Hannah and Patsy, the two girls that were standing in the corner before Steph and the man's conversation intensified, reenter the veranda. They curtsy with their heads bowed and whisper at the same time, "Yes, Mas'r?"

"Fetch me a pail of soapy water and some clean rags to clean up this lemonade. Already the flies are enjoying their free sugary lunch. The Man smiles at the girls, and then he says in a lighthearted tone, "And bring us another pitcher of lemonade and some of those terrific cookies your momma baked this morning, okay? Miss Josephine and I are going to have ourselves a little chat along with Missus Gray. Keep a dozen or so cookies for yourselves and share them with your friends."

The girls do not move. They simply stare at the man in disbelief. They glance at Steph, the expressions on their faces ones of, "What in the world should we do?"

She says in a soft tone, "Hurry now, girls. Please do what he says."

Hannah and Patsy curtsy once more, and then they rush out of the veranda. They glance over their shoulders at Steph and smile. Making certain the Man is not looking at her, she winks at the girls in return.

Despite her joy with the Man's sudden change of heart, from bad to good, at least as it concerns this conversation, Steph is in a panic. The last thing she wants right now is to sit down and have a chat with Missus Gray and the Man.

She whispers, "But sir, I said I would clean up my mess."

The Man chuckles.

"The girls and I will clean up your mess for you. After all, I am the one who caused you to get angry with me. It is my fault." His tone suddenly turns sincere.

"So, Josephine, why don't you skedaddle up to your room and freshen up a bit." He points to Steph's dress adding, "It appears you have spilled half the pitcher of lemonade on yourself." Then, to Steph's

92

complete surprise, he says in a joking manner, "Do I have to call you Missy once more to get your attention?" He laughs.

Steph laughs as she happily replies, "No sir!"

She dashes out of the veranda. She cannot wait to get to her room to read more of the letters written by the mother of the real Josephine. She hopes they provide her with more information. What she is supposed to say and do as the supposed Josephine visiting from across the Atlantic Ocean!

*****

Part II: A Mother's Cry for Help

Steph is frantically going through some of the letters written to Missus Mary Gray by her sister, Polly. From the contents of the letters, Spirit's remark that Polly is much older than Mary is indisputable. Her use of the English written word is phenomenal. Not only is her prose articulate, but her use of metaphors and delightful sayings is also extraordinary. Steph guesses the woman is highly educated.

"Long before we contemplated Josephine's voyage, I had warned her about the slavery issue in the country of her birth. It seems to be in the newspapers every day here in England. I told Josephine, 'Counter your hatred of slavery with the breathings of your benevolent heart. Try to go easy on your aunt's husband and those that work for him. For a man's conscience is his roadmap to his deeds, both good and evil.'"

Steph is stunned by the last metaphor. She reads the words again.

"For a man's conscience is his roadmap to his deeds, both good and evil."

Goodness, I must admit. It is almost as if Polly knows what makes the Man's heart and mind tick!

She flips the paper over to read what is written on the other side.

"And I dare say, my dear sister, nary a soul on this side of the Atlantic supports slavery. We find bondage of humans detestable. I, in particular, know that slavery is a friend of the devil. And this much I also know. America's slave owners have tossed their souls deep into the soil of bigotry where they will rot in the annals of history.

"I recognize your standing on the matter. I recognize you have no tolerance for the abuse of those of colour. In spite of this, I also appreciate you are unable to voice your loathing of the topic openly. As far as my daughter Josephine is concerned, she shall keep her nose out of everyone's business. At least that is what I told her."

Josephine's mum goes on to mention some of her daughter's likes and dislikes. Josephine likes strawberry jam the best. She enjoys horseback riding. She is very opinionated, and she does not take kindly to insults or flirting. She is a true lady, but she acts like a tomboy whenever she can.

Well, Steph ponders. At least Josephine and I have a few things in common although I prefer grape jam over strawberry any day. But nowadays I will devour just about anything.

She rummages through the drawer. She finds another letter buried beneath some papers. It is sealed, but it appears to have been opened and then carefully resealed. She opens the envelope and begins to read. An expression of panic suddenly appears on her face. She begins to tremble. Her trembling dramatically increases the further she reads down the lines.

"I think you will like our Great Uncle George. He willingly volunteered to accompany Josephine. He will probably stay for one or two nights. Afterward, he will journey up north to Boston where he will conduct business with his shipping partners. The old codger may be old, but he is as strong as a bull and even more bullheaded. He always tells Josephine and me, 'I shall live to be at least a hundred!' I declare, my dear sister, I believe he shall!'"

Oh, my God. I am, well, Josephine, is supposed to travel with Great Uncle George! How am I going to explain my way out of that, that he is not accompanying me? No proper young lady in her right mind travels anywhere alone during this day and age. Someone always escorts her as a chaperone. What in the world am I supposed to do, to say?

She stares out the window at the massive, well-manicured grounds of the plantation's mansion. Off in the distance scores of African Americans are toiling in the fields. She is perspiring as she sits in the relative comfort of the room. She can only imagine how the African

Americans must feel as they toil in the scorching sun. She is in a panic. She wants to jump from the balcony to the ground below, call out to Spirit, and get as far away from this bad dream, and as quickly as she can.

Spirit's thoughts suddenly are in her mind.

"You will have to tell a white lie, Steph. Make up some truly outlandish but believable story about Josephine's Great Uncle George being called away immediately after the ship docks. After all, you supposedly arrived in the Port of Charleston, South Carolina, so your story should be convincing to others. Just make it a doozy of a white lie, so far-fetched it is true-to-life."

"Lie?" Steph says in a firm tone. "I cannot lie. You know that. It is against everything in which I believe. It is deceitful. It is bad enough I am pretending to be someone I am not. I do not want anyone to think I am a liar."

She discerns Spirit's unmistakable whinny from somewhere off in the distance. He is probably grazing in the pasture. She immediately knows he is going to say something sarcastic. She impulsively cringes.

"Well, Steph, as the famous British poet and writer, A. A. Milne once said, 'If one is to be called a liar, one may as well make an effort to deserve the name.'"

"Thanks a lot for nothing!" Steph says. "Alan Milne hasn't even been born yet, at least not in this time zone!"

"You are correct," Spirit's thoughts say in her mind. "Then again, Milne was an English author, best known for his books about the teddy bear Winnie-the-Pooh. Sort of fits the script if you know what I am saying since you are supposed to be the British girl Josephine and all. Give it your best shot. Missus Gray already suspects something is not right about you even though she hasn't seen you. Playact, girl, playact."

Spirit's thoughts pause for a moment.

"As Ralph Waldo Emerson once said, 'Truth is beautiful, without doubt; but so are lies.' Be careful, Steph. And try to remember why you are here, why Jordyn brought you to this terrible age.'"

Steph replies, "I wish I knew. I honestly wish I knew why she sent me, us here. I have an inkling, but I am not certain. What is more, I wish I knew why Jordyn is silent this time."

From her literature classes, Steph knows that Emerson's quote about lying, as so kindly passed on to her by Spirit, may prove useful. After all, Emerson is a well-known American philosopher and poet who routinely makes newspaper headlines during the period in which Steph finds herself. If she gets in a bind, she can always quote Emerson to draw attention away from herself. Many Southerners in the present era vehemently hate Emerson because of his unwavering views regarding individualism and anti-slavery.

Steph stares at the envelope that she has unsealed.

Goodness, gracious! How am I going to reseal this envelope to make it look like nobody's opened it?

Her train of thought suddenly is interrupted by a soft knock on the door. She hastily stuffs the envelope back into the drawer.

"Yes, who is it?"

A woman replies in a loud voice, "Mistress Josephine, it is me, Janette. Mistress sent me to assist you."

Steph quickly undresses. She tosses her soiled dress into a corner. She slips on a robe draped over the bedpost. The beautiful cream-colored robe is handmade. A lovely bouquet of expertly embroidered buttercup flowers is above each of the pockets. The loose-fitting robe is much too large for her, but she could care less. After feeling unbelievably grungy in the dirty clothes she wore in Germany, and when she was lying on the stable floor, she now feels hale and hearty in clean and comfy girly apparels.

She finally replies to the woman that knocked on the door.

"Ah, I am sorry, Janette. I am undressed right now. I am still in my robe, freshening up. Can you come back in a little while if you please?"

Janette whispers at the door. She is speaking so softly her muffled words are hard to understand.

"I beg Miss Josephine's pardon. I must urgently speak with her. I beg of you. Please open the door!"

Steph cannot make out all of Janette's words. All she can discern is that the woman said the word *beg* two times. She moves closer to the door. She whispers in a hushed voice.

"I am sorry, Janette. What did you say?"

The woman's soft, whispering voice muffles through the door.

"I must speak to you. I beg of you. There is trouble. Please help me!"

Steph quickly opens the door. Standing in the doorway is a very frail African American woman. She appears to be in her late fifties. Steph senses she is much younger than that. Perhaps in her late thirties, early forties. She recognizes the woman from the earlier whipping. She was the first person to rush to Joseph's aid. By the manner in which she lovingly cradled the young man in her arms, Steph assumed she was Joseph's mother or, at the least, kinfolk. Tears of anguish were gushing from the woman's eyes as she lovingly held Joseph's trembling body.

Unlike the other African Americans that Steph has seen today, Janette's attire is handsome. Like Hannah and Patsy, a gaily-colored wrap covers the top of her head. She has fixed her grey-streaked hair in a neat bun on the back of her head. She has a freshly cut yellow rose tucked into the locks behind her right ear. She is wearing a thin, white blouse and a blue, pleated skirt. She is also wearing shoes, something that is very uncommon for servants. Steph rightly assumes someone, undoubtedly the plantation's wife, Missus Gray, thinks highly of Janette despite her servitude.

Janette is holding a bundle of clothes in the crook of one arm and a nearly full pitcher of water in the other. Steph takes the pitcher from the woman and carefully places it on the side table near the door. Water sloshes onto the floor.

Janette smiles brightly, flashing her many chipped and decayed, yellowed teeth. She curtsies elegantly.

"Good afternoon, Miss Josephine. My mistress, your Aunt Mary, sent me here with some extra clothes you may like. She also said I should appeal to you if you need anything. Mas'r and the mistress ask you to join them in the east side veranda as soon as you can. Perhaps in twenty minutes if it is okay. The east side veranda is much cooler than the west side this time of day. Prettier too."

Her expression turns solemn. She leans in close to Steph. Her words are barely audible.

"Miss Josephine, I beseech you. I desperately need your help." She looks Steph squarely in the eye as she cocks her head to one side.

"Or, would you prefer that I address you as Miss Steph?"

Steph's face suddenly flushes. The hairs on the nape of her neck stand on end. The door is open wide, so she knows it is prudent to act normal in case anyone catches them whispering. Despite her shock with Janette saying her real name, she manages to remain calm.

She says in a normal tone of voice, "I thank you, Janette. That is very kind of you and Aunt Mary. Please come in. You are correct. My hair is full of tangles. There are bits of straw in it as well. Thank you for offering to comb my hair."

Janette glances behind her at an African American boy outside the room. He is pretending to dust a writing table in the hallway. The boy looks up and down the hallway. He nods his head and gives Janette a thumbs up.

Janette says in a strong voice, "Well, Miss Josephine, if you need my assistance, it would be my pleasure to comb the tangles and straw out of your hair." She quickly enters the room and quietly closes the door behind her.

Steph reaches out to embrace Janette. As she hugs the older woman, she says in a guarded tone, "Janette, how is it you know my real name? That my name is not Josephine - that I am Steph?"

"I knew you were coming, Miss Steph," Janette says. Her words are void of emotion.

Steph gently pushes away from her. She stares at the woman incredulously. Her tone is skeptical.

"How in the world could you know that I was coming? I didn't even know where I was going - well, where I was until I woke up in the pasture this morning. Who told you?"

"Jordyn."

Steph is stunned. She suddenly feels faint, so she grabs the bedpost to keep from falling.

"Jordyn told you? How could she tell you when she does not even talk to me? And how is it you know Jordyn?"

"She cannot talk with you because she is ill, Miss Steph, seriously ill. She is unconscious, in a coma."

Tears immediately well up in Steph's eyes.

"Jordyn in a coma? That is horrible! What has happened to her? Do you know?"

"No, I am not at all sure. All I know is that Jordyn cried out two words before she fell unconscious. The words sounded like a boy's first and middle name."

Steph shakes her head disbelievingly.

"It is Roger Clyde, isn't it?"

"Yes, ma'am, Miss Steph. That's right. Roger Clyde. That is what the child said. She said, 'Roger Clyde.' Heard it as clear as a bell in my head, yes ma'am, I sure did. It was very spooky like a ghost was talking to me. Nevertheless, my heart knew the child, Jordyn, was gracious, not evil at all.'"

Steph plops down on the edge of the bed. She buries her head in her hands and begins to cry. After a few moments, she looks at Janette. She wipes her tears with the sleeve of her robe.

"Roger Clyde. If what you say is true, that it was Roger Clyde, then this isn't the first time he has injured Jordyn. He is a terrible bully. I wish I could get my hands on him to teach him a lesson."

"Perhaps, someday you shall get to meet him, Miss Steph," Janette replies. She sits on the bed beside Steph. She lovingly squeezes Steph's shoulders. Then she begins to comb her hair.

"You shall meet him, Miss Steph. Something tells me, sure enough, you will understand why that nasty boy torments the poor child the way he does. You need to remain patient until you do."

"Please, Janette, call me Steph."

Janette replies in a whisper, "But I must address you as Miss Steph. You are like a queen to us. Jordyn has sent you here for a purpose."

Steph thinks to herself, yes, I know.

My raison d'être.

Janette takes Steph's hand in hers. "It is dangerous enough that I call you Miss Steph. And I dread what would happen if I slipped up in front of the others. Nevertheless, I must call you Miss Steph in private because I know if I call you Josephine it will make you feel uncomfortable."

"Yes, you are correct. While the name Josephine is very pretty, I do not feel right when others call me by that name. It makes me feel guilty like I am an imposter. Do you understand what I am saying, Janette?"

Janette nods her head.

"You said Jordyn sent me here for a specific purpose," Steph asks. "Why was I sent here, Janette? Do you know? Because I do not know."

"Jordyn sent you here in my time to save my two little girls from the auction block."

"Oh, my goodness," Steph whispers. Her facial expression is one of sheer panic.

"The auction block! Do you mean the Man is going to sell your children to the highest slave bidder? That is horrible, detestably horrible and unjustly inhumane! I am very sorry, Janette. Have I met your girls? What are their names?"

"Yes, you have met them. My girls are the precious children you saw on the veranda. Hannah and Patsy." Now tears are welling up in Janette's eyes.

"After what happened to Joseph today, with your interruption during his lashing, I believe Mas'r plans to sell all three of my children!"

She notices the startled look on Steph's face.

"Yes, Joseph is my son. I know you guessed that. Because of your intervention today my three beloved children will meet their horrible fate at the auction. And knowing how Mas'r does things, each of them will be sold to separate white slave owners. That is the way Mas'r does things. Mas'r is evil, through and through evil."

Now anguished tears that mirror the profound grief of her breaking heart are escaping freely from her deep brown eyes.

"White folk do not take too kindly to us negros having the upper hand, defying authority and the lash. I fear Mas'r may think that your rescuing Joseph from the lash's fury will inspire others of my kind to rebel. It is what the white man does. It is his way of protecting himself from us. It is hateful retribution, revenge." She looks at the floor.

"It is against God's will to break up loved ones and friends."

Steph says in a whisper, "I cannot believe this is happening! Not Hannah and Patsy. The girls are innocent. They are very pretty and oh, very young! While I have no regrets about interfering during the horrible whipping, all the same, I feel terrible! Like all of this is my fault!"

She reaches out to embrace Janette. The two of them hug each other for a few moments. At last, Steph gently pushes away from her.

"But, Janette, what can I do? I know nothing about these things. Sure, I have read about the many atrocities of the way slave owners mistreat African Americans during this era. I also have read of the way they break up families for profit or because they want to wound family members. And yes, perhaps in Joseph's case, to get revenge and to warn other African Americans against any thoughts of defying the white man's lash. However, I do not know enough about the practices, the procedures, and rules and regulations to be of much help. I will not know how or where to begin to save your children!"

Janette looks her squarely in the eye. When at last she replies, her tone is comforting and convincing.

"Spirit will guide you. He knows what to do. He has a plan."

"Spirit? How do you know about Spirit?"

"Spirit has spoken to me in my mind. At first, I had no idea who or what was entering thoughts into my head. I thought it was the devil himself. I figured it out when Spirit moved closer to me. I was hanging laundry after the whipping. Spirit gently pushed against me, and then the strangest thoughts entered my mind. The thoughts said, 'Hello, Janette. My name is Spirit. I am Steph, or I should say, Josephine's horse Abraham. We are here to help you with Hannah and Patsy.'"

Janette giggles, and then she says lightheartedly, "As you can imagine, I nearly dropped a load of laundry onto the ground." Steph giggles as well.

Steph says in a sarcastic tone, "Yes, Spirit tends to surprise you when you least expect it. And he has some of the world's worst horsey quips I have ever heard. But how is it his thoughts can enter your mind? I assumed, incorrectly I see, that I was the only one with whom he could communicate."

And, of course, with Jordyn.

Janette takes Steph's hand in hers. As she stares into Steph's eyes, Steph suddenly feels as if she is being hypnotized or something similarly bizarre. The lazy feeling in her head is like floating in a vertical position in a breathtaking dream. She is not lightheaded or dizzy, but she feels like she is drifting off. She slowly shakes her head, but the weird feeling does not diminish. She continues to stare into Janette's eyes as if she is charmed, spellbound, hypnotized. When Janette finally speaks, her words sound very distant. The faraway words are like soft echoes of a gentle breeze in a quiet forest in the dead of night.

Spooky? Yes.

Comforting? Definitely.

Janette says, "Before the white man enslaved me like a prisoner and brought me to this strange, wicked land, I was an African enchantress. I still possess the magic. There are two forms of enchantress'. Good and evil. I am a good enchantress. I can hear in my mind voices; voices others cannot hear." She looks away from Steph.

Steph immediately awakens from her trance. She shakes her head a few times. Once her head clears a bit, she says in a soft tone, "Like Jordyn and Spirit's voices?"

Janette nods her head. She says, "Yes, like Jordyn and Spirit's voices." She adds, "And yours."

"Mine?" Steph asks with a surprised tone of voice. "You can tell what I am thinking?"

"Yes, I can. To a point. As an example, take the unopened letter you found earlier. I had never allowed my mistress to read the letter. I hid it from her view." She adds with a sly grin, "Because I knew its contents. I opened it, read a few lines to confirm what I had thought, and then I resealed it with a dab of sticky rice."

She walks over to the bureau and opens the drawer containing the letters from Polly. She withdraws the letter Steph had read a few moments ago.

"The letter arrived yesterday. I left this letter for you to read along with the others. Now that you have read it I shall discard it."

She carefully folds the envelope in half. Then she slips it beneath her foot into the sole of her shoe.

"I feel bad for deceiving mistress. She is very kind to me, kind to all of us, particularly Hannah and Patsy. She detests slavery. She even told me so. Nevertheless, if she had read the letter, you would be in danger. She could have said something to Mas'r or others. Then it would have been most difficult for you."

Steph nods her head knowingly.

"Because the letter mentions Missus Gray's Great Uncle George and my, I mean Josephine's escort."

"Yes, Miss Steph. You would be in danger because the letter mentions Josephine's Great Uncle George. You would have one terrible time trying to explain that." She softly laughs as she adds, "You are very intelligent, but I fear even you would not be able to respond well if they were to ask you about your Great Uncle George."

Steph sighs deeply. She is relieved to have the topic of Josephine's Great Uncle George dismissed.

"Whew, that is a load off my mind. The others will assume I was unescorted, yes?"

"Yes, they will. However, Mas'r will ask you the reason why you were unescorted. As you correctly assumed, as you read the letter, no young lady of decency travels without an escort. Therefore, you must lie, Miss Steph. Your safety and the lives of my two daughters and son are in peril if you do not."

Steph grimaces.

"But I do not want to lie. There has to be a better way."

*****

Part III: Slavery is a White Man's Bigoted Shackle

Steph is once again sitting at the table on the veranda. She is munching on delicious cakes while sipping lemonade. The cakes remind her of Petite Fours she had eaten while on vacation to Ohio. Except these cakes are round instead of square. The delicious confections are jam-packed with velvety yellow filling and topped with walnuts. A dusting of confectioners' sugar mixed with a hint of cinnamon is on top of each cake.

Her supposed Aunt Mary is sitting to her left. The Man is to her right. Steph marvels at Missus Gray's natural beauty. The woman appears to be in her mid-twenties. She is at least twenty years younger than the disheveled, overweight Man.

She has closely cropped auburn hair and lots of freckles. Her dark blue eyes seem to glow in the ambiance of the early afternoon's light. If Steph did not know better, that they were in the mid-Nineteenth Century, Missus Gray's hairstyle would look like something straight out of a fashion magazine of the Twenty-first Century.

Perhaps it is because she is half-British, Steph considers. Even now, in my time, many British women wear their hair short. Some even wear their hair like a boy's crew cut. But, here I go again, stereotyping. Teenagers my age and older women are empowered to do what they want with their appearance. Who am I to assume that women of this age cannot do the same?

Missus Gray says with a carefree tone, "What I do not understand is what compelled you to do it."

She eyes her husband, the Man. He does not look at her. He continues to stare across the veranda to his slaves working in the fields.

She says in a disgusted tone, "I too despise it, slavery that is. Be that as it may, I never had the mettle to interfere. Lord knows I wanted to."

She throws her hands up into the air. The expression on her face reflects the disgust in her tone of voice.

"Whipping another human. How horrible." She ignores her husband's disapproving expression as she adds, "So, Josephine, please tell me. What was your motivation to intervene, to try and stop the whipping, a whipping that you successfully terminated? You do know you were putting yourself in a dangerous situation. I hope you understand that."

She glances across the table at her husband. He is staring at Steph and slowly nodding his head. Missus Gray gives him a dirty look.

Steph ignores his stare, and she addresses Missus Gray.

"Well, as I was walking alongside William, I heard excruciating screams. William told me they were whipping a boy who allegedly had stolen from the pantry. I initially thought the screams were from the boy.

"When I entered the stable I realized it was not the boy that was screaming. Yes, he was whimpering a bit. By the look of the horrendous, crisscrossed welts on his back that were oozing dark red blood it is a miracle he hadn't fainted. I would have been screaming to high heaven if it were me. That is if I hadn't fainted after the first lash bloodied my back."

Now it is her turn to give the Man a dirty look. He simply smiles in reply.

"The blood-curdling screams that I heard came from a woman. I think they came from the boy's mother. The screams were horrible. Full of anguish and terror. Naturally, I ran toward them."

She places her half-eaten cake on the plate. She stares at the Man once more. Her expression is one of extreme repulsion. His expression, as he stares at her in return, is one of *I do not care.*

"Any decent human being would have run toward those screams. They were horrible - incredibly horrible!"

Now her voice is trembling. She shakes her head back and forth a few times.

"I had the sudden urge to vomit when I saw what was happening. Luckily, my stomach was empty." She glances at the Man adding, "How anyone could do that to another human being is beyond words. It is disgusting, inhumane, against everything good in this world. It is contrary to God's teachings."

She is about to say something else when the Man interrupts her. He says in a matter-of-fact tone of voice, "William said you ran toward the screams after he told you one of my overseers was whipping a slave. You had not moved an inch before then. At least that is what William said to me. In my view, you wanted to be the heroine, Josephine." He pronounces Josephine's name slowly and with loathing.

"Maybe you ran toward the stable after William said it was a boy." He eyes Steph for a few moments, and then he says with sarcasm, "You do like boys, do you not? Despite your boyish, ridiculous clothing?" He sneers as he adds, "Negro boys who are disgustingly black? You like their kind, yes?"

"Yes, I like boys," Steph says.

She wants to add *even if they are of color.* But she doesn't. She figures saying what she is thinking will only serve to enrage the Man even more. She wants to keep this conversation as civil as she can in the presence of Missus Gray.

"It is only natural for a girl to like boys and vice versa. Nonetheless, despite what you say, I had wanted to run toward the screams as soon as I heard them."

She glances over at Missus Gray. The woman seems to be eyeing her up and down more closely than before. Missus Gray's sudden keen curiosity, at least that is how Steph interprets it, is starting to make her nervous.

"As soon as William said a slave was being whipped, for something as trivial as stealing from the pantry, I could not help myself. I had to do something. Call it instinct if you must call my reaction to the screams anything at all. From where I come, people instinctively react when someone is screaming. Also, from where I come, people do not whip other people. I am certain you appreciate the British peoples' attitude regarding slavery of African Americans in your country."

She looks at Missus Gray. The young woman is nodding her head. Steph has the uncomfortable feeling that the woman continues to size her up much too carefully.

Then again, maybe Missus Gray is nodding her head because she agrees with what I said.

She decides to go on the offensive, a matter of speaking, to interrupt Missus Gray's thoughts.

"And you, Aunt Mary," she inquires in a whisper, "why is it you do not interfere, meddle as you say, when you hear the horrible cries of slaves?" She looks at the Man adding, "Especially when there is no legitimate cause to whip them in the first place? When they are innocent?"

She places her hand on Missus Gray's hand and squeezes it.

"Something tells me you are against slavery. Am I correct?"

The Man promptly says in a nasty tone, "Now listen here, Josephine. What my wife, your Aunt Mary, thinks about slavery is none of your business. You may be her kin, but you have no business asking her how she feels about slavery."

He intently stares at Steph with his piercing, dark eyes for far too long. It makes her feel very uncomfortable. For she instinctively knows. If she were an African American, one of his slaves, she would already be hanging lifeless from the nearest tree for talking back to him.

Much to her surprise, the Man suddenly leans across the table. His face is less than a foot from hers as he points his finger threateningly.

"I thought you and I had an understanding." He nastily smiles as he sarcastically adds, "Missy?"

Steph says in a calm voice, "An understanding, sir? I know of no understanding between us. And once more, please do not call me Missy. I am nobody's Missy. I am Josephine."

She gives the Man a nasty look, and then she addresses Missus Gray once more.

"So, if you do not mind me asking, Aunt Mary. Why is it you do not, as you say, meddle?"

"Because I know my place here in the household on the plantation that my husband owns. I am the wife. My husband is the provider. Here in America, especially down South, we women are not as liberal as women like my dear sister, Polly." She smiles meekly adding, "And you."

She warily glances at the Man as if she is expecting him to reach across the table and slap her. She looks at Steph once more. Her eyes are misty with tears.

"Does that make sense to you, Josephine?"

Steph wants to scream ugly obscenities followed by hearty, "No, no, no's!" Then follow up those no's with, "That does not make sense to me!"

However, she does not use curse words. She also knows there is no sense starting another argument with the Man. He will probably take his anger out on his wife when they are alone.

Besides, I cannot trust anyone who directs the whipping of a boy - especially for a crime he did not commit!

"Yes, it makes sense to me," she finally replies in a whisper. "I do not like it, but I understand that is the way it is here in America."

She looks the Man squarely in his face.

"But know this. The wheels of freedom may turn slowly, but their end result will be the death of slavery. You can mark my words."

As she expected, the Man reacts as someone has poked him in the eye with a hot branding iron. Despite his inner anger, he doesn't say anything. He manages to keep from lashing out at Steph as he continues to stare.

Surprisingly, Missus Gray's reaction also remains passive. She seems to be eyeing Steph suspiciously once more like she knows Steph is not Josephine.

That she is closely eyeing me should come as no surprise. After all, Josephine is her sister's daughter. Why wouldn't she be suspicious? Especially considering I do not look anything like her niece.

She decides to go on the offensive a second time. This time more aggressively.

"Why are you looking at me like that, Aunt Mary?" With a pretending, timid smile, she adds in a dismissive tone, "I dare say it is making me feel a bit uncomfortable."

She touches the top of her head.

"Did Janette fix my hair incorrectly? Did she not get out all of the tangles? Is there still bits of straw and dirt in it?" She wipes the corners of her mouth with her napkin.

"Or do I have something on my face? I tend to scarf down sweets like they are going out of style."

"It is your accent, Josephine," Missus Gray says. "It almost sounds, well, how can I put it? It almost sounds like the way folks talk down here in the South. It is like you were born right here in the South instead of up North. To be honest, I would expect your accent would be more British by now." She adds with a grin, "Considering you have lived in England for the past ten years or so."

Uh oh! Missus Gray is on to something. I was born and raised in the South. It does not get more country Southern American than that! Does she know I am not Josephine? That I am an imposter?

Steph laughs even though her knees are shaking like crazy beneath the table. She quickly pretends a British accent with a Southern drawl. She is not sure how to do it or how it will come across, but she decides she will give it her best shot.

"Well, my dear Auntie Mary, I do declare. We British-American folk sometimes assume the accents of those with whom we are conversing if you know what I am saying!" She covers her mouth with her hand and pretends to burp adding, "Yes ma'am, we do dat, we sure do." She looks at the Man.

"We even burp like Southern folk menfolk, we do at dat. Now, when's we gonna eat that squirrel?"

Missus Gray and the Man roar with laughter. Steph pretends to join in with their laughter even though she wants to run away and take cover in the quiet and peaceful haven of her room.

Or, better yet. Go home!

The Man's eyes suddenly narrow. He says in a somber tone, "I have to ask you something, Josephine. It has been bothering me since you arrived."

He leans across the table once more. He takes Steph's hand in his. She tries to pull her hand away, but his grip is purposely strong.

She can feel the evil of the Man's heart and soul oozing from the palms of his calloused hand into hers. She suddenly feels sick to her stomach. She wants to puke.

Part of her wants to scream, "Get your hands off me, you bigoted slob!" But the other part of her manages to mask her emotions.

"Why is it no one is escorting you as you travel, Josephine? Womenfolk, particularly young girls like you, must have an escort when traveling. That is especially important when traveling abroad." With a disgusting, guttural snigger he adds in a mocking tone, "Otherwise, people will think the young lady is anything but a respectable lady. You are a respectable lady, are you not? Despite wearing clothes like a boy."

Steph releases her hand from his clutch. She quickly reaches for her glass of lemonade. She can barely keep the lemonade from sloshing out of the glass. She is that nervous. And angry. As she slowly gulps her lemonade, she considers how she should answer the Man.

There he goes again insulting me. And yes. Leave it to the cunning Man to dash all hopes of me avoiding any mention of an escort! Now I am in a tight spot for real. All the same, it is a legitimate question, one that Janette said may force me to have to lie. But, I do not want to lie. It goes against everything in which I believe.

She looks at Missus Gray. It is obvious to her that the woman also is waiting for an answer.

She whispers, "First off, sir, please do not touch me again. You are a married man."

The Man replies in a nasty tone, "But, Josephine. I am your uncle, after all, the husband of your Aunt Mary. I have every right to take your hand in mine. Besides, I would never do anything to make you feel uncomfortable, to hurt you."

He tilts his head to the side, and then he adds in a contemptuous tone, "You must believe me when I say that." He sniggers adding, "You do believe me, do you not? That I do not want to hurt you?"

Steph replies to his words by way of a contemptuous tone of her own.

"I seriously doubt that you would never do anything to make me feel uncomfortable. Just sitting here at the same table with you makes me want to vomit."

She places her elbows on the table. She leans toward the Man, and then she looks him straight in the eye.

"Plus, let us get one thing straight right here and now. You are not my uncle, neither by blood or via relationship. I would never admit to having an uncle who keeps people of color in bondage and has them whipped for a crime they did not commit."

She continues to glare at the Man. She cannot help but notice that his eyes are twitching.

Good. Hopefully what I am saying is sinking in! But, goodness! He looks like he wants to strangle me!

She instinctively draws back. Her eyes begin to well up with tears triggered by the anger and disgust that are boiling in her heart. It is all that she can do to stifle the urge to reach out and slap the Man senseless.

If only my insulting words could somehow move his heart - compel him to free his African American servants no matter how much it hurts him in the eyes of his peers or financially. I can only hope and pray.

She addresses the Man once more saying, "Besides, I think it highly improper that you should take my hand in yours, especially in the presence of your devoted, lovely wife. That you did so makes me uncomfortable and very nervous."

She looks at Missus Gray adding, "I am very sorry, Aunt Mary. But it does." She pats Missus Gray's hand. "And I apologize about saying cruel things to your husband. Please forgive me."

She glares at the Man. His face is expressionless. She decides that she will attempt to get a reaction from him yet again. When she speaks, her voice is firm.

"Nonetheless, as God is my witness, I cannot help but feel utter repulsiveness toward one who willingly keeps others as slaves! Slavery is a white man's bigoted shackle." She points her finger. "You, sir, are that bigoted shackle!"

She leans back in her chair. She crosses her arms over her chest.

Goodness, what is wrong with me? I did not mean to say all of that, especially in front of his wife. But I am glad that I did. Maybe what I said will explain my sudden nervousness when he asked me why I did not have an escort. But how should I reply to his question? It is a valid question that needs answering.

The Man continues to stare at her fixedly.

Something she considered earlier crosses her mind. She leans across the table yet again.

"To answer your question as to why I am unescorted, I must say this rather emphatically. As my idol, Ralph Waldo Emerson, once said, 'Truth is beautiful, without doubt; but so are lies.'" With a mischievous smile, she adds in a sarcastic tone, "Contrary to what my hero Emerson says, I cannot tell a lie."

The Man grumbles loudly as he angrily pushes his chair away from the table. Like Steph did before when she abruptly pushed the table, the pitcher of lemonade begins to fall onto its side. Except for this time Missus Gray manages to catch it before it summersaults onto the floor. Despite her grabbing hold of the pitcher, lemonade splashes onto the beautiful tablecloth.

Steph moans.

Well, two soiled tablecloths in one day must be a record in this household. Goodness, the Man and I simply cannot seem to get along!

The Man abruptly says, "Excuse me, Josephine, but I implore you never to mention that vile man's name around here or anywhere else in these parts. We do not like his kind, nor do we appreciate his violent, hawkishness words." He glances at his wife adding with a somewhat dubious smile, "Now, if the two of you will excuse me, I have pressing matters that I need to attend to."

He looks at Steph. His penetrating, dark eyes express evil.

"As for you, young lady, please try and stay out of trouble. I do not want to hear any more talk about you interfering in our business. Do I make myself clear? Yes or no?"

Steph does not reply. She smiles and gawps at the Man. The comical expression on her face seems to say something along the lines of, "Honestly, do you want me to go there - again?"

The Man admonishes Steph by saying, "Oh, forget it, Josephine. You probably will merely answer me with my question like before, yes or no."

With a loud grumble, he pulls up his britches that were dropping much too low over his fat rump. He briefly glares at Steph, and then he abruptly turns about on his heels. As he departs the veranda, he is cursing under his breath.

Steph wants to laugh at the Man, at the way she always seems to bring his quick temper to the surface. But she thinks better of it. That is because Missus Gray is staring at her and making her more nervous than before.

*****

Part IV: An Understanding

"So, Josephine," Missus Gray says as she dabs the spilled lemonade on the tablecloth with a napkin, "tell me how Aunt Margaret is. Last time I knew, she was trying to recuperate after her unfortunate fall last year."

Steph stares at Missus Gray with a blank face.

Oh, my goodness! Who in the world is Aunt Margaret? Josephine's mother never mentioned her in any of the letters! How am I supposed to answer Missus Gray's question?

Thankfully, Spirit's thoughts quickly enter her mind.

"Act surprised Steph. Ask her to whom she is referring. Tell her you do not know an Aunt Margaret." He whinnies. "Nor do I. Sorry."

Steph hesitantly replies with a questioning tone.

"Aunt Margaret? Who is she? I do not think I know an Aunt Margaret."

"Ah, so you do not know Aunt Margaret. I think she is a very distant cousin on your father's side of the family. Sorry."

She continues to stare at Steph.

"So, Josephine, how is your father? Is he still working at the accounting office? Your mother told me he was thinking of going into business for himself."

"Father?" Steph questions silently. "Help me out here, Spirit."

"Tell her Josephine's father is still working for Williams and Wilson. He is the night manager."

Steph replies nervously, "Father? Oh, he is okay. I do not see him much since he began working as a night manager at Williams and Wilson."

Missus Gray says, "Williams and Wilson? I thought the firm was Williams and Watson?"

"No, Steph," Spirit's thoughts seem to scream. "She is testing you, trying to trick you. The firm is Williams and Wilson!"

"Oh, Aunt Mary," Steph says with a smile, "I am sorry to correct you. It is Williams and Wilson, not Williams and Watson. The name of the firm is often confused given that there are two W's involved in the gentlemen's last names."

Missus Gray says with a slight nod of her head, "I see. I am mistaken. Thank you for correcting me." She pauses slightly, and then, as she looks Steph squarely in the eye, she purposely says her niece's name very slowly in a drawn-out manner.

"Jo-se-phine."

Steph is tiring of this cat and mouse game. She decides to put her supposed Aunt Mary on the offensive yet again.

It worked before, so maybe it will work again.

"Aunt Mary, something deep in here." She points her forefinger above her heart.

"And something up here." She points to her temple with the same forefinger.

"Is telling me that you do not like me very much. Am I correct? Please excuse me for saying this."

She crosses her arms over her chest.

"Also, you are making me feel very uncomfortable. It is like you are testing me or something. It almost is like you are cross-examining me. And the way you just pronounced my name slowly and sarcastically, well, it was offensive. It hurt my feelings."

She uncrosses her arms and gestures with the palms of her hands facing up. Then she hunches her shoulders.

"Have I done something to offend you? If I have insulted you in some way, I can return to my room and leave you with your thoughts. I do not want to upset you. And, if you wish…"

Before she can finish her sentence, Missus Gray takes her hand in hers. The expression on Missus Gray's face is sincere, gentle, understanding.

"No, please do not think that way. I am sorry if I offended you, upset you. It is just that you are nothing like my sister had described in her letters. You seem, how can I put it? You seem very different than the niece I had expected to be visiting me."

She manages a meek smile.

"Not in a bad way mind you. Just different." She smiles again. "A lot different. Your mannerisms. The way you talk. The way you conduct yourself. Argue with my husband. Stand up for yourself."

She takes Steph's other hand in hers. She squeezes both of her hands lightly.

"In all honesty, you seem stronger, more spirited, and wiser than the way your mother had described you. More so, I must admit, than I expected." She hesitates a few moments, and then she says, "And your knowledge of things, particularly of slavery in America, well, to tell you the truth - they are mysterious. All the same, I find your attributes fascinating."

She kisses the back of Steph's right hand. Steph finds this gesture very reassuring. Her heart seems to glow with Missus Gray's friendly gesture.

"Your fearless spirit amazes me. It truly does. The courage you displayed in the stable during the whipping inspires me. I am very truthful when I say that. How you confronted two men without hesitation. One pointing a rifle at you. The other holding a whip. How you stood up to them to stop the whipping of a negro. Struck out at Boss and crushed his knee. I have to admit. I am somewhat jealous of your nerve. I only wish I had your nerve, your courage. But, sadly, I do not."

Her facial expression instantly turns to sorrow. Tears begin to well up in her eyes. She wipes at them with her napkin. What she says next seems to Steph like a long overdue confession. An admission of everything that she loathes about the curse of slavery. As the wife of a slave owner.

"I have very little input when it comes to my husband's affairs, especially his running of his property. I detest slavery. I truly do. And my husband knows it. But what can I do? I am a woman. A woman who knows her place and minds her manners in a man's world. A woman surrounded by men who detest negros. A woman who watches horrified as the men verbally and physically abuse eleven hundred negros on this plantation every waking hour of *every single day!*

"Lashings, beatings, even lynching's! Selling off of family members at the auction simply for retribution or for money. Even children! Kicking and slapping children for no reason. Berating adults. Shackling negros just because the white man can. Having negros wear tags when they work on other plantations or in Charleston. My goodness, they even brand some negros with a hot iron!

"Yes, I have seen it all! Every imaginable act of terror that humans can inflict on other humans. If you can think of the atrocities, that they are possible, I have witnessed them, or at the very least, I knew about them. That makes me an accessory to this unspeakable cruelty. Why? I do not have the mettle to do anything about it, to stop it! Do you understand what I am saying?"

Tears are now freely flowing down her cheeks. She ignores them as she stares at the soiled tablecloth. She is trembling, almost hysterically. Her voice is harsh when she manages to speak once more.

"It is inhumane - against God's will to enslave others, to treat them brutally. I have no children of my own, but I instinctively weep for the negro mothers. I can see - almost feel their pain. Their hearts breaking as they bear witness to their precious children toiling day after day in the fields from sunup to sundown. Picking bushel after bushel of cotton beneath the scorching sun until their tiny hands are nothing more than bloody, fleshy tissue.

"Then, in the dead of winter, children huddling together as they shiver before the stove. As their mothers feed bits of scrap wood into the flames to try and keep them warm. So they can stay alive for one more day. And to face what the next day, I ask you? One more cruel day of slavery!

"Children going without shoes in the snow. Some losing their toes to frostbite. Others passing away quietly in the night. Children with clothes that are nothing but tattered, filthy rags. Children constantly hungry. Crying out in the night for one more morsel of food. Children wanting to be set free, to escape the horridness of bondage. It is an abomination I tell you! Slavery is an abomination that goes against God's will!

She lowers her voice noticeably.

"And Joseph! He did not steal from the pantry. I know that for a fact. I saw who did it. And by what you said to my husband, I know you also know the truth. How that you know baffles me. But you know. Just like me."

She stares into the distance, her sobbing intensifying.

"As you and I know, it was not Joseph who stole from the pantry. It was my step-son, Henry. I had told my husband about it. I thought it necessary to tell him because Henry is getting out of control. My husband and Henry barely talk. And Henry despises me. I understand why he does not like me, and I do not fault him. All the same, my husband needed to know who stole two days' worth of provisions from the pantry. Nonetheless, he directed that Joseph be lashed for the crime, the crime he did not commit!"

She looks up at Steph, her tear-filled eyes seemingly pleading for support from her supposed niece.

"But unlike your spirited, daring self, I do not dare to confront this horrible curse that goes against everything in which I believe! This inhumane abomination of slavery, the white man's complete domination over people of color simply for revenue! For ego. For bigoted hatred. I hate it. I truly, truly hate it! But, what can I do? I feel helpless. After all, I am a woman in a man's world."

Steph gets out of her chair and walks over to Missus Gray. Even though she is about the same height and weight as her supposed aunt, she sits on her lap. She places her arms around Missus Gray's neck and hugs her lovingly. Then she begins to cry. After a few moments of sharing in the woman's grief, she manages to regain her composure.

"Oh, Aunt Mary, I am very sorry. I am sorry this is happening to you, happening to the African Americans on this plantation and throughout the South. As you know, I agree with everything that you have said. Slavery is horrible. Despite its ugliness, someday it will end. I promise you. African Americans will become truly free one day and respected by their fellow Americans as equals. Someday in the future, they will prove their worth as indispensable pillars of America's democracy and strength. All people of color, African Americans, Asians, and foreigners of distant lands of diverse cultures and religions will prove their worth here in America as American citizens. I promise you, Aunt Mary. I promise you."

Missus Gray says in a whisper, "Josephine, I am my sister's kin. And there is something I must tell you."

She gently pushes away from Steph. She looks into her eyes.

"I know you are not my niece."

Steph is shocked by what Missus Gray says. She breathes in deeply, and then she exhales a long, drawn-out sigh. She suddenly feels cold even as her face flushes with hotness and her ears begin to burn like they are on fire. She begins to tremble. She tries to get up from Missus Gray's lap, but the older woman shakes her head.

"Please do not get up. I am not angry with you. Just confused."

Then, as she looks into Steph's tear-streaked eyes, Missus Gray says in a soft, soothing tone, "It is okay, my dear. I do not know who you are. Nor do I care. In this brief period, I have come to love you as I love my flesh and blood. Something in my heart tells me you are here for a very important purpose. I do not know what that purpose is, but I think you do." With a sincere smile, she says, "You do know what your purpose is. Am I correct?"

"Yes, ma'am, sort of," Steph says softly. "I am not one hundred percent certain why I am here, but I am getting these strange vibes that I have to save others."

Despite her nervousness, with a slight grin she adds, "But, how did you know, missus, I mean Aunt Mary? How do you know I am not who others think I am?" She pauses for a few seconds, and then she adds, "May I call you Aunt Mary? That is if you do not mind."

"Indeed, please do," Aunt Mary says. "I would like that. Nonetheless, before I answer your question, please tell me, my strange young friend, what is your real name?"

"I am Steph. It is short for Stephanie. My full name is Stephanie JoAnne Galanos. I miraculously have traveled from the Twenty-first Century to now, the Nineteenth Century. At least I think it is the Nineteenth Century.

"However, please call me Steph. Everyone calls me that. Except for my teachers of course." She timidly smiles as she says in a hopeful tone, "I hope you are not angry with me, Aunt Mary. I have no control over my being here. I did not want to be your niece, Josephine. You must believe me when I say that."

"Yes, I believe you, Steph. I am a deeply religious woman, and I believe in miracles and strange things that I am not supposed to understand as a mere mortal." She smiles adding, "And I truly like your name. Stephanie is a very pretty name." She hugs Steph lovingly.

"Now, to answer your question. You just said some things about the future as it concerns the negros. How did you put it, African Americans?"

"Yes, African Americans. People of color, those to whom you refer to as negros, will someday be referred to as African Americans and rightly so."

Aunt Mary says, "Well, my husband told me earlier you had talked about people of color. I detest the terms *slave, slavery and negro* as much as I detest the institution. You had said to my husband that people of color would someday be known as African Americans. He said that you had stated they would be free. That in the future there will be an American Civil War.

"My husband also said that you had mentioned a man named Abraham Lincoln. You had said Lincoln would become the President of the United States. That Lincoln, as President, will proclaim that people of color, the African Americans, will be free. He said you called the President's decree the Emancipation Proclamation."

She rolls her eyes, shakes her head back and forth, and smiles.

"Of course, my husband said you were either crazy or a youthful dreamer. Is all that you said true? Is everything you said going to happen? Will people of color be set free? Will they become American citizens?"

Steph nods her head.

"Yes, Aunt Mary, all of what I said is true. I do not know what year it is now, but all of what I said will happen in the future as sure as you and I are sitting here today."

Aunt Mary says, "Today is April 12, 1860, in the year of our Lord."

Steph exclaims in a surprised tone of voice, "Wow! All of this makes sense."

"What makes sense?"

Steph replies with certainty, "Exactly one year from today, on the 12th of April 1861, the American Civil War will commence. In fact, the war will start right here in South Carolina. It will begin when Confederate troops - that is what the Southern Army will call itself - attack Fort Sumter right here in South Carolina. The Northern troops in the fort will be known as the Union Army. Confederate troops of the South and Union troops of the North will fight the Civil War. Fort Sumter will fall to the Confederates."

She adds solemnly, "I found a pair of handcuffs earlier. They were disgusting reminders of the cruelty of this era. The handcuffs had the words Property of Georgetown County Plantation Police imprinted on them. I assume the Georgetown County is in South Carolina. That we are in South Carolina?"

Aunt Mary replies, "Yes, you are correct, and yes, we are in South Carolina. And Fort Sumter is located in the port of Charleston." She chuckles. Then she says with a huge grin, "Of course, you would have known that since you supposedly arrived in the Port of Charleston.

Charleston is a day's journey, maybe one and one-half day's journey by coach."

"Well, I did not arrive via the Port of Charleston as you probably know," Steph says with a grin. "I woke up in the pasture this morning and wouldn't you know it? Here I am.

"My class at school recently studied the Civil War. Much of what I know about the Civil War is still fresh in my mind. Jefferson Davis, as President of the Confederate States of America, will lead the South. That will occur in February 1861. Less than one month later, Abraham Lincoln will be sworn in as the President of the United States.

"The Civil War will last a little over four years, from April 12, 1861, to May 1865, when Confederate troops finally surrender, and America is once more reunited. Tragically, over 600,000 Americans will die during the war. Disease will kill more than twice that many. Over 50,000 will be amputees. Then, happily, on December 6, 1865, the Thirteenth Amendment to the United States Constitution will be ratified, and slavery will end throughout the land."

Steph smiles as she says in a confident tone, "As I said, I know all these facts by heart, including the dates because we had four quizzes and one test during our study of the Civil War. It was a tough history lesson but very interesting."

Not to mention extremely useful considering I am here in South Carolina a year before the Civil War!

She gets up from Aunt Mary's lap to return to her chair. Her lips and throat are dry. She takes a long drink of her lemonade.

"Goodness, this lemonade is delicious and refreshing. And the cakes are scrumptious. Anyway, now that you know the truth about me, Aunt Mary, I must say this. I honestly cannot explain what or why all of this is happening to us, but I must trust the one who has sent us here."

"Who is us?" Aunt Mary asks.

"Oh, I am sorry. When I refer to *us,* I am referring to Spirit and me." Steph cannot help but notice the surprised look on Aunt Mary's face.

"Spirit is my horse. Your stepson, William, thinks Spirit's name is Abraham."

"Ah, I see," Aunt Mary says. "I was going to ask you about your horse, Abraham. I mean, Spirit. William does not know this, but Josephine's horse is black. Yours is not. At first, I had thought you maybe had borrowed the horse. After William told me about your horse traveling with you across the Atlantic, I had my doubts.

"Anyway, I must tell you something. I must tell you why I believe what you say is true. Do you want to know why I believe you?"

"Yes ma'am," Steph replies. "I would like you to believe that everything I am telling you is the truth. It is important to me. I do not lie. At least not on purpose." She grins adding, "Then again, when I have to lie I call it a white lie. That gives me an excuse for telling a harmless fib."

Aunt Mary reaches beneath her chair. She retrieves a leather pouch. Steph had not noticed it was there. She places the pouch on the tablecloth.

"This pouch belonged to my grandfather. He was an abolitionist. Do you know what an abolitionist is?"

"One who detests slavery like you and me?"

Aunt Mary nods her head.

"Also, abolitionists during this era are actively in involved in seeing that slavery comes to an end. Through their writings, speeches, protests, and political gatherings. My grandfather, even my dad, was very vocal when it comes to slavery. They are long gone now. My grandfather passed away last year. My dad passed away a few months ago.

"I wish my father and grandfather were here. We could use their bright minds." She adds with a sincere smile, "They would have loved meeting you, Steph. Could you imagine what abolitionists could do with your modern-day, futuristic knowledge of slavery's eventual demise? The Civil War? Lincoln, and as you say, the Emancipation Proclamation and the Thirteenth Amendment to our Constitution?"

Perhaps, Steph thinks to herself. But I seriously doubt it. The Emancipation Proclamation did not end the persecution of African Americans. Nor did the Thirteenth Amendment. No more so than the fall of Nazism ended the persecution of the Jews. Unfortunately, today, there are those who still openly discriminate against people of color and different religions and cultures. Like the white supremacists who protested in Charlottesville, Virginia. Like those who discriminate against Muslims and attack their faith, culture, and mosques.

Here in America, in the land of the supposedly free, where there is supposed to be liberty and justice for all. Why cannot Americans learn from the past and change the future for the better?

Aunt Mary carefully undoes the leather laces of the pouch, and then she removes a few documents. To Steph, the documents look like political pamphlets from the current era. Aunt Mary places one of the documents face-down on the table. She holds the other documents in her hand.

"Given that you are very young, I seriously doubt you would have access to what is in these pamphlets or even know that they exist. The pamphlets concern a man who I have come to respect very much. Do you know who the man is?"

Steph's heart is beating a mile a minute. It feels like it will soar out of her chest like a pinwheel that has lost all control over its spinning gyrations. She guardedly replies in a very low whisper.

"Abraham Lincoln?"

"Yes, my dear, you are correct. The man is Abraham Lincoln. These pamphlets address some of his views about slavery. They are the very same pamphlets that were handed out by Lincoln's supporters before one of his debates. Please allow me to tell you a bit more about Lincoln as it concerns his debates.

"Lincoln was an Illinois House Representative for nine years, 1834 - 1842. Then he became a U.S. House of Representatives member in the late 1840s. Two years ago, he was involved in seven debates known as the Lincoln-Douglas debates. The debates are now known as *The Great Debates of 1858.*

"The seven debates primarily focused on the issue of slavery in the United States. Lincoln was the Republican candidate for the United States Senate from Illinois. Douglas was the Democratic candidate. Douglas won the nomination. Despite Lincoln's loss to Douglas, his anti-slavery views propelled him to the forefront of the slavery issue."

She hands the pamphlets to Steph.

On the outside of one of the pamphlets is an image of a kneeling, distressed female slave. She is naked from the waist up. She is clasping her hands in prayer. She has a collar around her neck. A thick chain links the collar to her right ankle. The caption below the image reads, "Am I not a woman and a sister?"

The image on the outside of the other pamphlet is of the Liberty Bell. The caption reads, "Proclaim Liberty for all the Inhabitants."

Aunt Mary hands Steph the third pamphlet, the one that was lying face-down on the table. From the caricature of Abraham Lincoln on the outside of the pamphlet, Steph immediately recognizes that the pamphlet is Southern pro-slavery propaganda. The printed words below the silly-looking drawing of Lincoln remind Steph of ongoing, controversial topics back home about freedom of speech.

"Like Free Speech, this Northerner is the Enemy of the People and Fake News."

Aunt Mary says, "As you can see there are two sides of the slavery issue. Two controversial sides that can rile up even the most easygoing gentlemen."

Steph nods her head.

She can hardly catch her breath as she holds the pamphlets in her trembling hands. With tears of sheer excitement welling in her eyes, she says excitedly, "Oh, my God, Aunt Mary. I am holding the original, historical documents published over one-hundred-fifty years before my birth! I cannot believe this is happening! I am a history buff, and I must say this is incredible! I am honored to be holding these. Even if the topic, slavery, is an abomination. Thank you for allowing me to see them, to hold them!"

She hands the pamphlets back to Aunt Mary.

Aunt Mary replies, "You are welcome. Perhaps if you had the time, you could read what is inside the pamphlets. She pulls a book out of the pouch. A sly grin appears on her face. "The pamphlets are nothing compared to this, my dear." She hands the book to Steph.

Steph wants to jump up and down with absolute joy when she reads the words on the cover of the book she is holding in her shaking hands.

Collected Works of Abraham Lincoln, Volume 3

With a gasp, she says, "Oh, Aunt Mary, I cannot believe this! Abraham Lincoln wrote this book! That I am holding it in my hand is unbelievable!" With an unassuming tone accompanied by a huge grin, she adds, "Almost as unbelievable as I am sitting here with you today in the year 1860!" She hands the book back to Aunt Mary.

"Yes, Steph, it is remarkable. There is no way you could have known about Abraham Lincoln. At least I seriously doubt you could have known, that is if you were born during this era. True, Lincoln's collected works and his stand on the slavery resulted in the soaring of his popularity. But that is up North.

"His works would never be read here in the South, at least not by common folk Southerners. Maybe politicians but never common folk. White folk here despise anyone who opposes slavery. Bigotry begets blindness as far as the truth is concerned."

Steph mulls over what Aunt Mary has said.

"Bigotry begets blindness as far as the truth is concerned."

Goodness, the uncanny use of metaphors and interesting sayings runs in Aunt Mary's family.

She asks, "So, how did you come about the book and pamphlets, Aunt Mary? I mean, you are the wife of a white man who owns a plantation. Who has slaves."

"A friend of mine who lives in Boston sent them to me. She and I went to college together, Harvard University. It is in Cambridge, Massachusetts. Perhaps you have heard of it in your time and place in the future?"

Steph chuckles as she says, "Heard of it? Goodness, Aunt Mary, everyone in my time has heard of Harvard University. Harvard supposedly is America's oldest college. Some of our greatest presidents attended Harvard!"

Aunt Mary says, "Yes, I know. So, Steph, what are your plans? Your purpose. Do you know?"

Steph thinks to herself, everyone seems to know that I have a purpose.

My raison d'être.

"Well, I am not exactly certain. However, I think it has something to do with Hannah and Patsy and maybe even their brother Joseph."

Could it be? Are Hannah, Patsy, and Joseph my purpose, *my raison d'être?* Are they truly the reason Jordyn has sent Spirit and me back in time - exactly one year to the day before the commencement of the Civil War? A Civil War that began right here in South Carolina? It must be.

Aunt Mary replaces her pamphlets and Lincoln's book into the pouch. She carefully re-ties the leather drawstring and sets the pouch on the floor beneath her chair.

"Yes, Steph, I do believe that is the reason you are here. But you do not have much time, my dear. The dreaded auction is tomorrow. The girls do not even know what is supposed to happen. My husband decided to join the auction after you intervened in this morning's whipping." She suddenly stands. As an automatic sign of respect for her elder, Steph stands as well.

"I must return these to my secret hiding place. If my husband were to find them, I would hate to think what he will do. I would not be surprised if he told me to leave the plantation. Then he would probably divorce me. I do not enjoy my marriage. I think you can see that. I was forced into this marriage. However, I will not bore you with the details. After all, it is what it is."

She moves to the other side of the table. She opens her arms out wide, and then she embraces Steph. After everything Steph has been through, in Germany and now in the slavery era, Aunt Mary's warm hug feels mightily good.

Aunt Mary whispers, "I do not want to know anything more about you. I respect your privacy." As she moves away from Steph, she looks her squarely in the eyes.

"But I need to know one thing if you can tell me."

Steph nods her head.

"Anything, Aunt Mary, anything. That is if I can tell you."

From off in the distance, Steph can hear the distinct whinny of her beloved Spirit. She smiles. She knows he will tell her what she needs to say soon after Aunt Mary asks her question. How he knows what to say puzzles her, particularly since Jordyn has been silent this entire time. At this point, however, she does not care.

As long as he knows what I am supposed to say, I am good with it.

Aunt Mary moves away from Steph. She gently grips Steph's shoulders as she looks her squarely in the eye.

"Josephine, my niece. Is she okay? Is she safe? Will I see her soon?"

Spirit whinnies, and then his thoughts begin to enter Steph's mind. She closes her eyes.

"Just one second if you please, Aunt Mary. Spirit is speaking to me in my mind."

Spirit's thoughts say, "She is delayed. Their ship had to dock in Norfolk due to repairs of the main topsail. Aunt Mary's Great Uncle George is accompanying her. The two of them will arrive tomorrow evening by coach."

Steph can hear Spirit's neigh from across the pasture once more. She automatically cringes. She knows something sarcastic is coming.

"And tell her, Abraham, the elusive horse, is not accompanying them. He does not have what it takes to make the cross-Atlantic trip like me!"

Steph repeats to Aunt Mary what Spirit told her. She purposely leaves out the part about Josephine's horse, Abraham. It would take too much explaining to do otherwise.

Aunt Mary breathes in deeply and exhales with a long *whew!*

"That is a relief. I haven't seen Josephine since she was a young girl. It was when my dear sister Polly visited me up in Cambridge many years ago. And I cannot wait to meet my Great Uncle George, too." Then, with a questioning look, she says, "It is your horse, Spirit, isn't it? I heard his whinnies timed to your responses. He is the one who is guiding you. Am I correct?"

"Yes, Aunt Mary, you are correct. Spirit can speak to me in my mind. He always could. And now, for some strange reason, I think he can communicate with Jordyn even though she is unconscious."

She frowns adding in a troubled tone, "Jordyn is the deaf orphan girl who has entrusted me with this mission, one other passed mission, and probably at least one additional mission if not more in the future. She communicates with Spirit and me telepathically. I have never met her. Hopefully, someday I shall. She is incredible."

With a gentle smile of understanding, Aunt Mary says softly, "I see. It has been a pleasure meeting you, Steph. Something tells me you will succeed in this mission. From my perspective, there is no greater mission in life than helping those in need. You are like an angel from God. I will pray for you tonight and every night after that."

She clutches the black crucifix that is hanging from her neck.

"While I do not dare to change things around here, at least not yet, I trust in my God. I know He is merciful. He will give me courage. Do anything you have to do to save the children." As tears well up in her eyes she adds in a sad tone, "I will miss you. Think of me often after you return to your home in the future. I love Hannah and Patsy. I love their mother, Janette. And I love Joseph, too." She smiles.

"But, most of all I love you, my dear, spirited and brave, pretend niece Steph. I love you more than you will ever know. You have given me purpose and courage, and as it pertains to the scourge of slavery, hope. You have changed my life owing to your love, compassion, spirit, and fearlessness. I thank you."

Steph replies, "Thank you, Aunt Mary. I will miss you very much, and I promise I will think of you often from my world in the future." She reaches up to kiss Aunt Mary on her cheek. "I love you, too."

Aunt Mary embraces Steph yet again. She whispers into her ear. Her tone is somber.

"Your best chance for success is to wait until after dark, say around nine o'clock. Waiting until it is later is even better. The men gather in the veranda for their nightly round of merriment and drinking. Since tomorrow is the Sabbath, they will remain on the veranda until well past midnight. I will inform Janette to have Joseph and the girls ready to travel. Good luck and Godspeed."

"Thank you, Aunt Mary. I will need all the luck I can get. I will try my best to succeed. Maybe I cannot change the course of history, but at least I can change one of its many tales."

After all, it is my purpose.

My raison d'être.

Aunt Mary turns to leave. Just as she is about to exit the veranda, she abruptly turns around. She is shaking her head as she stares at Steph straight-on. She begins to giggle.

"Oh, there is one other thing, Steph. Something you need to know."

"Yes, ma'am?"

Aunt Mary's face is beaming with amusement.

"Just so you know, my make-believe, impersonating niece, Steph. With her gorgeous golden-brown locks and light brown skin tone." She giggles once more.

"Josephine is a redhead just like her Aunt Mary.

"Blue eyes.

"Fair skin.

"And lots of freckles."

CHAPTER SIX

FREEDOM DEFIES BONDAGE

"Four Score and seven years ago our fathers brought forth
on this continent, a new nation, conceived in Liberty, and
dedicated to the proposition that all men are created equal."
- Abraham Lincoln, November 19, 1863

Part I: He has no Concept of Dignity!

"I do not care what you say. There is no way I can accompany you if we are to save three African Americans from the auction block! The girls are small in stature, and they are not very heavy since they haven't eaten well all these years. Therefore, the two of them and Joseph can safely ride on your back. But add a fourth to your company - that would be me - and either Joseph or I will have to walk. That will slow the process far too much. The element of quickness as we escape, which is essential if we are to succeed, will be lost.

"Besides, their safety, their quest for freedom is more important than my welfare. I may find myself in danger once the others figure out who let the threesome escape, but I will remain free. Surely, I will have some explaining to do once the two girls and Joseph are gone. But, whatever happens to me is nothing in comparison to what will happen to them at the auction. They will end up in three separate homes of intolerable servitude.

"The three of them have lived their entire lives in bondage. I am free, and I will remain free no matter what happens. Do you understand what I am saying? So, Spirit, I have made my decision, and it is final. I cannot accompany you. Nor will I."

Spirit replies to Steph in her mind. "But Steph, I cannot leave you here. When the real Josephine shows up tomorrow evening, you will have some serious explaining to do. The Man will be especially unforgiving." He whinnies softly adding, "And you will be in a world of hurt since the Man will be missing three slaves, three young, healthy slaves. I am afraid he may physically hurt you."

Steph plucks another long stalk from the tall grass. She sneers as she sticks the sticky end of the stalk into her mouth. She shakes her head. Her tone is defiant when she answers Spirit.

"Oh, he will get over it. And I seriously doubt he will hurt me physically. If he tries to hurt me, I will fight him. You know that. He is fat and puny. If nothing else I will outrun him." She silently ponders what she said has said.

If I run very fast and the Man chases me, he will probably keel over with a heart attack. If he does keel over, I simply will say *good riddance to bad rubbish!* Then again, if he were to shoot me, I would be in a world of hurt, physically and metaphorically speaking. I will not even think about the possibility that he would shoot me!

Naturally, Spirit has read her mind.

"Steph, you cannot outrun a bullet. Please do not make light of it. What is more, I doubt, as you say, 'he will get over it.' You are stealing his property from him. The Man may have appeared agreeable before he dined with you and Aunt Mary. But his nastiness showed once more when you touched on slavery by mentioning Emerson's name.'"

Steph shakes her finger at Spirit. She says in a sarcastic tone, "I am not stealing anything. Humans do not *steal* humans. Period. It is unnatural. I would like to think that what I am going to do is natural. Allowing the children to be how God intended them to be when they were born. To be free.

"As far as Emerson is concerned, do not blame that on me. You were the one who told me to reference his name. Well, maybe not exactly. But you did plant the idea into my brain. The fault lies with you - one hundred percent of it."

Spirit's thoughts say in reply, "I guess I have to take credit for that. Just the same, mentioning Emerson's name brought out the Man's wicked bias for the umpteenth time. I was not on the veranda, but I could sense his loathsomeness, his undeniable hate, particularly his hatred of you and everything for which you stand. So what will you do? Where will you go? And when will we see each other again?"

Steph replies with a deep sigh, "I guess I will have to remain here until Jordyn wakes up and sends me home. As far as when we will see each other again, I have no clue. It is all up to Jordyn and fate."

Spirit's thoughts say, "What if Jordyn does not wake up? She may be dead for all we know. You could be stranded here forever."

"Yeah, I know," Steph replies. "I will have to take my chances. Aunt Mary likes me, so she will not allow anything bad to happen to me. Surely, the Man will get angry with me since I set his *property* free."

Steph purposely said the word *property* in a protracted, disgusted tenor.

"Nonetheless, he will figure out a way to recover his lost income. I am certain of it. He probably will auction off a couple of Hannah, Patsy, and Joseph's relatives if there are any left behind." She pauses adding with a grimace, "I hope he does not auction off Janette. That would be horrible! It would break Aunt Mary's heart. The two of them love and respect each other very much. I can tell."

"Be reasonable," Spirit thoughts say. "The Man does not care about recouping his income. He is selling his property, as you put it, because, in his evil manner, he wants retribution. By hurting others, he is free from blame for Joseph not receiving his allotted lashes. It is all about ego."

Steph nods her head. She replies out loud in a whisper, "You are the second one to have said that to me."

"Said what?"

"That the Man wants vengeance, retribution for my interfering in Joseph's whipping."

"Yes, he wants retribution, Steph. By force of habit, he is carrying on the rituals of the uncaring, cruel white slave owner. The Man thinks by auctioning off Joseph, Hannah, and Patsy - by hurting the other slaves who remain behind - he will restore his dignity."

Spirit's thoughts cease for a few moments, and then they convey, "The slave owner's custom reminds me of the old proverb, 'out of sight out of mind.'"

Steph replies angrily, "His dignity? What dignity? He has no dignity, no self-respect, at least in my opinion. History will prove that. The Man is a slave owner and a disgustingly cruel one at that. And out of sight out of mind as you say. Hah! Nothing that happens will be out of sight and out of mind. Especially as it concerns Janette and her relatives.

"And what about the other African Americans with small children? Nothing that has ever happened to them before today, right now, and in the future will be out of their minds. What will be in their minds, every waking moment of their sorrowful lives, every single day, is the fact that evil became even eviler if that is possible. And in the back of their minds, haunting them every day, there will be the fear that they too will lose their loved ones to the auction block. No, Spirit. I fear that the Man's evilness we are experiencing today will only get worse as time goes by."

Spirit's thoughts say, "Yes, you are correct. Sending slaves to the auction block will serve to remind other slaves to stay in line. It is all about power and control. If a child rebels they punish the child by sending one or more of his siblings to the auction block. Or, maybe, they send the child's mother or father, perhaps a very close relative or friend, to the auction block. Nonetheless, slave owners attempt to keep one or more relatives or close friends unmolested. That way they can continue their control over the rebellious child and others."

"It is disgusting!" Steph cries. "As Aunt Mary said, it is an abomination." As she shakes her head she adds in an offended tone, "It is beyond my imagination how a kind and caring woman like Aunt Mary could marry a slave owner. In contrast, compared to her, her husband has no concept of dignity!

"Aunt Mary is very sweet. I love her with all my heart like she is my real aunt. I know for a fact she is hurting. Her heart is breaking. I can tell by her sorrowful words, her sincere tone of voice, her gentle touch. She is a good woman. Well-schooled, intellectual, caring. I truly feel sorry for her, and I wish that she could somehow rid herself of the evil she sees every day. I fear that her life as the wife of a slave owner will be forever bursting with torment and sadness."

*****

Part II: Samuel and the Others

The nighttime air is hot and muggy. A storm is threatening from the west. In between the frequent, far-off rumblings of thunder, raucous sounds of drinking and merriment creep from the other side of the mansion.

Whew! Thank goodness the storm is approaching from the west. Otherwise, the men would be on the veranda that faces the stable. And the more the men party, the happier I am.

Steph listens attentively for any worrying sign that the men are getting ready to wind-up their nightly fun. The many rowdy guffaws and bawdy catcalls coming from the veranda remind her of a pack of snarling wolves surrounding their trapped prey. All the same, to Steph's ears, the ugly noises seem like a blessing in disguise.

Talk about idiots. Their gross language is bold enough to twist my earlobes! Especially the Man's vulgar language. His jokes are the crudest and loudest of all. I guess they must be, so he can prove to everyone he is in charge of this awful organization of human suffering.

Steph and Spirit are hiding in the shadows on the outside of the stable. An elderly slave named Samuel is with them. Samuel had said he would provide blankets and provisions for Joseph and his sisters. Steph told him, on more than one occasion, she was worried that he would be in trouble for assisting her. He had replied that he would not be in trouble.

"No, ma'am. Since they's be using yer mount, no horse be missing to rile Mas'rs temper. And, I's dare say, neither blankets nor provisions be missed by nary anyone either." He had laughed scornfully adding, "The blankets t'nothing more than rags. No white man gonna know they's be missing. But they's be good 'nuff to keep a small child's warm at night, to scare away's the fear."

Despite Samuel's reassuring words, Steph worried about his fate, and she told him as much. She did not want the Man to punish him. Samuel replied he did not care if he received punishment.

"I's be old, Miss Josephine. I's see too much. I's too have longed my's entire life to escape dis suffern'g. Any punishment I's be due is fine with me. If Joseph, Hannah, and Patsy be free, I's be free from worries." He had pointed above his heart. "No ma'am, I's fear no punishment da devil may inflict on my's body. No devilish deed can hurts my's soul, nor can it take away my's pride. Be I's alive or dead."

With a smile, he had said, "Nor do I's see punishment in any form a'coming to me's anyways. Mas'r not gonna knows dat it be I's who helped." He grinned, and then he said somberly, "I's know da sting of the lash. I's know da tormenting pain of my's heart when my's ankles be blood'd in da white man's irons, my's wrists knotted till they's sleep'n. A noose 'round my's neck. Nothing can hurt me's now, now dat's the children's they's be free."

Steph had thanked Samuel, and then she embraced him. She kissed his cheek softly.

"May God bless you for your kindness, Samuel. It is wonderful for you to assist Hannah, Patsy, and Joseph in this manner. I would not know how to begin if it weren't for your help."

"We be da ones who be blessed, my's dear child. God sent an angel of H'ven to save three of His beloved chil'ren from da clutches of bondage. The Lord's love and guidance will d'liver them's to safety. Yes, ma'am, I's be certain they's safely make da journey. They's feel da beauty of freedom. Then they's freely tell their stories to the world."

He kissed Steph on the forehead and disappeared into the night.

Steph never saw Samuel again. Nor did anyone else except for Boss and Jess. As fate would have it, Samuel was lynched by the two white overseers the next afternoon. Samuel's murder occurred beneath the very tree Steph had found herself this morning.

What Steph did not know at the time, Samuel was Janette's husband. He was the devoted father of Hannah, Patsy, and Joseph. Like all fathers who love their children, then and now, he was willing to sacrifice his life for them. Samuel's lynching was but one more shameless, evil act of man's dark brutality during America's ugly slave era. The murder of a fellow human being whose only crime was love for his children. To allow them to be free.

Steph is very sleepy. She sits down in the dirt and rests her head against the wall of the stable. The day has been tiring and very emotional. She is just about to close her eyes when Spirit's thoughts enter her mind.

"The Man is telling an offensive story. You probably do not want to know this but…"

"Then do not tell me if you please," Steph curtly says out loud as she yawns. "If, as you say, I do not want to know it, then I do not want to hear it. Please keep your thoughts to yourself. Thank you."

Spirit whinnies softly.

Steph frowns in response to Spirit's whinny. She knows he is not going to take no for an answer. She appreciates that he is just as stubborn as she is. She reckons that is why they get along very well.

"Oh, go ahead, Spirit. You are going to tell me whether I want to know or not. There is no way I can selectively block your thoughts. Lord knows I have tried on many occasions." She laughs adding, "Maybe someday I will succeed. I can only hope and pray."

"Sorry, Steph, but this is what the Man is saying right now."

A sudden chorus of wild laughter and boisterous, manly guffaws echoes from the veranda disgustingly.

Steph winces in response to the sickening noises. She says in a halting voice, "He's talking about me. Am I correct?"

"Yes, he is. He is telling the other white men that he intends to drag you to tomorrow's auction. He wants to see the look on your face as the other slave owners bid for Joseph. Then, after he auctions Joseph, and he says it should be a quick auction since Joseph is strong and young, he will give you another shocking surprise."

"Well, doesn't that just beat all," Steph says in an indifferent tone.

She yawns. Goodness, I am exhausted. How long has it been since I had some good, quality sleep?

She resumes conveying her thoughts to Spirit.

"Thank you for the head's up. I will make certain that I am impossible to find. But then again, I am curious. What is my other shocking surprise supposed to be?"

"The Man plans to announce during the auction, without any forewarning to the partakers, that Hannah and Patsy are also up for auction. He will force the two girls to attend Joseph's auction with Janette. The Man says he cannot wait to see the anguished look on your face when the girls and Janette start bawling. He wants revenge for you interfering during Joseph's lashing. He also wants revenge for the kindly way you treated the girls on the veranda."

Spirit whinnies. Steph patiently waits for his rejoinder.

"Also, so that you know. The Man did not help the girls clean up the broken glass and lemonade after you dashed to your room to read Polly's letters. In fact, he slapped both girls across the face when they returned to the veranda. Then he grabbed the extra dozen cookies Hannah had on a plate, the cookies intended for her friends. He threw them onto the floor and stomped them to crumbs with his boots. Then he scolded the girls and departed the veranda. His pretend kindness to you was nothing more than a scam. He is a truly evil person."

Steph says in a sickened tone, "That is horrible to know - that he slapped the girls for no reason and trashed their cookies. He is detestable! Utter wickedness! So tell me. How does he intend to ensure that I will go along with him to the auction? It is not like he can force me. And I will not go voluntarily. You can count on that."

Spirit replies, "He says he will lock you in your room later tonight. He will post a guard outside your door and below your window. Then, if he must, he will bind your wrists together and, again, if he must, drag you to the auction even if you are kicking and screaming."

"Oh, he better not attempt to bind me, Steph says. "As far as kicking and screaming are concerned, he can bet his bottom dollar I will do just that. I will crush one if not both of his kneecaps or worse!" With a grin, she adds, "I am getting pretty good with that maneuver. Tell me more."

Spirit's thoughts say, "Yes, you are tough. You have proven that on more than one occasion. In spite of your toughness, you will be in mortal danger if the Man has a rifle. He will not hesitate to hurt you if Aunt Mary is not nearby." He pauses briefly, and then his thoughts say, "That is about it. Another man is telling a story. It is very uncouth."

Steph laughs.

"Well, keep that one to yourself if you please. Unless, of course, it is about a horse that cannot mind its manners. That is one story I would like for you to repeat!"

"They are here," Spirit's thoughts say.

Steph's weary mental state snaps wide-awake. She stands up and brushes the dirt from her dress.

"Who is here? The Man? Others?"

"No, Steph. It is Joseph and the girls."

Hannah and Patsy run up to Steph. Patsy gives her a strong hug around the waist. Hannah hugs her around the shoulders. Joseph is standing behind them.

Steph says, "Oh, Hannah and Patsy! It is very good to see you! And these are much better circumstances, too." She looks at Joseph adding, "You too, Joseph!"

"I cannot b'lieve t'all is happening," Patsy whispers. "I's very scared, Miss Josephine. Mas'r will be very mad when he finds out we be miss'n."

Steph says, "My real name is Steph. Please call me Steph. I come from a different place. From a different time. Many years from now in the future. And do not worry about him. He will never find you. I promise."

Hannah looks at her questionably. When she speaks, it is obvious to Steph that she, like her mother Janette, has had some schooling. Her English is nearly perfect.

"Ma'am, I thought you were the mistress' niece, Josephine. But you's said you's are Steph. Either way, you's are a wonderful child. A gift from heaven." She strokes Spirit on his mane. "You's horse is also a gift from heaven. I do not have enough words to thank you's for you's kindness and for risking you's life for my little sister Patsy, Joseph, and me."

"True, Hannah, I am not Josephine. Your mistress and I had a very long conversation. She knows who I am. And she knows that her real niece, Josephine, is safe and sound." She adds with a warm smile, "In fact, Josephine will arrive here tomorrow. And I thank you for your kind words, and you are most welcome."

Patsy cries, "Well, makes no bother to me who's you's be. I love you's just the same." She gives Steph another hug.

"I love you too," Steph replies. With her arms held out wide, she gestures for Joseph to move closer, so he can join them in a four-person hug.

"In fact, I love the three of you like you were my brother and sisters. And I am very sorry you had to experience such pain, Joseph. No person should whip another."

Joseph replies in a whisper, "Tis okay, Miss Steph. I's get my revenge for the deceitful lies and the uncalled-for lashing someday." He searches Steph's eyes. "When my sisters and I's be free I's will tell all about you's bravery and you's compassion. Thank you."

"You are welcome, Joseph. Take loving care of your sisters. And trust everything that Spirit does, even if you doubt his decisions. He is a special, magical horse. He will ensure you arrive at your destination safely.

Spirit whinnies.

"You bet I will. There is no man alive that can out trick me!"

Steph kisses Joseph on his cheek.

"Remember what I said. Trust Spirit. He will not fail you. I promise." Then she reaches down and kisses Patsy on her forehead. Lastly, she kisses Hannah on her cheek.

Hannah, tears streaming down her face, says, "Steph, thank you's. God bless you's always. I will never forget you's."

Steph declares, "Okay, mount up. I want Joseph in front. Patsy, you get behind Joseph. Hannah will ride behind you."

After the threesome has mounted on Spirit, she hands the provisions to Hannah.

"Keep these safe. Spirit will guide you to drinkable water. Something tells me he will also find refuge for you if necessary. Whatever he does, it is important for you to trust him." She hands Patsy a cloth sack. "This contains enough food for two days. If you have to, stretch it to three or four."

She pats Patsy on her thigh.

"Once again, Spirit will guide you to places where friendly people will give you food and shelter. Take it readily. But, whatever you do, stay close to Spirit and your brother and sister. Never leave sight of them. Do you understand?" Patsy nods her head.

"Well, I guess this is goodbye, Steph," Spirit says. He whinnies softly adding, "See if you can stay out of trouble for one more night. Okay? And please be careful. Do not go trying to be the heroine like before. I do not want to hear later that you made more trouble for everyone around here."

Steph hugs Spirit on his mane. Tears are now flowing down her cheeks freely. She kisses Spirit on his forehead.

"I love you, Spirit. Do not think of this as a goodbye. We will be reunited soon. I am certain of it." With a chuckle, she says in a sarcastic tone, "Besides, who will harass me with his lousy jokes if you and I do not get together again?"

Spirit throws back his head and whinnies softly.

Steph says, "Okay, Joseph. Take loving care of the girls. Keep them safe. Stay off the main roads if possible and only travel at night. Spirit will know beforehand if trouble comes your way." She pats Spirit on his mane. "He has this uncanny ability to sense danger."

She blows a kiss to Hannah and Patsy.

"Listen to your brother. Do what he says. And always know, and I promise you this. Someday I will tell your story. And I hope that someday you will also tell your story as well. For the world and future generations must know. What happened here tonight is but one small chapter of humanity's freedom over bondage."

Patsy whispers something to Joseph. Joseph smiles, and then he nods his head. She reaches with her hand to the back of her neck. She unties a bit of twine that is supporting a necklace. Steph had not noticed the necklace before now since Patsy had it tucked beneath the collar of her simple gown. Patsy gathers the necklace in her hand. She kisses it, and then she hands it to Steph.

"This be my good luck charm. I's like you's to have it. It is not too much, just glass beads and cowrie shells. I's trust it brings you's good luck as well." She bends to kiss Steph's cheek. "Thank you's, Miss Steph. May our God bless you's and keep you's safe from harm."

With tears welling in her eyes, Steph replies, "Thank you, Patsy. I will cherish this precious gift for the rest of my life."

She fastens the necklace around her neck. Then she hugs Spirit on his mane one last time. As she smacks him on his backside, she whispers, "Now off with you, Spirit. Godspeed. I will see you when we get home."

Steph watches them as they disappear into the night. Her heart is heavy. She reenters the stable. Samuel had cautioned her to remain inside the stable for a few moments after Spirit and the others had departed.

He had said, "In case someone no'tices as your horse gallops off. You's not want to be seen anywhere near the stable when that happens. If someone comes you's way, you's skedaddle in the opp'site direction. Then circle and enter the back of the house. Be careful."

Steph stretches her arms as she yawns. She sits down on a bale of hay. As she tucks her legs beneath her, she leans her head against the wall.

Ah, this feels very nice and comfy. I will relax here for a few moments and then sneak back into my room before the men depart the veranda from their nightly shindig.

She closes her eyes, and then she is sound asleep in less than a minute.

*****

Part III: Overdue Punishment

Slap!

A vision of Roger Clyde slapping Jordyn suddenly enters Steph's senses.

Her mind reasons. This slap is not that bad. It is sort of gentle, not too painful. It feels like someone is trying to wake me.

Her eyes suddenly snap wide open. The mid-morning sun pouring into the stable from the entranceway is blinding her with its brilliance. She tries to shield her eyes with her right hand, but she cannot. She begins to scream.

"What in the world! My hands are tied!" She shakes her head and narrows her eyes. When the figure standing before her comes into focus, she yells, "Oh, I should have figured it would be you! You are a detestable, poor excuse for a human being. How dare you bind my hands! How dare you slap me!"

"Serves you right, Missy. And if it were not that you are a white girl, I would tie you to the rafters." He points over Steph's head.

"String you up from the highest one myself! By your scrawny English neck."

He leans in close. Steph suddenly feels sick to her stomach as she gets a whiff of his foul-smelling breath. It reeks of cheap whiskey and stale cigars.

"How dare you free my slaves. But do not concern yourself with them, Missy. My men will catch up to them soon enough. And when they do, I will whip all three of those children myself. And you will watch. And so that you know, I will thoroughly enjoy a delicious horsemeat steak for dinner." He guffaws, adding in a mocking tone, "Compliments of your dead horse. In fact, I will spoon-feed some of the horsemeat to you. Then the two of us can dine together like a loving uncle and his wife's disobedient niece. How would you like that, eh? Now get to your feet, Missy!"

He grabs the ropes binding Steph's wrists. As he attempts to pull Steph to her feet, she kicks out with her right foot viciously. Being bound at the wrists and in the sitting position causes her to miss. She was aiming for his groin.

She screams, "I swear to you. I will haunt you every day while you are awake and every night in your dreams. How dare you bind me, slap me! You are more wicked than I thought. You are the devil himself! Besides, you do not scare me. You may have me at a disadvantage right now. But I swear to you. I have but one life to give, and it isn't mine. It's yours!"

She looks the Man squarely in the eye. She begins to laugh wildly. When she addresses him again, remarkably, her tone is calm. But it is teeming with intense contempt.

"As far as the three African Americans and my horse Spirit are concerned, my horse has more intelligence and gumption than all of your men combined. You will never catch them, nor will you find them. Spirit will know your men's every move before they can even decide to make them." She smiles adding sarcastically, "And your former slaves, my fellow Americans, will be free!"

The Man attempts once more to grab the ropes binding her. She kicks out with her foot a second time. This time she connects with his midsection. He doubles over in pain. Nonetheless, much to Steph's dismay, he quickly recovers. Just as she is about to stand and kick at him again, the Man reaches to his right. He grabs a rifle off a bale of hay and places the end of the barrel against Steph's thigh. Steph winches in pain as he gradually increases the pressure on her muscle.

He snarls, "Make one more move, try one more kick, say one more word, and I will make you wish you were never born. I cannot kill you, but I can always say I accidentally shot you in the thigh. Everyone will believe me when I say it was an accident."

Suddenly, a voice cries out, "You will do nothing of the kind! You will not hurt that child!"

In response to the shout, the Man hurriedly whirls around in place. Steph jumps to her feet. She kicks out hard at the back of the Man's knee with her right foot. She misses and falls onto the floor. She lands on her left side. In the blink of an eye, she lashes out with her right foot and trips the Man. He falls hard in a heap onto his right side. Steph can hear the wind sail out of his lungs as he lands with a muffled, *harrumph!* The rifle slips from his hand and careens across the straw-covered floor. Aunt Mary picks up the rifle.

The Man is lying on the floor perpendicular to Steph, his face toward hers. Before he can recover his senses, she quickly positions the ankle of her left foot beneath the right side of his neck. Then she moves her right foot, so it is on the other side of his neck. She applies just enough pressure to get his attention. She does not want to incapacitate him, although she knows that she could. Her legs are that powerful.

She shouts in earnest, "How does it feel to be restrained? I do believe you are feeling the shameful horror of subjection like those who you enslave! Make one move, try one blow, say one word, and I will make you wish you were never born! Do I make myself clear? Grunt your response two times. After all, you are as lowly as a pig."

The Man does not reply. He desperately clutches at his neck with both of his hands. His face is turning beet red, and his eyes are bulging with the enormous pressure Steph is applying with her strong muscular legs.

"I want you to respond to me. Answer me yes. Or answer me no. I honestly do not care, but you must make a choice. Do I make myself clear? Do you surrender? If you do not, I will increase the pressure on your neck until you are unconscious!"

The Man still does not reply. All he does is stare as he frantically tries to free himself.

Steph knows that the hatred in his eyes reflect what he is thinking. She knows he would kill her if he could. She stares back in return as she applies a bit more pressure to his neck. In response to the increased pressure, he begins to pound the calf muscle of her right leg with his fist.

Steph yells, "I must tell you. You do not have enough strength to hurt my legs with your puny fist. Years of roller skating, many months of rugby, and the fact that right now I do not care, make me immune to pain."

She applies a bit more pressure with her legs. The Man begins to beat the floor with his fist. Clouds of dirt mixed with straw fly in the air. He is starting to panic, and Steph instinctively knows what is happening to him. He can hardly breathe. And he is about to concede.

"Answer me by saying either yes or no. Do you surrender? Yes or no?"

The Man manages to whisper in a harsh voice, "Yes. Yes, I surrender. Let go of me!"

Steph releases the Man from her legs' crippling vice grip. She kicks at his torso for good measure. He rolls over onto his side.

She scrambles to her feet. It is then that she notices Aunt Mary is pointing the rifle at the Man. Surprisingly, she seems calm.

Steph shouts to the Man, "Get up. And do it slowly." Then she looks at Aunt Mary straight on.

"Please, Aunt Mary, remain calm. I got this. Please lower your rifle. And whatever you do, do not shoot. It will only make things worse."

The Man clutches at his throat with both of his hands for a few moments. Then he manages to roll over onto his stomach. Soon he is perched on his hands and knees. After a few seconds, he stands. He continues to massage his throat. His coal-black eyes bespeak hatred as he stares at Steph.

Steph says in a quiet voice, "Untie these ropes." She stretches out her hands.

"Do it slowly, and no funny moves or I will kick you someplace on your body you will forever wish I hadn't."

As the Man unties the ropes binding Steph's wrists, he turns his head to look at his wife. The hatred in his eyes has intensified.

"And what in the name of god do you think you are doing? Lower that rifle, woman! Do you think for one moment you are going to shoot me?" He motions with his head to Steph. "This wench, this so-called niece of yours just let three of my slaves go free. She is evil I tell you and worse than a thief!"

Aunt Mary says in a soft tone, "Yes, Judas, I know she let Joseph, Hannah, and Patsy go free. I told her when to do it. She also had my permission." She adds with a nasty grin, "As far as my lowering your rifle, I am sorry, Judas. I will not."

She looks at Steph. The expression on her face is one of courageous resolve.

"Not as long as Steph is in danger. Now back away from her! And do it slowly, Judas or I swear to God. I will shoot you."

Judas slowly backs away from Steph. He throws the ropes onto the floor that were binding her wrists. He gawks at his wife. Then he places his hands on his hips. He begins to laugh hysterically. After a few moments, his feverish laughter dies out. A wicked-looking smirk follows. He points his finger at his wife.

"Now you are defying me?" he says slowly. "For god's sake, I am your husband, Mary Grace. I will not. I repeat - I will not allow this young lady's thievery, her complicit aid to free three of my slaves to go unpunished." He takes a few steps toward his wife.

"Besides, if you even so much as graze me with a bullet, you can kiss your comfortable life goodbye. I will divorce you before you can say I am sorry."

Then, with an evil eye as he points to Steph, he says in a mocking tone, "This girl's name is Steph, eh? She is not your niece, Josephine after all. Figures. I knew she was an imposter as soon as she started calling my slaves African Americans. Yes, my negroes came from Africa.

But my negroes, my slaves as Americans? Never! Slaves will never be Americans and live as equals with white men as long as I am alive."

He spits on the floor.

"Not only is this girl a charlatan, but she is also a witch. Reading minds and knowing things and predicting the future. A civil war, Abraham Lincoln, and other rubbish. It ain't natural. She's an occultist!" He turns his head toward Steph as he spits on the floor yet again. His spittle lands between her feet.

"Do not tempt me, Judas," Aunt Mary scolds. "Let the girl go, and then you and I can talk."

Judas laughs once more. He glances at Steph with a look of contempt in his eyes. His contemptuous look could easily slay ten men.

"Let her go? You must be kidding, Mary."

He stares at the ground as he slowly shakes his head. Steph reasons he is considering, given that his wife is pointing the rifle at him, he should try to negotiate and stall for time. After all, his wife is the one holding the rifle. She is in control. At least for now.

He points his finger at Steph.

"Okay, I will tell you what, Mary Grace. I want her gone. Before nightfall on this godforsaken day. But before I allow her to go, I want her beaten, whipped, lashed. I do not care how or where or when, but I want her physically punished. What she did deserves punishment. She stole from me!"

His tone suddenly changes as he takes another tentative step toward his wife. He smiles as he reaches out his hand to her.

"Now, my dear, sweet Mary Grace, please hand me that rifle before you do something you will regret for the rest of your miserable life."

In response, Missus Gray shakes her head. She raises the rifle to her shoulder blade, and then she repositions her finger on the trigger. Judas glares at her. He abruptly stops in his tracks.

Steph suddenly feels lightheaded as she distinguishes a soothing, familiar voice in her mind. She firmly presses her fingertips against her temples. Then she closes her eyes tightly. A grin appears on her face. Her thoughts begin to race.

"Jordyn! You are back! You are alive! Oh, thank you, God. Thank you!"

"Yes, my darling, Steph, I am here. Just as you did when saving Adalard's life, you gave this mission everything you had. You used your cunning, intelligence, strength, and your unselfish love and compassion to help those in need. Once more, thanks to your remarkable fearless spirit, which radiates from within your loving heart, good has triumphed over evil."

Steph is standing six feet from both Judas and Aunt Mary. They are in a semi-circle. Judas is to her left, and Aunt Mary is to her right. Judas has his arms folded over his chest as he stares straight ahead at his wife. Aunt Mary is pointing the rifle at him. The couple's unblinking eyes are locked. The rigid expressions on their faces are a mirrored image of antipathy and obstinacy.

The fact that Steph is deeply absorbed with her thoughts has not gone unnoticed by Judas. He has been watching her from the corner of his eye for the past few moments, waiting for the right time to pounce. With a devilish grin of absolute hatred and his arms outstretched before him, he abruptly turns to his right and lunges at her. He intends to choke her until she surrenders or, and he could care less if it comes to pass until she expires.

Steph, with a huge grin on her face and her eyes tightly closed, does not know Judas is lunging at her, that he is reaching out at her with his bare hands. But she is mindful of one thing. She is mindful of the thunderous sound of a rifle's gunshot. A gunshot echoing within a place that has borne witness to humankind's sinfulness far too often.

Before she can even open her eyes, she is gone.

CHAPTER SEVEN

THE GOOD 'OLE USA

"You are, as they say in these times, in the groove, hip, outta sight!"
Jordyn - May 10, 1964

Part I: Amazing Sights and Sounds

Steph is sitting on a bus stop bench off to the side of the sidewalk along a busy, two-lane avenue. The warm springtime breeze is gently caressing her hair. People walking by on the sidewalk, as well as a few in their cars that are stopping for a red light, take a quick look at her with interest. Some, mostly elderly women, seem to turn their noses up at her as they pass. Others, in fact, the majority, smile approvingly and move along quietly.

Steph does not know that people are looking at her. That is because she is sound asleep as she sits up with her legs folded beneath her. That, in and of itself, is not an uncommon thing, and it is not the object of the passerby's attention. Nor is her naturally pleasing good looks.

What is getting passersby's attention is the plaid miniskirt she is wearing. Because she has her legs folded beneath her, more of her thigh is showing that is proper in public. This despite the relative open-mindedness and liberalism of this day and age.

Jordyn's thoughts abruptly rouse Steph from her sleep.

"Steph! Wake up. It is time for you to get started."

Steph nods her head in response, but she does not open her eyes. She replies in her mind, "Geez, Jordyn, you know I am very tired. I haven't had but a few hours' sleep in, what is it? Going on two days now? Quite frankly, I completely have forgotten how many days it has been. Besides, I'm very worn out from fighting those soldiers and dealing with Judas! I need more sleep. Please leave me be so that I can get some more shut-eye."

"There is not enough time. It is time for you to go to work. Wake up now! And sit up straight. People are staring at you! You are showing too much thigh!"

Steph opens her eyes with a start. She looks down at her exposed thigh and abruptly sits upright. She squirms in place as she frantically tries to pull the miniskirt lower down her legs. It is of no use. The skirt does not get any lower on her legs than it already is.

"Goodness, Jordyn, what in the world am I wearing?"

"It is called a miniskirt. It is the fashion right now. Every girl who is somebody wears one."

"Well, I do not want to be a somebody. This thing is too darned short! It is too revealing. And where are my other clothes, the ones I wore at the plantation?"

"They are beneath the bench," Jordyn replies, "in the suitcase." She pauses, and then she says, "Well, a few of them anyway. I disposed of the hopelessly soiled clothes from when you were lying on the stable floor. Besides, they stunk like horse poo. You have more modern clothes in the suitcase as well. Fashionable stuff."

"Suitcase? How in the world did you manage to give me a suitcase?"

Steph glances beneath the bench.

"The suitcase is ginormous, Jordyn! What in the world is in it? A Sherman tank? Maybe a fighter jet? Geez, Jordyn, this thing is absurdly too darned big!"

Jordyn replies via telepathy, "Please allow me to answer the first question. Do not underestimate me. If I can have you and Spirit travel back and forth across the Atlantic Ocean between two centuries, I think I can manage an ordinary suitcase filled with clothes and whatnots. In response to your saying that the suitcase is huge, I beg to differ. It is a medium-sized suitcase, and it is just the right size for you. Besides, it has a set of wheels, so it is easy to pull behind as you walk. In reply to your second question, open it. Look to see what you have inside. It contains all sorts of goodies!"

Steph says in a disgusted tone, "But it is gross-looking! Whoever heard of a pink suitcase? And those round things plastered all over it - are they what I think they are?"

Jordyn's thoughts reply, "Pink is the rage these days, Steph, especially for world travelers like you. As far as the round things go, you are correct. They are stickers of 45rpm LP records that represent today's musical hits. The stickers are all the rage these days. Girls plaster them on just about anything that does not move - purses, wallets, hats, sneakers, books."

Steph hauls the suitcase onto the bench. She sets it beside her and snaps the hinges open.

"Oh, my goodness, Jordyn! Roller skates!" She removes one of the roller skates from the suitcase to examine it. She says with a grimace, "Oh, come on now. Give me a break! Roller skates with tall, white boots? You have got to be kidding me!" She laughs as she spins one of the four wheels.

"And are these what I think they are? Are these wooden wheels with old-fashioned ball bearings?"

"Yes, they are wooden wheels with old-fashioned ball bearings," Jordyn's thoughts reply. "The wheels you use at home, either for skating outside or inside, have yet to be invented in this day and age. Nor have the fancy bearings been invented. So wooden wheels with ball bearings it must be. As long as they go round and round, you should be satisfied.

"As far as the color of the boots is concerned, women and girls wear nothing but white boots these days. Only guys wear roller skates with black boots. You are very lucky I didn't put colorful, fluffy pink, azure, or purple pompoms on them. I have to admit the thought crossed my mind."

Steph's thoughts say, "If you had, I would have removed them immediately. Let there be no doubt about it!" She rummages inside the suitcase.

"Oh, there is at least three days' worth of clothes. Thank you, Jordyn!" Before Jordyn can reply, she adds, "And check this out. It is a darling change purse. I have never seen anything quite like this!"

She snaps open one side of the two-pocket purse.

"Goodness, Jordyn, there must be a few hundred dollars in here. Twenties, tens, and fives!" She snaps open the other side of the change purse. "And will you look at this? There are two Morgan silver dollars, and there is plenty of smaller change, too!" She removes a nickel from the purse. "I cannot believe this. This coin is a buffalo nickel! And the ten cent pieces are mercury dimes. Talk about being totally cool! Thank you, Jordyn."

"You are welcome," Jordyn replies. "You will need money to buy things near the end of your assignment. You will not have to worry about buying food. Someone will provide food to you as you will find out later. And, so that you know, your food is free where you will be working. Now, you must get going. Look at your wristwatch. It is nearly noon. You are supposed to report to work at noon. It is your first day on the job."

Steph glances at her wristwatch. She had not noticed it before now. It is an outmoded windup Timex with a brown leather band. Her Daddy has a similar watch tucked away in his drawer. Steph always thought the windup wristwatch her Daddy owned was out of this world, totally cool. But very old, an antique.

And here I am - wearing a wind-up wristwatch just like Daddy's!

The time reads 11:32.

Her thoughts convey, "Having a place to work sounds interesting. I hope it is somewhere where I have always wanted to work to earn my money for the future. So, Jordyn, where am I going to work?"

"At a place called Jimmy's. It is a block up the street to your left. Jimmy is your boss. He will have a business outfit for you to wear. A stylish skirt but not as short as the miniskirt you are wearing. Naturally, he will ask you a few questions after you report to work. He also will ask you to give him some paperwork. The necessary paperwork is in a blue folder inside your suitcase. Just hand the folder to him when he asks for the paperwork. Do not, I repeat, do not offer him any additional information unless it is imperative that you do so. Please get a move on, or you will be late for work!"

Steph closes the suitcase and starts up the sidewalk. She is pulling the heavy suitcase behind her. Even though the suitcase is on metal wheels, it is a chore to pull. It also makes one heckuva racket as the wheels pass over the cracks in the sidewalk. To make matters worse, her destination, Jimmy's, is one enormously long city block away. And it's all uphill from here!

Why couldn't Jordyn deposit me closer to Jimmy's? Maybe on the other side of his establishment, so that I could walk downhill? This climb is tough!

To make matters seem even worse, at least in Steph's mind, people stare and smile as they pass her by on the sidewalk. She feels awkward because she does not know why they are looking at her that way.

I bet they think I look ridiculous because of my pink suitcase smattered with stickers of LP records. Or maybe because of my miniskirt and bright purple boots. And what was that? Dang, some guy in a flashy red convertible just whistled at me! How nasty is that? Thank God I am a stranger to them. Otherwise, they would be laughing at this three-ring circus walking up the sidewalk!

Jordyn's thoughts in her mind say, "Laughing? I seriously doubt it, Steph. You are, as they say in these times, 'in the groove, hip, outta sight.'" She pauses briefly. "As it concerns the young man that passed by you in his car a few seconds ago, he said in his mind that you are 'choice!' The word choice means you are very pretty. And the boots you are wearing are also in the groove. They are called go-go boots. Go-go boots are the rage now. To be frank with you, Steph, you are very fashionable.'"

Making certain no one is near her as she whispers, Steph says, "In the groove, hip, and outta sight? What in the world does all that gibberish mean?"

Jordyn replies, "All of the words I said are complimentary. The people you are passing on the sidewalk envy you because you are, what they call nowadays, a contemporary hipster. A hipster is a young, pretty girl who is with the times, in this case, the Sixties.

"And I need to tell you this. Your future boss, Jimmy, is a cool head. That means he is a nice guy. But he can get hacked very easily. The word hacked means he can get very angry." Jordyn's thoughts pause briefly once more, and then what she says via telepathy seems like a scolding. At least that is how Steph interprets it.

"Especially when his workers - that would be you, Steph - are late for work on their first day of the job! So, as I said earlier, get a move on, or you will be late."

As she trudges uphill huffing and puffing (and complaining under her breath), Steph's head is twisting and turning every which way. She is nearly overwhelmed with what she sees. The things that impress her the most are the cars whizzing by on the two-lane avenue.

Glitzy cars of all shapes and sizes with two-toned and even three-toned paint jobs of every imaginable color. All barreling down the avenue like they are in an Indy 500 race. Powerful-looking monsters. Roomy and comfortable. Bizarre, gas-guzzling, four-wheeled oddities (gas is only 31 cents a gallon). With huge V8 engines and loud, backfiring mufflers.

Now and then a car whizzes by that resembles a sleek rocket ship with air intakes protruding from its rear side panels (the first prototype of the Ford Mustang). Others with painted black stripes that race down the middle of their sloped hoods. Sleek, hipster convertibles with steel-rimmed, brightly gleaming, fancy hubcaps and quad headlamps. Just about every car with white-walled tires!

The cars glisten in the late morning sunlight - streams of shining jewels whizzing by as if they do not have a care in the world. Some seem to have wings. That is what Steph calls them. Automobile buffs in the day, and even now, refer to the added, aerodynamic additions on either side of the cars' rear end as fins. Many of the cars are belching grayish smoke from their noisy mufflers, particularly those idling alongside the curb.

Now and then Steph hears the backfire of a car engine. The sudden reports remind her of the gunfire she heard in Germany.

And the horrible sound of a gunshot I heard just before I disappeared from the stable. I wonder if Aunt Mary killed Judas? Hopefully not! I was not there to defend her if she had to stand trial. Goodness, she couldn't even say that she was trying to protect me. I had disappeared. Oh, poor Aunt Mary. I bet she was in serious trouble!

Steph is about to walk by a drugstore. For some reason, she feels compelled to stop if only briefly. She glances up the street toward her destination. The large, unlit neon sign in front of Jimmy's establishment is partly visible. She does not yet know what kind of establishment Jimmy's is. That is because all she can make out from behind the foliage of trees are the last four letters of Jimmy's name - *mmy's*. But one thing she does know, and it causes her to grin. Jimmy's must be a popular place because there are a lot of cool-looking cars turning into his parking lot.

This drugstore is too cool! I must stop here to catch my breath if only for a few moments.

She glances at her Timex. It reads 11:46.

I should be able to make it to Jimmy's before noon with plenty of time to spare.

Steph fully expects Jordyn will admonish her for dawdling. Much to her surprise, the orphan's thoughts do not enter her mind. That Jordyn is silent is not to say that she is unaware of what Steph is doing. On the contrary. She is allowing Steph these few brief moments to rekindle the compassionate part of her spirit. It also will make Steph aware of her purpose.

Her raison d'être.

I have seen black and white photographic images of drugstores from the 1960s on the Internet. But I never thought I would be standing outside one in the flesh. That I am is totally awesome!

The store's façade is weather-beaten. Even so, it continues to shine in its own distinct way with vibrant hues of every color of the rainbow. The word DRUGS, in bold letters, is on the extreme left-hand side of the façade. The word SODA, in identical bold letters, is on the façade's right-hand side.

A giant crest of a bottle cap is in the middle of the two words. Centered on the bottle cap is a painting of a frosty bottle of Coca-Cola with its cap removed. A bent straw is sticking out of the neck of the bottle. Beneath the trademark is the price of a bottle of Coca-Cola back in the day - 10¢.

Ten cents! Goodness, I can go without water and drink Coca-Cola all day and night, and I will never go broke with the money I have on me! Talk about neato!

Steph looks askance, and then with a chuckle, she says aloud in a whisper, "Neato? Where in the world did I come up with that word? I was thinking the words totally cool and out of my mouth comes the word neato! Talk about nifty!" She chuckles once more. "There I go again. Nifty. Now that is a neato word!"

She looks up at the horizontal unlit neon sign that is hanging above her head. The sign spans the entire width of the sidewalk. It reads:

"Barber's Rexall Drugs"

A circular blue sign is attached to a vertical pole next to the building.

"American Telephone & Telegraph Co. and Associated Companies"

The image of a bell is in the center of the sign.

"Local and Long-Distance Telephone"

The telecommunication words do not spark Steph's interest. But the two words beneath the bell do.

"Booth Inside"

There's a booth inside? Awesome. I bet it is one of those tall wooden booths with an old-fashioned pay telephone. Just like in the Harry Potter movies. I cannot wait to use it! Then again, who would I call?

She glances at her Timex once more. It is 11:48.

I have just enough time to peek inside the window.

She positions herself to look into the store window. As she does, her suitcase bumps against a bicycle held upright by its kickstand. The bicycle is painted yellow, and it has fat, balloon tires that are covered by chrome fenders pitted with considerable rust. She seizes the bicycle to keep it from falling over onto its side.

There are no brakes on this thing. How in the world does the rider stop it? Oh, look! Here's a little bell. But it's hanging upside down. The screw on the handlebar bracket must be loose. I'll straighten it.

She twists the bell until it is in its upright position on the handlebar. She giggles, and then she pulls the lever.

Ting-ting

She pulls the lever once more.

Ting-ting

Then three more times.

Ting-ting - Ting-ting - Ting-ting

Just as she is about to turn away to look inside the window, a small boy with sandy hair brusquely opens the exit door to her left. The boy appears to be around seven or eight-years-old. He is wearing tattered jeans and a short-sleeved yellow shirt with horizontal blue stripes.

He has black canvas high-top Pro-Keds brand name sneakers on his feet. The sides of the canvas sneakers are threadbare. No surprise, since sneakers of the day seemed to wear out from the top-down.

Just about every boy in the Sixties wears Pro-Keds. They are very affordable. However, in Steph's modern time, used Pro-Keds sneakers from the 1960s sell for anywhere between one hundred and two hundred dollars on eBay!

"Whatcha think 'ya are doing there, girlie? 'Ya tryin' to rip off my bike and then split? This is unreal! Besides, it is a boy's bike. Girls can't ride a boy's bike." He points to a red bicycle on the other side of the double doors. The bicycle is missing a kickstand, so its rider leaned it against the wall.

"See that? Now that's a girl's bike. Ain't got no support crossbar on it. It is made sissy-like for girls who wear dresses and all." He points to Steph's miniskirt.

"Like you. See?"

Steph says with an accompanying chuckle, "I am not going to steal your bicycle. I just wanted to hear the bell ring. So, I pulled the lever a few times. I hope you do not mind." She glances at her suitcase. "Besides, how could I ride your bicycle and haul this ridiculous suitcase around as well?"

The boy eyes her suspiciously, and then he mutters, "Okay then. But don't 'ya be ringing my bell, 'ya hear? Or I am gonna be ticked off and go ape. And I mean it!" The boy gives Steph one final dirty look, and then he disappears into the store.

Just as Steph is about to peek inside the store window, the boy reappears. She notices he has been crying.

"Hey, girlie."

Steph replies in a calm tone, "Yes, son?"

"My momma says I gotta apologize to 'ya. She heard what I said to 'ya. She said I was shoutin' which ain't the way she brought me up. She won't buy me an ice cream fudge sundae wit 'xtra fudge n whipped cream 'less I apologize."

Steph smiles. "That is not necessary. But go ahead and apologize."

The boy spins on his heels to reenter the store. He calls over his shoulder a split-second before the door closes behind him.

"I just did."

Steph cannot help but laugh at the gutsy, little boy's cute mannerisms.

Now that he is gone, she finally can look inside the drugstore window. She presses her nose against the window pane. She positions her hands on either side of her head to block the sun's reflection. As she stares, she too is about to, as the saying of the times has it, "go ape." Go ape means to lose control over one's emotions.

Four-tiered shelves stocked with the sundry items they sell in drugstores are everywhere. A long lunch counter is on the far right-hand side of the store. A thin man with a pink-striped, paper soda jerk hat is waiting on customers from behind the counter. He looks to be around twenty-five, give or take a few years. He is surrounded by various snack bar contraptions.

Three cast-iron milkshake mixing machines, presumably for chocolate, vanilla, and strawberry shakes. A line of soda dispensers. (Steph counts six dispensers in all) Five countertop jukeboxes that swallow a customer's quarter to belch five metallic-sounding songs.

And everywhere the eye can see paper napkin holders, glass containers containing paper straws, and salt and pepper shakers. Row after row of green-tinted glasses and at least a half-dozen or so plastic squeeze bottles of ketchup and mustard. All of these objects are emblazoned with the Coca-Cola logo.

The young man also is attending to an old-fashioned cash register at the far end of the counter. It is the only register in the store, so it is apparent that he has triple duties - waiting on customers at the counter, ringing up their food sales, and ringing up sales for shoppers. Steph decides, if she ever gets to meet him in person, she will refer to him as the waiter-cash register man.

She watches spellbound as the waiter-cash register man rings up the sale for a departing customer. The customer hands him a receipt. The waiter-cash register man reads it, and then he smashes a few buttons on the register. Little dollar and cent numbers appear in the register's glass window. He quickly compares the numbers in the window to the receipt. Then he pulls a lever on the right side of the register. The drawer pops open with an accompanying, loud *ping!* He takes the customer's bills, dolls out a bit of change, plops the receipt on a pin next to the register, and then he scurries back to his server duties.

Two elderly African American men are working in the kitchen. They have a line of menu tickets lined up at the top of the opening that separates the kitchen from the waiter-cash register man's workspace. When an order is ready, they push a little bell to alert the waiter-cash register man. He examines the ticket to compare it with what is on the plate. Then he turns around and gives the plate to the customer along with the receipt.

Steph is amazed at how busy the waiter-cash register man is. He is sweating profusely.

From the wonderful aromas hurtling from inside the drugstore as customers come and go through the double doors, she figures the cooks' fare must be delicious. She envisions scrumptious cheeseburgers and crispy fries; fried fish smothered in tartar sauce; perhaps the piping hot soup de jour; and all sorts of sandwiches - BLTs, clubs, tuna and egg salad, and many more scrumptious what-have-you's. The wonderful aromas surrounding Steph cause her stomach to growl loudly.

On the customers' side of the counter, a line of about ten or so round stools of a bright red color sit atop slender, brightly shining, chrome-colored cylindrical stands. Patrons are sitting on every stool.

The little boy who owns the bicycle is slowly spinning round and round on one of the stools. He has a half-eaten burger in his right hand. A plate of French fries is on the counter in front of him.

Steph marvels at his childish but very effective technique when it comes to eating his French fries. He is performing what he and his friends like to call "The three-rotation French fry technique."

When he is facing the counter after a complete rotation on the stool, he quickly grabs a French fry off of his plate. Then, when his second slow spin has him facing the counter once more, he speedily dips the French fry into a dab of ketchup on the side of his plate. He stuffs the French fry into his mouth on the third spin. Then he repeats his three-rotation French fry technique once more. All the while he continues to take small bites out of the burger.

The man to the boy's left scowls a dirty look at the boy from time to time. Even though Steph thinks the boy's spinning and eating technique is hilarious, not to mention very inventive, she cannot blame the man for being annoyed. The boy's antics must be very maddening when one is trying to read his newspaper while he eats. All the same, she already knows from her two brief encounters with the boy outside the store that he has spunk.

I think he has enough spunk for two or three boys. Nevertheless, there is no doubt in my mind that he knows how to enjoy his meal. His spinning on the stool, while he eats, looks like fun! If I were younger, I would probably spin on my stool, too!

She notices that a middle-aged woman is sitting to the boy's right. She has some of the same facial features as the boy. Another boy, with similar facial features, who appears to be Steph's age, give or take a year or two, is sitting to the woman's right. Steph is not certain, but the woman seems to be breaking the older boy's burger into small, bite-sized pieces. Steph correctly guesses the woman is the mother of the two boys.

The little boy suddenly stops spinning on his stool. He has noticed Steph with her face pressed against the window. She can only imagine that she looks ridiculously silly with her face squashed onto the window pane. The boy says something to the woman, and then he points in Steph's direction. The woman and the teenaged boy look at Steph. The woman smiles as she waves her hand. Since his mother is looking at Steph, the little boy sticks his thumbs into his ears and wiggles his fingers. Then he sticks his tongue out at Steph.

She cannot help but wonder yet again at the little boy's naughty but cute antics. She cheerfully waves her hand in return at the threesome.

It is then that she notices something odd. The teenaged boy, who she cannot help but think is very handsome, is waving his hand in an unnatural, floppy manner. His movements seem spastic to her. And his head seems to jerk from side to side just as he beams the most attractive, sincere smile she has ever seen.

Suddenly, cold shivers run up her spine. Then they race across her shoulders causing her to tremble. Goosebumps crawl down her shoulders to her forearms. And now awareness is beginning to engulf her psyche. For, at this precise point in time, she is certain she knows her purpose.

Her raison d'être.

The teenager who is smiling at her as he sits at the counter, and at whom she is happily smiling at in return, is her next assignment. He is the reason why the deaf orphan Jordyn has transported her to this time and place.

To a typical, small American town in the mid-1960s.

But one more opportunity for Steph to rekindle the spirit within her - to reveal her fearless, compassionate, and loving heart.

Jordyn's words in her mind say, "Okay, Steph. Now that you know, it is time to head up to Jimmy's. Good luck!"

Steph turns away from the window, grabs the handle of the suitcase, and resumes walking up the sidewalk as quickly as her tired legs can go. She nervously glances at her watch.

Goodness, I should not have taken so much time being nosy. I hope Jimmy does not get mad at me if I am late.

She suddenly begins running. The suitcase noisily follows closely behind making one horrible racket as it meanders back and forth on the sidewalk. She is running because she can now see all of Jimmy's brightly-colored sign.

"Welcome to Jimmy's Drive-in!"

She loudly shouts as she huffs and puffs up the winding sidewalk at a complete sprint.

"Jimmy's is a drive-in burger joint! That is why I have the roller skates in my suitcase! I am going to be a carhop! I have always wanted to be a carhop! People will drive up in their cars, and I will wait on them while wearing my roller skates! I cannot believe my good fortune. It is like a dream come true!"

She turns into the parking lot, her suitcase nosily bumping along behind her. She sees a gigantic man with an enormous belly standing in the doorway of the office. She can tell in a flash that the man is the owner, Jimmy. His huge abdomen tells of too many burgers, milkshakes, and fries. That he is shaking his head back and forth while staring at his watch is another dead giveaway.

As she sprints the few remaining yards to the office, Steph yells in the lingo of the times.

"I am going to be an outta sight, far out hipster, groovy carhop! How neato is that?"

*****

Part II: Jimmy's Drive-in

Steph skids to a stop a few feet from Jimmy. Her suitcase continues to roll and smashes into his knee. Then it tips over and crashes onto his foot with a frighteningly loud *thump!* She frowns as he grabs his knee. Even though she doesn't hear any words, she can tell he is cursing softly beneath his breath.

Gosh, all I seem to do is smash people's knees - this time with a heavy suitcase. When am I going to stop being so brutally physical?

"Oh, sir, I am very sorry. I should have known my suitcase would keep on rolling after I stopped running. It has some pretty nifty wheels, well oiled. Plus it is very heavy. I kid you not."

Her face turns beet red. She quickly removes the suitcase from the top of Jimmy's foot. He immediately begins hopping up and down on his other foot.

"Does it hurt, sir?"

"Hurt? You gotta be kidding me? What in the devil do you have in there? The kitchen sink? A bowling ball perhaps? Maybe a V-8 car engine?"

Steph replies bashfully, "Just a few things. Three-day's worth of clothes, a pillow, my roller skates, a few books, money, some odds and ends."

Jimmy continues to massage his knee as he flexes his injured foot.

"Okay, I guess you are the new girl, Steph. Am I right?"

Steph snaps to attention. She gives a sharp salute.

"Yes, sir. Steph is reporting for duty, sir!"

Jimmy says with a straight face, "Well, you have one heckuva way of introducing yourself - smashing my knee and crushing my foot. Furthermore, you were almost late for your first day on the job. Another minute or two and I would have told you no go. What kept you, anyway? I expected you a half-hour ago."

"I stopped to look into a drugstore window," Steph confesses. "I nearly was drooling when I smelled all the delicious aromas coming from inside. I had to peek through the window to see what the customers were eating. I have not eaten a thing today. I am very hungry, to say the least." She sniffs the air. "And the wonderful aromas here aren't helping very much when it comes to my hunger pangs."

Jimmy says, "Well, I must agree. We have some super-terrific aromas here at Jimmy's Drive-in, I dare say." He sniffs the air as he licks his lips.

"Burgers anyway you want them. Crispy, salted fries, large and small portions. Tangy onion rings. Twelve flavors of shakes. A wide variety of ice cream sundaes and sodas, Coca-Cola and Pepsi. We even have the new sugar-free soda called *Tab*. The Coca-Cola Bottling Company makes Tab. If all that isn't enough to whet your appetite, we also sell homemade brownies and the most delicious chocolate chip cookies on the planet."

He adds with a haughty laugh, "Barber's Drugs cannot beat us when it comes to delicious varieties of tasty food. Besides, when you dine here, you can sit in your car and eat in private. At Barber's you have to dine alongside people that you do not know. Plus there is not much elbow room." He pats his behind lovingly adding, "And those stools are too small for people like me."

Steph is tempted to challenge what Jimmy has said.

Yes, all of what you said may be true. But when you dine at Barber's you get to watch the little boy as he spins round and round on his stool while he skillfully grabs French fries off his plate. Only to expertly dip them in ketchup during his second spin and scarf them down on his third. All the while he is happily munching on a burger!

Considering Jimmy is her employer she holds her tongue and keeps her thoughts to herself.

Jimmy offers his hand. Steph takes his hand and shakes it heartily.

"Welcome aboard, Steph. I am Jimmy, Jimmy Peters. But of course, you probably have figured that out for yourself." As he smiles, he says enthusiastically, "Come on inside and let's talk for a spell in my office. It's down the hall."

He holds the entranceway door open for Steph. She thanks him, and then she enters the restaurant. Her heavy suitcase noisily follows behind, its steel wheels skidding on the waxed linoleum.

"I assume you have all the necessary paperwork that I sent you? Filled out correctly? No spelling errors? Tax forms okay? Your temporary place of residence here in town legit?"

Steph nods her head as she pretends to agree with what Jimmy has asked her. But the thoughts zipping through her mind state otherwise.

Goodness, Jordyn mentioned paperwork that is inside my suitcase. But I have no clue what it is, what it says. I have never seen it no less have I read it! And what is this about my temporary place of residence? Where could that be? I do not even know the name of this town not to mention where I am supposed to reside!

To get to Jimmy's office, they must pass on the outside of the serving counter. If Steph thought the food smells she sensed outside the drive-in were mouthwatering, these aromas, in comparison, are out of this world! Her stomach instantly begins to growl loudly as she takes in the delicious scents.

Three girls and two boys on roller skates are busily collecting their orders. Steph briefly pauses as she watches them in action.

The carhops doublecheck what is given to them by the cooks with what they had written on the ticket when the customers placed their orders. Then they scoop everything onto a plastic tray. The trays are designed to hold drinks without them spilling, a maximum of four drinks per tray.

Credit and debit cards were not readily available in the Sixties. So a little cup filled with dollar bills and coins for making change are on the trays. The trays are just the right size, shape, and weight for the roller skaters as they expertly carry them at shoulder level in the palm of their hands. Steph watches in awe as one of the carhop's skates out the door with a yellow tray heavily loaded with four tall drinks and an equal amount of burgers and fries.

I wonder if I can do that without tripping over myself or dropping everything? Yeah, I guess I can. If he can do it, so can I.

Jimmy gestures for Steph to enter his cramped office. There is just enough room in the office for a small metal desk, two chairs, an undersized wooden credenza, and a four-drawer metal filing cabinet. Then there is Jimmy, who, in Steph's opinion, takes up nearly half of the office space with his huge frame.

Every imaginable item one would expect to find in an office, most of it heaped on top of the credenza and filing cabinet, adds to the office clutter. The wastepaper basket is overflowing with crumpled up paper balls, discarded hamburger wrappers, and crushed cardboard drink containers. All of the drink containers still have paper straws sticking out of their openings.

A three-tiered stack of wooden boxes sits on the right corner of Jimmy's messy desk. The boxes are labeled from top to bottom in bold letters, "IN," "OUT," and "HUH?" A beat-up, Underwood manual typewriter sits in the middle of the credenza. To the typewriter's left and right are important-looking books and ledgers.

A framed family photograph is near the far right-hand corner of the credenza. The photograph is of Jimmy, a lovely woman, and two boys. Steph immediately recognizes the woman and the boys. They are the same threesome that she waved at through the drugstore window.

Talk about a coincidence! Jordyn sends me to this town. She lands me a job doing something I always wanted to do - working as a carhop at a drive-in burger joint. And wouldn't you know it? Jimmy is married to the women I saw at the drugstore. And the two kids are his kids! Way to go, Jordyn. It doesn't get any more convenient than this!

Jimmy squeezes behind his desk and sits in his chair. The chair seat objectively murmurs with a long, muffled *whooooooooosh!*

Then he pushes away a few inches from his desk. He opens the middle drawer in search for a pen. The four swivel casters on the bottom of the chair legs seem to object loudly with high-pitched squeals with his every move. Even the slightest of moves! The squeals cause Steph to cringe. She is tempted to stick her fingers into her ears to stifle the obnoxious squealing.

Squeak - Scrunch. Squeak - scrunch. Squeak, squeak - scrunch!

Steph notices that Jimmy does not seem to hear the obnoxious squeaking sounds whenever he moves in his chair.

Either he cannot hear those horrible squeaking sounds because they are too high-pitched, or he chooses to ignore them. Either way, I want to scream, *please oil those wheels or don't move!* The squeaking sounds are worse than someone scraping their sharpened fingernails on a school blackboard!

Jimmy motions to the chair on the other side of the desk. He says in a polite tone, "Have a seat, Steph." He glances around his office.

"I'm sorry about my messy office. I help the boys in the kitchen most of the time, so I have little chance to do my paperwork." He adds with a laugh, "And Lord knows, once I finally get to my paperwork, and I have completed it for the night, the last thing I want to do is clean up this mess!"

Steph says, "It looks fine to me."

She gestures to the framed photograph.

"Is that your family? If so, you have a lovely wife and handsome boys."

Jimmy removes the photograph from the credenza. Surprisingly, despite Steph's compliment, the tone of his voice sounds a trifle sad when he answers.

"Yes, this is my family. I love them to death." He points to the images one by one. "My wife Marcia, my son Christopher, and my son Eddie. Christopher is seventeen. He will turn eighteen next month. Eddie just turned nine." He manages a slight grin despite tears misting his eyes.

"I will not tell you Marcia's age. She'd kill me if she found out that I had, and then I would be sleeping on the couch for at least a week." His face brightens a bit.

"You will meet them soon enough once we get home. All of them are anxious to meet you. Your room is ready for you."

His facial expression suddenly changes.

"Steph, there is something I need to tell you. Please do not be alarmed when you meet Christopher. He is disabled. He has spastic cerebral palsy. He is not as bad as some kids, thank God. Nevertheless, it is very difficult for him. Despite his disability, he is strong-willed. Be that as it may, he gets depressed very often which is understandable."

He points to Eddie's image on the photograph.

"That is why his brother can be a handful at times. Eddie acts up a lot, probably because we must, by necessity, devote a lot of attention to Christopher. Eddie also has a habit of talking in *I'm a totally cool guy* sort of way.

"His mother gets after him all the time, but his excuse for talking like his peers is characteristic of kids his age. He usually replies to her scolding with an excuse like, 'All my friends talk like this. It's cool.' In contrast, Christopher does not succumb to peer pressure. Since he has cerebral palsy, he has difficulty pronouncing some words. Despite his difficulty with certain words, he is super smart, a straight-A student. So is Eddie, smart that is.'"

Jimmy laughs loudly, and then he jokingly adds, "A smart-aleck. Yes, Eddie is your classic example of a smart-aleck. Despite his wise-guy attitude, he is very well-behaved in school. He knows the teachers will not tolerate his way of speaking and his antics that he gets away with at home. In fact, he is an A/B student.

"As far as Christopher is concerned, like I said, it is difficult for him given his disability. Especially at school. He gets bullied a lot. But I guess that is the way it is these days. It was far worse when I was a kid. Far worse. At least they do not gang up on Christopher and beat him to a pulp like they did to me when I was in school. I have been heavy all my life, so you can imagine the bullying that I had to suffer.

"Let there be no doubt in anyone's mind. I am very proud of Christopher. Proud of them both." He adds with a sly grin, "Christopher graduates in two weeks. Never thought I would see the day. Then he is off to college in the fall. He has a handful of letters in the mail to universities. Given his grades, I am confident he will be accepted at one if not more of the universities."

He turns in his seat to place the photograph on the credenza.

Steph frowns as the caster wheels scream once more.

Squeak - Scrunch. Squeak - scrunch!

Jimmy says, "Okay, what do you have for me?"

Steph replies, "What do you mean?"

"Your paperwork." He eyes Steph's suitcase. "You do have it, don't you?"

"Oh, yes sir."

She reaches around to pull her suitcase through the open door. She sets the suitcase on its side and releases the latches to snap it open. She withdraws the folder and hands it to Jimmy.

"Here you are, sir." She crosses her fingers on her left hand. "I hope you will find that everything is in order."

Jimmy replies with a smile, "Me too. But if your paperwork is not in order, we will get you some new forms to fill out. Not a problem." He opens the folder and begins to shuffle through the forms.

"Sir, may I ask you something?"

Jimmy says, "Sure." He looks up from the paperwork. "But first, Steph, please call me Jimmy. Sir and Mister Peters are too formal for my liking." As he returns his attention to the paperwork, he mumbles, "So, what do you want to ask me?"

"You had mentioned that I would get to meet your family. I look forward to it. In fact, they were the ones I saw at the drugstore. They were sitting at the lunch counter. They waved to me, and I waved back." She giggles.

"I had the pleasure of meeting your son, Eddie. In person. I can see what you mean when you say that he likes to talk as if he is cool or something. But I can tell he is a good kid. He thought I was going to steal his bicycle since I had rung the bell on the handlebar a few times. He got after me pretty good but in a respectful way."

Jimmy laughs. "Yeah, do not mess with Eddie's bike. He will fight you tooth and nail for it. He loves the blasted thing. More so than his new Mickey Mantle baseball bat we got him for his birthday. As far as eating at the drugstore, it is okay by me that they eat there. Even though I would like them to eat here more often since I can feed them for free and save Marcia a bundle of money."

He looks up from his paperwork. He stares at the wall with a blank look. Steph notices that his eyes are misting yet again.

"Christopher gets a little upset when people stare at him whenever they eat at the outside tables of my drive-in. When they are out and about the town shopping, like they are today, it is more comfortable for him if he eats inside. Like at the drugstore where you saw them. That way people do not stare at him as much.

"As you probably know, people nowadays are not used to seeing someone in a wheelchair. Especially someone who has spastic cerebral palsy. Most disabled kids, grownups too, hide away from the public. They are forced to dine behind closed doors which is very sad. Because people stare, and then they whisper God knows what behind their backs.

"Most disabled kids in this town go to special schools. But not my Christopher. Oh no. Marcia and I insisted that our son attend public school. The school officials fought us tooth and nail at the beginning, but we were victorious in the end.

"Christopher started to attend public school when he was in fourth grade. He has been a straight-A student ever since. And he has had perfect attendance the whole time. Never late for classes either. But people tend to stare at him and say nasty things whenever he is in public places. It hurts him, hurts all of us. But what can I do?"

"That is horrible people stare and say nasty things to Christopher," Steph says in a whisper. "I bet he is a strong-willed boy, and I can tell you are very proud of him."

"Yes, he is very strong in more ways than one. He refuses to sit in the wheelchair at home when we eat. He sits on a chair at the kitchen table as the rest of us. He is adamant that he uses his crutches as much as he can rather than the wheelchair. Especially at home. But when he is in town, like today, he must use his wheelchair. He is one tough kid, much tougher than I would have been if I were in his shoes."

Steph nods her head. "And one other thing sir, I mean, Jimmy." She takes a deep breath. "What did you mean when you said, 'Your room is ready for you?' Am I staying with you and your family?'"

"Why yes, I thought you knew that," Jimmy says with a surprised look. "In fact," he holds up a sheet of paper, "it says right here in your very own handwriting, 434 Marigold Avenue. That is where we live. Where else would you stay if not with us, at least until you find a place of your own?"

Steph is in a panic. She ponders silently.

Find a place of my own? Goodness, how is that possible? I am not of legal age yet!

She throws her hand in the air and says with a pretending happy tone, "Why, of course, how silly of me. I guess all the traveling I have done has clouded my mind. You are correct. Where else would I stay if I weren't staying with you?"

Jimmy laughs. "Yeah, I can imagine you are beat. After all, you traveled all this way from South Dakota." He removes another sheet of paper from the folder. He begins to read it.

During the brief lull, Steph's thoughts are running frantically like a scared rabbit trying to outrun a fox.

South Dakota? Am I supposedly traveling from South Dakota? I have never been to South Dakota. South Carolina, yes. But South Dakota? No. I hope his family members do not ask me questions about South Dakota! If they do, I will be in a world of hurt!

Jimmy interrupts her thoughts.

"Steph, it says here you were born nineteen years ago this past February. And all this time I thought you were eighteen-years-old." His face blushes as he says in a somber tone, "If you do not mind me asking, do you have identification on you? You sure do not look like you are nineteen. If I had to guess I would say you are around sixteen, seventeen at the oldest. I hate to ask for ID in your case since you're attending college soon. But I must see some ID. Please excuse me for asking."

Steph can feel her heart is now racing a mile a minute. Her face feels hot, and her throat is as dry as a bone. She has no clue if she has an ID in her wallet. Moreover, she has no clue that if she does have an ID what it will say!

"Why yes," she says in a high-pitched voice. She reaches into the suitcase to withdraw the small wallet she had noticed when she was sitting on the sidewalk bench. She clears her voice. "Let me see what we have here."

She removes two plastic ID cards from the wallet. One is a college ID. The other is a driver's license. Thanks to Jordyn's amazing magic, her birthdate on both documents say she is nineteen-years-old as of February the 14th.

With a broad smile that is accompanied by a huge sigh of relief, Steph happily inquires, "Which do you prefer, Jimmy? College ID or driver's license?"

"Driver's license will do just fine," Jimmy says. He takes the ID from her, studies it a bit, and then, with a nod of his head, he hands it back to her.

"Looks okay to me. Sorry I had to ask. I do not want the child labor board breathing down my neck. It is bad enough the health inspectors give me a tough time. All the same, I cannot blame them. They are more helpful than hurtful. In fact, last month we received a perfect score - a one hundred! I gave all the workers a bonus. I could not do it without their conscientious, hard work."

He gestures with his hands at his cluttered office as he makes a complete 360-degree turn in his chair. Steph cringes as the chair wheels cry out in protest for the umpteenth time with horrible squeals.

"But I have to thank God the health inspectors never come in here. If they did, they would give me one heckuva tough time for having a messy office. And as sure as you and I are sitting here, they would quarantine my office for good measure. Just look at this mess!"

He closes the folder. As he stands, he removes a key from his pants pocket. He unlocks the filing cabinet and inserts Steph's folder into the top drawer. After locking the cabinet, he turns to look at Steph. A huge grin is on his face. He places his hands on his hips and stares at her for a few moments.

"Yes, Steph, I think you will work out just fine. In fact, I think you are perfect for the job. Athletic, great personality, people-oriented, and smart. Yep, you will do fantastic. Plus I know your fellow crewmembers will like having you working here as well."

He squeezes from behind his desk. He pauses briefly to rummage through the papers stacked high in his inbox. Steph stands, and then she backs away to the door to give the huge, overweight man more room to maneuver.

She is very relieved that Jordyn miraculously had prepared all the paperwork to Jimmy's satisfaction, in addition to providing her with two ID's, both with up-to-date photos! While Jimmy rummages through his inbox, she considers Jordyn's miraculous magical abilities.

I do not know how she does it! She can send thoughts to me and others telepathically, transport me back and forth through time and space, and speak in a foreign language! She also can transport a heavy suitcase filled with clothes, roller skates, and money, from wherever to here, and even make ID's with a picture of me on them!

I cannot wait to meet this amazing child! I must admit I feel a bit guilty assuming the identity of a nineteen-year-old imposter named Stephanie JoAnne Mahoney! It was bad enough during the last adventure that I was Josephine. But hey! It is not my fault. I have a purpose here, and Jordyn is not cutting any corners to ensure that I accomplish it without a hitch or a glitch.

Jimmy has completed rummaging through his inbox paperwork. He growls something under his breath as he irritably crumples a piece of paper into a ball. He tosses it at the overflowing trash can. The crumpled ball lands on top of the other trash, and then it tumbles to the floor. It comes to rests beside a half-dozen other wadded-up paper balls.

Steph giggles.

In response to Steph's giggles, Jimmy turns to face her. He laughs.

"Yeah, I thought I would give it the 'ole college try - try to make the half-court basket sort of speaking." Then his tone turns serious. "I really must do something about this office. It truly is embarrassing. You must think I am an overweight slob."

Steph immediately shakes her head forcefully.

"It looks okay to me, Jimmy. A bit messy, but at least you seem to know where everything is." She looks at him questionably adding with a grin, "You do know where everything is, yes?"

"Yeah, most of the time. But things do get lost. It is such a small office." He gestures to the open door.

"Okay, Steph, I know you are bushed. We will leave here in a bit and head for home. I cannot stay for too long. Maybe grab a bite to eat. Depends what leftovers are in the refrigerator. But Marcia will get you settled in comfy-like. But, before we head for home, I want to show you around and introduce you to some of the crew. You will start working at noon tomorrow." He extends his hand to shake Steph's.

"Congratulations, Steph. All your paperwork is in order. And I must compliment you on your neat penmanship. I did not see any grammatical or spelling errors on your forms. Yes, I cannot wait for you to start. The customers will be driving in here all day and all night to have the college-bound Steph carhop for them!"

He winks.

"And I bet you will get loads of tips, too. Just make sure you try to draw attention to that nifty dimple of yours whenever you smile! When it comes to my customers, I know from experience. A courteous attitude, lots of please's and thank you's, lots of ma'am's and sir's, and a heartwarming smile with a nifty dimple gets them every time!"

CHAPTER EIGHT

LOVE AND COMPASSION

"You may need crutches for support as you walk, but someday others
will seek your support and willingly walk in your footsteps."
- Steph, May 24, 1964

Part I: Home Away From Home

The 1950s were a decade filled with optimism which resulted from
the United States victorious post-war recovery. The American economy
was booming, and America's outlook on life was expectant of good
things to come. As such, the Peters' home, from its gaudy, pastel-
painted walls to its modern furnishings, reflect the country's optimism
of the last decade, the 1950s. Along with its emphasis on leisure,
comfort, and aesthetics.

There is no surprise here considering the Peters bought, decorated,
and furnished the house seven years ago - 1957.

Unfortunately, the optimism of the 1950s did not carry over into
the 1960s. Despite the Peters' home décor and furnishings.

Quite the opposite.

The year 1964, where Steph finds herself, reveals a deeply divided
America. The country is awash with controversial topics - politics,
women's rights, sexuality, inequality, poverty, and the most controversial topic of them all, Vietnam.

Conversely, 1964 also introduces popular culture - Muhammad
Ali, the Beatles, the Ford Mustang, color television, to name but a few
positive aspects of the year.

In spite of the political and societal storms wracking America in 1964, it does no good to belabor the issue as it concerns Steph. All the same, the Peters' home and the inhabitants' mindset, along with the societal aspects of the 1960s, set the foundation for Steph's visit.

Steph's boss, Jimmy, along with his wife Marcia and his two sons, Christopher and Eddie, live in a modest, two-story brick house - 434 Marigold Street. The house is on a medium-sized corner lot in a middle-class neighborhood of a small upstate New York town. The house has four bedrooms, two full baths, and spacious living and dining rooms.

The rooms are gaily-decorated with dried flowers, porcelain cat and dog figurines, framed pictures of lovely country settings, and colorful fabrics of flowers, fruits, and abstract designs. The overall theme inside the house, to include the furniture, is indicative of the age when the house was built and furnished as mentioned earlier - 1957.

There is a large concrete patio in the fenced-in backyard complete with a built-in charcoal barbeque pit. It is seldom used except on holidays when Jimmy's Drive-in closes. A small gazebo sits in one corner of the backyard. A small vegetable garden plot is to the right of the gazebo.

Marcia had mentioned to Steph that spring came early this year, and the days and nights have been unseasonably warm. As a result, tiny, bright green sprouts of all kinds of vegetables - tomatoes, radishes, carrots, and lettuce, to name a few, already are peeking from beneath the rich, well-tilled soil.

The kitchen, where Marcia spends most of her time when she is not running errands, is Steph's favorite hangout after work. Similar to all of the other rooms in the Peters' house, the kitchen is a cheerful, colorful place. Its walls are bright turquoise. Pastel colors of pink, turquoise, blue, and yellow are the craze of homeowners during this era.

Like most kitchens of houses built in the late 1950s, the Peters' kitchen is designed with convenience in mind for the stay at home housewife. It has abundant cabinet space - six cabinets on the left and four on the right. A string of spacious drawers is beneath each of the cabinets. The cabinets and drawers are a mint green. The kitchen also is equipped with the most modern conveniences. Jimmy made certain of that when he bought the major appliances, electronic gadgets, and room furnishings.

"A happy kitchen makes for a happy wife who makes a delicious supper, and, consequently, for a happy man of the house when he comes home to roost."

The Westinghouse shiny refrigerator, that makes round ice cubes by itself, and a natural gas Sears and Roebuck double oven stove complete with glass, see-through doors are Marcia's favorite appliances - even better than the Maytag washing machine.

The Peters do not own a clothes dryer. Marcia does not believe in owning one. Jimmy is glad because he thinks having a clothes dryer will double their already out-of-sight electricity bill. He probably is right.

Marcia hangs her laundry outside in fair weather. During inclement weather and throughout the winter months, she hangs the laundry in the attic.

"A clothes dryer is not for me," Marcia is fond of saying. "I like the exercise when I haul the laundry basket outside or up the stairs to the attic. And stretching my arms above my head keeps those triceps sags away, too. Besides, did you ever consider that clothes dryers ruin your clothes? Just look at all that lint residue if you don't believe me!"

Smaller electronic gadgets, the most modern gadgets Jimmy's money can buy, sit on the longest of the two counters in the kitchen. There is the electric can opener, coffee maker, mixing machine, blender, four-slice toaster, and an electric carving knife with its very own stand. Marcia sewed made-to-fit turquoise coverings for all the gadgets.

The shortest counter plays host to varying sizes of canisters that contain dry goods - flour, white sugar, brown sugar, ground coffee, coffee beans, tea bags, loose tea leaves, a huge glass jar of chocolate chip cookies (Marcia bakes a batch three times a week), and a small canister of Oreo cookies (Marcia's favorite).

A small serving island sits in the middle of the room. Tall stools flank two of its sides. The Peters' family eats dinner at a large, six-seater kitchen table located in a small enclave of the expansive kitchen. The wooden table and chair, like the kitchen cabinets, are mint green.

Marcia made the pretty - you guessed it, turquoise - tablecloth that adorns the table. A plastic turquoise vase filled with blue, red, gold, and yellow plastic tulips adorns the middle of the table. Marcia replaces the flowers every three months to correspond with the seasons.

It is no small wonder that the road on which the Peters lives is named Marigold Street. Bouquets of marigolds of every imaginable color seem to grow in front of nearly every house. Large, fully mature elm trees also line the street. Their broad leafy canopies shade the entire roadway as well as both sidewalks. Well-kept, manicured lawns, most with beds of tulips, gladiolas and, unsurprisingly, marigolds, reflect the self-worth of the close-knit community.

It is May, and the lilac trees are in bloom. The distinct, fragrant, sweet-smelling scent of their vibrant blossoms of violet, blue, lavender, and white fill the air. Steph loves walking along the street, especially early in the morning. The morning is when the divine lilac scents are the most potent.

Marigold Street is a very quiet neighborhood. Except on weekends and after school lets out for the day. Since the temperature is warm, kids of all ages are playing outside. Happy shouts fill the air.

There is not much thoroughfare traffic on Marigold Street, so the kids ride their bikes up and down the roadway without fear of being hit by cars.

Now and then, usually on weekends, groups of five or six boys play rowdy games of street baseball on the asphalt. They use soft rubber balls, so they do not break the windshields of neighborhood cars parked along the street. The ballplayers outline home plate and the three outlying bases in white chalk. Sliding on the asphalt is not advisable for obvious reasons. Even so, there are plenty of skinned knees as the boys slip and slide on the asphalt to score a game-winning hit or home run. After all, boys will be boys and games are meant to be fun despite the risks.

Younger girls and boys roller skate along the sidewalks, and there seem to be nonstop games of hopscotch as well. Steph marvels at the sidewalk roller skates the kids wear. The roller skates are clip-on with metal wheels and steel bearings. The children must wear their Sunday best or school shoes while they roller skate. If they were to wear sneakers, the roller skates would easily slip off their sneakers causing them to fall or twist an ankle.

Also, there are the many sidewalk cracks, pebbles, sticks, and stones to contend with while skating. Consequently, like the boys playing games of street baseball, the skaters are often rewarded with skinned knees and elbows as they happily skate on the sidewalk.

Steph's accommodations at the Peter's home are very nice. She has a bedroom to herself which is kept spic and span each day by Marcia. She has a full-sized bed adorned with crisp sheets of pink and two super-fluffy, down pillows. Her bed has a lovely comforter with embroidered red roses. She has a chest of drawers, a standup looking glass mirror, and even a small bookshelf stocked with classics. She also has an adjoining bathroom which is very convenient. That is because Jimmy and the boys seem to hoard the other bathroom. In fact, Marcia has to ask to use Steph's private bathroom on occasion. Whenever she does, she usually mutters something like, "Men! I should have had all girls!"

Marcia is the nicest lady and the most charitable host. She is small in stature maybe five-foot-three-inches. Unlike her husband, who is very much overweight, bordering on obese, she is very thin. Her slightly graying blonde hair falls in wavy curls to the middle of her back. She has blue eyes and an inviting smile that seems to say, "Give me a hug," which she often does, even to those who she meets on the sidewalk.

Marcia treats Steph like a daughter. In fact, when her friends see her and Steph together on the sidewalk - Marcia always walks Steph to and from work - she refers to Steph as her adopted daughter. When introducing Steph, she usually says something along these lines.

"I would like you to meet my nineteen-year-old adopted daughter, Steph. Well, not really as you know. I have always wanted a girl. So Steph it is! She will not be staying with us long. Nevertheless, while she is here, I intend to spoil her as if she is my flesh and blood."

And spoil Steph she does! She bakes cookies and cupcakes just about every day, and her cinnamon-flavored pecan waffles are out of this world! Her spaghetti with made-from-scratch sauce is fantastic, and her meatballs are juicy and spicy, just the way Steph likes them.

Marcia keeps a plate of leftovers warming in the oven for when she and Steph arrive at home, which is usually around 8:30 pm. They eat dinner together. As they dine, Marcia occasionally whispers in a loving tone, and in a joking manner, the reason why she keeps Steph's dinner warming in the oven.

"I do not want you eating all those burgers and fries for dinner. It is bad enough you eat that greasy garbage for lunch. Otherwise, you will turn out to be big, plump, and sassy just like my darling husband!"

Steph does not want to offend Marcia, but she loves Jimmy's Drive-in burgers and crispy French fries. She cannot seem to get enough of them. Then again, she also loves Marcia's cooking, so she knows she is enjoying the wondrous delights of both worlds - Jimmy's greasy burgers and fries and Marcia's wholesome, homecooked, healthy meals.

Marcia and Steph have very interesting and fun-filled conversations as they walk the twenty-minutes back and forth to Jimmy's Drive-in. Since Steph works six days a week, and she and Marcia eat dinner together, they spend a considerable amount of time chatting away. They also stay up late talking while the men of the house, as Marcia jokingly refers to them, watch television or play a game of cut-throat spades. As a result, they have become the best of friends.

Marcia is the typical mid-Sixties housewife, at least that is how others in Steph's modern age have stereotyped stay at home moms from the early 1960s. Even the television programs such as *The Donna Reed Show* depict the housewife as the center of the family. Ironically, *The Donna Reed Show* is the only program that Marcia watches. As a devoted housewife, she is busy in the kitchen or laundry room into the late hours of the evening. Despite her late-night schedule, she is up and adam at the break of dawn. Steph loves waking up to the pungent aromas of fresh, made from scratch hot chocolate, bacon and eggs, and toast with a heaping pile of cinnamon-flavored pecan waffles on the side.

Steph loves her job at Jimmy's Drive-in. She earns the minimum wage of $1.25 an hour. However, Jimmy has given her a bonus of ten dollars the past two paydays. She gets to keep all her tips as well. Jimmy explained that she is a temporary hire, so she does not have to combine her tips with the other employees.

"Nevertheless," he had said, "You may have to report your tips for tax purposes. I'll check the regs for you."

Steph was worried about having to report her income and tips to the State and IRS. After calling his tax consultant, Jimmy allayed her fears.

"You will not make enough money in wages or tips. Therefore, you will not have to file a tax return with either New York State or the IRS."

Steph was relieved, especially when she considered she was not the person who everyone thought she was.

Jimmy and Marcia assume that Steph will not be working much longer at Jimmy's Drive-in. Steph assumes this as well. In fact, she almost is certain. Even so, the reasons why Jimmy and Marcia think Steph will soon depart are miles apart from reality.

Everyone assumes that Steph will depart for the college summer session in a couple of weeks. Steph knows otherwise. She is fairly certain she will depart this Friday night, Saturday night at the latest.

At least I hope so because I miss Mom and Daddy, my sister, my friends, my bed, and yes, I miss Spirit as well.

Jordyn has not communicated with Steph since Steph saw Marcia, Christopher, and Eddie having lunch at the drugstore on her first day in town. Even so, subsequent events have set in motion Steph's purpose.

Her raison d'être.

Christopher's cerebral palsy is not as serious as Jimmy and Marcia had feared a few months after he was born. He has motor and speech limitations, and his eyesight is poor, but, happily, he has above average intelligence. He tends to drool when he eats but not always. He has poor coordination, stiff and weak muscles, and he suffers occasional tremors, commonly referred to as twitching. When he walks, he is at risk of falling because his legs tend to move in a scissor-like manner. For that reason, he usually uses a wheelchair to get around in school and around town. He uses crutches at home, but only when he feels particularly weak.

Christopher likes to venture outside for fresh air. Whenever he does, he usually remains in the backyard where he can enjoy himself without neighbors and passersby gawking at him. Jimmy installed a tall wooden fence years ago. It faces the two streets. Whenever Christopher is outside, he practices walking without his crutches. He will place his arms out wide as he cautiously takes tiny steps. He knows doing so will enhance his motor skills, strengthen his leg muscles, and improve his balance. Whenever he falls, and it happens from time to time, he crawls to the picnic table, pulls himself up, and walks some more.

Notwithstanding Christopher's disability, he is courageous, determined, and upbeat. More importantly, his self-esteem, at least in his mother's opinion, has increased ten-fold since Steph arrived.

Undeniably, at first, Steph felt uncomfortable when she was alone with Christopher. But then, owing to her compassionate manner and Christopher's affable personality, quick humor, and superior intelligence, she quickly overcame her unease. Even now, whenever Christopher drools, Steph, without consciously thinking about it, nonchalantly reaches across the table with a napkin and wipes the sides of his mouth or the spittle off his chin. They also have the most interesting conversations about every subject imaginable. To say they have become very close friends is an understatement.

Steph used to have difficulty understanding what Christopher was saying. That is because he sometimes slurs certain words. Now she can comprehend just about everything that he says. Whenever she cannot discern a word that he has said, the two of them play a game. They have affectionately dubbed the game *talk and write*. Talk and write is, by all accounts, an oral teaching process to assist Christopher with the pronunciation of difficult words. Talk and write, using the simplest explanation, goes like this.

Christopher will say a word that Steph does not understand. She will first ask him to repeat it. Most of the time, on the second go-around, she knows what he is saying. If she still cannot understand the word, she makes use of a small chalkboard that is lying on the kitchen table. She writes the word she believes he has said on the chalkboard. If what Christopher said matches what she writes, he responds silently, either by nodding his head or giving her a thumbs up.

When the word he said does not match what she has written, he shakes his head or gives a thumbs down. They repeat the process a few more times until Christopher's spoken word and the chalkboard's word match. Whenever the spoken word and written word do not agree, which happens from time to time, they move on with their conversation.

Christopher sometimes gets frustrated when the words he has spoken and what Steph has written do not agree. Steph usually calms him down by writing silly puns on the chalkboard or drawing emoji happy faces. There was one time, however, that Christopher got very angry. He had shouted.

"Sometimes I get sick and tired of having cerebral palsy, Steph. Being disabled sucks! It honestly sucks!"

Steph had replied in a calm voice as she kissed his cheek, "Yes, Christopher, you are disabled, but your heart is no different than mine."

*****

Part II: Jordyn's Miracle

"Yes, ma'am, I would like to invite Christopher to the senior prom. Do you think he will accept? I do not want to embarrass him. Boys are supposed to ask girls on a date, not the other way around."

Marcia is sitting on the opposite side of the kitchen table. She jumps out of her chair and rushes over to Steph. She gives Steph the most loving hug.

"Embarrass him? I should think not. He will be thrilled. I am certain of it. And I am positive he will accept your kind invitation." She gently pushes away from Steph and looks into her eyes.

"But, please tell me. Why are you doing this? You know you do not have to invite him to the prom. True, he has been talking about it for months. Even so, I do not want you to invite him for the wrong reasons."

Steph's reply is in a questioning tone that reflects the puzzled look on her face.

"The wrong reasons? What could those be?"

"You know to what I'm referring. Out of pity. I know the two of you have become the best of friends. Christopher thinks the world of you. He has told me as much. He has also told me on more than one occasion that he wishes you were his sister. I am certain he would love for the two of you to go to the prom together. However, if you want to invite him, please ensure you are going to do so because you are his friend. Not because you pity him."

Steph laughs as she throws her hands high into the air.

"Pity him? No, Marcia, I do not pity Christopher. Not at all. Sure, I feel a bit sad even angry at times that others ostracize and bully him, but I am confident he will persevere. He is strong-willed and as tough as nails. Besides, he is a genius, at least in my eyes. Anyone who can get straight A's in Latin, calculus, trig, biology, and chemistry has to be a genius.

"Sure, he is an A-minus student in English, but that is because his penmanship is very poor. The teachers have trouble reading his literary writings. It is not his fault. I have read a few of his compositions. They are perfect in every way, grammatically. And there are no spelling errors either. Besides, he has a richly creative mind. I believe he has all the qualities of an accomplished writer. In my heart, I know he will achieve remarkable things in the future."

Steph shakes her head as she adds in a confident tone, "No, ma'am, I would not invite him out of pity. That would be deceitful, and until you mentioned it, the word pity never crossed my mind. I would invite him out of respect and yes, out of love as a very dear friend."

Her look suddenly turns serious. She looks Marcia straight in the eye.

"May I tell you a secret? Promise you will not get mad, and you will not tell Jimmy or your boys?"

Marcia crosses her heart with her hand.

"Cross my heart and hope to die.'

"I am only sixteen years of age not nineteen like everyone thinks."

Steph notices the surprised look on Marcia's face. She quickly adds, "But do not let that upset you. I am here for a short visit; you know that. But the reason I am here is Christopher. Since I am sixteen, I am not ready for college. In fact, I still have two more years to go in high school. So when I depart from here soon and depart I definitely will, I will not be going to college. I will be going back home to my time and place in the future. My actual life is more than fifty years from now."

"But your IDs say you are nineteen," Marcia says matter-of-factly. She crosses her arms over her chest. The look on her face is stern. Steph winces in reaction to her look. She has seen that motherly, stern look more than once in her life. It is a look that can stop you in your tracks.

"Steph, please tell me you do not have forged IDs. That is my worst fear - that you are an underaged minor with forged IDs." She adds, "And Jimmy only hired you because he thought you were at least eighteen years of age. He even told me he suspected you were only fifteen or sixteen. That is why he asked you for your ID."

She pauses adding, "And, as I recall, Jimmy said you seemed very nervous when you took the IDs out of your wallet. He said your reaction was very strange. It was like you didn't even know what was on the IDs. Your nervousness only diminished when you handed your driver's license to him. He said you appeared to be very relieved as well."

"I did not make the IDs," Steph replies. "And yes, admittedly, I was nervous. I had no clue what was on the IDs. You must believe me.

"As far as working at Jimmy's is concerned, sixteen-year-olds are permitted to work the hours that I work. I checked. As long as they do not work past nine o'clock in the evening on a school day, everything is okay. In fact, Jimmy asked me last Friday night to stay past nine o'clock. I told him no. I said I had a headache. I did not want him to get in trouble for having a sixteen-year-old working past nine. If anyone was to get in trouble given my true age, I wanted it to be me. Not Jimmy.

"As far as my IDs are concerned, they were made for me by a deaf orphan named Jordyn. And I swear, Marcia. I never knew that she made them, and I never asked that she do so. What is more, I never posed for the two completely different pictures that are on the ID cards. Jordyn somehow superimposed them on the IDs. How she did it without me posing for the photos, I probably will never know. The photos are nothing like anything I have ever posed for in the past. My real driver's license back home even has a different photo than those.

"But this much I do know. Jordyn has super magical powers. She can perform miraculous things that are astounding, truly unbelievable. Not only can she communicate with me telepathically, and me with her in my mind, I think she also has psychokinetic powers. She can move things, do things, even make others do things, simply by - I am not quite certain how it works - but I guess by using her telepathic and psychokinetic powers. Even though she is thousands of miles away!

"Thanks to Jordyn's magical powers, I was able to save a little German boy named Adalard from the ruins of Cologne, Germany, during World War Two. I also was able to help two little girls named Hannah and Patsy and their brother Joseph escape slavery a year before the Civil War. It happened in South Carolina. And all of that occurred over the course of one or two days. I kid you not.

"And now I am here for Christopher. Not necessarily to invite him to the prom, although I am excited to do so. I am here because I want to have a positive influence on his life like he has had a positive influence on mine. You probably do not believe me, and I do not blame you if you don't. But I swear, Marcia. I do not lie, and I would never lie to you. You have been very kind to me. I would never deceive you. You must believe me. All of this - my being here, my two other actions in the past, everything - has been orchestrated by the deaf orphan, Jordyn."

Marcia's face suddenly pales as she begins to tremble. She staggers to her chair on the other side of the table. Then she grabs the back of the chair for support. She slowly slides into it. She stares at Steph for the longest time. Tears begin to well up in her eyes.

She whispers, "Steph, you are incredible! Amazingly incredible! And what you have just told me is even more incredible, almost unbelievable. Despite that, yes. I do believe you. I honestly do. And I am honest with you when I say that. Now it is my turn to tell you something. And I think you will believe every word that I have to say."

She closes her eyes. She is about to recount something that will even astound Steph.

Steph has no idea what Marcia is going to say, but her heart is telling her that whatever it is, it must be very important. The look on Marcia's face is like she has seen a ghost. She is shivering, and she has her hands clasped before her on the table. Her lips are moving. Steph assumes she is saying a silent prayer. At least she hopes so.

Steph moves to the other side of the table. She quietly slides a chair next to Marcia. She slides into the chair. She puts her arm around her shoulder and gives her shoulder a gentle squeeze. She whispers, "What is it? Are you okay? A few seconds ago you looked like you were going to faint."

Marcia smiles and nods her head. Her eyes remain closed as she continues to pray. After a few moments, she says in a whisper, "I am okay, Steph, thank you. What I am about to tell you is too far-fetched to believe. At least for anyone but you."

She opens her eyes. But her hands remain tightly clasped on the table.

"I had a dream last night. It was the most vivid dream I have ever had in all my years. A lovely girl, a deaf orphan who introduced herself as Jordyn, approached my bedside. Jimmy was fast asleep snoring like there was no tomorrow." She adds with a laugh, "I sometimes have to sleep on the couch or in the guest bedroom. His snoring is that loud. You undoubtedly know what I mean."

Steph nods her head. "Yes, I know what you mean. The first night I heard Jimmy snoring I thought a freight train was barreling down the street. It was super loud and kept me awake for hours. But eventually, I got used to it. Turning the fan on helps."

Marcia smiles.

"Anyway, this girl Jordyn begins to talk to me in my mind. Naturally, I am paraphrasing here, but this is the gist of what she said. She said, 'Marcia, please do not be frightened and do not speak aloud. I cannot hear you anyway because I am deaf. But you can ask me questions in your mind if you would like. I will understand them.

"'I am here because of Steph. Tomorrow she will tell you a secret. She will tell you about how she saved a little Jewish boy during World War Two. She will also mention two former girl slaves' names, Hannah and Patsy along with their brother Joseph. She will not go into much detail, but you must believe everything that she says. What she will say is the truth. She is present during your time on a mission for Christopher. I would not be here tonight except for this. It is important that you do not contact the authorities as it relates to Steph's age. You are a law-abiding citizen, and when she tells you she is sixteen, your first reaction will be to contact the authorities. Not out of meanness. I know that. But in consideration of Steph's welfare as a minor. Where she is at and what she is doing is no fault of her own. She has spent the past two weeks in your home and working at Jimmy's Drive-in because I sent her on an assignment. For Christopher.'"

Tears begin to fall freely from Marcia's eyes. She dabs at them with the hem of her apron. She takes Steph's hand in hers and squeezes it.

"And then she says, 'If you need proof that Steph and I know each other, well, that we communicate telepathically, ask her what Patsy gave her just before she and her brother and sister rode off into the night to freedom. She will reply that it was a gift, and then she will tell you what it was. You must do this, Marcia, to complete my conveyance and further the bond you share with Steph.'"

Marcia looks Steph squarely in the eye.

"Then she told me what it was that Patsy gave you. Please tell me what the gift was, Steph. Jordyn said it was important for me to ask you. To complete the transference and to further our bond."

Steph says, "Yes, Patsy gave me a gift a few moments before they departed. It was a handmade glass beads and cowrie shells necklace. Patsy said it was her good luck charm."

"Oh my goodness!" Marcia whispers. "Yes, that is what Patsy gave you, a glass beads and cowrie shells necklace. Jordyn also told me that Adalard gave you a German coin that used to belong to his father. I cannot recall the exact name of the coin. It was in German. It started with an "R" if I remember correctly."

Now Steph's eyes are full of tears. She says in a nearly inaudible whisper, "Yes, Adalard gave me a Reichspfennig. The coin, like Patsy's necklace, did not travel with me as Jordyn moved me through time and space. I wish they had. They are very precious mementos."

And the only proof that what I think I did, what I think I saw, and everything else I experienced, actually happened. That I haven't been dreaming all this time.

Marcia says, "Isn't this truly amazing?" Steph nods her head. Marcia continues tell her story.

"Most astonishing, the next moment I was wide-awake. I could not believe my eyes! I was looking straight on at Jordyn! She was kneeling on the floor next to my bed! Naturally, in the dim light, she was nothing but a shadow. Just the same, I knew she was real and not a figment of my imagination.

"Because she was kneeling, I could not determine her height. If I had to guess, I would say she was about five-foot-six, give or take an inch. She looked very frail, skinny in fact. Her eyes were closed, and her hands were clasped together in front of her face. She looked like she was praying. I could not make out the color of her hair in the dim light, but I think it was a dark color, maybe a mahogany brown. The color of her skin was a light-brown.

"Then, and you will not believe this. Jordyn went on to say something that I will never forget. Her words are etched in my mind like carvings on stone. It is like she wanted me to remember her words forever. Like she wanted to caress my heart with loving, exciting words that only a mother could understand.

"She said, 'And I must tell you this, Marcia. Due in large part to what Steph will soon do for Christopher, because of the love and compassion she has in her heart, your son's self-esteem will soar to new heights. He will attend Yale University where he will excel amongst his peers. He will attain a biomedical degree and graduate a year early. Then he will go forward to discover new therapies and treatments for those inflicted with cerebral palsy and related neurological diseases. He will also champion research into the dreaded scourge of childhood cancer.'"

Marcia reaches across Steph for an official-looking envelope that is lying on the far end of the table. She hands the envelope to Steph.

"And do you know what else she said?"

Steph shakes her head as she stares with disbelief at the envelope. It is addressed to Christopher Peters, 434 Marigold Street. The return address is Yale University, New Haven Connecticut. She looks up at Marcia.

"What else did Jordyn say?"

"She said, 'The postman will deliver a registered letter to Christopher in the morning. It will be from Yale University. It is an acceptance letter. Acceptance letters from other universities will follow, but Christopher will choose Yale. Congratulations!'"

Marcia stares straight ahead. The color of her face slowly turns ashen white.

"Then, and you will not believe this. In the blink of an eye, Jordyn disappeared before my very eyes! One moment I was looking at this miraculous, god-like child kneeling next to my bed. The next moment she disappeared into thin air! I had to pinch myself to make certain I was fully awake, that what I saw with my eyes and heard in my mind were real. Yes, I was wide-awake, and everything I had experienced was real."

Steph is choked up and barely able to speak. She is a slight bit jealous that Jordyn had appeared before Marcia. Even so, she is thrilled that Jordyn told Marcia what she did. She hugs Marcia. Then she closes her eyes and says in her mind, "Thank you, Jordyn, for what you have done, to bring untold joy to this family. I love you!"

*****

Part III: We are Going to Crash the Party!

"Well, did he accept?" Marcia asks excitedly. The expression on her face is animated. Steph notices she has crossed her fingers on both of her hands.

Steph replies with a smile, "Why of course." She slowly motions with her hands alongside both sides of her lovely face. "Now who, may I ask, could resist this lovely smile and beseeching brown eyes?" Then she points to the cute dimple on the right side of her cheek. "And this gorgeous dimple? As Jimmy had said, it gets them every time! And that includes Christopher."

Her expression turns serious.

"To be honest with you, I think Christopher was more excited than me. In fact, I think he was more excited about my asking him to the prom than he was about receiving the acceptance letter from Yale." She takes Marcia's hand into hers.

"And I thank you for allowing me to give him the acceptance letter from Yale. It was an honor for me to do so. I was trembling when I gave it to him. I was thinking, 'What if Jordyn was incorrect? What if the letter is a denial?' But then I figured Jordyn hasn't let me down up till now, so I took it from behind my back and, as I handed it to him I said, 'Look, Christopher. You have an acceptance letter.' He looked at me like I was crazy or something. Once he read the letter he was all smiles. I was all smiles as well and very relieved it was an acceptance letter and not a denial.'"

Marcia says, "It was the least I could do - for you and Jordyn's love for him. So are you ready to buy your gown? I do not have too much extra money in my household piggybank. But we can get you something delightfully pretty. Maybe from JC Penny or even from Sears. And, of course, we will have to buy Christopher a tuxedo."

She suddenly shouts, "Goodness. This is very exciting! My boy is going on his first date, to the prom with the most beautiful girl in the entire universe - my lovely adopted daughter, Steph, the most caring girl in the whole wide world!"

Steph's face turns beet red.

"Aw, shucks, Marcia. What a delightfully wonderful thing for you to say. Thank you. And I mean that from the bottom of my heart!"

She walks over to the chest of drawers, and then she withdraws her change purse. She opens the purse and removes a wad of bills. She shows the wad of money to Marcia.

"As far as the gown and tuxedo and shoes and whatnots are concerned, I want you to use this money for the expenses."

Marcia shakes her head from side to side. She shoves her hands into her apron pockets.

"That is very kind of you to offer. Nevertheless, I am sorry." She shakes her head once more. "I cannot accept your money. I will ask Jimmy to advance me some cash from next month's household account. We will manage just fine by budgeting over the next several months. But I thank you just the same. Please, you keep your money."

"Marcia, I must insist. This money is not mine. I did not earn it. Jordyn gave it to me - to us, which includes Christopher - as a gift. For the prom and maybe more."

She pulls Marcia's right hand out of the apron pocket. Then she places the wad of money into her hand and gently closes her hand into a fist.

"Besides, whatever money I do not spend on something tangible will disappear as soon as I leave. Just like the gifts from Adalard and

Patsy disappeared. So the money might as well be used now for something worthwhile rather than go to waste. I bet there is enough money for a gown, tux, shoes, a corsage, maybe even dinner after the prom. And that dinner should include everyone - you, Jimmy, and Eddie. Of course, the three of you need not be all dolled up in a gown and tux. So please keep the money. I give it to you to manage for me. Please."

Steph reaches into the chest of drawers once again. She retrieves two envelopes and hands them to Marcia.

"You might as well have these, too. Unlike the money that is leftover, if any, from what Jordyn gave me, this money will not disappear when I leave. And I already know from past experience, it will not travel with me when I depart. Anyway, it is my earnings from working at Jimmy's. And let me tell you, being a carhop was like a dream come true. I loved every minute of it."

She removes the pay stubs from the envelopes and tears them into little pieces. She drops the pieces into the trash can. Then she removes the bills and holds out her hand.

"Please take this money. There only is fifty or so dollars left. As you know, I treated Christopher and Eddie to lunch a couple of times. I also bought Eddie a new bell and fenders for his bicycle. The other fenders were pretty much shot."

Marcia says, "No, I cannot and will not accept your earnings. You earned every penny of it. And from what Jimmy has told me, he hates to see you leave. You are his best carhop, and that is saying a lot because Jimmy does not give out compliments as you probably know."

Steph laughs. "Yes, I know. He is very demanding which is good. He expects a lot from his employees which is also good. I respect his work ethic very much. It has been loads of fun for me to meet the people that I serve as a carhop. I always have a smile on my face as I enjoy the experience. And I hope my positivity brings the customers joy. Certainly, I must be focused to make sure I do not spill their drinks, but it brings me happiness to see everyone is having an enjoyable time with their family and friends. I love my job."

She stuffs the bills into Marcia's apron pocket. With a huge grin on her face she says excitedly, "And wait until Jimmy gets home

189

tonight. I pretty much can guarantee he will be in the happiest mood ever."

Marcia asks, "Why is that?"

"Last night, after he fell asleep in his easy chair, I removed his office keys from his fancy Jimmy's Drive-in jacket. Then I skated off to the drive-in. You did not know that I was gone. You were at your friend's house helping her prepare for her daughter's graduation party.

"I spent nearly three hours cleaning Jimmy's office. It is now spic and span, like new. I even polished his desk, emptied his trash can, and scrubbed the tile floor on my hands and knees. He probably did not even recognize his office when he entered it this morning. I hope his clean office makes him happy."

Marcia says, "That was very thoughtful of you. And I bet he will love it. I hope he keeps it neat and tidy. I'll stay after him to make certain that he does." She hugs Steph adding, "You are too sweet. I love you. I hope you know that."

"Yes, ma'am, I can feel it in my heart. And I love you and the men in your family as well. And I thank you for your wonderful hospitality. Your kindness has made this assignment the best one yet." She rubs her belly adding, "I especially love your homecooked, delicious food and desserts. I think I may have put on some weight!

"Also, please use all of the money for whatever you need. As I said, it will not travel with me." She adds, "But no worries. Something tells me I will earn my own money when I return home. I am going to apply for a job at a place called Sonic. It is sort of like Jimmy's Drive-in except Sonic has drive-ins just about everywhere throughout the country. I will be a roller-skating carhop just like here. At least that is my intention."

Marcia says with an unhappy tone of voice, "I do not want you to leave. This house will never be the same without you. I truly mean it. Your gown? Will it also disappear when you leave?"

"No, I do not think so," Steph replies. "I think everything that has occurred here up until now and will occur in the future, at least from a physical standpoint - the money I earned, the gown, tux, shoes - all of it will remain behind after I leave. It's just that it will not travel with me. Perhaps you can keep my gown as a memento of how much fun we have had up to this point, that we are going to have!"

She suddenly grabs Marcia by the elbow. She has a huge grin on her face as she steers Marcia to the door and down the stairs.

"The prom is less than six hours from now. And let me assure you, Missus Marcia Peters. Your son Christopher and I are going to crash the party! There is no doubt in my mind. We will be the most handsome couple in this town's history! So let us gather up Christopher and head to the stores for some serious shopping."

She pauses on the stairs. "I want the prettiest but cheapest purse money can buy with a gazillion of those glittering sequins on it, too!"

A few hours later the threesome emerges from JC Penny. Steph is pushing Christopher's wheelchair. As they walk, the three of them are chatting away nonstop. To say Steph and Christopher are excited is an understatement. The huge grins on their faces confirm their excitement.

Marcia says, "Well, I think it will only take me a half-hour to take up the hem on your gown. I honestly love the cream color. The sequins on your gloves and the purse match those of the gown perfectly. We lucked out getting the three items as a set. I guess waiting until the last minute paid off. Everything was on sale." She glances at her watch.

"But I wish I had more time to perm your hair." She glances at the sales slip she is holding in her hand. "But oh! Everything was so very expensive! One-hundred-fifty-seven dollars and sixty-three cents! I dare say that is a lot of money!"

"Oh, it is okay," Steph replies. "As I said earlier, it is money that Jordyn gave to me to use for this very purpose. For the senior prom. Plus, to tell you the truth, I do not think it all that expensive considering we got a gown, matching purse and gloves, a tux, and shoes for the two of us. In my day the amount of money we spent would be lucky to cover the cost of the gown. You should have plenty left over for a nice meal after the prom.

"In fact, I think there should be enough left over for a nice family meal after tomorrow's graduation ceremony as well." After a brief pause she adds, "As far as my hair is concerned, I think a quick shampoo and combing it out will do just fine."

Steph taps Christopher on his shoulder. "And you, Christopher, how do you like your tux?"

"I think it is the niftiest thing in the whole wide world," Christopher says. "I particularly like the bright red bowtie you picked out for me."

He looks up at Steph. "And I thank you for asking me. Your invitation and my acceptance letter from Yale have made this the best day of my life."

"Oh, remember what we agreed to," Steph says in a whisper. "If anyone asks, you invited me to the prom. Not the other way around. Sure, it is a little fib, a little white lie if you will. But I want you to shine tonight. It is the least I can do for you and your family for being so kind to me." She pauses briefly and then she adds, "And for being my awesomely handsome date."

She unexpectedly stops pushing Christopher's wheelchair. She spins his wheelchair around so that it is facing her. She bends over and kisses Christopher's forehead.

"And just so you know, Christopher, I am going to be the proudest girl at tonight's prom. Although you have a disability, you always put the feelings of others before your own. I respect that. Not only are you super intelligent and handsome, but you also have a gentle heart."

Christopher says, "You also have a kind heart, Steph. In fact, I would dare say; you have a kindred spirit and a fearless heart." Steph looks surprised at what Christopher has said.

"Yes, I said that. While you were in the dressing room trying on one of your umpteenth gowns," he chuckles, "Momma told me about her dream - about your friend Jordyn appearing at her bedside." He looks up at his mother.

"She told me how you saved the Jewish boy's life. She also told me how you risked getting yourself killed by saving the three slaves. So yes, I know why you are here. And I respect both you and Jordyn for what you are doing. I am deeply humbled.

"You cannot even begin to imagine how your friendship and inviting me to the senior prom have enhanced my self-esteem. Thanks to you, I know I can do anything if I put my mind to it. I dream of wonderful things happening in my life despite my cerebral palsy. And I think I have what it takes to make those dreams come true. I love, respect, and admire you, Steph. Please never forget that."

Steph replies in a whisper, "I love you too, Christopher. More than you will ever know."

She quickly turns Christopher's wheelchair, so it is facing the other way. Then she begins to jog slowly on the sidewalk all the while yelling in a singsong voice, "We're going to the prom! How do you like that? Yes, we're going to the prom! And we're going to show 'em how to dance!"

Christopher sings along as best as he can.

*****

Part IV: The Senior Prom

Steph is pushing Christopher's wheelchair the four blocks to their destination. The two of them are engaged in a high-spirited conversation interspersed with much laughter. Christopher is clutching Steph's high-heels shoes and her purse in his lap. That is because Steph is wearing roller skates as she pushes Christopher's wheelchair along the sidewalk.

A few moments before Steph and Christopher left the house, Steph had asked Marcia to pin up the hem of her gown with safety pins.

She had said, "I will remove the safety pins once we arrive at the prom."

Marcia had asked incredulously, "Why in the world would you want me to do that? Even though you are going to push Christopher's wheelchair wearing your gown, I seriously doubt you will trip over your own two feet." With a chuckle, she added, "Unless you have trouble walking in high heels. Do you?"

"No, ma'am," Steph replied. "I can walk and dance in high heels just fine. The reason I would like you to pin up the hem of my gown is very simple. I am going to push Christopher's wheelchair wearing my roller skates!"

"You're going to do what!" Marcia exclaimed. "Steph, you cannot skate along the sidewalk wearing a gown. It is bad enough you turned down a ride by Jimmy and his offer to hire you a taxi." She added in a scolding tone of voice, "There is no way you can skate on the sidewalk wearing a gown."

"Says who?" Christopher chimed. "Steph and I think it is a grand idea. We will turn a few heads, but that is the purpose."

"Well, I am not certain," Marcia said. Her tone was somber. "Christopher, people will laugh at you. I honestly do not want them to laugh at the two of you."

"Oh, I seriously doubt it, Marcia," Steph said with a grin. "In fact, if I were a betting teenager, which I am not, I would bet that people will look at us with awe, especially our fellow promgoers. Think about it. Two excited teenagers are on their way to their senior prom. A sweet female in a lovely gown is wearing roller skates while pushing a handsome boy in a wheelchair wearing a tux. Think of the positive message it will send to others with disabilities. Besides, if some onlookers laugh what is it to us?" She laughs offering, "As the saying goes - sticks and stones no break our bones."

Christopher said, "Yes, Steph is correct. I have been laughed and stared at all my life. I am immune to it. And, as you know, Momma, those of us with disabilities are expected to hide from view from those who are, at least in their minds, normal. Well, not anymore. Not as far as I am concerned. I broke the mold when you and Dad insisted that I attend public school rather than hide from view by attending a special school. I firmly believe I have received an outstanding education as a result.

"Sure, I was challenged. And yes, classmates bullied me. But those obstacles made me work all the harder in comparison to my peers. I also have a thick hide now. You know that better than anyone. So tomorrow I will receive my diploma, and today I will dance." He had looked at Steph admiringly adding, "With my beautiful, roller skating girl as I hold my head up high."

"You are going to dance?" Marcia had asked. "I have never seen you dance, Christopher. Do you even know how?"

Steph immediately answered on behalf of Christopher. She said in a tone of voice that was full of pride, "Yes, and I must say, Marcia, Christopher is a terrific dancer. His movements are not the most graceful due to his spastic cerebral palsy. However, in my opinion, he gets along just fine. We have been practicing in his room. You undoubtedly heard the phonograph playing our favorite rock 'n' roll songs the past several nights until well past midnight."

Marcia nods her head.

"Yes, I heard the music. But I never, in my wildest dreams, thought the two of you were dancing. I thought you were listening to the music."

Christopher had added with an accompanying hearty laugh, "And when it comes time for the fast songs during the prom I already have most of the latest weird and jerky teenager dancing moves down pat! I dare say, I am a natural!"

Marcia and Steph had laughed wildly at Christopher's comment.

As a result of their three-way conversation, Marcia shortened the hem of Steph's gown with a half-dozen safety pins.

The Goodfellow High School senior prom is in the gaily-decorated banquet hall of the Blessed Trinity Church. Walking from the Peters' house to the church normally takes twenty-five to thirty minutes. Since Steph is on roller skates, the trip takes a little over fifteen minutes.

As they approach the church, Steph notices that most of the couples are arriving in family cars or taxis. A few of the more affluent (or show-off) promgoers arrive in limousines. A handful of couples, seven to be exact, are walking alongside Steph as she pushes Christopher's wheelchair. She had slowed her skating speed to a crawl as a result of their company. She and Christopher are now engaged in amicable conversations with the other couples. Their fellow promgoers are admiring Steph and Christopher's fearlessness just as the couple had expected.

One of the boys says, "Well good for you, Christopher. I always knew you were a sport, and I dare say, a tough one at that." He glances at Steph's roller skates. Then he says to his date, a lovely brunette with a huge wrist corsage, "Why in the world didn't we think of wearing our roller skates? Talk about neato!"

A girl offers, "Yes, what a cool idea. Had we known you would be on wheels all of us could have worn roller skates. It could be a roller-skating senior prom instead of dancing and having to drink watered-down fruit punch and eat stale Wise potato chips and salty pretzels."

Steph is beside herself. Her heart is beaming for Christopher as they close in on the church. She and Christopher had made their point, at least as it concerned those who saw the two of them rolling along on the sidewalk.

Passersby on the sidewalk, even some in their cars, and some neighbors sitting on their porches, gleefully cheered as Steph skated along the sidewalk pushing Christopher's wheelchair. Two onlookers scurried inside their houses, and then they reemerged with their Polaroid cameras. They raced after Steph and Christopher to take pictures. Steph, all smiles, obliged by slowing down her skating pace.

Some of the comments from onlookers were unforgettable.

"Way to go, girl!"

"Hey, Christopher, your date is beautiful!"

"You two must be the neatest teenage couple in town!"

"Gosh, I wish I had skated to *my* prom!"

"Here, let me take another photograph. I want to show it to my wife!"

The most memorable comments came from a man who was wearing a flashy black suit. He had made an illegal U-turn in the middle of the street. He stopped his car alongside the curb, tires screeching and rubber burning. He was holding a Polaroid camera when he emerged from his car.

"Hey, you two. I declare! Skating while pushing a wheelchair is very clever. My name is Mitchell, Gerald Mitchel. I work for *The Evening News.* If you do not mind, I would like to take your photograph, maybe a half-dozen. I bet my newspaper will print them." Naturally, Steph and Christopher consented.

To the Peters' delight, the front page of the Monday edition of *The Evening News* featured a photograph of Steph on roller skates pushing Christopher's wheelchair. The caption beneath the photograph said it all when it came to Steph and Christopher's audacity.

"Why dance when you can roll? A couple on wheels head to the prom!"

Steph carefully wheels Christopher to the bottom stair of the twenty-six stairs that lead up to the entrance of the banquet hall. The cheerful sounds of rock 'n' roll music are already streaming from inside the open door. She quickly removes her roller skates and slips on her high heels. As she lifts Christopher by his armpits to help him stand, she notices that he is smiling broadly from ear to ear. That he is smiling makes her happy. Then his eyes mist with tears. Steph notices this and her heart sinks.

Something is causing his eyes to fill with tears! Is something wrong? Are they staring at him? Are they making fun of him, his disability? Oh, they better not!

She slowly turns around to face the stairs. Her heart seems to jump for joy.

Their fellow promgoers are standing on the stairs. They are smiling admiringly. Suddenly, as if prompted by some unseen force, they begin to clap loudly. Steph is now all smiles as she helps Christopher tackle the first stair tread. Lifting his leg is an effort, so she must take her time. As they negotiate the second stair tread a shout of a young man's voice breaks the inelegant silence.

"Three cheers for Christopher and his beautiful date."

Then fifty or more couples lining the stairs and standing in the church entranceway chime in with resounding cheers.

"Way to go! Way to go! Way to go!"

Christopher is already perspiring with the herculean effort to negotiate the third stair tread. Two boys rush to assist him. The larger of the two boys says, "Christopher, we can carry you up the remaining stairs if you would like."

Christopher replies, "No, but I thank you just the same. I want to do this," he looks at Steph, "for her."

Steph ponders what Christopher has said.

Oh, my goodness. That is the most darling, loving thing anyone has ever said to me. I am glad I am not wearing makeup. Otherwise, I would be a dreadful mess.

She whispers, "Thank you, Christopher."

"So," Christopher says to the boys, "if one of you will get to my right and the other to my left, and then if you will slip your hands beneath my armpits," he looks up at the remaining stair treads, "we should be there in no time." He adds with a hearty laugh, "And don't worry guys. I used deodorant after I showered."

As Steph walks behind the three boys, to say she is enormously happy is a huge understatement. Along with Christopher, she wants to press home a premise tonight. It is one of her primary principles when it comes to those who are disabled or less fortunate than others. That she is doing so, and fearlessly at that, is particularly important in this day and age, the 1960s.

People of this era are unaccustomed to seeing people in wheel-chairs. They are unaccustomed to seeing anyone with a physical, emotional, or mental disability. Adults, as well as kids, stare at the disabled, even mock them and talk behind their back for being less fortunate than themselves. They are not mean-spirited. On the contrary. They do not know any better. That is because society hides most of the severely disabled from public view. The disabled are a novelty. To some, almost like strange people in a traveling, three-ring circus.

Until the Congress passed the American Disabilities Act in 1990, the disabled were subject to wholesale discrimination. The Act addressed the needs of people with disabilities and prohibited the discrimination of the disabled in employment, public services, public accommodations, and telecommunications.

And so it is. Steph and the boys' assisting Christopher to climb the twenty-six stairs to gain entrance to the hall is a purposeful act of resolution. Unlike in Steph's era, the disabled have to climb those twenty-six stairs like it or not. The alternative is to be left behind. It is that simple.

So Steph and Christopher, by their bold actions tonight, are making a likewise bold statement. And that statement is crystal clear. People with disabilities need not hide behind closed doors. They need not cower in public. They need not be ashamed. And they need not fear the stares, jeers, and jokes. They have an equal right to be who they are and who they want to be just like anyone else.

The prom lasted for precisely two hours and twenty-nine minutes. During this time Christopher and Steph danced to three fast rock 'n' roll songs and one slow dance. Christopher was very tired after dancing. Despite his weariness, he and Steph had a wonderful time. They told silly jokes, laughed boisterously, and enjoyed engaging conversations with Christopher's fellow graduates.

Then the impossible happened.

At precisely 9:29 pm, Mister Donald Brown, the school vice principal, who is serving as the prom's master of ceremonies, calls Freddy Steward to the microphone. Freddy is the graduating class valedictorian. He also is the star quarterback on the school's football team. Thanks to his accuracy when throwing the football and his know-how when calling the plays, the Goodfellow High School football team won the district football championship two years in a row.

His date is Shirley Jones. Shirley is a tall, gorgeous blond. She attends Goodfellow's rival school, Milliard Fillmore High. Like her date, Freddy, she also is a valedictorian.

Steph ponders, it just goes to prove that even the most competitive of rivals can be best friends.

Mister Brown removes a carefully folded three-inch-square piece of yellow lined paper from his pocket. A chorus of loud moans and groans radiate from the dance floor as he slowly, and very purposely, unfolds the fourteen-inch-long paper.

After he finally unfolds the paper, Freddy moves next to him to glance at it. He whispers into the mike that Mister Brown is holding in his hand.

"It's okay folks. There are only three bulletized entries." He places his arm around Mister Brown. "He is not going to talk on and on and on like he does at the assembly."

Freddy's lighthearted decree elicits enthusiastic applause from the promgoers along with the cheer of, "Way to go, Vice Principal Brown!"

As he glances at his notes, Mister Brown begins his spiel by thanking the promgoers for behaving themselves during the dance. His pronouncement results in good-natured but extremely loud, energetic boos from the promgoers. When he teasingly points his finger at the promgoers, a chorus of friendly, respectful laughter replaces the boos.

Then he singles out a few parents in attendance for their assistance in the prom's preparations. A polite round of applause follows the mention of each name. At last, he pays tribute to Missus Sheila Ferguson for baking the delicious, seven-tiered graduation cake.

The cake, which is now nothing more than a few crumbs, resembled a large wedding cake. Porcelain figures of a teenaged boy and girl wearing caps and gowns were on the top tier. A printed placard at the base of the cake read, "Well Done Goodfellow High School Graduating Class of 1964!"

Before Mister Brown can even finish his tribute to Missus Ferguson, the promgoers begin to cheer and clap loudly.

Missus Ferguson is the proprietor of the neighborhood bakery, "Sheila's." She is very popular with the Goodfellow high schoolers, and her establishment is their preferred hangout. Sheila's has twelve, four-seat tables, a ten-seat counter, and in the opinion of the teenagers, the best jukebox in town with all the latest rock 'n' roll hits. Her hangout also sports a ten-foot-square dance floor for those who are in the groove.

The teenagers' favorite fares at Sheila's are double cheeseburgers, fries, onion rings, tater tots, a variety of sodas, and seven flavors of milkshakes. Sheila's also specializes in homemade cakes, cupcakes, eclairs, brownies, and many kinds of donuts. It is a favorite family place to dine, especially on Sunday's. It is on Sunday's when Sheila's three-person bakery crew bakes the Sunday special donut affectionately dubbed the Monster. The Monster is a nine-inch, perfectly round, chocolate-covered vanilla cream donut. It only costs fifteen-cents. What is more, if a customer purchases a dozen of the Monster's, Sheila throws in one extra donut, making the customer's purchase a true baker's dozen - thirteen donuts in all.

After the applause finally dies down, Mister Brown says into the microphone, "So, Freddy, have you reached a verdict?"

Freddy is renowned for his friendly sarcasm and being very quick with the jokes. He takes the microphone from Mister Brown.

"Yessir, we have reached a verdict. And it is unanimous. We find you, sir, Mister Brown, Vice Principal of Goodfellow High School, guilty of dereliction of duty." As he lightly smacks the vice principal on the back he adds, "For not spiking the punch bowl!"

Freddy's fun-loving pronouncement elicits the second chorus of boos from the promgoers.

"On a more serious note, sir," Freddy says at last. "Yessir. We have a winning couple. Those of us from the graduating class of nineteen-sixty-four have decided on the prom king and queen."

"I see," Mister Brown says as he takes the microphone from Freddy. "By secret ballot I take it?" He tilts the microphone toward Freddy.

"Yessir. Everyone voted in secret. Shirley and I carefully counted the votes to make certain there was no cheating."

Mister Brown asks, "How did you make certain no one cheated?"

"Every piece of paper we handed out during the dance was numbered sequentially. No one couple could vote twice."

Mister Brown begins to ask another question. Before he can, a girl calls out, "Oh, come on now, Mister Brown. You are purposely keeping us in suspense. Let Freddy tell us who won!"

With a grin, Mister Brown says, "It's all yours, Freddy. Take it away!" Then he hands the microphone to Freddy.

Freddy's voice is loud and clear as he says boldly, "The Goodfellow High School graduating class of nineteen-sixty-four is proud to announce…" He looks at the promgoers.

"Somebody - please give me a drum roll."

The promgoers start to intone in unison loudly.

Da-da-da-da-da-da-da-da-da!

After a few moments, Freddy waves his hand. "Okay, that was terrific." He clears his throat. "Ahem. The king and queen of the Goodfellow High School graduating class of nineteen-sixty-four prom are." He pauses slightly, and then, pointing to the back of the hall, he shouts, "Mister Christopher James Peters and his lovely date, Stephanie JoAnne Mahoney!"

Steph and Christopher are sitting in the back of the hall just to the left of the doorway. They are planning to make a quick getaway right after the announcement of the prom's king and queen. Everyone is looking at them, clapping their hands, and cheering loudly. Steph and

Christopher stare at each other for a few moments. The expressions on both of their faces are ones of categorical surprise. Steph suddenly begins to giggle wildly.

"Christopher, can you believe it? They voted us the senior prom king and queen! Isn't that amazing?"

"Yes, it truly is," Christopher says. He manages to get to his feet, and then he takes Steph's hand in his. "All because of you, Steph. Because of you and your fearless, spirited heart." His face flushes. He quickly adds, "Besides, and I hope you do not mind me saying this. You are the prettiest girl in the entire place! So it comes as no surprise you are the queen. They only made me the king because I am with you."

Steph stands. Her face is beet red. She kisses Christopher on the cheek.

"Aw, thank you, Christopher. That is very sweet of you to say. But then, I cannot take an iota of credit. Your handsomeness would make it easy for any girl in your company to look pretty."

The applause is deafening as Steph and Christopher slowly make their way to the stage. Their fellow promgoers move to the side to allow them to pass. Steph is skillfully grasping Christopher's forearm with her right hand. Her left arm is around his waist. She knows that Christopher is very tired from standing so long and for dancing four songs. About halfway to the stage, he stumbles. But Steph's grip on his forearm is sure.

She mumbles, "I gotcha, Christopher."

He whispers, "Gosh, Steph, what would I do without you? I almost fell. Thank you."

"You will never fall, Christopher. You may stumble from time to time, but in my eyes, you will never fall. And you will never fail. No matter come what may."

*****

Part V: Graduation

It is Saturday, the day after the prom. The Peters' house is abuzz with frantic excitement. Everyone slept in because they were very tired from staying up until the wee hours of the morning. Because Christopher was exhausted after the prom, they did not go out for dinner. In spite of this, since everyone was hungry, to include Christopher and Steph, who had nothing but cake and punch at the prom, Jimmy ordered three large pizzas from Boche Club Pizzeria. Then the five of them played Scrabble until 2:00 am.

"Hurry up!" Marcia cries. "We do not want to be late for the graduation ceremony. We have less than fifty minutes to go!"

Fortunately, everyone is ready to go by 9:30 am. That includes Christopher smartly dressed in his graduation cap and gown. They arrive at Goodfellow High School twelve minutes later.

After the Pledge of Allegiance and a few remarks by the vice principal, the band plays *Pomp and Circumstance.* Handing out of diplomas begins shortly thereafter.

The school principal, Mister Frederick Carlson, is calling graduates up to the stage to receive their diplomas. The program Steph is holding in her hand lists the last names of graduates in alphabetical order. Christopher is graduate forty-three. It takes approximately twenty-seven minutes for the first forty-two graduates to receive their diplomas. Finally, after what seems like forever to Steph, it is Christopher's turn.

The principal says into the microphone, "Mister Christopher James Peters."

He glances out to the graduates that are sitting in the first five rows. His eyes fix on Christopher. He is sitting in the aisle seat in the third row of the graduates. Mister Carlson's brow furrows slightly, and then he hands Christopher's diploma to the school secretary, Miss Victoria Walters. He is about to announce the next graduate when Steph shouts at the top of her lungs. She is sitting with the Peters around ten or eleven rows behind the graduates.

"Sir! Please do not announce the next graduate! Mister Peters and I are coming. Hold on a few seconds if you please!"

Steph is sitting to Marcia's left. Nine other people are between her and the center aisle. She quickly stands, and then she scoots in front of those seated to her left. She is apologetic as she slides in front of them.

"Excuse me."

"I am sorry."

"Oh, I didn't mean to step on your foot."

"Thank you for standing so I can pass."

"Hello, Missus Flowers. It is nice to see you. Please give my best to Bobby."

"Oops, I apologize for stepping on your toe."

"Thank you, ma'am. I like your dress as well."

"Well hello, Jack. How's your mother feeling?"

"Thank you for standing. Whew. Finally!"

It takes Steph less than fifteen seconds to scoot in front of the nine people. As soon as she is in the center aisle, she shouts once more.

"I am sorry about the delay, sir, but it is only proper and fitting that Mister Peters receives his diploma on stage like everyone else. Please give me a few more seconds to fetch him."

Once Steph is standing beside him, Christopher says, "Goodness, Steph. What in the world are you doing?" He glances up at the principal who looks incredibly annoyed. He is unconsciously tapping his left foot as he stares down at Steph and Christopher.

"Shush. Just because you are disabled, and they do not have a handicap ramp to gain access to the stage, does not mean you cannot get your diploma like your fellow graduates." She takes him by the elbow.

"Please get to your feet. It is important to show everyone that, even though you are disabled, you are no different than everyone else."

Christopher says, "Naw. But thank you just the same, Steph." He looks up at the principal who now has his arms folded across his chest. "It will take too long to get up there."

Steph says in a scolding tone, "Too long? How about four years of a nearly 4.0 average, Christopher? Now that is long. A two-minute walk to the stage to receive your diploma like everyone else is nothing in comparison. Now get to your feet. Please!"

He slowly gets to his feet. Steph takes him firmly by his forearm. She places the hand of her other arm around his waist.

Christopher whispers, "Hey, wait a minute, Steph. Aren't we going to use my wheelchair?"

Steph says, "Nope. We are not. You are going to walk to the stage with your head held high. All we have to do is take one hundred or so steps to the stage, climb the five or six steps of the stairway, and then proceed a dozen or so steps across the stage. Besides, and I want you to listen closely to what I am about to say.

"You may need crutches for support as you walk, but someday others will seek your support and willingly walk in your footsteps. I promise you that will come true." She lightheartedly laughs as she looks up at the principal. "Now let's get going before I change my mind!"

As they advance toward the stage, Steph is conscious of many rustling noises to their right. She glances out at the audience. Her heart soars at what she sees. The men, women, and children in the audience - there must be a few hundred of them - are slowly getting to their feet. So are the graduates.

Christopher is looking down as he laboriously takes one tentative step after another. He does not seem to notice that everyone in the audience is standing.

Once they arrive at the foot of the stage staircase, Steph says, "Okay, here we are." She moves slightly to her left, so she is directly behind Christopher. She slips her hands beneath his armpits. "There are but six steps, six measly steps. You can do this."

"Okay, that is one," Steph whispers. "Number two will be a breeze. You got this."

Christopher whispers, "You have to be the kindest person in the whole wide world. I mean it." He adds with a chuckle, "And perhaps the craziest as well."

"Shush, Christopher. Save your strength and concentrate on what you are doing. Okay, that is step two. Once again use your hands to help lift your legs like before. That is the way to do it. Perfect! Okay, three down. Halfway there."

Finally, after a minute or so, Christopher has successfully negotiated the six stairs to the stage.

"See, Christopher? Just like I said last night. You may have stumbled a bit. But you did not fall. You did not fail. Now, let me move a bit to your right, so I can support you as you walk along the stage."

Christopher whispers, "Wow, Steph. I need to tell you. This is amazing." He begins to chuckle.

"What is so darned funny?" Steph whispers.

"This is the first time in four years of high school I have been on this stage." He glances out at the audience. "What a view. And will you look at that? Everyone is standing, even the graduates! Why are they standing? Do you know?"

"My dear friend, Christopher James Peters. Do you not know? They are standing as a tribute to you. They are paying tribute to your amazing display of courage despite your cerebral palsy. Indeed, they, to a man, woman, and child, like me, know you have what it takes to succeed." She gently places her left knee behind Christopher's leg.

"Now walk silly man, walk! Everyone is waiting for your big moment to take place! Especially me!"

As they near the center of the stage, the principal, who is now all smiles, takes Christopher's diploma from Miss Walters. Once Christopher is standing next to him, he hands the diploma to him. Christopher manages to grasp it with both of his hands. He awkwardly clutches it against his chest.

He says, "Thank you, sir. Thank you. What an honor!" Then he shakes the principal's hand.

Mister Carlson replies, "The pleasure and honor are all mine, son. What you achieved during the last four years, and what you accomplished here today, all of it tells me you will succeed beyond expectation in the future." He turns to face the audience.

"Ladies and gentlemen, esteemed graduates of the Goodfellow High School class of nineteen-sixty-four, I give you graduate number forty-three, Mister Christopher James Peters!"

What happens next makes Steph's heart leap for joy. The entire audience gives her dear friend Christopher, a disabled teenager with spastic cerebral palsy, a two-minute-long standing ovation!

*****

Part VI: The Bracelet

"That was the most moving part of the entire evening," Jimmy says. He removes his glasses and wipes the corners of his eyes with his handkerchief. He looks at Christopher.

"I have to tell you, son. My heart was thumping like crazy when Mister Carlson called your name. I was the proudest father in the audience." He looks at Marcia adding, "I know your mother was equally proud."

Marcia nods her head in agreement.

"You had done it, Christopher, notwithstanding the overwhelming odds against you given your cerebral palsy! You graduated from high school with a near-perfect average." He wipes his eyes.

"But then, when Mister Carlson handed your diploma to his secretary, well. I must tell you. My heart sunk deep into my chest. All of my joy disappeared if you know what I am saying."

He takes Steph's hand in his.

"At first I was shocked when Steph called out. I was like, 'What in the world is she doing?' Then it dawned on me. She was going to escort you to the stage so that you could get your diploma! I think what she said will remain in my memory, in my heart forever.'"

He smiles at Steph adding, "Correct me if I am not quoting you verbatim. You had yelled at the top of your lungs, 'Sir! Please do not announce the next graduate! Mister Peters and I are coming, sir. Hold on a few seconds if you please!'"

Tears are now falling freely from Jimmy's eyes. He ignores them.

"But then, when everyone stood up as the two of you approached the stage, well, I mean to tell you Steph, Christopher. I lost it. I was the happiest father on the planet."

Marcia says, "Yes, my heart soared as well. And then, when the principal announced that Christopher was the 1964 graduating class' forty-third graduate, I could not believe my ears. It was like a dream come true." With a chuckle, she adds, "I could not see what was happening on the stage. My eyes were too blurry with tears."

She takes Steph's other hand in hers and squeezes it.

"Thank you, Steph. Thank you. You are the sweetest, most spirited, fearless teenager, I have ever met. I am very proud to call you my daughter, the daughter I never had but who I always wished for in my dreams. I am going to miss you when you leave. I swear to you."

Steph is all smiles.

"Thank you both. What I said and what I did was totally on impulse. I originally had thought that Mister Carlson would ask Christopher to slide into his wheelchair and proceed to the foot of the stage. I thought he would give him his diploma that way. Or, more appropriately, he would leave the stage and go to Christopher.

"When he handed Christopher's diploma back to his secretary I was, for lack of a better word, shell-shocked. I just knew I had to do something - anything for Christopher to enjoy the special moment like his classmates!" She looks at Christopher.

"To be honest with you, there was no way I was going to allow you to remain in your seat as an onlooker. I wanted you to have your well-earned diploma handed to you personally by the school's principal in front of everyone. Because you deserved nothing less."

Steph goes on to say, "As for me, I thought the standing ovation was the coolest part. I mean, I had noticed earlier everyone had stood up as Christopher and I walked to the stage. But a standing ovation? Now that was something. The scene of all those smiling, appreciative faces, and the rhythmic clapping for nearly two minutes will remain etched in my memory forever."

She takes Christopher's hand in hers.

"What you accomplished tonight was nothing short of amazing. I am very proud of you. Your grit showed the world that someone with spastic cerebral palsy, or any other debilitating disability or handicap, can do anything if he puts his mind to it."

Christopher says, "I have to admit, it was enormously difficult to navigate those six stairs to the stage. I was terrified I would trip and embarrass you. But we did it thanks to you." He beams a warm smile.

"Yes, I owe it all to you, Steph. I honestly do." With a frown, he adds, "I have something to confess to you. I have been one stubborn disabled person all these years. I have had my good days, and I have had many more bad days. However, what you have done for me over the past two weeks has boosted my self-esteem to new heights. Thanks to you, my self-confidence has soared. Thank you, Steph."

He looks at his mother. Steph cannot help but notice that he is smiling a silly grin.

"Momma, if you please."

Marcia reaches into her purse. She hands a small box to Steph. It is wrapped in pink tissue paper.

Steph says to Christopher, "What is this?"

"It is a little something I asked Momma to buy for you with my allowance. Go ahead and open it."

Steph's hands are trembling as she removes the tissue wrapper. Even though she is smiling outwardly, her heart is breaking, and her thoughts are troubled.

Another gift from another friend. Christopher's gift is wonderful and very thoughtful, but then again it will only disappear into nothing more than a memory like Adalard and Patsy's gifts. Nevertheless, as the saying goes, it is the thought that counts.

"Oh, my goodness! This charm bracelet is delightfully beautiful. And it's silver - my favorite. I love it! And oh, these three charms are adorable. A charm of two intertwined hearts, a horse, and will you look at this? A miniature wheelchair!"

She kisses Christopher on his cheek, and then she unclasps the bracelet and slips it onto her wrist.

"Thank you, Christopher. Thank you very much! This lovely gift is one of the niftiest gifts I have ever received in my entire life."

"You are welcome," Christopher says. "I hope that every time you put it on, you will remember me and our friendship." He points to the bracelet.

"The two intertwined hearts represent your love and compassion. Not only do they mirror your display of love and compassion for me," he glances at his mother, his father, and then at Eddie, "but to my entire family. And yes, Steph, your love and compassion for Hannah, Patsy, Joseph, and Adalard as well.

"The horse charm signifies your constant, daring spirit as you journey through time along with your trusted steed by the same name, Spirit.

"And the wheelchair," he laughs, "signifies how your amazing gift of love, your spirit, and your compassion combine to reflect your fearless soul. How you, in turn, have made my soul fearless as well. Despite my disability."

Steph says, "Thank you, Christopher. Thank you very much, especially for mentioning the four children who have influenced my life more than I could ever imagine. And honestly, there is no way I could ever forget the four of you as well. These past two weeks have been fourteen of the most pleasurable days of my life. I thank each one of you from the bottom of my heart for your kindness, for your love, and for your friendship. When I set off to my next assignment, if there is to be one, I know that my heart will be breaking."

She looks at Jimmy adding with a grin, "And car-hopping at Jimmy's Drive-in has been like a dream come true. I only hope I can land a similar job when I return to my other life."

Eddie suddenly cries out, "Mushy-mushy. Ugh! But I guess it is good for everyone to get it off his chest. So, Steph, are you really leaving us? If so, when? And why? Why do you have to go?"

Steph replies, "Don't tell me you are anxious to see me go, Eddie. I still haven't had a chance to take a spin on your bike." She notices that Eddie's eyes are welling up with tears.

"Naw, it is okay if you take a spin on my bike. Just do not wreck it, okay? And no, I am not anxious to see you go." He looks at Christopher, and then he glances over at his mother and father.

"In fact, I wish you could stay a bit longer. It is slick having a big sister around the house. You seem to come to my rescue every time I get in trouble." He looks at his mother adding, "Which seems to be just about every day lately."

Marcia says in a soft, understanding tone, "Well, if you would do your chores and clean up your room when I ask, maybe I would not have to ground you as much as I do. Plus, your slang, trying to be hip talk drives me crazy. I hope you know that. I am very pleased you are doing away with that."

Eddie says, "Yeah, you are correct. I have been a bum lately. I am sorry. I will try to talk more civil. I promise."

Steph suddenly says, "Please excuse me for a few moments. I have to use the restroom." As she pushes away from the table and stands, she is surprised that Jimmy, Christopher, and Eddie also stand.

"You three are the perfect gentlemen," Steph says with a giggle. She looks at Marcia adding in a joking tone, "If I am not mistaken, I do believe there is hope for your three men despite the odds. I won't be long."

After walking a few steps, she turns around.

"And oh, please do not order dessert until I get back. I want to try a piece of that delicious-looking cheesecake. I'll be right back."

A few minutes later Steph is standing in front of the restroom mirror. She is combing her hair. She is softly singing lyrics to the latest Beatles hit melody *She Loves You.*

Oo, she loves you, yeah, yeah, yeah.
She loves you, yeah, yeah, yeah.
With a love like that.
You know you should be glad.

Suddenly, from out of nowhere, a grayish-white mist begins to form on the mirror. She leans forward to draw a smiley face in the mist. Surprisingly, her smiley face does not appear. Thinking that steam may be escaping from a pipe somewhere behind her in the restroom, she turns around.

Hmm, strange. There is nothing here. Must have been my imagination. Too much excitement these past two days.

She turns around to comb her hair once more. When she looks in the mirror, she notices that the strange mist has disappeared. She squints her eyes. Something is materializing behind her reflection in the mirror. She begins to tremble. Her legs feel weak. Her throat is dry as if she has just inhaled a blast of hot desert air.

Oh no. I would recognize that building anywhere!

She sets her brush on the sink counter. Because she is beginning to shudder, she places her hands on the countertop to keep from falling. She watches with nervousness as the restroom slowly transforms into a frightening panorama. What she sees next immediately overwhelms her sense of normalcy.

It's the Orphanage.

CHAPTER NINE

SAINT MARY'S HOME

"The cogs of a clock are timeless turnings never ceasing."
- Steph, February 13, 1904

Part I: Missus McAllister

Steph is standing in a spacious courtyard. Unlike the other occasions when she traveled through time and space, this time she did not fall asleep. The last thing she remembers is staring into the mirror as the bathroom slowly disappeared from view, while, at the same time, the orphanage gradually began to appear.

She looks down with disbelief at what she is wearing.

Gone are her flashy 1960s attire and the hipster go-go boots that she had come to like during her time with the Peters. In their place are drab-looking, old-fashioned garments that resemble something a grandmother would wear way back when.

Her frilly dress is a dowdy, deep brown. It is heavily pleated and hangs at least six inches below her knees. She lifts the hem of her dress up a bit. Black, tightly-woven, woolen stockings are completely covering her legs. The thick stockings are already beginning to itch. She can feel the sweat oozing from her pores like the apertures of a slowly squeezed sponge. Her legs, rear end, and even her feet feel cold and clammy. The high-top black leather shoes she is wearing have seemingly endless eyelets. The eyelets are laced halfway up her shins. She also is wearing white cotton gloves. The gloves seem wholly out of place given her unadorned, drab-looking dress and hideous-looking, old-fashioned shoes.

If it weren't that I am standing outside in full view of the world, I would strip off these unbearably hot stockings and ridiculous shoes in a flash! Then I would go bare-footed.

She quickly tugs at the cuff of the glove on her right hand. Her eyes immediately begin to mist.

Christopher's gift is gone! No surprise there! It happened just as I predicted. Just like the two other times when Jordyn moved me through time and space.

She notices her stretched out shadow creeping in front of her on the sidewalk. Her heart seems to skip a beat when she sees in her shadow something shockingly outrageous on the top of her head.

What in the world is that monstrosity? My goodness, no! It is a dagburned hat!

She unties the wide, silky ribbon from around her neck that is holding the hat in place. She slips the hat from her head to examine it. Then she begins to rock from side to side with loud laughter.

The hat is a large, dull-yellow, oversized collection of plums of blue feathers, multi-colored bows, and three fake flowers. The king-size flowers resemble roses. She does not know it, but the hat she is wearing is the rage of fashionable women in the early 1900s.

Oh, my goodness, this is ridiculous! I cannot wear this. Just look at those ugly, bright red flowers, bunches of bows, and all those stupid-looking feathers. I will be the laughing stock of everyone who sees me in it!

She is tempted to toss the outlandish hat onto the ground. After a moment's reflection, she thinks better of it. She places the hat on her head and fastens the ribbon around her neck.

I am wearing this atrocious stuff for a purpose. But my God, I look like something from a horror movie!

Now that she is no longer focusing on her ludicrous attire and bizarre hat, she looks around at her surroundings. From her recurring dreams back home she vaguely recognizes most of what she sees. The building before her does not look like the same looming, frightfully imposing limestone building of her dreams. Nevertheless, she knows that it is. It has the same profile, and it is seven stories tall. But it looks newer, less blemished, and much better maintained.

The windows on the three upper floors do not have the prison-like corroded bars Steph envisioned in her dreams. And the first four windows are clean, crystal clear. All the windows in the seven stories are cheerily reflecting the late afternoon sunrays and countryside behind her.

The courtyard is neat and clean. Flowers are growing in wooden flowerpots on either side of the entrance of the building. And, unlike in Steph's dreams, the sidewalk is not crumbly and infested with thorny weeds. Clumps of manicured, verdant grass line both of its sides. Also missing is the ten-foot-high fence topped with inward-facing barbs.

She notices a painted wooden sign to the left of the building's entranceway.

SAINT MARY'S HOME
VISITING HOURS NOON TO EIGHT
CLOSED WEEKENDS
RING BELL ONCE FOR ASSISTANCE

Steph quickly walks on the sidewalk toward the entrance. She presses the doorbell with her thumb. From somewhere off in the distance she can hear the loud echoing of a ringing bell. The bell's dreadfully shocking, ten-seconds-long screech sounds like an angry fire alarm one hears during fire drills at school. She sighs with relief once the bell stops ringing.

Goodness, that was super loud. I pity the person sitting beneath the alarm. I am glad I did not push the doorbell button more than once. I can only imagine how it would have sounded if I had!

She hears the creak of a window opening on the second floor. She backs away a few steps from the entrance and looks up. A disgusted voice speaks through the open window. Steph cannot make out if the owner of the voice is a male or female.

"Yeah, what do ye want?"

Steph says politely, "Good afternoon, sir or ma'am. I would like to visit someone."

"Sir or ma'am?" The voice blurts out in a hoarse squawk.

Then whoever it is that is speaking suffers a ten-second coughing fit. The cough is full of throat-rattling, disgusting-sounding phlegm traveling up and down within the person's irritated throat.

"I ain't a man. I have a deep voice, that be all. Ye got a problem with that, Missy?"

That the woman is calling her Missy gives Steph the creeps. The last person who called her Missy was Judas.

And most likely Judas is dead.

Steph replies in an apologetic tone, "No, ma'am, I do not have a problem with that. I am dreadfully sorry. Please excuse me. I did not imply any disrespect. I am very tired from traveling."

The woman with the hoarse voice appears at the window. Steph wants to laugh when she sees her, but she thinks better of it. The woman looks like she has just awakened from a year's long hibernation. Her gray-streaked, thinning black hair is up in huge curlers. The heavy bags under her eyes make her look like a washed-out, dripping wet raccoon. She is wearing gaudy, bright red lipstick. Steph can tell by her wrinkled, leathery skin that she is a smoker.

Probably a chain smoker at that, Steph muses. If the woman is a chain smoker that would explain her deep, husky voice.

And the disgusting smoker's phlegm traveling up and down within her luckless throat!

The woman growls, "Can't ye read the darn sign, Missy? We be closed for visitors on weekends."

Steph glances at the sign. She knows that she had disappeared from the restaurant ladies room on a Saturday evening. Unless she had slept, which she doubts, it still should be Saturday - Saturday evening!

But then, how to explain my arriving here earlier in the day while the sun is still shining? By the shape of my shadow cast on the sidewalk, it is late afternoon. Perhaps four or five o'clock. However, it could be Sunday. Or any other day for that matter. There is no way I can know for certain. But the woman did say this is a weekend. Strange.

The cogs of a clock are timeless turnings never ceasing.

She looks up at the woman.

"Oh, I am sorry, ma'am. I just arrived a few minutes ago, and I had no idea the orphanage closes on weekends."

"Well, we be closed. Goodbye."

The window slams shut offensively.

Steph is shocked by the woman's rudeness.

"Now wait a minute here, ma'am," she yells.

"I have traveled far and wide to be here today. And I have no place to stay either. At least not yet. Allow me the satisfaction of visiting if only for a spell. I promise I will not be a bother. Please, I beg of you."

The window creaks open once more.

"Who do ye want to visit? Orphans come and go and in and out like rag'n storms on a summer night. Maybe who ye want to see be no longer here. Ever think of dat? Who be it anyway?"

"A girl named Jordyn."

"Jordyn who?"

"I am sorry, ma'am. I do not know Jordyn's last name. She is a deaf child. That is all that I know."

"Ye want to visit someone, and ye ain't got her last name?" the woman cackles. "Dat's pretty stupid if ye ask me. Besides, only one deaf girl here, and her name ain't Jordyn. Her name be Jennifer, Jennifer Steward or something like that."

The window slams shut a second time. Steph notices the woman continues to stare down at her. She considers her next move.

No wonder Jordyn conveyed in her mind that Roger Clyde abuses her. This woman is the epitome of nastiness. And those hideous screams of this god-awful place I imagined in my dreams seem to confirm it. If this woman's sorry, nasty attitude is any indication of what the orphans must endure; this orphanage is worse than the *Little Shop of Horrors!* True, I have never seen the movie. But comparing this woman, and what I know of the orphanage, to something horrible seems appropriate enough!

She rings the doorbell once more. This time she roughly smashes it with her thumb three times. The doorbell alarm screams from off in the distance three times longer than before. Steph takes satisfaction knowing she undoubtedly is annoying the woman.

The window opens with a fuming mad, forceful *swish-slam!*

"What in tarnation be yer problem, Missy?" The woman screams. A lit cigarette is now dangling from the left side of her scowling lips.

"I told ye, we be closed on weekends. Can't ye hear how loud the blasted doorbell alarm be? Ye pressed it long enough, and three times in

216

fact, 'nuff noise to wake up the dead brats, and they be buried in the cemetery two hundred yards behind the dagburned building!"

She glowers at Steph for at least thirty seconds.

She probably expects me to turn away. But I'm not going anywhere. She won't bully me! Besides, I have no clue where I am or what I am supposed to do!

"I told you, there be no girl named Jordyn here. Period. Now go away. Ye are bothering me. I am listening to a romance story on the radio. It be a goody, too. Goodbye."

"Perhaps I am mistaken with her first name," Steph cries out forcefully. Her tone is apologetic, although she is getting more riled up with this woman's foul attitude with each passing second.

"I have never met her. I just sort of know her. Please do not ask me how. But trust me if you please. We are dear friends. Besides, it is hot out here in the sun, and I am very thirsty."

The woman stares at Steph for the longest time. Steph is afraid she is going to close the window and leave her standing outside.

Goodness, what will I do if she does not let me inside? Not only do I not have any money for transportation or to eat, but I don't even have a handbag! Only these ridiculous clothes and this absurd-looking hat! Dang, I do not even know what day it is, no less the month and year!

"What's yer name, Missy?"

"My name is Steph."

"You gotta last name, Missy Steph?"

"Yes, ma'am." Steph lies, "It is Johnston. Stephanie Johnston."

"Okay, Miss Stephanie Johnston. My name is McAllister, Missus McAllister to you. Glad to meet yer. My husband, Doctor Reginald McAllister runs this dump. Tell ye what I will do for yer. I will see if I can find Jennifer and ask her if she knows ye. My radio program be over anyhow." She cackles with a less than sincere tone, "It may take me a bit. The kid be always up to some nasty trouble, hiding from us. She be a sneaky Pete she be, always getting hurt and stuff. She got hurt a few weeks ago. Banged up her forehead pretty good too. Be right back."

She sneers at Steph, and then she slowly closes the window.

Always getting hurt, Steph muses. That sounds like Jordyn. But whenever she gets hurt, it always seems to be Roger Clyde's fault.

Roger Clyde Brewster!

She suddenly yells, "Also, ma'am. I am sorry to bother you." She pretends the most adorable smile. "I did not want to ring the doorbell a third time. It is very loud as you say. I clearly can hear it from where I am standing. I am also here to see Roger Clyde, Roger Clyde Brewster."

Missus McAllister slams the window open once more. Steph knows she could be wrong, but the expression on the nasty woman's face seems to have changed. Dramatically. What was a disgusted look a few seconds ago is now one of outright curiosity. Maybe even satisfaction.

"Roger Clyde? Ye know Roger Clyde? Ain't no one been here to see him for Lord knows how long. Not since his drunken father came to visit three years ago. Never came back he did. Ye sure yer know him? He be a pretty rotten kid given his mis'bavior. Deserves a visitor occasionally nonetheless."

"Yes, ma'am. In a way, I know him quite well." Steph laughs adding, "I think he will love to see me."

"Hmm, Roger Clyde ain't ne'er mentioned knowing a Miss Johnston. Do not think it be on his record either. Sort of keeps to himself be he a youngster. Ye two kinfolk or some'thin? Maybe a rich aunt or some'thin? Dressed like that ye be made of money I bet. We sure could use a donation. We be almost broke!

"Anyhow, ye ain't got the same last name, so I know ye ain't his older sister. Then again, some orphans are adopted. 'Fact, most be 'ventually."

A rich aunt, an older sister? Steph thinks to herself. She glances down at her outrageous-looking dress and her stupid-looking mid-calf shoes. Do I look that old in this ridiculous outfit, old enough to be a teenager's older anything? Hopefully not.

She replies to the woman's questions with a tone of complete innocence. "No, ma'am, just a friend, an acquaintance."

"Well, we do have a Roger Clyde. Cute little fella as yer know."

Steph ponders. Cute little fella? Is this the same Roger Clyde Brewster? What in the world is going on here?

Missus McAllister rudely tosses her burning cigarette out the window. It lands in the grass next to Steph's foot.

Cigarette smoke has the uncanny ability to waft toward nonsmokers. If you are a non-smoker, you probably know this. The woman's smoldering cigarette lying in the recently mowed grass is no exception to this phenomenon.

The horrid thing's whitish-grey, nasty-smelling smoke begins to greet Steph's nostrils. She has the sudden urge to cough or, at a minimum, to get rid of the wafting smoke from her face with a wave of her hand. But she fights the temptation. She does not want to make the woman angrier than she already is.

Missus McAllister coughs a few more times as she continues to stare at Steph. Then her head tersely rears back as if someone has smacked her in the jaw. She is trying to clear the phlegm out of her throat. It sounds to Steph as if she is gargling with a cupful of horrible-tasting, dribble mouthwash. The disgusting sound causes her skin to crawl.

If the ghastly sound the woman is making is not bad enough, her head suddenly lurches forward. Then she spits a glob of yellow mush out the window with a nauseating *pthu!* The glob of mush smashes onto the sidewalk a few inches next to Steph's foot with a revolting *splat!*

Steph cannot help herself as she glances at the nasty glob of mush that is sitting next to the smoldering cigarette. Her stomach lurches as if it wants to spew out the last meal she had with the Peters.

Missus McAllister says, "Oops, sorry, Miss Johnston. Was aiming for the other way. Guess the wind caught it. Ye didn't get any on yer, did ye?"

Steph replies with a pretend smile, "No, ma'am. Sure didn't." She wants to shout, "But I felt the gross mist as it smacked me in the face on its way to the grass!"

"Dat's good. I would not want to soil yer pretty dress, yer being rich and all. Okay then, I should not do it, since it is a weekend and all and we be closed for visitors. But you look like a very nice girl all dressed pretty and proper like ye be heading off to church or some'thin.

Rich too. We sure could use money I tell yer. Things be rough with all these brats to feed. Wish half of dem be dead I do."

She howls with a long, drawn-out snigger. Her snigger is sprinkled with another, less-dramatic coughing fit. The woman's suggesting laugher and ghastly smoker's cough unnerves Steph yet again. Nonetheless, she continues to smile up at her.

"Roger be happy to see yer, pretty made-up and all. Like an older sister or some'thin. Rich too. Hold on a sec. I will be right down to let yer in." She slams the window down. Then she reopens the window. Without bothering to look down at Steph, she yells from the other side of the open window.

"And fix yer bonnet why don't ye. Ye got it on backward. The flowers suppos'd to be in the front, not the back."

*****

Part II: Roger Clyde Brewster

When Missus McAllister finally opens the door, another cigarette is dangling from her lips. Its nasty, putrid smoke immediately wafts toward Steph's nostrils. She stifles a sneeze.

Missus McAllister eyes Steph up and down with a look that is anything but pleasant.

"Where be yer stuff?"

Steph replies questionably, "Stuff? What do you mean, ma'am?"

"Yer stuff. Ye said yer just arrived. Don't ye have a suitcase or some'thin? And why ain't ye got a purse? Ye one of those Califor'a girls are ye? They be weird, fashion-wise. Read it in *Cosmopolitan* magazine. Yer Merry Window sort of confirms it."

"My what? Steph asks skeptically.

"Yer Merry Window. Yer hat, yer bonnet. The only one on yer head, Missy. Gee, what's wrong with ye, girl?" She reaches with both hands to adjust Steph's hat. Smoke from the cigarette drifts into Steph's right eye stinging it.

"Don't ye know what it is called? I read in *Cosmopolitan* yer hat is called the Merry Window hat. It became popular last year. Some hats, with stuffed dead birds, be called bird nests. But I do not like those.

Kill'n birds just to put them on hats be cruel to me. So where ye from, Steph?"

Steph crosses the fingers of her left hand behind her back.

"You are very observant, Missus McAllister. And you are correct. I am from California. As far as my suitcase goes, well, I think it may have missed the train."

Missus McAllister eyes Steph suspiciously.

"Train? What ye talking 'bout? We ain't got no train service here. Only got bus service, and it ain't too good at dat. Always late it be. Sorry service."

"Oh, that is what we call it in California," Steph quickly says. She pretends to grin. She still has her fingers crossed behind her back.

"Yes, a bus-train. Exactly."

"So, they lost yer luggage when ye transferred busses."

Steph nods her head.

"Poor child. Come on inside. I will fix yer some'thin to eat. Ye said ye be thirsty too. Got some lemonade. It not be very cold, 'cause there be no ice delivery on weekends. But it be refreshing. Made it myself this morning. Freshly squeezed."

As Steph enters the spacious anteroom of the orphanage, she feels as if she is going to faint. The inside of the orphanage looks frighteningly like what she envisioned in her dreams. Unquestionably, the inside is not as rundown as she dreamt it, but in a dozen or so years it will be the same. She is sure of it.

"Don't ye mind the mess," Missus McAllister says. "Not too many people donating like they did years ago. We be lucky to have enough funds to keep the stupid brats fed."

A handsome boy maybe four or five years old hobbles down the stairwell.

"You's called me, did you's, Missus McAllister?"

Steph recoils as soon as she hears the youngster's voice. She instantly knows the little boy is a younger version of Roger Clyde Brewster.

"I's sure did, Roger. This nice young lady is here to visit with ye. Her name is Stephanie, Stephanie Johnston. Says she knows ye." She looks at Steph adding, "If yer excuse me for a minute. I have a pot of stew on the stove for the brats." She departs leaving Steph and Roger Clyde by themselves.

Steph is beside herself. In each of her dreams where she envisions Roger Clyde, he is a few years older than Jordyn. She always thought Roger Clyde was at least fifteen or sixteen years of age.

If what I am seeing is true, and this truly is Roger Clyde, Jordyn would be - what? Right now Jordyn would be three years old at the most! That's because this kid standing in front of me is no more than five or six years old! There is no way a three-year-old Jordyn could have scrubbed floors! What I am seeing cannot be happening!

She wants to dash through the open door, run through the courtyard as fast as her legs will carry her, and escape this latest nightmare. But, she does not. For she knows Jordyn has sent her here for a purpose.

My raison d'être.

She crouches down onto her knees. Then she opens her arms out wide gesturing for Roger Clyde to come to her, to be hugged.

He eyes her suspiciously as he slowly walks toward her. Steph notices he has a serious limp. It is as if one leg is shorter than the other.

Then again perhaps he has been abused! And my God - those bruises on his forearms. And the one beneath his right eye! This child is physically abused!

She immediately notices that Roger Clyde has a serious tic which causes his left eye to blink rapidly. Plus his head occasionally jerks back and forth.

Oh my God! I cannot believe my eyes! Not only do I think Roger Clyde Brewster is savagely abused, but I also think he has Tourette Syndrome! This poor child.

Roger says, "Do I know you's?"

Steph notices he also has a distinctive lisp when he talks.

He suddenly grunts as he tries to clear his throat. Now he is trembling.

Steph replies lightheartedly, in the sincerest tone of voice, "Oh, Roger Clyde, you probably do not remember me." She gestures with her hands as she tells another white lie.

"Last time I saw you, you were about this tall. Boy how you have grown! You are very handsome and very strong-looking too!"

Roger Clyde says, "If I be that tall then that would make me's like I was a baby or something last time you's saw me."

"Yes, you are correct," Steph lies. "So tell me, Roger Clyde Brewster, how old are you now?"

"Five, five and one-half going on six in August."

He reluctantly allows Steph to embrace him. As they embrace, Steph notices that his trembling has stopped. After a few moments, she gently releases him from her embrace. She stands. As she looks down at him, he abruptly looks away. And then he lets out the loudest scream imaginable. He is unaware that he has screamed.

Yes, he definitely has Tourette Syndrome. And now I know why I am here.

Jordyn wants me to see for myself why Roger Clyde turned out the way that he did. Why he became a bully and the leader of the Trio. Because she is deaf, she could not tell me via telepathy about Roger Clyde's actual voice intonations. However, she must have known all along that something was wrong with him, that he had a disability, that he was, and still is, horribly abused.

Tears begin to well up in her eyes as she addresses Jordyn in her mind.

Jordyn, all this time I have been mistaken, terribly mistaken. None of what I dreamed, what I thought, what I did - none of it had anything to do with your predicament as a bullied, deaf orphan. On the contrary. All of what I experienced, what I am still experiencing at this very moment, has been about everyone else. None of it has been about you. How sad it is for me to realize this at last. Yet how wonderful to bear witness to your amazing compassion and endearing love for others!

So now I know, Jordyn. I know why you have brought me back to this time and place. While it makes me somewhat sad to learn the truth, I am glad you brought me here. I respect you very much. And I love you with all my heart and soul.

Steph notices Missus McAllister has returned.

"Okay, Roger. Go ahead and see if 'ya can locate Jennifer. She be hiding, trying to get out of work."

"Aw, do I have to?" Roger says. He has a tormented look on his face.

"I do not like her. She is mean to me. She is worse than the Trio."

Steph is stunned by Roger Clyde's reference of the Trio. She asks in a soft tone, almost in a whisper, "Roger Clyde, is Jennifer mean to you? What does she do to you? And what is the Trio?"

"She is always kicking me and stuff. Sometimes she hits me with her fist." He points to the bruise beneath his eye. "She is a bully she is."

His head suddenly jerks back and forth.

"The Trio are bullies. Jennifer is the boss of the Trio."

Missus McAllister says in a stern voice, "Now, that be 'nuff of those nasty, evil lies, Roger Clyde. Git yer lying behind out of here. Scoot up them stairs and find Jennifer. Or do I have to use the belt?" She eyes Roger sternly.

Steph notices she has clenched her hands into fists.

"Like last night? Yer do remember don't ye? Yer must. Yer screamed to high h'ven!"

Roger Clyde's eyes are now wide-open. The expression on his face is like he has seen a ghost. He begins to tremble uncontrollably once more. His eyes well up with tears as he backs away slowly. Then he abruptly turns around and stumbles up the stairwell.

Steph asks Missus McAllister, "How old is Jennifer?"

"I honestly have no clue. Maybe she be sixteen or so. She should be leaving soon. Kids her age don't fit in too good once they be adults." As an afterthought, she says, "And don't 'ya go believing Roger Clyde when he talks about bullies. There be no bullies here."

I am certain this woman is lying through her teeth! It is obvious someone is bullying Roger Clyde. He even said that someone was bullying him. That is why the much older Roger Clyde turned into a bully, the supreme bully, the eventual leader of the Trio! Because he was bullied as a little boy!

Missus McAllister grins the evilest smile Steph has ever seen.

"Don't yer go thinking 'bout what Roger Clyde said. He be a liar he be. Worst of his kind. Deserves a good whip'n from time to time."

She eyes a thick, leather belt lying on the table. "Yep, dey all do. A whip'n be good for der soul."

Steph shakes her head vigorously. She begins to rub her temples with her fingertips. She notices beads of sweat are covering her forehead. Her entire body feels hot and sticky, principally her legs. She wishes she could rip off the woolen stockings. While she believes she has not yet finished her assignment here, the feelings she has right now are telling her Jordyn is up to something.

She says in a somber tone, "Missus McAllister, I am very sorry, but I do not know what to think. Can I please have that lemonade now?" She fans her face with her open hand. "I feel like I am going to pass out."

Missus McAllister leads her into the kitchen. Steph immediately notices a calendar on the wall. She walks over to look at it.

Today is Saturday, February 13, 1904.

CHAPTER TEN

HOME AT LAST

"Every day is a journey, and the journey is home."
- Matsuo Basho

Part I: On the Porch

When Steph wakes up, she is sitting on the floor in the far left-hand corner of her front porch. It is the exact spot she was sitting at when she began her journey.

She knows for certain she is home when she sees the school crossing sign in front of her house. She has a watch on her wrist. She sighs with relief. It is the same watch she had on the morning she disappeared.

Her watch reads 4:27.

It must be 4:27 in the morning since it is still dark out here.

She glances to her left.

What are those? Oh, they're only the blinking lights on the school zone warning sign. But wait a minute here. Something weird is going on!

She stands to look across her front yard at the elementary school across the street.

There are no cars in the school parking lot. So why are the lights of the school zone warning sign blinking?

Unexpectedly, she senses familiar thoughts in her mind.

It's Jordyn!

"The note, Steph! You need to get into the house quietly and get the note you left on the kitchen table for your parents."

"The note? Goodness. Is it still there? Didn't they read it? And after all this time?"

"No. Your parents did not read it. Now get inside and get the note before it is too late. Crumple it up and stick it in your pocket. It is important no one sees it."

Steph stands, and then she quietly walks across the porch to the front door. She groans.

Darn! The door is locked. No surprise considering the time of day. And I do not have a key.

She suddenly hears the unmistakable click of the latch as the door is unlocked. Thinking someone unlocked the door from inside she quickly steps away from the door and presses her back along the wall.

"I unlocked it, Steph. Get inside. Get the note. Then return to the porch. Please hurry!"

Steph quietly walks to the kitchen. She spots the note on the table. She crumples the note into a ball and squashes it into her pocket just as Jordyn had told her. She returns to the porch. Once she is back on the porch, she leans over the railing.

"What now?"

Jordyn replies in her mind.

"Over here. On the other side of the school fence across the street. Can you see me? I'm sitting in the extreme left-hand corner of the fence as you are facing me."

Steph notices a shadow of what looks like a person on the other side of the fence. A hand of the shadow is waving. She waves back. Then she whispers excitedly.

"I can see you! Is it really you, Jordyn?"

"Yes, Steph, it is me. In the flesh. Well, sort of anyway."

"Can I go to you? Can you come to me?"

"No, Steph. Stay where you are. It is safer for you if you remain on the porch. Please sit back down in the corner where you woke up a few minutes ago. We need to talk before everyone in your house wakes up."

Steph turns, and then she sits back down on the floor in the corner of the porch. She stretches her legs before her. It is then she notices that the makeshift knapsack is beside her. She opens it.

What is this? Nothing is missing! But - but! I ate out of it! I changed my clothes! What is going on?

Jordyn's words in her mind suddenly interrupt her thoughts.

"Hello? Hello, Steph. Remember me? I am over here."

"Aw, sorry Jordyn. I got sidetracked. Hey! When I sit here in the corner of the porch, I can no longer see you. Is it okay if I stand up?"

Jordyn's thoughts say, "After all this time together and now you want to see me rather than communicate with me in our minds? Goodness, Steph. You are something else."

Steph hears a faint giggle from across the street.

"No, Steph. I would rather you remain where you are. Out of sight."

Steph hears the giggles once more.

"Okay, Steph. I bet you have a ton of questions. Fire away. But make sure your questions are in your thoughts. Please do not ask them aloud, even in a whisper. We do not want to wake up your parents."

"Well, I do have a few questions. Here comes my first question.

"Why weren't you at the orphanage? I was very sad I did not get to see you. True, I think I met Roger Clyde. And I am fairly certain the poor boy had Tourette Syndrome, and that he probably was bullied if not worse by Missus McAllister. Perhaps others as well. The orphanage, while not in a brutal state of decline like I imagined it earlier in my dreams, was well on its way to ruin. But you were nowhere to be seen. Why weren't you at the orphanage, Jordyn?"

"There is a simple explanation for that. I was only three-years-old at the time. I was still with my parents. I did not enter the orphanage until a year after your visit. My parents died in a car accident. It was only after their death that I entered the orphanage. My grandmother could not take care of me. Next question."

"I am very sorry to know your parents died, Jordyn. Please accept my sincerest condolences."

Jordyn replies, "Thank you. I appreciate it. It was a very long time ago. Time heals wounds. Please ask me your next question."

Steph's thoughts inquire, "Please tell me more about Adalard. What happened to him? Also, can you tell me about Hannah, Patsy, Joseph, and Christopher? In spite of everything that happened for real, or I imagined that happened in a dream, my purpose was to assist those five children. Am I correct in my assumption? That I had a purpose?"

"Yes, you are one hundred percent correct," Jordyn's thoughts convey. "Since he was your first assignment it is only natural that I start with Adalard."

*****

Part II: Adalard

"As you know, Adalard was a very industrious, strong-willed lad. He had to be to survive the repeated bombing of Cologne by Allied bombers. He could not escape the bombs, so he hid away beneath the rubble. He prayed a lot, Steph. He knew that the rubble could cave in on him at any time. All the same, as you know, he miraculously survived. Virtually without a scratch except for his broken arm.

"Since you saved him from certain death by the Jew-hating Nazis soldiers inside the Cologne Cathedral, you gave him another chance to live. Before he met you, he was very discouraged. He wanted to die. He even thought about standing in the middle of Cologne square during the next bombing.

"Thank the heavens he was encouraged by your kindness and your genuine display of love and compassion. Over the course of the next six months, after you had departed, Adalard avoided German troops. It was extremely difficult, but he did it. He slept during the day and traveled at night. He stole food from houses, and he killed, cooked, and ate rodents. Even bugs. Sometimes weeds like dandelions.

"He crossed the border into Luxemburg. It was there that he found refuge in a safe house with a wonderful, caring family. They too were Jews but somehow managed to escape persecution. Thanks to the family's hospitality and having access to relatively decent, nourishing food, Adalard became stronger. And bolder.

"He set off once more on a southwesterly path toward France. A few months later, after walking along trails only at night, he crossed into France. The Germans continued to occupy France. So he was extra careful. His trek finally ended outside the French City of Reims. It was at Reims that a French soldier of German ancestry befriended him. The soldier took Adalard under his wing. After the War, shortly after German forces surrendered to the Allies, the soldier and his wife adopted him.

"Adalard eventually moved to Paris, fell in love, and finally he married. He was thirty-one-years-old at the time. The couple had four children. Their oldest daughter gave birth to a daughter named Emma. Emma is an internationally-known actress. So you see Steph, by risking your life to save Adalard from certain death and, with the help of Spirit, relocating him to the countryside most certainly saved his life. Thanks to you, untold millions around the world now enjoy the wondrous acting and benevolence of his granddaughter Emma."

Steph says in her mind, "Wow, Jordyn. That is an incredible story. Is Adalard still alive?"

"Sadly, no. Adalard passed away in 1978. He was only forty-four years old when he died. Pancreatic cancer. When you saw him in 1942, you assumed he was nine or ten-years-old. He was only eight-years-old. He truly was a remarkable boy to have survived the war and the journey to France - and only eight-years of age at that."

Steph's thoughts say, "Jordyn, you know better than anyone that I loved Adalard. I still do. And I am sad that he is gone. On the other hand, it is comforting to know his granddaughter Emma is entertaining people."

Jordyn replies, "Okay, let me speak briefly about the African Americans that you and Spirit set free."

*****

Part III: A Spirited, Fearless Heart

"I did not do too much for the three children," Steph conveys. "Spirit did most of the work along with Samuel. He was very happy to know that the three children would be free."

"Samuel had a vested interest in seeing that they escaped slavery, Steph."

"How's that?"

"Samuel was married to Janette. He was Joseph, Hannah, and Patsy's father."

"He was? Gosh. He never told me. I bet he was very happy to see them set forth for their freedom."

Jordyn is tempted to tell Steph that Boss and Jess lynched Samuel the same day that Steph had disappeared from the Gray Plantation. However, she knows there is no reason to make Steph feel bad about Samuel's murder. Besides, everyone that Steph befriended during her journey, except Christopher and Eddie, are deceased.

Jordyn conveys, "Before I talk about the three children I need to say this. And I say it with conviction and with the strongest words possible. So listen to me very carefully. You are incorrect when you say you did not do too much for the three African American children! On the contrary. What you did was nothing short of incredible."

"How's that?" Steph inquires. "All I seemed to do was get myself into more trouble as time went on. And all of that trouble occurred over the course of fewer than two days!"

"You are too humble, Steph. Consider what I am about to say very carefully. You faced up to Judas time and again. You even did so in front of his wife, your Aunt Mary. As a result, you provided her with the courage to confront her bigoted husband as it concerned slavery and his role as an owner of slaves. Do you think for one moment she would have gone along with you to allow the three children to escape had you not voiced your disgust of slavery so vehemently?"

"Well, I guess I was sort of outspoken when it came to the slavery issue," Steph replies.

"Outspoken? You underestimate yourself, Steph. You were anything but outspoken. You were adamant, unbending, and as resolute as anyone who stood on the right side of the slavery issue at the time.

"My goodness, Steph! You had just witnessed and then stopped the whipping of an innocent child! You had risked your life for that child even though you had no clue who he was at the time. That took guts. What you did took courageous, spirited, fearless guts. And each time you spoke to Judas, your heart was livid with hatred for his bigoted ways. I could sense the passion in your voice. I could sense your vehemence in my mind. So could your Aunt Mary.

"So let there be no doubt in your mind with what I am saying. Do not think for one moment that you had nothing to do with Hannah,

Patsy, and Joseph's escape. You were the reason *why* they escaped. Besides, do you not recall what you said to Spirit the night the foursome fled?"

"Not really, Jordyn," Steph replies.

"Your words still ring true in my heart. And they still move me as well. What you said sounded like something out of a play or a movie. Your words were heartstrings, Steph - passionate, sincere, and unselfish. Period."

Steph replies, "Wow, Jordyn. I had no idea. To be honest with you, I do not recall what I had said."

And why is it you sound very angry with me?

"Well, let me refresh your memory for you, Steph, and then you will know. You said to Spirit, and I am going to quote you verbatim."

"You can do that?" Steph inquires before Jordyn can complete her thoughts. "Wow, you are more than amazing. What I said to Spirit outside the stable happened more than two weeks ago."

Jordyn replies, "Yes, I can quote you word for word even if you said it a decade ago. This is what you said. 'I do not care what you say. There is no way I can accompany you if we are to save three African Americans from the auction block! The girls are small in stature, and they are not very heavy since they haven't eaten well all these years. Therefore, the two of them and Joseph can safely ride on your back. But add a fourth to your company - that would be me - and either Joseph or I will have to walk. That will slow the process far too much. The element of quickness as we escape, which is essential if we are to succeed, will be lost.

'Besides, their safety, their quest for freedom is more important than my welfare. I may find myself in danger once the others figure out who let the threesome escape, but I will remain free. Surely, I will have some explaining to do once the two girls and Joseph are gone. But, whatever happens to me is nothing in comparison to what will happen to them at the auction. They will end up in three separate homes of intolerable servitude.

'The three of them have lived their entire lives in bondage. I am free, and I will remain free no matter what happens. Do you understand what I am saying? So, Spirit, I have made my decision, and it is final. I cannot accompany you. Nor will I.'"

"Thank you for refreshing my memory," Steph conveys. "I had no idea." She adds with a smile, "And just so you know. Your recollecting something verbatim that was said weeks ago - and consisted of many words - truly is amazing!"

"Well, now you should understand, Steph, and I thank you for your compliment. So, please get it out of your head that you did not have much to do with the children's escape. You are the reason they escaped slavery. Standing up to the Man. Sympathizing with Janette. Consoling your Aunt Mary. Speaking out heatedly against slavery. What you said and did were important. And they reflected your fearless heart and your amazing spirit to do what is right no matter the risk to you personally.

"You risked your life to save Joseph from being tortured further by the lash! Then, of all things, you stood face-to-face with a man holding a rifle. And then you dared him to shoot you. Steph, you did that two times! The first time was with Jess, and the second time was with Judas! That takes guts, Steph. Don't you ever forget it."

Jordyn's thoughts briefly halt. The pause makes Steph feel very uncomfortable. Steph fully understands that Jordyn is a tad bit angry with her for what she had said about not having much to do with the three children's escape to freedom.

She whispers in a soft voice, "I am very sorry, Jordyn. I truly had no idea - that what I said and did made that much of a difference. Now I understand, and I thank you."

Finally, after at least two minutes of silence, and to Steph's relief, Jordyn resumes sending her thoughts to Steph once more.

"Okay, now I will tell you about the three children."

*****

Part IV: Freedom!

"The children made it to Boston safely. Their trek was difficult and full of danger. Thanks to Spirit, however, they were able to avoid those who wished to do them harm. They also found friends along the way. They were sheltered, fed, and clothed. As you had directed, they never left sight of Spirit during their journey, and they stuck together. They were a close-knit foursome on the run to freedom.

"When they arrived in Boston, they were met by your Aunt Mary's Great Uncle George along with your Aunt Mary's friend. Uncle George and the real Josephine had arrived at Gray's Plantation in the evening on the day you disappeared. It was the day after the children and Spirit departed on their journey.

"Your Aunt Mary told her Great Uncle everything about you and the children. The next day he departed for Boston. He vowed to meet the children when they arrived. Since he did not need to hide out and avoid the Reverse Underground Railroad, he arrived in Boston ten days before the children. He greeted them with open arms upon their arrival. He also sheltered them. Now, about the children. I will start off with Joseph.

"Shortly after President Abraham Lincoln signed the Emancipation Proclamation on January 1, 1863, Joseph enlisted in the 54th Massachusetts Infantry Regiment. The regiment was the first African American unit that fought during the Civil War. Recruiting was conducted at a camp outside of Boston. The regiment consisted of African American enlisted men. White officers, led by Colonel Robert Gould Shaw, commanded the regiment. While Joseph was in camp, he met Frederick Douglass and his two sons. Douglass' sons had also enlisted in the regiment.

"As you know from your history lessons, Frederick Douglass was a national abolitionist leader in Massachusetts. He also wrote many works, to include *Narrative of the Life of Frederick Douglass, an American Slave*. He also wrote the novel that you have read, *Times of Frederick Douglass*. Anyway, I digress. Back to Joseph.

"Joseph fought gallantly alongside his African American comrades. Ironically, the 54th Massachusetts Infantry Regiment saw action in Charleston, South Carolina, seventy-five miles or so from where Joseph and his sisters were enslaved. Then, two days later, on July 18, 1863, the Regiment assaulted Fort Wagner, once again in Charleston, South Carolina. Twenty of the Regiment were killed, 125 wounded, and 52 missing, presumed dead. According to a ledger that exists to this day, Joseph was one of the 52 soldiers missing in action.

"While his life was cut short due to his service to our country, he died a more noble and dignified death than he would have as a slave. All thanks to you, Steph. And oh. Before I forget to mention it, a 1989 movie entitled *Glory* portrays the heroic actions of the 54th Massachusetts Infantry Regiment. It stars some notable actors of which you are familiar. I know you have seen the movie. Watch it again when you have the chance. It will bring back fond memories of the courageous former slave, Joseph - the young man you rescued from the lash and eventually allowed him to become a freedman."

"Thank you for telling me that story," Steph conveys. "It is very sad to know that Joseph was one of the missing, presumed dead during the battle of Fort Wagner. Nevertheless, I am very proud of him. He not only proved his grit by not crying out when Boss was whipping him; Joseph also volunteered to serve his country - the very country that enslaved him. He will forever live in my heart as a hero. A true American hero."

"Now for the girls," Jordyn's thoughts say. "Let me start with Patsy. Her story is the easiest to tell of the two sisters.

"Patsy married a freedman after the Civil War. The couple moved to Philadelphia, Pennsylvania. Patsy's husband was very talented. He worked at the naval shipyard. They had two children, a girl and a boy. Their offspring had seven children among them. Like their uncle, Joseph, three of Patsy's grandchildren served in the military - one in the army and two in the navy.

One of Patsy's great-great-great-grandchildren received a commission as one of the first African American admirals in the United States Navy. So once again, Steph, your actions to help another in need resulted in wonderful things happening for our country. I cannot think of anything nobler than serving one's country."

"Once again, that makes me very happy and proud," Steph conveys.

"Isn't it amazing? Joseph volunteered to serve as did Patsy's grandchildren. And to think Patsy's descendant was one of the first African American admirals in the Navy. That is very awesome. What an accomplishment that the descendant of a former slave would rise to such a distinguished position in the military!"

"That is not all," Jordyn's thoughts say. "Let me tell you a bit about Hannah. She, like her brother Joseph, was a true patriot.

"Hannah volunteered to serve as a cook in the Union Army's 2nd South Carolina Volunteers. Few people know this, but the famous former slave and abolitionist, Harriet Tubman, also served as a cook and then as a scout for the Union Army. Tubman led an assault on a collection of plantations along the Combahee River. Ironically, one of the plantations was the Gray Plantation. By that time, however, in 1863, the Gray Plantation had been sold.

"Hannah was present when Tubman led the assault. It was called the Combahee River Raid. The raid freed more than 750 slaves. Some of the former slaves were friends of Hannah's parents. Later, and somewhat sadly, the Volunteer Regiment was involved in the looting and burning of the pro-Confederate town located at Darien, Georgia. I must stress at this point, however, that Hannah was but a volunteer cook during this sad chapter of Civil War history. She never held a torch. Despite her noninvolvement, she was present during the carnage. Like her brother's regiment, the burning of Darien is told in the Civil War movie *Glory*."

Steph asks, "Did Hannah survive the war?"

"Yes, she did. She moved back to Boston after the Civil War. She never married."

*****

Part V: Recapping the Journey

"Now for Christopher. As you know, after he graduated from Goodfellow High School, Christopher attended Yale University. He graduated a year early with a biomedical degree. He continued to struggle with his cerebral palsy. Nevertheless, as you also know, he was never a quitter. His courage was and still is, unfathomable. Even though he is seventy-two-years-old, he remains very active. He presently is employed as an invaluable research scientist at the National Institute of Neurological Disorders and Stroke (NINDS), Bethesda,

Maryland. His primary focus at NINDS is to find more advanced methods to assist children with cerebral palsy. He also is actively involved in the research and treatment of childhood cancer.

"Once again, like Adalard whose granddaughter is a famous actress, and just like the patriots Hannah and Joseph, and Patsy's descendants, your successful efforts to assist others have changed the course of history. Certainly, in a small way. Nevertheless, the world would not be as grand if you had not succeeded. I salute you, Steph. And I love you from the bottom of my heart."

"I love you as well," Steph replies in her mind.

"I really should not ask this, but I will. Did Christopher ever find someone who would love him despite his spastic cerebral palsy? Did he ever marry?"

"Matter of fact he did. He married a co-worker twenty-four years ago."

"Did they have any children?"

"Yes. One boy. He is in university studying to be a doctor."

Steph conveys, "That is wonderful. I am very happy for Christopher and his wife. And I am very happy he has a child. You do know I loved him as only one friend could love another, yes?"

"Yes, I know. By the way, Eddie owns a bicycle shop in Texas. He is married with four children, all girls."

Steph laughs. "I am not surprised he owns a bicycle shop. He certainly did love his bicycle when I was there. No question in my mind."

"Perhaps I do not want to know the answer to my next question. Nevertheless, I will never quit wondering unless I ask. Did Aunt Mary kill her husband, Judas? I heard the awful report of the rifle just as I disappeared."

"Your Aunt Mary only wounded him, Steph. The bullet grazed his left shoulder. Nothing serious. She was aiming for his heart. She had never shot a rifle before, so she did not know how to aim it properly. Knocked her clear across the stable when the rifle discharged.

"Judas did not have her arrested. Naturally, he divorced her. Then he sold the plantation in 1863. Regrettably, he joined the Ku Klux Klan a few years after the Civil War ended. He was out-and-out evil.

You know that better than anyone except, perhaps, your Aunt Mary and, obviously, the poor souls that he enslaved. He passed away in 1872 during a gun battle."

"And Aunt Mary. What happened to her?"

"She lived with her friend in Boston for a few months. Then she met the love of her life, a doctor. She married at the youthful age of twenty-nine. The couple had three children, two boys, and a girl. They named the girl Stephanie after you."

"No kidding? That is very cool. Knowing that makes me very, very happy. It truly does. And Josephine? What became of her?"

"Well, given all the commotion at the Gray Plantation, the shooting and all, Josephine boarded the next ship heading back to England. She spent but one night on the plantation. Just like you."

Steph conveys, "To think Josephine traveled all the way across the Atlantic Ocean to see her Aunt Mary and step-cousins William and Henry, and then she had to leave. I feel bad for her, and it makes me feel sad as well."

"Yes, it is very sad. I do not know what became of Josephine. Now, it is time for you to ask me some more questions. Fire away."

"Why was my note on the kitchen table? Why didn't my parents read it?"

"Did you notice the time, Steph, you know, when you woke up a while ago?"

"Yes. The time was twenty-seven minutes past four, 4:27."

"What time was it when you disappeared on your journey? Do you remember?"

"I do. It was exactly one o'clock in the morning when I disappeared over two weeks ago. You had told me to make certain I was on the porch before one o'clock. I remember looking at my watch a few seconds before it disappeared. It said the time was one o'clock. I am certain of it. Then everything in my neighborhood disappeared. Next thing I knew I was on Spirit. We were in Cologne, Germany during World War II."

Jordyn replies in her mind, "Exactly."

"So," Steph conveys, "what I think you are saying is this. I never left my house. None of what I experienced happened. I probably imagined or dreamt everything! After all, I thought I disappeared at one o'clock in the morning, and when I woke up a few moments ago it was twenty-seven minutes past four, 4:27 - in the morning!

"Was everything I thought I experienced a dream, Jordyn? Did I fall asleep on the porch before one o'clock? A few minutes before my departure time? And did I awaken a while ago? At 4:27?"

"I never said you had not left your house, Steph. And I did not say that you fell asleep. But, please allow me to ask you this. Do you think everything that happened in your mind was a dream? Or do you think everything was real?"

"I would like to *think - to believe* everything that happened was real. Do you understand what I am saying? Well, thinking?

"However, now that I am here at home sitting on the floor of my porch, I have my doubts. Besides, I do not own a horse named Spirit. You know that. Although I once rode a horse named Spirit in Ohio. Goodness, now that I think of it, I rode a horse named Spirit near a town called Saint Mary's! All the same, maybe Spirit was the same horse that was with me as I journeyed. And then there was the scene in the book of an elf named Enna riding a Pordanas, a flying horse named Spirit.

"To tell you the truth, Jordyn, I seriously doubt everything."

"If you rode a horse named Spirit in Ohio, Steph, then the horse is real."

"But Jordyn, a horse that could read my thoughts! A horse's thoughts that I could interpret? Like I said. Now that I am home everything I thought happened sounds too far-fetched to be real."

"Really?" Jordyn replies. "But here you are right now. Sitting no more than one hundred feet from me while we are having a telepathic conversation. What makes you think you cannot have a telepathic conversation with a horse, a magical horse at that?"

"So what you are telling me is that I did have a telepathic conver-sation with a horse?"

"Do you think that you did, Steph?"

"Yes."

"Okay. Next question."

"Despite everything you told me a few moments ago about everyone I allegedly helped, did everything that happened to me actually occur? Did I go with a horse named Spirit to Cologne, Germany? Did I fight three soldiers, almost get shot, and save the Jewish boy Adalard? And did I then go through time and space across the Atlantic Ocean one more time to confront Judas? Did Spirit and I help Hannah, Patsy, and Joseph to escape slavery?

"And did I make friends with Aunt Mary and sit on her lap? Cry with her? Hold in my hands a book written by President Abraham Lincoln? Make friends with Christopher and his family? Go to a prom? Help Christopher walk across the stage to get his diploma? Meet Missus McAllister at the orphanage?

"And this is very important. Did I meet the younger Roger Clyde Brewster? Did I do all of that, Jordyn? Was everything real? Or was everything simply a figment of my imagination?"

"Do you think you actually experienced all of that, Steph? Do you think it was real?"

"I want to think that I did experience everything, that it was real. I honestly do. After all, it felt very real at the time. In fact, in my mind, I can still smell Adalard's musty clothes. I can still smell the gunpowder from the exploding bullets. I am still sore, but not too bad, from fighting those soldiers. My calf still hurts where the shard of wood pierced my leg when I was in the cathedral."

She unconsciously licks her lips as her stomach growls.

"Oddly, it is almost as if I can taste Jimmy's mouthwatering, greasy burgers and fries, and Marcia's delicious spaghetti and meatballs, and those scrumptious, homemade waffles. Yes, Jordyn. I think I experienced everything. And yes, I think all of it was real."

"Then it was real, Steph. Next question. But please hurry. It will be light soon. I need you tucked in your bed and sound asleep before five o'clock. We do not have much time."

Steph says in her mind, "Why, Jordyn? Why must I be in my bed before five o'clock?"

"Because I said so."

Steph hears another giggle from across the street.

"Trust me, Steph. That is all that I ask of you - to trust me. Next question. Hurry now. We do not have much time."

Steph hesitates a few moments before she asks her next question. When she finally does, she decides to whisper as softly as she can rather than sending her thoughts to Jordyn. She knows Jordyn can interpret her thoughts either way. She begins to weep softly.

"Jordyn, this is very important to me. Please answer me honestly, okay? Are you real?"

"Steph, do you think I am real?"

"Yes, I do. At least I want to think you are real and not a figment of my imagination." Her thoughts pause for a few moments, and then she says, "Especially considering what I experienced the past couple weeks. Well, if it were a couple of weeks. I lost track of time.

"How you saved my life on more than one occasion. How you introduced me to remarkably interesting people of former times. How you enabled me to see and experience things no one else my age could ever imagine witnessing. More importantly, how you allowed me to realize my raison d'être, as I like to refer to it, my purpose - to help children in need.

"Yes, my sweet, beloved, honest to God, faithful friend Jordyn, I wish for all my heart for you to be real. To be alive like me full of life and happiness. I truly do. I have come to love you like a sister. Please, Jordyn, please tell me you are real because I want you to be real. I truly do.

"Also, please tell me I will meet you someday. Because, other than what I think are memories of everything, I have nothing to prove what happened. Even my knapsack is the same. It is as I never left. If only I had Patsy's necklace, Adalard's coin, and Christopher's charm bracelet. Those things would prove to me that you are real and that everything I think happened actually occurred!

"Yes, Jordyn. I want you to be real! With all my heart and soul."

Steph hears a faint giggle from across the street.

"Steph, if you want me to be real. I am."

CHAPTER ELEVEN

TRUTH

"Steph, as I said earlier if you want me to be real. I am.
And I shall never leave your side. I promise."
- Jordyn, the present and until the end of time

"Steph! Steph! Wake up, sleepyhead! Today is your big day."

Steph awakens with a start. Her mother has opened the bedroom curtains wide. The morning sunshine fills the room. Her first impulse is to shield her eyes from the brightness. She places her hands in front of her face.

"Huh? What am I doing here?"

Her mother laughs.

"What do you mean when you say, 'What am I doing here?' Where else would you be but right here in your bedroom lying in your bed?'"

Steph rubs her eyes.

"Oh, sorry, Mom. I guess I was dreaming." She shakes her head to rid her sleepiness from her mind. "At least I think I was." As she rubs her eyes some more, she looks up at her mother.

"What do you mean by today's my big day? What time is it? And what is so special about today?"

"Oh, come on now, silly. You have been waiting weeks for this day to occur. It is your birthday, and let me tell you. We have a super-fun day planned!" She hands Steph a manila envelope.

"This came via UPS yesterday. I was going to give it to you last night. However, I guess you went straight up here after work. After I returned from grocery shopping, I came here to give it to you, but you were sound asleep. I have no clue who sent it. There is no return address. Probably one of your friends."

Her mother turns to leave. She calls over her shoulder.

"Now, take your time getting ready, sleepy head birthday girl. We are off to church in about two hours. The noon service. So you have plenty of time to get yourself ready. There is fresh cocoa powder in the pantry and a box of donuts on the kitchen table if you are hungry."

Steph retrieves her cell phone from her bedside table. It reads 9:42 am. She shakes her head once more as she ponders everything her mother just said.

Is today my birthday? Goodness, how in the world could I forget something as important as that? And I wonder who sent this to me?

But wait a second! How in the world did I get from the porch to my bedroom? Oh no! This cannot be happening. Not again!

She reaches down to the side of her bed to grab the pants she wore the night before. She frantically searches the pockets for the crumpled ball of paper. The crumpled ball of paper is the note informing her parents that she was leaving - leaving to help Jordyn.

I found it!

She uncrumples it. She verifies that it is the same note she wrote to her parents.

Suddenly her heart sinks when she sees the partly concealed knapsack beneath her bed. It is the knapsack she prepared the morning she departed on her journey. She grabs it, and then she unwraps the checkered tablecloth. She begins to cry.

Everything she packed is still in the knapsack - Twinkies, peanut butter and jelly sandwiches, hard candy, her clothes, changes of underwear.

Everything.

I should have known! I never left. Adalard never ate Twinkies or a peanut butter and jelly sandwich. I never sucked on the hard candy.

I never left!

She angrily points to random places in her bedroom.

I never went there, or there, or there, or there, or there! Nor there, darn it!

Nowhere! Nowhere at all!

Everything I thought happened was nothing more than a stupid dream. But how to explain those other dreams, the ones of Jordyn and the orphanage? Of Roger Clyde? Did I dream all of those dreams in one night as well? Or was everything nothing more than a figment of my wild imagination?

She sighs deeply.

I guess I'll never know.

Tears of total distress fall from her eyes as she rips open the envelope. The envelope contains a sealed card and a small square box. The box is wrapped in white tissue paper. She gently shakes the box.

Oh goody! It sounds like there are a few things inside. I cannot wait to see what they are! But first, I must look at the birthday card assuming that is what it is.

She manages a meek smile and begins to calm down even though tears continue to fall from her eyes.

She carefully slides her fingernail beneath the flap of the envelope. She removes the card. On the cover of the card is a lovely sepia silhouette image of a teenaged girl kissing the forehead of a horse. She opens the card.

Her hands begin to shake as she reads the beautiful, handwritten cursive script.

> "Happy Birthday to my one and only friend in the entire universe, Steph!
> Steph, you touched the lives of five children and, in your unique way, you changed the world!
> Owing to your boundless spirit, compassion, love for others, and your fearless heart.
> I hope you enjoy seeing your gifts as much as I enjoyed returning them to you.
> Love always until the end of time, Jordyn.
> PS. Steph, as I said earlier if you want me to be real. I am.
> And I shall never leave your side. I promise."

Steph's heart is beating so fast her entire body is trembling. Like so many times before while she was journeying, for real or in her dreams, her lips are bone dry. Her throat is parched, and she can barely breathe.

She carefully removes the white tissue paper wrapping from the box. A yellow post-it note is taped to the lid of the box.

"My dearest Steph - Here is proof of your purpose, *your raison d'être.*"

Resting on a bed of velvety cotton are three unforgettable items - of the past.

- The weather-beaten Reichspfennig coin from Adalard

- The glass beads and cowrie shells necklace from Patsy

- The silver charm bracelet from Christopher

Oh my God, Jordyn! You truly are real! Everything I thought I experienced must have happened! These precious gifts prove it. You must know how happy you have made me, and how much I love you! How can I ever thank you?

Steph excitedly stares at the ceiling for the longest time.

She is hoping with all her heart and soul for an answer.

That never comes.

The End

EPILOGUE

Steph has never sensed Jordyn's thoughts in her mind after that day. Even so, she continues to treasure her memories of the unseen deaf orphan as she telepathically guided Steph on the journey of a lifetime. And, even though something tells her she may never again sense Jordyn's words or meet her in person, she knows.

Jordyn's absolute love for her has made her a better person.

Steph cherishes the three gifts given to her as tokens of love by the children whose lives she touched as she traveled through time and space - the children whose precious lives touched hers as well, made her an even more compassionate and loving person.

She wears the lovely, handmade glass beads and cowrie shells necklace given to her by Patsy when she attends church. As she prays, she clutches the necklace between the palms of her hands. People, to include her parents and her sister, occasionally ask why her eyes well up with tears as she lovingly clutches the necklace when she prays. Her simple reply.

"I am truly blessed to be free."

The coin Adalard gave her, the weather-beaten Reichspfennig that belonged to his father, has a special place in her jewelry box. Whenever she takes the coin out of the box to examine it or to show it to her friends, her friends ask why it is very precious to her.

"It reminds me how kindness and tolerance can make the world a better place."

She seldom removes the silver charm bracelet from her wrist that Christopher gave to her. When family and friends ask about the meaning of the three miniature sterling silver charms - the horse, the wheelchair, and the two intertwined hearts - her reply is instant. Confident. Indisputable.

"Spirit."

246

"Fearlessness."

"Love and compassion."

Her raison d'être.

NOTABLE QUOTES AND METAPHORS

As Concerns Sexism

"The officer's insulting, bigoted comment and the soldiers' rude laughter feel like sexist daggers piercing my heart!" - Steph to herself

As It Concerns Nazism

"Nazism is a human parasite. Altruism will eradicate it soon enough." - Adalard to Steph

"That you survived the bombings proves that nothing can scathe your impenetrable will to survive." - Steph to Adalard

As it Concerns Slavery & Bigotry

"Freedom without health is infinitely sweeter than health without freedom." - *New York Daily Tribune*, March 9, 1859

"A man's conscience is his roadmap to his deeds, both good and evil." Polly to Josephine

"America's slave owners have tossed their souls deep into the soil of bigotry where they will rot in the annals of history." - Polly to Mary

"You do not scare me. No more than an elephant fears a flea." - Steph to Judas

"As far as I am concerned, you are a nobody, a detestable slave owner. Nothing more than a figment of history's scorn. Your threats mean nothing to me." - Steph to Judas

"Counter your hatred of slavery with the breathings of your benevolent heart." - Polly to Josephine.

"Slavery is a friend of the devil." - Polly to Mary

"The wheels of freedom may turn slowly, but their end result will be the death of slavery." - Steph to Judas

"Slavery is a white man's bigoted shackle." - Steph to Judas

"Maybe I cannot change the course of history, but at least I can change one of its many tales." - Steph to Aunt Mary

"Slavery's detestable bigotry is like intolerance turned upside down" - Steph to herself

"Bigotry begets blindness as far as the truth is concerned." - Aunt Mary

"I do believe you are feeling the shameful horror of subjection like those who you enslave." - Steph to Judas

"I have one life to give, and it isn't mine. It's yours!" - Steph to Judas

As it Concerns the Disabled

"Deaf and dumb t'gether mean you can't hear or talk. I can talk. Not too good, but I talk just the same. Ain't my fault I talk funny sometimes. It is normal for deaf people." - Jordyn to Roger Clyde

"Yes, you may have a disability, but your kind heart is no different than mine." - Steph to Christopher

"You may need crutches for support as you walk, but someday others will seek your support and willingly walk in your footsteps." - Steph to Christopher

As It Concerns Friendship and Life

"Every day is a journey, and the journey is home." - Matsuo Basho

"You will never fall, Christopher. You may stumble from time to time, but in my eyes, you will never fall. And you will never fail. No matter come what may." - Steph to Christopher

"Steph, as I said earlier if you want me to be real. I am. And I shall never leave your side. I promise." - Jordyn to Steph

"The cogs of a clock are timeless turnings never ceasing." - Steph to herself

LIST OF FICTIONAL CHARACTERS

Steph (Stephanie) JoAnne Galanos - Leading Character. (Steph also has three aliases' in the story - Stephanie JoAnne Mahoney, Stephanie Johnston, and Josephine. See the aliases' below for more information.

Adalard - Protagonist. Adalard is an emaciated Jewish boy sought by Nazi soldiers during World War II. Steph saves Adalard from certain death in Cologne, Germany, when she enters the Cologne Cathedral. Adalard tells the story of the persecution of Jews by the Nazi's during World War II. Shortly after German forces surrender to the Allies, a French soldier of German ancestry adopts Adalard. Adalard moves to Paris, France where he completes his education. He marries a French woman. They have four children. His oldest daughter gives birth to a daughter named Emma. Emma is an internationally-known actress and an advocate for women's rights.

Aunt Margaret - (no speaking part in the story) Missus Gray mentions Aunt Margaret during her talk with Steph. Steph assumes Missus Gray is trying to trick her by mentioning Aunt Margaret since she suspects Steph is not Josephine.

Benjamin - Benjamin is a friend of Josephine's step-cousin, William. Benjamin witnesses Steph's intervention during Joseph's whipping by Boss.

Boss - Boss also goes by the name of Jim. Boss is a ruthless white overseer of slaves on the Gray Plantation. Steph initially encounters Boss as he whips a young slave named Joseph. Boss, along with Jess, lynches Samuel, the father of the escapees, Hannah, Patsy, and Joseph.

Christopher James Peters - Protagonist. Christopher is the oldest son of Jimmy and Marcia Peters. Brother of Eddie Peters. Christopher has a mild form of spastic cerebral palsy. Steph befriends Christopher as she moves back in time to a small town in the mid-1960s. Christopher graduates from Goodfellow High School. He attends Yale University and graduates a year early with a biomedical degree. Later in life, Christopher is employed as a research scientist at the National Institute of Neurological Disorders and Stroke (NINDS), Bethesda, MD. Christopher's primary focus at NINDS is finding a cure for children who have cerebral palsy.

Donald Brown, Mister - Mister Brown is the Vice Principal of Goodfellow High School. Master of ceremonies during the Goodfellow High School Graduating Class of 1964 senior prom.

Eddie Harold Peters - Eddie is the youngest son of Jimmy and Marcia Peters; brother of Christopher Peters.

Edith - (no speaking part in the story). Edith is the deceased wife of Judas Gray.

Freddy Stewart - Freddy is the class Valedictorian of the Goodfellow High School Graduating Class of 1964. Freddy announces the names of the Goodfellow High School Graduating Class of 1964 senior prom.

Frederick Carlson, Mister - Mister Carlson is the Principal, Goodfellow High School. He is the master of ceremonies during the Goodfellow High School Class of 1964 graduation.

Gerald Mitchell - Gerald is an employee of *The Evening News*. He takes photographs of Steph and Christopher as Steph, on roller skates, pushes Christopher's wheelchair to the senior prom. Steph and Christopher's photograph appears on the front Page of *The Evening News* the following Monday, two days after Steph departs the town.

Great Uncle George - (no speaking part in the story) Polly mentions Great Uncle George in a letter to her sister, Mary Gray. George is Josephine's escort to the Gray Plantation. He will travel to Boston, Massachusetts to meet Hannah, Patsy, and Joseph.

Hannah - Hannah is one of three African American slaves freed by Steph and Spirit. Daughter of Janette and Samuel; sister of Joseph and Patsy. During the Civil War, Hannah volunteers, alongside the famous abolitionist Harriet Tubman, as a cook and then as a scout for the Union Army's 2nd South Carolina Volunteers. Hannah is present when

Tubman leads an assault on a collection of plantations along the Combahee River. More than 750 slaves are set free in the Combahee River Raid.

Hauptmann Rittmeister - A German Army Captain. The Hauptmann Rittmeister confronts Steph, Spirit, and Adalard inside the Cologne cathedral. The Hauptmann Rittmeister is accompanied by two soldiers.

Henry - (no speaking part in the story) Henry is the son of Judas Gray; brother of William Gray; step-son of Mary Gray. Henry's theft of food from the Gray mansion pantry results in his father falsely accusing the slave, Joseph, of stealing food for his sisters, Hannah and Patsy. Essentially, Henry's theft prompts everything that unfolds - Joseph's whipping and, ultimately, the escape to freedom of Hannah, Patsy, and Joseph; and also the lynching of their father, Samuel.

Jess - Jess is a white man who works on the Gray Plantation. Jess is present during the whipping of Joseph by the white overseer Boss. He brandishes a rifle to ensure the African Americans do not protest during the whipping. After Steph threatens him, in response to his pointing a rifle at her, he yields.

Jimmy Peters, Mister - Protagonist. Jimmy is the owner of Jimmy's Drive-in. Steph's employer. Husband of Marcia Claire Peters; father of Christopher and Eddie Peters.

Jim Shane Dewitt - Jim goes by the name Boss. (See "Boss" for more information.)

Jordyn - Protagonist. Jordyn is a magical deaf orphan that miraculously transports Steph and Spirit across time and space, first to Germany during World War II; and to South Carolina one year before the American Civil War. Then she transports Steph to a small New York town in the mid-1960s; then to Ohio during the early 1900s. Jordyn communicates with Steph and Spirit via telepathy. She also communicates telepathically to Adalard in German. She also can see what is happening in the environs where Steph finds herself. While not substantiated in the story, Steph assumes that Jordyn has telekinetic abilities.

Joseph - Joseph is an African American slave set free by Steph and Spirit. He is the brother of Hannah and Patsy; son of Janette and Samuel. Shortly after President Abraham Lincoln signs the Emancipation Proclamation, on January 1, 1863, Joseph enlists in the 54th Massachusetts Infantry Regiment. He fights gallantly alongside his African American comrades. Joseph is one of the 52 soldiers gone missing in action and never accounted for after the assault on Fort Wagner, Charleston, South Carolina - July 18, 1863.

Josephine - (no speaking part in the story) Josephine is the niece of Missus Mary Gray; daughter of Polly. Josephine is scheduled to visit the Gray Plantation. However, she is delayed. Steph is forced to assume Josephine's identity before Josephine's arrival. Everyone but Missus Gray assumes Steph is the real Josephine.

Judas Gray, the Man - Antagonist. Judas Gray is the owner of the Gray Plantation, South Carolina. Husband of Mary Elizabeth Gray; father of William and Henry Gray.

Marcia Claire Peters, Missus - Protagonist. Wife of Jimmy Peters; mother of Christopher and Eddie. Steph and Marcia become best friends.

Mary Elizabeth Gray, Missus - Protagonist. Mary is the second wife of Judas Gray; sister of Polly; stepmother of William and Henry Peters; aunt of Josephine. Steph and Mary become best friends. Steph ultimately refers to the woman as Aunt Mary.

Missus McAllister - Protagonist. Missus McAllister is the supervisor of the Saint Mary's Home.

Overleutnant - A senior lieutenant of the German Army. The Overleutnant confronts Steph, Adalard, and Spirit outside of the cathedral, Cologne, Germany.

Patsy - One of three African American slaves freed by Steph and Spirit. Daughter of Janette and Samuel; sister of Hannah and Joseph. Patsy marries a freedman after the Civil War. The couple moves to Philadelphia, PA. One of Patsy's great-great-grandchildren receives a commission as one of the first African American admirals in the United States Navy.

254

Polly - (no speaking part in the story) Polly is Mary Gray's sister and Josephine's mother. She lives in England. Steph reads Polly's letters addressed to her sister to gain insight as to her pretender role as Mary Gray's supposed visiting niece, Josephine.

Reginald McAllister, Doctor - (no speaking part in the story) Doctor McAllister is mentioned by his wife, Missus McAllister, as the manager of the Saint Mary's Home.

Roger Clyde Brewster - Antagonist. Roger Clyde is the supreme bully and head of the Trio bullies at the Saint Mary's Home. In Steph's dreams, Roger Clyde bullies Jordyn unmercifully. Roger Clyde also appears later in the story as a young boy. Steph correctly assumes Roger Clyde is bullied and abused as a young boy. Roger Clyde suffers from Tourette's Syndrome and has a noticeable limp, the latter condition probably due to physical abuse at the orphanage.

Samuel - Samuel assists Steph in collecting blankets and provisions for Hannah, Patsy, and Joseph. Samuel is the husband of Janette and the father of the three children. Samuel is lynched by Boss and Jess the day after his children escape to freedom.

Sheila Ferguson, Missus - (no speaking part in the story) Proprietor of the neighborhood bakery, Sheila's. Sheila's is a favorite hangout of Goodfellow high schoolers. It is also a family gathering place on weekends.

Shirley Jones - (no speaking part in the story). Shirley is Freddy Stewart's date at the Goodfellow High School prom.

Stephanie JoAnne Mahoney - A false name created on Steph's driver's license and college ID by Jordyn.

Stephanie Johnston - A false name given to Missus McAllister by Steph.

Victoria Walters, Miss - (no speaking part in the story) Victoria is the secretary of Goodfellow High School.

William - William is the first person to meet Steph when she arrives at the Gray Plantation. William pulls Steph away from the scene in the stable after she intervenes during Joseph's whipping. William is the son of Juda Gray; brother of Henry Gray; step-son of Mary Gray.

CITED WORKS AND REFERENCES

The following cited and referenced works are used in this novel to add realism to the story. Mention of these works in no way endorses their products or organizations; nor does the author have any affiliation with their writers, musicians, producers, business owners, or products.

In Chapter Three, a brief description of the bombing of the German city of Cologne during World War II is provided. Statistics and historical background came from wikipedia.org.

In Chapter Three, mention is made of the Cologne Cathedral which remained standing during the repeated bombing of the German city of Cologne during World War II. Statistics came from rarehistoricalphotos.com.

In Chapter Three, mention is made of *die Endlösung der Judenfrage*, the "Final Solution." After extensive research of various references, the author decided that the most useful reference material came from wikipedia.org. This material includes passages in the same chapter that reference Herr Erich Kilbansky. Kilbansky was the Schulleiter (Headmaster) of Jawne, otherwise known as the Jewish Gymnasium of Rhineland, Cologne, Germany.

In Chapter Four, the quote below the chapter title is attributable to the *New York Daily Tribune* of March 9, 1859. A *New York Daily Tribune* reporter was present during the Slave Auction of 1859. The auction was held on the outskirts of Savannah, Georgia. The quote is from eyewitnesstohistory.com. Reprinted by Albert B. Hart in *American History told by Contemporaries* v. 4 (1928)

In Chapter Four, mention is made of the Gray Plantation located on Pawley's Island, South Carolina. The plantation and the white men and women, as well as the enslaved African Americans, are fictional. Nevertheless, fictional information portrayed in the novel is based upon actual data contained in the publication, *Atlantic Black Star*. The *Atlantic Black Star* publishes daily Black news and narratives.

In Chapter Four, mention is made at length of the Slave Auction of 1859. The auction was at the *Race Course* on the outskirts of Savannah, Georgia. Four hundred thirty-six slaves were on the auction block. These included men, women, children, and infants. The Slave Auction of 1859 mentioned in the story is complete fiction with the exception of the auction's title. Details of the auction came from eyewitnesstohistory.com.

In Chapter Four, mention is made of the Georgetown County Slave Patrol and the Reverse Underground Railroad. While portions of the material are fictional, some of the material is truthful based upon research of wikipedia.org.

In Chapter Four, mention is made of Mister Cleveland M. Grouse, a maker of slave tags. While mention of the Gray Plantation is fictional, according to Dr. Lori (www.drloriv.com), a resident of Charleston, South Carolina made slave tags for South Carolina plantation owners during the 1850s.

In Chapter Five, Steph provides detailed facts about the Civil War. The facts were derived from historyplace.com.

In Chapter Five, Steph and Spirit discuss the English author Alan Alexander Milne (1882 - 1956). Milne was an English author, best known for his stories at Winnie-the-Pooh. He was also a playwright. Milne served in both World Wars.

In Chapter Five, Steph and Spirit discuss Ralph Waldo Emerson (1803 - 1882), to include one of his famous quotes. Emerson was an American essayist who led the transcendentalist movement of the mid-19th Century. He also was an outspoken critic of slavery.

In Chapter Eight, mention is made of the rock 'n' roll group, Beatles', hit song "She Loves You." The song was written by John Lennon and Paul McCartney. It was released as a single in 1963. The song "She Loves You" was one of the top five Beatles songs in the United States on 4 April 1964.

In Chapter Eight, mention is made of the 1986 rock musical comedy horror film *Little Shop of Horrors*. It was produced in December 1986 by David Geffen and released by Warner Bros. In the story, Steph admits she has never seen the film. However, comparing the orphanage to the *Little Shop of Horrors* seems appropriate given Steph's first impression of the fictional character Missus McAllister.

In Chapter Ten, mention is made of the 54ᵗʰ Massachusetts Infantry Regiment. Information for the passages in the story came from many sources. The predominant source was wikipedia.org.

In Chapter Ten, mention is made of the 1989 American movie *Glory*. The movie was directed by Edward Zwick and starred Matthew Broderick, Denzel Washington, and Morgan Freeman.

In the Preface, two quotes are provided. The first quote is by Theodore Roosevelt ("Believe you can and you're halfway there."). The second quote is by Lou Reed ("There's a bit of magic in everything, and some loss to even things out.").